PRAISE FOR
Lori Wilde's
NOVELS

You Only Love Twice

"Fast-paced adventure, sexy situations, and lots of suspense will make Wilde's book appeal to a wide spectrum of readers."

—***Booklist***

"[A] funny, fast-paced tale . . . Readers will be . . . laughing at the shenanigans."

—**Publishers Weekly**

"Super fun romantic suspense . . . YOU ONLY LOVE TWICE [is] a . . . humorous contemporary thriller worth reading."

—*Midwest Book Review*

"YOU ONLY LOVE TWICE is a thrill ride from page one . . . An exciting tale, [this] is a book I highly recommend."

—*Romance Reviews Today*

"Wilde is a master of snappy prose . . . I was amazed at how much just plain fun this book was."

—**TheRomanceReader.com**

more . . .

"Lori Wilde dishes up a perfect combination of great characterizations, action, zingy dialogue and plenty of humor . . . If you're up for a fun, fast-paced and thoroughly engaging read, then make sure you pick up a copy of YOU ONLY LOVE TWICE."

—Bookloons.com

"Pick up this book for a great read!"

—Freshfiction.com

Mission: Irresistible

"Fun, romantic . . . humorous and fast-paced . . . Fans who appreciate a breezy, lighthearted romantic suspense . . . will enjoy reading the adventures of the wilder Cooper twin."

—Blether.com

"4 stars! This novel has a nice balance of humor, sexy romance, and a large splash of danger."

—*Romantic Times BOOKclub Magazine*

"Sexy . . . An action-packed, fast-paced adventure."

—*Booklist*

Charmed and Dangerous

"This zany romantic comedy will steal your heart . . . sexy, fun, and hard to put down . . . It's pure delight."

—TheBestReviews.com

"With a deft hand, Wilde blends humor and suspense, passion and mystery into a story both charming and dangerous."
—BookLoons.com

"Fans will take immense pleasure [in] this FBI art romance."
—Harriet's Book Reviews

"An exhilarating romantic suspense."
—Midwest Book Review

"A plot that is sure to win [Wilde] more readers."
—Southern Pines Pilot (NC)

"Quite the exciting romp. Fans will be charmed."
—Romantic Times BOOKclub Magazine

"Witty . . . the chemistry between David and Maddie is hot enough to satisfy those looking for light summer reading."
—Publishers Weekly

"Sexy, fun . . . Had me laughing out loud and sitting on the edge of my seat . . . If you're looking for the perfect summer read, look no further. Lori Wilde has already written it."
—TheBestReviews.com

more . . .

License to Thrill

Also by Lori Wilde

You Only Love Twice

Mission: Irresistible

Charmed and Dangerous

License to Thrill

There Goes the Bride

❦

Lori Wilde

NEW YORK   BOSTON

Copyright © 2007 by Laurie Vanzura
Excerpt from the Wedding Veil Wishes series copyright © 2007 by Laurie Vanzura. All rights reserved. Except as permitted under the U.S. Copyright Act of 1976, no part of this publication may be reproduced, distributed, or transmitted in any form or by any means, or stored in a database or retrieval system, without the prior written permission of the publisher.

Cover design by Diane Luger
Book design by Giorgetta Bell McRee

Warner Forever
Hachette Book Group USA
1271 Avenue of the Americas
New York, NY 10020
Visit our Web site at www.HachetteBookGroupUSA.com

Warner Forever is an imprint of Warner Books, Inc.

Warner Forever is a trademark of Time Warner Inc. or an affiliated company. Used under license by Hachette Book Group USA, which is not affiliated with Time Warner Inc.

Printed in the United States of America

First Printing: March 2007

10 9 8 7 6 5 4 3 2 1

To my wonderful editor, Michele Bidelspach, who gently pushes me to reach my highest potential. Thank you so much for caring!

Acknowledgment

Many thanks to super agent Jenny Bent. Her support and encouragement were invaluable in the writing of this book.

There Goes the Bride

Prologue

The summer issue of *Society Bride* declared the marriage of Houston's hottest bachelor, Dr. Evan Van Zandt, to his childhood sweetheart, oil heiress Delaney Cartwright, a classic friends-to-lovers fairy tale.

Texas Monthly, in its trendy yet folksy way, decreed their union the high-society equivalent of beef barbecue and mustard potato salad. Delaney and Evan simply belonged together.

A sentimental write-up in the *Houston Chronicle* dubbed their romance a heartwarming Lone Star love story.

Delaney's mother, Honey Montgomery Cartwright, pronounced them the perfect couple. Lavish praise indeed from a Philadelphia blue blood with impossibly high standards.

Her father grumbled, "This thing's costing us more than her liberal arts degree from Rice," as he wrote out a very large check to cover the nuptials.

And her long-deceased sister Skylar, who occasionally popped up in Delaney's dreams to offer unsolicited advice, whispered with unbridled glee that the ceremony was a glorious train wreck just waiting to happen and she insisted on front-row seating.

Skylar, being dead, could of course sit anywhere she chose. Everyone else had to cram into the River Oaks Methodist Church.

The cherrywood pews overflowed with five hundred invited guests, plus a dozen members of the press and a sprinkling of enterprising wedding crashers. The laboring air-conditioning system was no match for the double punch of a too-thick crowd and sweltering one-hundred-degree heat.

"Who gets married in Houston during August?" Delaney heard a woman murmur.

"I'm getting a heat rash in these panty hose," another woman replied.

Feeling chastised, Delaney ducked her head. She stood just outside the open door of the chapel waiting for the wedding march to commence, her arm looped through her father's.

"I heard it was originally supposed to be a Christmas ceremony, but the bride postponed it twice," the first woman said. "Do you suppose we could have a runaway situation?"

"Hmm, now that would make an interesting spread in tomorrow's society pages."

At that comment, her father tightened his grip. *No turning back now,* his clench said.

Delaney's hopes sank. Her mind spun. *A coyote would gnaw her paw off.*

The bridesmaids reached their places. Her best friend,

Tish, wedding videographer extraordinaire, was filming madly. Every gaze in the place was glued to Delaney.

Everything was perfect. It was a true celebrity-style wedding, just as her mother had planned. The purple orchids, accented with white roses, were on lavish display—in bouquets and boutonnieres, in vases and corsages. Her size-four, ten-thousand-dollar Vera Wang wedding dress fit like a fantasy. The flower girl was cute. The two-year-old ring bearer even cuter. And both children were on exemplary behavior. Delaney's antique wedding veil fetchingly framed her face, even though her scalp had been tingling weirdly ever since she put it on.

This was it.

Her big day.

The seven-piece orchestra struck the first notes of the wedding march. Dum, dum, de-dum.

Delaney took a deep breath and glanced down the long aisle festooned with white rose petals to where Evan stood at the altar. He looked stunningly handsome in his long-tailed tux, love shining in his trusting blue eyes.

Her father started forward.

But Delaney's beaded white Jimmy Choo stilettos stayed rooted to the spot. No, no, this was all wrong. It was a big mistake. She had to call it off before she embarrassed everyone. Where was her cell phone?

"Delaney Lynn Cartwright," her father growled under his breath. "Don't make me drag you."

A hard throb of distress surged through her temples. *What have you done? What have you done? What have you done?*

She forced herself to move forward. Her gaze

searched for the exits. There were two on either side of the altar, and of course, the one directly behind her.

But Daddy wasn't letting go.

Closer, closer, almost there.

Evan made eye contact, smiled sweetly.

Guilt whirled like a demon tornado in the pit of her stomach. She dragged in a ragged breath.

Her husband-to-be held out his palm. Her father put her hand in Evan's.

Delaney's gaze shifted from one corner exit to the other. Too late. It was too late to call this off. What time was it anyway?

"Dearly beloved," the portly minister began, but that's as far as he got.

A clattering erupted from behind the exit door on the left.

And then there he loomed. Dressed head to toe in black. Wearing a ski mask. Standing out like crude oil in a cotton field.

Thrilled, chilled, shamefaced, and greatly relieved, Delaney held her breath.

The intruder charged the altar.

The congregation inhaled a simultaneous gasp.

The minister blinked, looked confused.

"Back away from the bride," the dark stranger growled and waved a pistol at Evan.

Excitement burst like tiny exploding bubbles inside her head. *Prop gun*, Delaney thought. *Nice touch.*

Evan stared at the masked intruder, but did not move. Apparently he had not yet realized what was transpiring.

"Move it." The interloper pointed his weapon directly at Evan's head. "Hands up."

Finally, her groom got the message. He dropped Delaney's hand, raised his arms over his head, and took a step back.

"Don't anyone try anything cute," the man commanded at the same moment he wrapped the crook of his elbow around Delaney's neck and pressed the revolver to her temple. The cold nose of it felt deadly against her skin.

Fear catapulted into her throat, diluting the excitement. Delaney dropped her bouquet. It *was* a prop gun, wasn't it?

The crowd shot to its collective feet as the stranger dragged her toward the exit from whence he'd appeared.

"Follow us and the bride gets it," he shouted dramatically just before the exit door slammed closed behind them.

"You're choking me," Delaney gasped. "You can let go now."

He ignored her and just kept dragging her by the neck toward the white delivery van parked at the back of the rectory.

A bolt of raw panic shot through her veins. What was going on here? She dug her freshly manicured fingernails into his thick arm and tried to pry herself free.

He stuck his gun in his waistband, pulled a pair of handcuffs from his back pocket, and one-handedly slapped them around her wrists.

"What is this?" she squeaked.

He did not speak. He wrenched open the back door of the van just as the congregation came spilling out of the rectory and into the street. He tossed her onto the floor, slammed the door, and ran around to the driver's side.

Delaney lay facedown, her knees and elbows stinging from carpet burn. She couldn't see a thing, but she heard anxious shouts and the sound of fists pounding the side of the vehicle.

The engine revved and the van shot forward, knocking her over onto her side.

"What's going on?" She struggled to sit. The veil fell across her face. She pushed it away with her cuffed hands and peered into the front of the van. "What's with all the rough stuff?"

He didn't answer.

She cleared her throat. Perhaps he hadn't heard her. "Nice execution," she said. "Loved the toy gun, but the handcuffs are a definite overkill."

He hit the street doing at least fifty and she tipped over again.

Her heart flipped up into her tightly constricted throat. She dragged in a ragged swallow of air. This guy was playing his role to the hilt.

When they made it to the freeway entrance ramp, he ripped off the ski mask, threw it in the seat beside him, and then turned to look back at Delaney.

Alarm rocketed through her. Saliva evaporated from her mouth. Something had gone very, very wrong.

Because the man who'd just taken her hostage was *not* the kidnapper she'd hired.

Chapter 1

Two Months Earlier

"Glasses up, girls. A toast to the bride-to-be," bubbled Tish Gallagher. She smiled at Delaney, tucked a dark auburn corkscrew curl behind one ear studded with multiple piercings, and raised her drink. "May your marriage be filled with magic."

Delaney Cartwright and her three best friends were celebrating the final fitting of the bridesmaids' dresses by dining at Diaz, Houston's trendiest new restaurant hot spot. They'd already slurped down a couple of margarita-martinis apiece and noshed their way through blue corn tortilla chips dipped in piquant salsa and fire-grilled shrimp enchiladas laced with Manchego cheese and Spanish onions.

Everyone was feeling frivolous.

All except for Delaney.

Tequila made her edgy, but it was what her friends were drinking, so she'd joined in.

"Third time's the charm." Jillian Samuels winked and lifted her glass.

Her friend was referring to the fact Delaney had postponed the wedding twice. No matter how many times she explained to people that she'd delayed the ceremony because she was trying to get her fledgling house-staging business on solid ground, everyone assumed it was because she'd gotten cold feet.

But that wasn't the reason at all.

Well, okay, maybe there was a tiny element of an icy pinkie toe or two, but mostly Delaney didn't want to end up like her mother. With nothing to do but have kids and meddle in their lives.

"To the most perfect wedding ever." Die-hard romantic Rachael Harper sighed dreamily, her martini glass joining the others in the air. "You've got the perfect dress, the perfect church, and the most perfect man."

On paper, it was true. Rich, good-looking, affable. Dr. Evan Van Zandt was kind, generous, and thoughtful. Her family loved Evan, and he adored them.

The only thing not perfect in the whole scenario is me, Delaney thought and anxiously reached up to finger the bridge of her nose.

Rhinoplasty might have ironed out the hump, bestowing her with a flawless nose, but it hadn't straightened out her insecurities. She felt like a fake. No matter how many people raved about how gorgeous she was, Delaney didn't believe it.

The emotional repercussions of being a chubby, bucktoothed, nearsighted girl with a witchy nose resonated deep within. Never mind the weight-loss programs, intensive exercise sessions, braces, veneers, elocution lessons, LASIK, and liposuction. Inside, she still felt the same.

"To happily-ever-after," Tish said. "Come on, up with your glass, Del."

"To happily-ever-after," Delaney echoed and dutifully clinked glasses with her friends.

Remember, it's just like Mother taught you. Perceiving, behaving, becoming. Perceive yourself as happy and you'll behave as if you're happy and then you'll become happy.

Happy, happy, happy.

Tish lowered her drink and narrowed her eyes at Delaney. "What's wrong? Don't tell me you're getting cold feet again, because I'm counting on your wedding paying off my Macy's card."

She might be teasing in that devil-may-care way of hers, but it was impossible to slip anything past Tish. Her street-savvy friend had come up the hard way, but she'd never let poverty stop her. After years of struggling, she was finally gaining the reputation she deserved as one of the best wedding videographers in the business. Delaney was so proud of her.

"Nothing, nothing. I'm fine."

"You lie. Everything's not fine. Spill it."

"Honestly. Just pre-wedding jitters."

Tish didn't let up. "What's wrong? Is your mother driving you around the bend with her everything's-gotta-be-perfect-or-my-high-society-world-will-implode routine?"

Delaney cracked a half smile. People joked about Bridezilla, but no one ever mentioned that Mother-of-

Bridezilla could make Bridezilla look like Bambi on Valium. "There is that."

"But it's not all. What else?" Tish pushed the empty salsa bowl aside, leaned forward, propped her elbows on the table, and rested her chin on her interlaced fingers. Jillian and Rachael were also studying her curiously.

She shrugged. "No relationship is perfect. I'm sure I'm making a mountain out of a molehill."

"You let us be the judge of that. Go on, we're listening." Tish waved a hand.

Talking about her romantic life made Delaney uncomfortable. Unlike her friends, she didn't enjoy freely swapping stories about her sexual adventures.

Um, could it be because you've never had any sexual adventures?

Besides, if she told them the truth, she couldn't keep pretending everything was fine. And yet, staying connected to those she loved was the most important thing in the world to her. If she couldn't share her fears with her friends, how could they remain close?

"Well?" Tish arched an eyebrow.

Delaney blew out her breath, trying to think of a delicate way to phrase it. "Things with Evan are . . ."

"Are what?" Jillian prompted when she took too long to continue.

Jillian was a dynamic young lawyer with exotic ebony hair, almond-shaped eyes, a body built for sin, and a Mensa IQ. She snared every man she'd ever set her sights on, but then dumped them just as easily as she collected them.

"Well, you know." Delaney shrugged.

"No, we don't. That's why we're asking."

"Okay, here goes. Not to complain or anything, but ever since Evan suggested we abstain from making love until our wedding night, I haven't been able to think about anything but sex. And now he's leaving for Guatemala next Monday with a volunteer surgical team to perform surgery on sick kids, and he'll be gone for six weeks."

"What?" Tish exclaimed. "You guys aren't having sex?"

"Evan thought it would make our wedding night special if we waited," Delaney explained.

"How long has this been going on?" Jillian asked.

Embarrassed to admit the truth, Delaney dropped her gaze. She wished she hadn't even brought it up. Evan was a saint. He was giving generously of himself to others, and here she was selfishly whining about their lack of a sex life.

She gulped and murmured, "Six months."

"Six months!" Tish exploded. "You're engaged, and you haven't had sex in six months?"

"I think it's romantic." Kindergarten teacher Rachael was a green-eyed blonde with delicate porcelain skin and a poetic heart. Her favorite color was springtime pink, and she favored flowing floral-print dresses. In the candlelight, through the haze of a couple of margarita-martinis, Rachael looked as if she'd stepped out of a Monet. "And very sweet."

"You think everything is romantic," Jillian pointed out.

"Oh," Delaney said quickly, "don't get me wrong. I was all for the idea."

"Why?" Jillian looked at her as if she'd said she was for a worldwide ban on chocolate.

Delaney shrugged. She wasn't all that into chocolate either. "Because honestly, our sex life wasn't so hot before and I thought maybe Evan was right, that time without physical intimacy would help us appreciate each other more. But now I'm thinking it was a dumb idea. What we really need are some techniques for spicing up our love life, not celibacy."

Her friends all started talking at once, each offering their version of how to rev up her romance with Evan before he left on his trip to Guatemala.

"Surprise him with floating candles in a hot bath," Rachael suggested. "Mood music. Massage oils."

"No, no, that's not the way to go," Jillian said. "Sexy outfits are what you need. Stilettos, thongs, a leather bustier."

"Make love outside," Tish chimed in. "Or in the laundry room or in the backseat of your car. Pick someplace you've never made love before."

"Sex toys," Jillian threw in.

"Write him X-rated poetry." Rachael giggled. "Mail him a naughty poem every day while he's out of town. He'll be crazed for you by the time he gets back."

None of this sounded like the Holy Grail of sexual experiences that her friends seemed to suggest, but Delaney was willing to give their ideas a shot. Anything to prove to herself that this impending marriage wasn't a big mistake.

"Wait a minute." Tish snapped her fingers. "I've got the perfect scenario. Kidnap Evan from his office during his lunch hour tomorrow. Do something really daring, something that feels mysterious and taboo."

"Yeah, yeah," Jill joined in. "I can see it now. Delaney calls Evan and then tells him to meet her in the parking lot outside his office for a luncheon date. She dresses up in something super sexy, but throws a coat over her outfit and . . ."

"It's June," Rachael pointed out.

"Okay, a raincoat then."

"And," Tish said, "Delaney hides behind the door and when Evan comes outside she throws a tarp over his head, puts a dildo to his back—you know, like it's a gun—and tells him if he doesn't do everything she demands then she's going to blow him away."

"She forces him into her car," Jillian continued, "and takes him off to a secluded spot and has her way with him."

"Or," Rachael added, "she could take him to a really nice hotel where they have a big spa tub and flowers and candles and room service."

Tish fanned herself. "Whew, I'm getting hot and bothered just thinking about it."

Actually, Delaney thought, it wasn't a bad idea.

Longing to find something to accelerate her low-voltage sex life, she mulled over their suggestions. What if she did kidnap Evan from his office and take him to a secluded spot and seduce him? It might just be the catalyst they needed, and it would make for a great send-off so that he didn't forget her while he was in the wilds of Guatemala.

Be realistic. This is straitlaced Evan you're talking about.

Delaney shook her head. "Evan would never go for it. He's too dignified for stuff like that."

"Which is precisely why you take him hostage. Don't give him a choice. Bring handcuffs or duct tape or zip ties." Jillian pantomimed binding her hands.

"You never know," Tish said. "Evan could very well surprise you. He might be thinking you're the one who's too dignified, and you'll both find out you're horny as rabbits."

"Tish!" Rachael exclaimed.

Tish grinned impishly. "I'm just saying."

"You know," Jillian said, "there's a sex toy store in the shopping center across the street. Why don't we go check it out? Find a dildo Delaney could use as a pretend gun."

"Excellent idea." Tish flagged down their waiter and asked for the check.

A dark sinking feeling settled inside Delaney. Blabbing about her fears may have drawn her closer to her friends, but she couldn't help thinking that in the midst of their plans, she'd once again lost sight of herself and what it was that she really wanted.

And apparently she was now off to buy sex toys.

Five minutes later Delaney found herself being hustled across the busy thoroughfare. By the time they reached the shopping center, all four of them were breathless and laughing from dodging traffic. The sex toy place was located in the far corner of the strip mall, its neon sign flashing out a vibrant red—Ooh-La-La.

They trooped past a jewelry store with engagement rings prominently positioned in the showcase. Delaney glanced down at her own four-carat marquis-cut diamond set in an elegant platinum band. Funny, try as she might, she couldn't remember how she'd felt the day Evan had slipped it on her finger. She must have been happy. Why wouldn't she be happy? She just couldn't remember being happy.

There was a party supply warehouse, then a discount shoe barn and a lingerie shop. Inset in the small space between the lingerie shop and Ooh-La-La was a consignment store specializing in wedding attire.

Delaney shouldn't even have glanced in the window. Her mother was such a snob she'd have a hissy fit if Delaney dared to buy anything from a consignment store, but an enigmatic force she could not explain whispered, *Go on, take a peek.*

Cupping her hands around her eyes, she pressed her face against the glass for a better look inside the darkened store. And then, just like that, she found what she hadn't even known she was searching for.

The wedding veil to end all wedding veils.

It was encased in glass and mounted on the wall over the checkout counter. For reasons she could not comprehend, Delaney felt as if she were standing on the threshold of something monumental.

She could not say what compelled her. She already had a perfectly beautiful wedding veil from Bergdorf Goodman's that her mother had picked out for her on their last foray into Manhattan, but she felt compelled. There was simply no other word for it.

Her friends kept walking, but Delaney stayed anchored to the spot. Transfixed. Unable to take her eyes off the veil. It was an ivory, floor-length mantilla style, and so delicate it looked as if it had been created for a fairy princess.

I'm the answer you've been searching after, the veil seemed to whisper. *The magic that's missing.*

For the first time since she'd agreed to marry Evan, something involving the approaching nuptials truly excited her.

The veil was absolutely perfect.

Delaney's fingers itched to stroke the intricate lace, but the store looked closed. The lights were dimmed. She couldn't see anyone inside, yet her hand was already pushing against the door handle.

Drawn by the sight of the wedding veil waiting just a few feet away, she stepped over the threshold.

"Delaney? Where did you go?"

Distantly, she heard her friends calling to her, but she did not turn around. She just kept moving, pulled inexplicably toward the veil. She reached out a finger and stroked the glass case.

Up close it was even more compelling. The delicate lace pattern formed a myriad of butterflies sewn with thread so fine it was almost invisible.

"May I help you?"

Startled, Delaney jumped and tore her gaze from the veil to meet the eyes of a soft-voiced, black-haired woman in her early forties. The shopkeeper wore a gauzy, purple crinkle skirt and a lavender sleeveless knit blouse. She studied her quietly.

Delaney felt a subtle but distinct atmospheric change. The room grew slightly cooler, damper, and she experienced a strange but familiar sense of connection. "Have we met?"

"Claire Kelley," the woman said with the faint hint of an Irish brogue. Her handshake was firm, self-assured.

"Delaney Cartwright."

Claire raised an eyebrow. Delaney knew that look. The woman recognized the Cartwright name, but to her surprise, Claire did not ask her if she was one of those oil money Cartwrights the way most people did.

"Tell me about the veil," Delaney said.

"You have a very discerning eye. It's a floor-length mantilla style made of rose point lace, created with a very fine needle. Rose point is considered the most delicate and precious of all laces."

"May I see it?"

The woman hesitated and then said firmly, "I'm afraid it's not for sale, Ms. Cartwright."

Delaney's father, the consummate oilman, had taught her that everything was for sale for the right price. "If I may just examine the design up close, I'd like to have one just like it commissioned for my wedding."

"That's impossible. It's one of a kind."

She couldn't say why this was suddenly so important, but need settled like a lead weight in her stomach. She curled her fingernails into her palms. "Please, I must see it."

Outside on the street she could still hear her friends calling to her, but they sounded so very far away—on another planet, in another dimension, far outside her realm of concern.

Reluctantly, Claire took a key from her skirt pocket and ticked the lock open. She removed the veil from the case and arranged it with great care on the counter in front of them.

The majesty of it hit Delaney like a softly exploding eggshell. For one incredible instant she felt as if she were floating. She forgot to breathe. She could not breathe. Did not want or need to breathe. Terrified that if she dared inhale, the veil would evaporate.

A second passed, then two, then three.

At last, she was forced to draw in a deep, shuddering sigh of oxygen.

"Butterfly wings," she whispered.

The design was constructed of tiny roses grouped to form the butterflies. The veil was so white, so beautiful—almost phosphorescent. At any moment she expected it to fly right out the door.

Isn't it amazing, she thought, *to live in a world where there is such a work of artistic beauty.*

Delaney blinked, blinded by the dazzle and the image of herself wearing the veil as she walked down the aisle to meet her groom. The image swept in and out before her eyes as if she were in a slow, dreamy faint. She stared at the veil, seeing her future wedding, seeing the man she was about to marry.

But it wasn't Evan.

In his place stood a hard-jawed man with piercing dark eyes and a world-weary expression. He looked like a guardian, a soldier, a warrior. He exuded a strong, masculine quality. For the first time in her life, she had an overwhelming urge to kiss a man she knew absolutely nothing about. And she sensed, without doubt, he would taste like caffeine—strong, brisk, and intense.

A hard shiver ran through her.

She hitched in another breath. Her vision cleared and she was aware that while only an instant had passed, a vast expanse of time had swayed before her. A chasm into an unknowable dimension.

Claire was watching her, concern reflected in her pale blue eyes, yet there was also warmth and a steady quietness that reassured Delaney.

Whatever you see, it's okay.

The shopkeeper did not speak the words, but Delaney heard them as clearly as if she'd shouted.

Like a magnet to metal, the veil tugged at something deep within her. Her body pulsed with buoyancy and desire. She shut her eyes and found the alluring pattern burned into the back of her eyelids.

"This veil is very special." Claire's voice grew sentimental and her mouth softened. "It's over three hundred years old."

An illicit thrill shot through her at the possibility. Delaney's eyes flew open. "Impossible. It's snow white. A veil that old would yellow with age."

A slight, knowing smile lifted the corners of Claire's mouth. "It's rumored to be magic."

"Magic?"

"There's a legend."

Delaney adored history and ancient lore and had a secret longing to believe in magic, to have faith in something beyond the five senses. She leaned in closer, her eyes swallowing the veil.

"A legend?" she whispered.

"Here you are!" Tish barged through the door, Jillian and Rachael following in her wake.

The interruption, like a knuckle scraped against a cheese grater, irritated her, but she loved her friends, so Delaney tamped down her annoyance and forced a smile.

"What's up?" Tish asked, coming to stand at her elbow.

"Shh," Delaney said. "Claire was about to tell me the story of the veil."

"Oh." Tish blinked, seeing it for the first time. Delaney heard her sharp intake of breath. "Wow, that's some veil."

Jillian peered over Tish's shoulder. "It's brilliant."

"Strangely mesmerizing." Rachael tilted her head to study it in the muted lighting.

"Go on with the story," Delaney pleaded.

Claire paused.

"We want to hear it too," Tish said.

The shopkeeper eyed them all, and then she cleared her throat. "Once upon a time, in long-ago Ireland, there lived a beautiful young witch named Morag who possessed a great talent for tatting lace." Claire's lyrical voice held them spellbound. "People came from far and wide to buy the lovely wedding veils she created."

"I can see why," Delaney murmured, lightly fingering the veil.

"But there were other women in the community who were envious of Morag's beauty and talent. These women made up a lie and told the magistrate that Morag was casting spells on the men of the village."

"Jealous bitches," Jillian said.

Claire arrowed Jillian a chiding glance.

"The magistrate," she continued after Jillian got the hint and shut up, "was engaged to a woman that he admired, but did not love. He arrested Morag, but found himself falling madly in love with her. Convinced that she must have cast a spell upon him as well, he moved to have her tried for practicing witchcraft. If found guilty, she would be burned at the stake."

"Oh, no." Rachael brought her fingers to her lips.

"It's just a myth," Tish said, but Delaney could tell that her friend, who pretended to have tough skin to hide a tender heart, was as enraptured with the story as the rest of them.

"But in the end, the magistrate could not resist the power of true love. On the eve before Morag was to stand trial, he kidnapped her from the jail in the dead of night and spirited her away to America, giving up everything for her love. To prove that she had not cast a spell over him, Morag promised never to use magic again. As her final act of witchcraft, she made one last wedding veil, investing it with the power to grant the deepest wish of the wearer's soul. She wore the veil on her own wedding day, wishing for true and lasting love. Morag and the magistrate were blessed with many children and much happiness. They lived to be a ripe old age and died in each other's arms."

"Ah." Rachael sighed. "That's so sweet. I was afraid they were going to burn her at the stake."

Tish snorted and rolled her eyes.

"Humph," Jillian said. "I don't think it's fair that she had to give up the very thing that defined her just for the love of a man."

"The magistrate gave up his job for her," Delaney pointed out. "And he was exiled from his homeland."

"Morag was exiled too." Tish narrowed her eyes at the veil as if she didn't trust it.

"You must remember," Claire said, "this was three hundred years ago. Things were much different then.

And the magistrate wasn't just any man, but her soul mate. There's a very big difference. You can love all manner of people, in all manner of ways, but we each have only one soul mate who not only completes us, but challenges us to grow beyond our fears."

Was it true? Delaney wondered. Was there really such a thing as a soul mate?

Whether it's true or not, muttered a saucy voice in the back of her head that sounded a whole lot like her sister, Skylar, *one thing's for sure. Evan Van Zandt is definitely not your soul mate. You're too much alike. Peas in a pod. No challenge. No emotional growth going on in that relationship.*

Delaney nibbled her bottom lip, disturbed by the thought. Maybe Evan wasn't her soul mate, but he was kind and good and honest. As children they'd played in the sandbox together.

Evan was the one person who had told her she was pretty when she was chubby and bucktoothed and nearsighted and had a hump in her nose. Both of their families heartily approved of the marriage, and she did love him. Maybe not with a magic-wedding-veil-soul-mate-for-all-eternity kind of love, but she did love him. So what if there was no red-hot chemistry? In Delaney's estimation sex was way overrated anyway.

Too bad you don't have a magistrate to kidnap you and take you away with him.

It's my fault, Delaney thought, *not Evan's.* She hadn't tried hard enough to make their sex life something special and then she'd gone and agreed to the celibacy thing and now he was going off to Guatemala to heal crippled children.

She pushed the troubling thoughts away and leaned down to examine the veil more closely. Poetry in lace. It spoke to her in a singsong of the ages. It might not be rational or practical or even sane, but she could feel an enchanted force flowing through the air.

Goose bumps spread over her arms. What if there was some truth to the legend? What if she wore the veil on her wedding day and wished that her sexual feelings for Evan would grow stronger, richer, deeper, and truer? Would it happen?

A compulsion quite unlike anything she had ever felt before gripped her. The feeling was much greater than an itch or a whim. It gnawed at her. No matter how much it might cost, she had to have this veil. Weird as it sounded, Delaney just knew that if she had the veil she would get the happily-ever-after she so desperately desired.

But what about her mother? How could Delaney begin to explain this to Honey and convince her to let her wear this veil on her wedding day?

You can figure out how to deal with her later. Just get your hands on it.

There it was again. The undisciplined voice that sounded like Skylar. A voice boldly inciting her to do things she wouldn't ordinarily dare.

"I'll give you a thousand dollars for the veil," she blurted, surprised at her feelings of desperation.

Claire shook her head. "I'm sorry, but it's not for sale."

"Three thousand," Delaney said firmly, acting as if there was no way the woman could refuse. Three grand was probably twice what this little consignment store netted in a month.

"It's not a matter of money."

"Five thousand." Enough haggling. She was determined to possess the veil.

"You would spend that much for a wedding veil?" Claire's eyes widened.

"Her grandmother left her a two-million-dollar trust fund and she just turned twenty-five," Tish interjected. "She can spend as much as she wants."

"No." Claire shook her head.

"If it's not the money," Delaney asked, "what is it?"

The shopkeeper took a deep breath and looked as if she wished they would all just go away and leave her alone. "There are complications."

"Complications?" Delaney frowned. "What kind of complications are we talking about?"

"Um . . . well . . . throughout the years the veil has . . . er . . . backfired," Claire stammered.

"Backfired? What does that mean?"

"There've been a few incidents."

"Like what?"

"Whenever people hear about the legend, they feel compelled to wish upon the veil."

"What's wrong with that?"

Claire nervously moistened her lips. "Nothing in and of itself. The problem occurs when people wish for one thing and what their hearts really want is another thing completely. Because you see, when you wish on the veil, you get whatever your soul most deeply hungers for. It's just that some people aren't ready to face what's truly in their hearts and souls."

"Be careful what you wish for because you just might get it," Jillian said.

"Exactly." Claire nodded.

"But this wedding veil is absolutely perfect," Delaney said, feeling wildly out of control, but unable to reel herself in. "I have to have it. Would seventy-five hundred dollars convince you?"

A long silence stretched across the room. All five of them were staring at the wedding veil.

"You really are desperately needin' a bit of magic in your life, aren't you," Claire Kelley murmured, her Irish brogue more noticeable now.

Delaney looked from the wedding veil to Claire and saw understanding in the shopkeeper's eyes. Eerily, it seemed as if the woman comprehended all of Delaney's doubts and fears concerning her impending marriage.

"Yes." *Far more than you can ever know.* Delaney raised her hands in supplication. "Please, sell me the veil."

"I cannot sell it to you."

An emotion she could not name, but that tasted a bit like grief, took hold of her. Why was possessing this particular wedding veil so important? There was no rational explanation for it, but an odd feeling clutched deep within her. The yearning was almost unbearable.

"Ten thousand." She felt like an acolyte begging a Zen master for enlightenment.

Claire sucked in her breath and looked around the shabby little shop. "You really want it that badly?"

Delaney nodded, too emotionally twisted up inside to speak.

"All right." Claire let out her breath in an audible whoosh. Her reluctance was palpable. "You may have it."

She felt as if someone had lifted a chunk of granite off her heart.

Delaney's breath came out on a squeak of pure joy. "Really?"

"Yes, but only under one condition," Claire cautioned.

"Yes, yes."

"You must swear that you will never, under any circumstances, wish upon the veil."

"I'll sign a waiver, a contract, whatever it takes. My friend Jillian is a lawyer; she can bear witness."

"Delaney." Jillian made a clucking noise. "Are you sure you want to do this? Ten thousand is a lot of money for a wedding veil."

Defiantly she met Jillian's eyes. "I want it, okay? Just back me up here."

Something in her face must have telegraphed her seriousness. Delaney rarely took a stand on anything, hardly ever expressed an opinion or even a strong desire, but because of this, whenever she did take a stand, people usually listened.

Jillian held up her palms and took a step back. "Hey, if it's what you want, I say go for it."

"Thank you." She turned back to Claire and reached inside her Prada handbag for her checkbook. "I promise never to wish on the veil. Now may I have it?"

Claire stuck out her hand to seal the deal. "Done."

And that was the moment Delaney realized that although she'd managed to find the special magic she'd been aching to believe in, she had just made a solemn vow never to use it.

Chapter 2

That night, Delaney dreamed of her sister.

Skylar had been dead for seventeen years, but she popped up in Delaney's dreams with surprising regularity. Although she couldn't say why her sister still played such a prominent role in her sleeping life.

Maybe it was because Skylar's passing had left her an only child. Afterward, her mother had tied the apron strings so tightly Delaney felt as if all the personality had been strangled out of her. Maybe dreaming of her outrageous sister was an avenue into her own subconscious. A way to express the feelings she'd learned to suppress.

Tonight, for some inexplicable reason, her sister wore roller skates, purple short-shorts, and a silver-sequined top hat. Other than the bizarre outfit, she looked exactly as she'd looked the last time Delaney had seen her—blond, beautiful, and sweet sixteen.

Skylar perched on the curvy footboard of Delaney's sleigh bed, enthusiastically chewing a persimmon.

"Who eats persimmons?" Delaney asked.

"I do."

"Of course you do."

"Persimmons are like me. Unique. If you were a fruit, Laney, you'd be an apple. Dependable, granted, but boring as hell."

"Watch what you're doing. You're dripping juice all over my new Ralph Lauren comforter."

Skylar rolled her eyes. "See? What'd I tell you? Boring. Go ahead and bitch all you want; you can't fool me. I know what you've been up to."

"I haven't been up to anything except protecting my expensive bedding from a persimmon-sucking ghost."

"Low blow, baby sis. But I am glad to see you're showing some spunk. Bravo," Skylar said. "However, insults aren't going to distract me from what you're hiding under the bed."

It was true. Delaney didn't want her sister poking fun at the wedding veil.

"Come on, pull it out. I know it's there. You might as well let me see it."

She sighed, knowing Skylar would pester her until she either showed her the veil or she woke up. "It's no big deal, just a wedding veil."

"Hmm, the plot thickens," Skylar mused. "What are you going to do about the veil that you've already got hanging in your closet? Remember that one? The veil Mother picked out for you."

"You're just trying to start trouble."

"But of course. Everybody knows stirring up trouble is what I do best." Skylar polished off the persimmon and chucked the remains in the trash can.

"I didn't know ghosts could eat," Delaney said, trying to deflect Skylar's attention.

"Technically, I'm not a ghost. Rather, I'm a figment of your dream imagination. You could send me packing if you really wanted to, but honestly your life would be pretty damn dull without me. So quit arguing and produce the veil." Skylar made "gimme" motions with her fingers.

Delaney flipped her head over the side of the bed and grappled underneath the bed skirt until she found the sack. She slipped it out, sat up, and cautiously handed her the sack. "Be careful with it."

Skylar peeked inside and whistled. "Holy shit, that's an awesome veil."

"I know." Her sister's approval meant a lot. Delaney felt eight years old again, full of wistful longing to be glamorous and grown-up. Hanging around Skylar's vanity, watching her apply makeup and change outfits as she got ready for a date.

"And I see that you found the veil at a consignment shop."

"Uh-huh."

"Mom's never going to let you wear it."

"I'm aware of that."

"You could fight her on this. Oops, oh, wait, I forgot. You're so into being the perfect daughter, you could never buck the flawless Honey Montgomery Cartwright."

"No need to get unpleasant." Delaney snatched the wedding veil away from Skylar and folded it back into the sack.

"Ah, perfect little princess. Lucky for me I died when I did. I would never have heard the end of how perfect you are, and how perfect I am not."

Skylar's comment shot her full of anger. Delaney

remembered the raw horror and agonizing grief she'd experienced over her sister's death. Nostrils flaring, hands knotted into fists, she faced off with her. "No, it was not lucky! It was terrible the way you died."

"Okay, sorry. Chill."

"I won't chill. The way Mother and Daddy were afterward was awful. Losing you was the worst thing that ever happened to this family. I had to be perfect because you got your silly self killed, sneaking off to a KISS concert, drinking with your friends, and then getting smashed up in a car crash. If you hadn't been so damn rebellious, you'd still be alive and I wouldn't have ended up spending my whole life making amends for something you did. I had to have chaperoned dates until I was nineteen. Mother wouldn't even allow me to go to sleep-away camp, much less a rock concert. She refused to let me get my driver's license until I was twenty-one. And it was your entire fault."

"Ooh, where's all this emotion coming from?" Skylar applauded. "I approve. Usually, you're so pent-up."

"I don't want your approval."

"Why not?" Skylar crossed her legs and the wheels of her skates left dirty marks on the sheets.

Delaney cringed. "Watch the linens, will you?"

"What? Scared you'll become like me? Scared Mommy won't love you anymore if you do?"

That's exactly what she was scared of, but Delaney couldn't tell her sister that. "I am going to wear this veil on my wedding day. Wait and see."

"Sure you are," Skylar scoffed.

"I am!"

"Nah." Skylar pushed the top hat back off her forehead and assessed Delaney with a pensive stare. "You'll cave and our mother will get her way yet again."

"I won't."

"We'll see."

Delaney clutched the sack to her chest, knowing her sister was right. If she responded true to form and accepted her mother's edicts for what constituted the perfect wedding, she would not be wearing the consignment shop veil.

"I have an idea on how to handle Mother." Skylar smirked. "If you've got the balls for it."

"There's no need to be crude." Delaney pressed her lips together. "What's your idea?"

"Why don't you sew a designer label on the veil, put it in an expensive box, and tell Mom someone very high up on the blue-blood food chain sent it to you. Like one of our Philadelphia relatives we've never met."

Delaney gasped. "But I can't do that. It's underhanded and sneaky."

"I knew you didn't have the balls for it. Night, Chicken Little." Skylar swung her legs off the bed, the wheels of her skates making a clacking noise as she stood. "See ya in your dreams."

"Wait, don't go."

Skylar paused. "Yeah?"

"Do you really think your plan would work?"

"Guaranteed." She winked.

Delaney worried her bottom lip. She wasn't a liar, but she wanted so badly to wear the veil at her wedding.

"I'll tell you something else," Skylar added.

"Oh?"

"I was hanging out tonight, eavesdropping on your

dinner conversation with your friends, and I think they're right."

"About what?"

"Seducing Evan. Making him your sex hostage. Sounds totally hot. Go for it. Maybe it'll be the jump start you two need."

"Your glowing endorsement is all the more reason not to do it." Delaney glowered.

"You sound just like her, you know." Skylar wrinkled her nose and stuck out her tongue.

"Just like whom?"

"Who do you think?"

Skylar was right. She did sound just like their mother. Judgmental, inflexible, overly concerned with appearances. And that was the last thing Delaney wanted.

She dragged a hand through her hair. "This is horrible! How can I stop from becoming like her?"

"Do the most outrageous thing you can think to do. Kidnap Evan from his office, take him to the woods, and have your way with him. I triple dog dare you."

"Fine," Delaney said. "If that's what it takes to prove to you I'm not like Mother, I'll do it."

Skylar snorted. "Seeing is believing, pipsqueak."

Following that snarky comment, Delaney woke up.

Detective Dominic Vinetti watched Dr. Evan Van Zandt stride into the exam room, frowning at the chart in his hand and shaking his head. A bullet of dread ricocheted through the ventricles of Nick's heart at the serious expression on the other man's face.

"I've received the results of your follow-up tests," Van

Zandt said, "and I'm sorry, Nick, but the outcome isn't as favorable as we had hoped."

Sweat broke across Nick's brow. He fisted his hands and swallowed hard. In this stupid paper gown he was nearly naked and felt too damn exposed. He scowled past his anxiety and mouthed toughly, "Whaddya mean?"

"It's been eight weeks since the injury and while your leg is improved, you're still healing at a much slower rate than I anticipated. I'm afraid I can't yet allow you to return to work."

Fear swamped him. Anxiety soup. Followed on its heels by a thick, rolling wave of despair. *Son of a bitch.* He could not spend one more hour watching bad television. Could not play one more video game or surf the net one more time or he'd lose his frickin' mind.

"I gotta go back to work, Doc. I'll take a desk job. Sit on my butt, no chasing suspects. I promise." He held up his palm as if he were taking an oath on the witness stand.

Van Zandt fidgeted with his tie, then flipped up the tail of his lab coat and took a seat on the rolling stool. He had the butter-soft face of a man who'd lived an easy life. "I can't in good conscience sign the release form."

Nick pressed his palms together, supplicating. "I'm going nuts, here. Please don't make me beg."

"Have you been doing your exercises?"

"Regular as a nun to mass."

Van Zandt threw back his head and brayed loudly at Nick's comment. "Well, at least you still have your sense of humor."

Irritation dug into Nick's gut. The guy laughed like a freaking barnyard donkey. "Yeah, lucky me. Ha, ha."

"Have you been taking your antibiotics?" Van Zandt asked.

"Morning, noon, and night."

"What about the pain pills?"

"Not so much."

"When was the last time you took one?"

"I never got the prescription filled when I left the hospital," he admitted.

"You're kidding."

Nick shook his head.

"There's no need to be macho. If you're hurting, take the Vicodin. Pain inhibits healing."

"Pills make me feel dulled."

"Take them anyway."

"I've seen a lot of people get addicted to those things."

"You're too strong-minded to get addicted."

"You have no idea how bored I am."

"Let's listen to your lungs." Van Zandt took a stethoscope out of his pocket. He placed the earpieces in his ears and pressed the bell of the stethoscope against Nick's back. The damn thing felt as if he'd just pulled it out of the freezer. "Deep breath."

Nick inhaled.

"Have you been eating a healthy diet?"

"I have a slice of pizza now and again, but otherwise I'm doing the whole rabbit food thing and staying away from beer like you said the last time I was here."

"Good, good." Van Zandt nodded.

"Why am I not healing? You really think it's just because I haven't been taking the pain pills?"

"Could be. How's your stress level?"

"I told you, I'm going stir-crazy with nothing to do."

"Anything else going on?" Van Zandt finished listening to his lungs and came around the examination table to lay the stethoscope against Nick's heart.

"You mean beside the fact my grandfather died two days after I got wounded on the job? And my income has been cut by a third while I'm on disability? And oh, yes, my ex-wife, who left me on our honeymoon last year, just sent me a wedding invitation. Guess what? She's three months pregnant, marrying a famous stand-up comedian, and moving to Martha's Vineyard."

Nick didn't like discussing his private business, especially that bit about Amber, but he was playing the sympathy card, hoping Van Zandt would feel sorry enough for him that he'd sign that release form.

"Really?" Van Zandt looked surprised and dropped his stethoscope back into the pocket of his lab coat.

"Yeah, my life's a regular soap opera. You've heard it on TV, maybe read it in the tabloids. I'm the schmuck who got cuckolded by Gary Feldstein." It occurred to Nick that he felt as empty inside as those new plastic specimen cups lining the shelf over the sink.

He'd closed himself off emotionally and he was dead numb. Talking about it was like poking your arm with a needle after it had been submerged in ice-cold water for a long time—you'd already lost all the feeling, it was the perfect time for more pain, before the arm woke up and started throbbing like hell.

"Ouch," Van Zandt said.

"Tell me about it. See why I have to get back to work? My mind's a mess. I need the distraction."

"I see why you're not healing. Excess stress takes a tremendous toll on our bodies. I'm getting married myself in August, so I do understand the anxiety involved. Although I can't imagine what it must be like to get dumped on your honeymoon." Van Zandt tried to appear empathetic, but only succeeded in looking constipated.

"I would say congratulations, Doc, but I'm sorta soured on the whole subject of marriage."

"Understandably so."

"Word to the wise. Watch your back."

"I appreciate the warning, but I can assure you my fiancée isn't like that."

"Yeah," Nick muttered. "That's what I thought."

"My fiancée and I have known each other since we were children. She's sweet-tempered, quiet, and modest. I've never met anyone so easy to get along with."

"Well, you know what they say about the quiet ones."

"I have no cause for concern."

The son of a bitch looked so damn smug. Like he had the world by the balls. As if he was so sure that something like that could never happen to him.

"Whatever you say." Nick shrugged. "Now that you understand where my tension is coming from, will you sign the form and put me back to work?"

Van Zandt's smile was kind, but firm. "Nice try, but no. Now let's have a look at that leg."

He pulled back the paper sheet to study Nick's injury, his fingers gently probing the knee. The wound was surprisingly tender, the scars still pink and fresh-looking. The kneecap was slightly puffy. Nick sucked in his breath at Van Zandt's poking.

"It shouldn't be this tender two months post-op." Van Zandt shook his head. "And you've still got a lot of swelling. You're going to have to baby it more. Take your pain pills. I know you're an intense guy, but for God's sake, man, try to find a way to relax."

Nick sighed. Dammit all. "How much longer?"

"I'm headed to Guatemala with a surgical team, and I'll be out of the country for six weeks," Van Zandt said. "We'll have Maryanne schedule you for an appointment the day after I get back."

"Six more weeks!"

"I know it seems like a long time, but it's what your body requires. If I allow you to go back to work too soon, you could have a relapse that would end your career as an undercover detective." Van Zandt scribbled something on a prescription pad, tore off the top sheet, and handed it to him. "This is the name of a good massage therapist. She'll teach you some relaxation techniques to get you through your recovery. In the meantime, try to find a low-key hobby to keep your mind busy."

Massage therapy? Relaxation techniques? Hobbies? What a load of crap. He needed his job back. It was the only thing that grounded him when the world was shifting beneath his feet.

"If you require anything more while I'm out of town, Dr. Bullock will be standing in for me."

Hmm, Nick thought. Maybe he could talk this Bullock character into signing his release form.

"And don't think Dr. Bullock will send you back to work," Van Zandt said. "I'm making a notation in your chart."

Ass wipe. "You know me too well."

"Go ahead and get dressed. You can leave through the doctors' entrance on the south side of the building. It's closer to the parking lot so you won't have so far to walk."

"Thanks," Nick forced himself to say.

Before he left the room, Van Zandt rested a hand on Nick's shoulder. "It's going to be all right if you do what I tell you. I promise. But if you don't . . ." He didn't finish his sentence. The warning was implicit.

Easy for him to say. He had a killer job and two good legs and a fiancée who loved him.

"Yeah." Nick nodded.

He'd come to his appointment with the expectation that he'd be returning to work on Monday. He was leaving with the realization he was stuck with himself for six more weeks, or risk losing his career forever.

Fuck it all. He felt like he'd just received a roundhouse kick to the head.

Again.

The sleek architecture of the Medical Arts Center in northwest Houston where Evan leased office space exuded a clean, faultless charm achieved only by brand-new buildings.

Feeling like an extra from *The Rocky Horror Picture Show* trying to sneak into the Oval Office for an audience with the president, Delaney paced the sidewalk outside the doctors' entrance.

The black, thigh-high, vamp boots Jillian had loaned her pinched her toes, and the pink raincoat covering her skimpy black bustier, garters, and fishnet stockings rustled noisily. A modest-sized dildo, which Tish had insisted she buy when they'd finally made it over to the sex toy store, rested in her raincoat pocket.

THERE GOES THE BRIDE

With both hands she carried a small, lightweight tarp pilfered from her father's barbecue grill. She had come fully prepared to carry out this sexy hostage-taking fantasy.

But doubt was making mincemeat of her already shaky self-confidence. Nervously, she nibbled her bottom lip, and then realized she was mangling her lipstick and forced herself to stop.

Remind me again why you're doing this?

To improve sex with Evan.

Is that really the reason?

Okay, if she was being truly honest with herself, she had to admit it was a last-ditch effort. Before she hitched her life to Evan's forever, she wanted to know if the possibility of sexual electricity even existed between them.

And if it doesn't?

Delaney shook her head. Tish and Jillian and Rachael and even her dead sister, Skylar, felt certain that taking Evan hostage for an afternoon of unexpected sexual delight was exactly the thing their relationship needed.

But what if they were wrong? What if Evan hated this surprise seduction? What if he refused to play along? Or worse yet, what if he did play along, but the seduction did nothing to spice up their sex life?

She checked her watch. Twelve-oh-five.

Where was he?

She'd phoned Evan early that morning and invited him to lunch. He'd promised to meet her in the parking lot outside of his office at noon.

He's a doctor, his time isn't his own. Patience, patience. He'll be here.

Good advice, except the waiting was ramping up her

nerves and making her palms sweaty. Quickly she peeked through the darkly tinted back door to see if she could spot Evan in the hallway.

Ooh, ooh, there he was, head down, ambling toward the exit.

Excitement spun through her. Pulse pounding, she jumped behind the door.

This is it.

She raised the tarp up in front of her, ready to toss it over his head when he came through the door.

Several seconds passed.

Where was he? What was taking so long?

Just as she was about to take another peek, the door swung open.

A thrill, unlike anything she'd ever felt, took swift possession of her. Delaney pitched the tarp down over his head, whipped the dildo from the pocket of her raincoat, and then pressed the tip of it against his spine.

"This is a gun," she growled in a movie moll voice. "Do as I say, or you're gonna get a bullet in your back."

In her imagination Evan's knees would quake. He would raise his hands over his head, beg her not to kill him, and then promise to do whatever she demanded. She was floored by the realization that having that kind of power turned her on.

But that was not what happened.

One minute she was teetering on her stiletto boots and the next minute she was lying flat on her back, pinned to the cool green lawn and peering up at the bristling stranger who was staring down at her. His hands were wrapped around her wrists and his knees were between her legs.

Everything had gone wrong. Her blood pumped crazily. Oh, God, oh, no, it couldn't be.

A bizarre sensation of déjà vu crushed her. This was crazy, insane, impossible.

Thunderstruck, she blinked, unable to believe what she was seeing. Instead of snaring her fiancé, she had bagged the man from that weird vision she'd had while she was in Claire Kelley's shop when she'd first touched the wedding veil. The hard-jawed warrior. The man she'd seen herself marrying.

You're imagining things. This can't be the same guy you saw.

But it was.

Same uncompromising chin, same dark mysterious eyes, same irresistible pull of attraction.

She gulped.

The barbecue grill tarp lay on the sidewalk beside them. Her raincoat hung open, revealing her scanty boudoir attire, and she was still holding that damnable dildo clutched in her fist.

Shame burned a red-hot blush up Delaney's neck, a rampaging forest fire of embarrassing heat consuming her entire face.

His gaze raked over her.

She watched him sizing up the situation with a look that told her he'd seen it all and done even more. Nothing surprised this guy.

Like her fiancé, he was dark-haired and had a similar build—slightly taller than average height, broad shoulders, narrow hips—but the resemblance stopped there. Evan's eyes were blue, but this guy's eyes were so brown they seemed black.

Like coffee. Or cocoa beans.

She sensed he was a man who felt everything intensely, and he didn't need much of a reason to fight. Or to make love. He was a man who dared. A man who took risks.

And he *was* the man from her vision.

Something in his face spoke to her. He would be fiercely loyal and protective, making his woman feel special and cared for. And, illogically, she wanted to be that woman.

His eyes kept drilling into hers as if on some level he recognized her too.

Silly? Fanciful? Or something metaphysical?

Delaney's chest tightened. It was as if every muscle in her body had converged around her heart and they were squeezing in rhythmic, synchronized contractions. Suddenly there didn't seem to be enough oxygen in the entire world to pacify her hungry lungs. She was breathless and struggling hard to regain some small shred of self-control.

Then again, he appeared to be doing some struggling of his own. Actually, he looked . . . *flattened.* As if she were a tornado and he was a trailer park.

His pupils constricted and he moistened his lips. His pelvis was pressed flush against her thigh and Delaney realized, to her total mortification, that he was halfway aroused.

"Is this the gun you were planning on shooting me with?" He wrenched the dildo from her hand and sent her a sardonic smirk. "'Cause it looks like it's already gone off half cocked."

Oh, God, kill me now. "I thought . . . I thought . . . you were someone else."

"Clearly."

He arched an eyebrow and took another look at her body, this one long and lingering. His eyes darkened from coffee-colored to inky black as he carefully cataloged the lacy details of her bustier.

Goose bumps dotted her skin at his appreciative stare. Her breasts prickled, her nipples tightened, and her throat closed off.

And Delaney was terrified he would notice how her body was betraying her desire.

She felt trapped, and the thought sent a shiver through her that she couldn't dismiss as being chilled. It was June in Houston. Hot, humid, sticky. Plus, she was startlingly aware that her thin plastic raincoat was molded tightly against her curves.

So was the good-looking stranger.

What had she gotten herself into? His lips hovered above hers, and she made the deadly mistake of staring at his mouth.

Anticipation raced her heart.

Perturbed by both his mocking and her stupidity for listening to her friends and dressing up like this, she splayed her palms against his chest and pushed. "Get off me, you big oaf."

Usually, she wouldn't have been so rude, but this was not a normal circumstance, and the roguish expression on his face was just begging for a bad-mannered comment.

"You're freakin' gorgeous," he murmured. "What gives? You shouldn't have to throw a tarp over a guy to get him to go out with you."

"Off!" She tried to sound tough and bitchy, but she

wasn't good at tough and bitchy, and she came off sounding more scared than anything else.

"Yes, ma'am." He rolled to one side.

"And give me that back." She sat up and snatched the dildo from his hand.

He laughed then, a rich, melodious sound rolling over her like a spring breeze, and she almost liked him for it.

Almost.

Then a shocking thought occurred. What if Evan came out of the clinic and caught her like this? Sitting half naked on the ground like some deranged Victoria's Secret model. The notion was enough to propel her to her feet. Quickly she belted her raincoat closed and jammed the lurid sex toy back inside her pocket. She had to get out of here. Her mission of seduction had failed miserably.

Well, it wasn't a totally failed seduction; the oddly familiar stranger was looking at her as if he wanted to eat her for dessert. Unfortunately, she'd managed to arouse the wrong man.

Breathing heavily, Delaney snatched up the tarp and spun on her high-heeled boots, striding for the sanctuary of her car.

"Hey, lady," the guy called after her.

She wanted to keep walking, but years of good breeding wouldn't allow her to ignore him. Frustrated, she turned and snapped, "What is it?"

He stretched out a hand. "Could you help me up here? Seeing as how you're the reason I ended up on my butt in the grass."

For the first time she noticed the brace strapped to his right leg. He was impaired.

Guilt flooded her. She slapped three fingertips across her lips. "Oh, my, I'm so sorry."

"'S'all right."

"How did you do that, you know, with an injured leg?" she asked, hurrying back toward him.

"Do what?"

"Flip me onto my back."

"I'll never tell." His smile was pure wickedness.

Delaney felt something start to unwind inside her. Something she could not name, but it had been bound up tight for a very long time. Her breath escaped her lungs, rushing out over her lips. She stepped closer. She was looming over him, but it felt as if he were the one dominating her personal space and not the other way around.

How was that possible?

Clutching the tarp to her chest with one hand, she put out her other hand to help him up.

He took it.

His palm was hard and calloused, his grip strong. Her skin burned. Dumbfounded, she felt herself dissolving. Becoming something else, someone else. Her jaw dropped open. No words came out. What was there to say?

"Give me a tug." His fingers closed more tightly around her hand.

She yanked him to his feet and then he was standing right in front of her. Eye level.

He wasn't but a couple of inches taller than her own five-foot-nine height. Barely but distinctly, he leaned in toward her. Close enough for his black T-shirt emblazed with the Harley motorcycle logo to brush the sleeve of her raincoat. And for Delaney to feel the heat of his breath on her cheek.

A thermal wave of energy hit her and she battled the urge to push her body against his. The sensation was so compelling, Delaney realized that if she didn't move away right this instant, this very macho male was going to kiss her.

Defensively crossing her arms over the tarp and holding it close to her chest, she turned. Moving as quickly as she could in the damnable stilettos, she raced for her silver Acura.

Fingers trembling, she fumbled the keys from her pocket, jabbed them in the lock, wrenched the door open, and tumbled inside.

Consumed by remorse, she squeezed her eyes closed. Her breath came in heavy, irregular gasps.

What if Evan had seen them?

Where was Evan? Her eyes flew open, her gaze tracking to the digital clock in the dash. Twelve-twenty.

She tossed the tarp in the backseat, then took her cell phone from the console and flipped it open. She started to punch in Evan's number, but then saw she had one missed call. She entered the code to hear her messages.

It was her fiancé.

"I'm sorry to do this to you, Laney," Evan's recorded voice said. "But I've got an emergency at the hospital. Rain check?"

Rain check.

Delaney looked down at her pink raincoat and then stared up at the cloudless sky. It might be sunny and hot, but she couldn't shake the feeling there was one hell of a thunderstorm heading her way.

Chapter 3

Two days had passed and for some bizarre reason, Nick couldn't stop thinking about the sexy vixen who had ambushed him outside the orthopedic clinic.

Whenever he closed his eyes, he could see how she'd looked walking away from him, rolling and swaying, as if she were gliding on an ocean wave. Serene, calm, untouched by external circumstances. He wished he'd had hours to watch her, study her—okay, all right, *ogle* her.

Her light brown shoulder-length hair, streaked with enticing blond strands, had been styled in a straight sleek style that underscored her cool-as-a-cucumber aloofness. She wasn't voluptuous like the women he usually dated, like his ex-wife, Amber. Yet in spite of her athletic figure, she had sufficient curves. He'd gotten a pretty good look at what she'd been hiding underneath that raincoat.

Not bad. Not bad at all.

Something about her compelled him in a way no one

woman had in a very long time, and it shook him. He thought he'd washed his hands of all that romantic junk.

She looked like a woman who had a lot to say, but never got to say it. Nick found himself wishing he could be the one to hear what was inside her head, learn the secrets she kept closed up behind those sphinxlike lips.

What was it about this particular woman that got to him? Was it her unflappable calmness that made him ache to rumple her? Maybe it was her wide, slightly crooked mouth that seemed out of sync with the rest of her? That mouth was the most interesting part of her beauty, precisely because it didn't fit.

Or perhaps it was her eyes—sharp, smart, and green as an oasis. Looking into the depths of her made him feel like a traveler lost in an enchanted forest. Of course, it could have just been the sizzling underwear peeping from behind the raincoat and her unexpected willingness for adventuresome sex play.

A shudder passed through Nick. Whatever the cause, the woman was F-I-N-E, fine.

He'd been damn tempted to ask for her phone number, but it was clear from the huge rock on her ring finger she was deeply involved with someone else. And to Nick's way of thinking, there was nothing more off-limits than a woman who was spoken for. Too bad. A little sexual healing would have been a very nice way to pass his recovery time until Dr. Van Zandt got back from Guatemala.

Yeah, right, like you would ever have a chance with her even if she wasn't engaged. She's filet mignon, and you're a hot dog.

Determined to burn her off his brain, Nick decided a workout was in order.

He ambled out to his pickup truck, favoring his achy knee, and drove over to Gold's Gym. Strenuous cardio was out of the question, but he could do upper-body strength training, and Doc Van Zandt had endorsed swimming.

After twenty minutes in the lap pool, Nick emerged winded with water trickling down his bare chest and abdomen. He dried off with a thin white cotton towel, his heart punching hard against his rib cage, his lungs burning. Fatigue weighted him, but his thoughts were still locked on his mystery woman. He kept picturing her on his bed, in that girly pink raincoat, knowing full well that she was wearing next to nothing underneath.

What was the inexplicable pull? Where had it come from, this continual, aching need that had dogged him for two long, agonizing days?

He hit the weight machines. Working out his triceps, his biceps, his pecs. He pushed himself until his arms quivered, desperate to sublimate his sexual desires with exhaustion. But this time, instead of easing his mental torture, exercise seemed to have fueled it. He was doubly aware of his body, of his physical needs.

Face facts, Vinetti, you can't have her. The woman is already spoken for. Maybe that was why he couldn't stop thinking about her. Because she was strictly off-limits. Dammit. What the hell was so special about this one?

His cell phone rang.

Relieved to finally have something else to focus on, Nick snatched up the cell phone from his gym bag and punched the TALK button. "'Lo?"

"Nicky, it's your nana."

Immediately the muscles at his shoulder blades tensed and his grip tightened around the phone. "Is everything all right?"

"Yes, yes. I just needed to talk to you about something."

"What's up?" Sweat ran down his forehead and he swiped it away with his gym towel.

"I'm ready to go through your grandfather's personal effects. Could you drop by tomorrow afternoon, say three-thirtyish, and help me start packing things up?"

Nick hesitated.

It wasn't that he had anything else to do tomorrow. Nor was it that he minded in the least helping his grandmother. He'd move heaven and earth for her. What he hated was the thought of saying good-bye to his grandfather once and for all.

Nick had been just seven years old when his father, his two younger brothers, Richie and Johnny, and his sister, Gina, had moved in with Nana and Grampa in their three-story Victorian on Galveston Island. Over the course of the last year, everything in Nick's life had changed. His bride had left him on their honeymoon. His knee had gotten mangled, forcing him off the job he loved for weeks, and his grandfather had passed away. He simply wasn't prepared to handle any more changes.

"Are you sure now is the right time?" he said. "It's only been two months."

"It's time," she said. "It's got to be done."

"There's no reason we can't wait a while longer."

"Yes, there is, Nicky. I'm selling the house," she said, her firm tone telling him she'd brook no argument.

Nick couldn't have been more stunned if she'd reached

through the phone and punched him squarely in the gut. "Nana, no, absolutely not. You can't sell the house."

"I can't talk about this now. There's someone at the front door. We'll finish this discussion when you come over tomorrow afternoon." And with that, she hung up on him.

The dial tone mocked his ear.

Nana had hung up on him!

Feeling as if he'd just gone fifteen pulverizing rounds with a heavyweight boxing champ, Nick slipped his cell phone back into his gym bag.

All right then, if that's the way it was going to be, he'd look at the upside. At least he had something to do besides fantasize about the woman in the raincoat and fret over his knee—confront his grandmother and convince her she couldn't sell the only real home he'd ever known.

On Sunday evening, Delaney got her rain check.

Evan took her to La Maison Vert, the only five-star French restaurant in Houston. He wore a tux. She had on a little black cocktail dress. The decor was elegant, the service impeccable. And the pan-seared, pecan-encrusted mahimahi bathed in a rich buttery caper sauce was definitely worth the three additional hours on the treadmill the extra calories were going to cost her.

It should have been a magical evening.

Instead, Evan talked nonstop about his work, spoiling the romantic mood. Any other time, Delaney wouldn't have minded. Evan was passionate about his job and she was a good listener, but tonight she found herself wishing that he were half as passionate about her as he was about medicine.

She'd still planned on seducing him, but extreme embarrassment—following what had happened outside Evan's office—caused her to give up on the hostage-taking fantasy and go for something a little lower key. She had reserved a room at the Hyatt and worn a dress that showed lots of cleavage with sexy underwear underneath, and she'd ordered oysters on the half shell for an appetizer.

But Evan hadn't wanted any.

Glumly, she'd sucked down the delicacies alone while her husband-to-be extolled the virtues of a new hip replacement procedure. Delaney zoned out on the details. She didn't know how to tell him he was boring her to tears.

This is how the meals are going to go for the rest of your life. Skylar's voice rang in her head.

Now that was a depressing thought.

It's okay, she reassured herself. She had her work too, and she loved it. Evan probably got just as bored listening to her talk about All the World's a Stage as much as his shoptalk bored her. Except she never really talked about her job with him.

She'd gotten into the business of staging houses quite by accident. She had received her master's degree in liberal arts and was trying to decide what to do with it when Tish, who'd been struggling to make a big mortgage payment after her divorce, asked Delaney to help her fix up her house so she could sell it.

She had given her friend's place a complete makeover, and it sold the following week at ten thousand more than the asking price—and that was after the house had been on the market for over a year. Delaney had found her niche, and on the plus side, it was also a career her mother endorsed.

Excited by the headiness of that first success, she'd borrowed money from her father and started All the World's a Stage last summer. But while the business was breaking even, it was only because of her mother's friends. To date, besides Tish, only one other of her clients had not come from the pool of people who regularly kissed up to Honey Montgomery Cartwright.

But Delaney was eager to change all that. She was determined to succeed on her own, without her mother's help.

She ordered another glass of wine to loosen her up enough to proceed with her plans for seduction. Evan was leaving for Guatemala tomorrow morning. If she couldn't coax him into bed tonight, she wouldn't have another chance before their wedding.

She assessed him through the glow of a pricey zinfandel. He was classically handsome—flawless to a fault, perfectly symmetrical features, manicured fingernails, complexion like a baby's, every hair combed smoothly into place.

And Delaney couldn't help comparing him to the rugged guy she'd tarped outside Evan's office.

Now there was a man. *Ha-cha-cha*.

Immediately her mind conjured up a picture of him. Beard stubbling his firm jaw, calluses on his hands, tanned skin, unruly hair curling around his collar. He put her in mind of Gerard Butler, the rugged British actor who'd played the phantom of the opera in the recent film version of the famous musical. It was one of her favorite movies. He possessed the same hauntingly mesmerizing quality of extreme masculinity that Mr. Butler did.

Her heart thumped faster just thinking about him.

He was everything she had never wanted. Bold, brash, cocky. And yet, again and again, over the course of the last couple of days, her mind had been drawn to thoughts of him.

He's a fantasy; forget him. Your future is sitting right in front of you.

But those biceps. Those piercing dark brown eyes. She sighed.

She squinted at Evan in the candlelight and tried to get worked up, but an undertow of anxiety tugged at her thoughts. He was a very good-looking man. Why couldn't she get stoked over him the way she did over this stranger? What was wrong with her?

"And by then," Evan was saying, "we'll be ready to have kids, and then you can give up your business and stay home."

"What?" Delaney blinked, realizing she'd spaced out. "What did you say?"

Evan repeated what he'd said.

"I'm not giving up my business. I love my business. What made you think I would give up my business?"

"We don't need the money, and our children will require your undivided attention."

"What about your undivided attention? Don't kids need a dad as much as a mom? Why don't you give up your job?"

He laughed, the braying sound affecting her like fingernails on a chalkboard. When had the sound of his laugh first started to irritate her? She'd never really noticed before what an unattractive sound it was.

"Okay, point taken," he said. "You can keep the business as a sideline and we'll hire a part-time nanny."

"Oh, thanks so much for your permission."

"You're mad?" Evan looked bewildered. "Why are you mad?"

"Nothing. I'm not mad." She held up her palms. He didn't even realize he'd been patronizing her. "Never mind."

"No, no, let's talk this through."

His calm rationality was getting on her nerves. Which was weird. His steady sensibility was one of the things Delaney liked most about him.

Thankfully, her cell phone picked that moment to ring.

Evan gave her a gently chiding look. "You left your cell phone on? This is our last dinner together for six weeks."

"You leave your cell phone on whenever we go out," Delaney said, feeling a little defensive as she searched in her clutch purse for the slim flip phone.

"I'm a doctor; there could be emergencies," he said. "You stage houses for a living." There it was again, that slightly condescending tone in his voice.

She found the phone and checked the caller ID. It was from Trudie Klausman, the one client who had not come to her from her mother's sphere of social influence. "Excuse me, Evan, I need to take this."

Delaney put her napkin on the table, pushed back her chair, and hurried to an out-of-the-way alcove to take the call.

"Trudie," she greeted her caller. "How are you?"

"Fine, just fine."

"How's the new condo?"

"Wonderful, I love it. There's so much to do here, so many activities, and lots of handsome widowers to chase after in my golf cart."

"That's great to hear."

"Listen," Trudie said, "I've got a friend who's looking to sell her house."

"Really." A smile flitted across her lips. At last, a referral that had nothing to do with her mother.

"My friend lives on Galveston Island in an old Victorian. It's a beautiful place, but needs work. Her husband died a couple of months ago and she's really lonely."

"That's sad," Delaney said. "I'm so sorry to hear it."

"It's been rough on her. They were married fifty-two years, and Leo was the love of her life."

Delaney made a noise of sympathy. "Tragic."

"Well," Trudie said, "they did get fifty-two wonderful years together. Most of us aren't so lucky. Anyway, a condo came open here at Orchid Villa right across the courtyard from my place. But she can't afford the condo until she sells her house. The condo won't last long. You know how quickly the properties are going around here, so she needs to sell the house as soon as possible. Can you drop by tomorrow afternoon and give her your expert opinion?"

"Trudie," Delaney said, "I'd be happy to do what I can for your friend."

"Can you come around three? Got a pen so I can give you the address?"

"Three would be perfect. Hang on, I've got my Black-

Berry right here." She dug the device from her purse and powered it on. "Go ahead."

"Her name is Lucia Vinetti." As Trudie gave her the address, Delaney felt her excitement growing. She hadn't had a project in a couple of weeks, and she was eager to work and get her mind off the wedding plans.

In the course of a two-minute conversation, Delaney had completely forgotten about seducing Evan. If she couldn't find the magic that was missing from her life through love, then she would do it through her work. Now, all she could think about was making sure Lucia Vinetti's house sold quickly and for the most amount of money possible.

And opening up a whole new aspect of her career.

Lucia Vinetti and her friend Trudie Klausman strolled through her garden in the gathering twilight, admiring the flowering bougainvilleas, inhaling the scent of red honeysuckle growing up the fence.

"I hope I'm doing the right thing. Messing with fate can be a risky proposition," Lucia Vinetti said as she pulled a small bottle of lavender lotion from the pocket of her apron and rubbed a dab of it into her hands.

She'd led such a wonderful life, she'd never really minded growing old. But these wrinkly brown spots on her hands, Mother Teresa, how she hated them. When Leo was alive, he would laugh about her vanity, kiss her hands, and tell her she was in luck, because brown was his favorite color. Remembering her husband, Lucia smiled while at the same time her heart welled with sadness. She was going to miss this place so much, the garden in particular where she and Leo had worked side by side, coaxing things to grow.

"I'm telling ya, Luce, Delaney is the one for your Nicky," her best friend Trudie said.

"But playing matchmaker? I'm not sure it's prudent to interfere in other people's love lives."

Even at seventy-five Trudie still dressed like the Las Vegas showgirl she used to be. Garish colors, styles made for women a third of her age, outrageous props. Tonight she had a lime green feather boa tossed around her neck. But Lucia never judged Trudie for her eccentric clothes. She might be outrageous, but she was the truest friend Lucia had ever had.

"The minute I met this girl, I knew she was the one for your grandson." Trudie sounded so certain. "But just to be sure, I did her astrological chart. The stars never lie. She and Nick are destined to be together."

"But you said she's engaged to marry another man." Lucia kept rubbing her hands long after the lotion had been absorbed. Nervous habit, but then playing around with fate was something to be nervous about. "That isn't a good sign. Nick's already been cut to the quick by one fickle female; the last thing I want is to see my grandson get hurt again."

"You were engaged to someone else when you met Leo," Trudie reminded her.

Lucia thought of Frank Tigerelli, the wealthy man her family had wanted her to marry. He'd ended up going to prison in some real estate scam. Thank God for her Leo. He'd saved her from making the gravest mistake of her life.

"If something goes wrong and Nicky gets hurt, I'll never forgive myself," Lucia said.

"We're just putting them together and letting nature take its course," Trudie assured her. "If they meet and the whammy doesn't strike, no harm, no foul."

Lucia nodded and took a deep breath. Her grandson needed something to jar him out of his doldrums.

"Will you tell me the story again about how you knew Leo was the one?" Trudie asked, absentmindedly twirling her boa. "I love that story. Look at me. I had to go through three husbands before I got it right, and then Artie up and dies on me. Men."

Lucia smiled. "Our first meeting was such a cliché, I don't get why it fascinates you so."

"You know why. Tell the story."

The truth was Lucia loved telling the story as much as Trudie loved hearing it. "I had just turned eighteen. A friend and I had been invited to a party thrown by a man in our office where we both worked as secretaries. The party turned out to be very dull. I looked at a clock on the wall and it was only nine-ten. I wanted so badly to leave, but my girlfriend who'd given me a ride didn't want to go. She'd found a fellow to flirt with."

"Not much of a party girl, were you?"

"No." Lucia smiled. "I seriously doubt that you and I would have been friends if we'd met back then."

"Probably not," Trudie agreed. "So then what happened next?"

"I was about to call my father to come get me, when Leo walked into the room. And then it hits me. A bolt from the blue. The whammy."

"What did the whammy feel like?"

"My heart started pounding and I wanted desperately to run away, but at the same time I couldn't take my eyes off him. Nor he me. He comes toward me and the crowd parts like the Red Sea. I'm barely breathing."

Trudie sighed happily.

"Leo introduces himself and we start talking and talking and talking. The room gets less crowded and quieter. We find a seat and keep talking. My friend shows up and wants to leave. Leo tells me he'll give me a ride home so I tell my friend to go on without me. Finally we're the only ones left at the party. Even the host went to bed. I looked at the clock and it says nine-fifteen. I'm starting to think I'm caught in some weird waking dream and then I realize the clock has stopped. It stopped the minute I saw Leo." Lucia's voice broke and tears sprang to her eyes.

"Aw, Luce, I'm sorry. I shouldn't have prodded you to tell that story," Trudie fretted. "I didn't mean to make you cry."

"It's all right." Lucia swiped at her eyes. "Even though it hurts, I like remembering Leo."

"See, don't you want that kind of love for Nick?"

"Of course I do."

"Then let go of your fears and put your trust in the magic that stopped that clock the minute you and Leo met. If Delaney Cartwright *is* Nick's soul mate, they'll know it."

"And if she isn't?"

Trudie shrugged. "She's still a whiz at staging houses."

Chapter 4

James Robert, what is this?"

Jim Bob Cartwright glanced up from the *Houston Chronicle* Sunday crossword puzzle he was working to help him fall asleep and saw his wife, Honey, standing in the doorway, holding something out in front of her as if it were going to give her a disease. Jim Bob pushed his reading glasses up on his forehead to see what she was talking about.

"Looks like a wedding veil."

"Exactly." Honey's lips were pressed together in a tight, disapproving line. If she hadn't just had a round of Botox, Jim Bob had no doubt she would have been frowning.

He slid his glasses back down on his nose. "What's a ten-letter word for flawless?"

"Perfection," she said. "I found it under Delaney's bed."

"What? Perfection?"

"No, the wedding veil. Perfection is a ten-letter word for flawless."

"So is Honey Leigh." He smiled at her.

"I doubt that's what the makers of your crossword puzzle had in mind," she said dryly. "Delaney bought this at a consignment shop. If she thinks I'm going to let her wear this shabby thing at her wedding, she's going to have to think again."

"I think it looks nice," he said.

"You would," Honey grumbled and set the veil down on the edge of the bed. "It's from a consignment shop."

"What's wrong with that?"

"It's tacky. It's been on other women's heads." Honey shuddered.

"What were you doing snooping in her room?"

"I wasn't snooping," she said defensively.

"No?"

"If you must know, I went to turn down her covers so she could slip right into bed when she gets home from her date with Evan. I expect they'll be out late since this is the last night they'll have together for six weeks. I saw the corner of the veil sticking out from underneath her bed and pulled it out for a look. What perplexes me is why she would want to wear a used veil. I've raised her better than that."

"You're too hard on her," he said, but thought, *Who are you, Martha Stewart?* "Cut her some slack."

"We've had this discussion a million times."

"And you always win."

"That's right, and don't make me say why."

Skylar.

Their eldest daughter's name hung in the air between

them, painful as a third-degree burn. Jim Bob blinked and stared hard at the crossword puzzle.

He couldn't say for sure when his marriage had started to unravel; certainly Skylar's death had been a pivotal turning point. But if he were being honest, Jim Bob would admit the marriage had been fraying long before then, and he had no real idea why. He still loved Honey, deep down inside, but they hadn't been close in a very long time.

In fact, when he thought back on their life together, he wondered if they'd ever really been emotionally intimate. Honey was always on guard, worried about presenting a glossy image of the impeccable wife, hostess, mother, or what have you. It felt like she was a consummate actress who'd perfected a role in a long-running play, and she was determined to get rave reviews each and every night.

And she expected him to play the perfect leading man, although she never hesitated to let him know how he failed to live up to the role.

He supposed her insistence on living what she called the "proper way" came from being a blue blood with a pedigree she could trace back to European royalty. While his family, before his great-grandfather had struck oil back in the 1920s, had been nothing but dirt-poor farmers. For reasons he couldn't fathom, foolish things like not allowing Delaney to wear a used wedding veil mattered greatly to his wife.

With a clarity undiminished by the passing years, Jim Bob remembered the first time he laid eyes on Honey. He'd been attending a summer seminar at the University of Pennsylvania, and he'd seen her striding purposefully across campus as if she knew exactly who she was and where she was going and she wasn't about to let anything or anyone stand in her way.

That strong sense of purpose was what had initially attracted him to her. She possessed a special something that he lacked—a driving force that pushed her to continually better herself. He admired the quality, but honestly did not fully understand it. Honey was a doer, whereas Jim Bob was just happy to be along for the ride. In that regard, Delaney had taken after him.

Growing up the youngest of the three Cartwright brothers, with a larger-than-life father, Jim Bob had gotten lost in the shuffle of his legendary family. He was laid-back and easygoing. Loved having a good time and believed that life took care of itself, that you really shouldn't have to work so hard at it. Unlike Honey, who discounted anything that came easily.

His family had loved Honey from the minute they'd met her. Both because her blue-blood status gave respectable cache to their oil field money and because they believed she was exactly what Jim Bob needed to give him some direction in life.

They were right on both counts.

Honey had taken to his family like, well, a duck to water. Her own mother had died shortly after they'd met and she had no other immediate family. She'd told Jim Bob she didn't get along with her distant relatives, since they'd forsaken her during her mother's long illness. Medical bills had drained most of the fortune her father had made in textiles. Even her family home had been mortgaged to the hilt. They'd never been back to

Philadelphia, and none of Honey's relatives ever called or came to visit.

But her high-society cache and Honey's unerring sense of direction hadn't brought Jim Bob the happiness he'd thought their marriage was supposed to provide. His children had been the only things that had given him real joy.

And then Skylar had been killed.

Honey blamed him wholly, completely. Blamed his permissiveness and what she called his screwed-up priorities. Putting fun ahead of safety. And he couldn't fault her for it. He'd actually pleaded Skylar's case for less restriction, convincing Honey to untie the apron strings and let Skylar go to that damnable rock concert. Jim Bob never regretted any decision more.

When Honey had told him he would get absolutely no say in raising Delaney, he'd stepped out of the picture as far as discipline was concerned. Even when he didn't agree with something his wife was doing, like putting Delaney on a strict diet, or pressuring her into plastic surgery, or egging her on to marry Evan, he'd kept his mouth shut. Jim Bob's ideas on child rearing had gotten his oldest daughter killed. What in the hell did he know? He couldn't buck Honey on anything.

Jim Bob peered over the top of his newspaper. Honey was sitting on the edge of the bed, staring at the wedding veil as if it were a poisonous viper. She was so damn determined this wedding had to meet some impossibly high standard she'd set up in her own mind. It was costing him a fortune, but the money wasn't what bothered Jim Bob. He worried that Delaney was getting married simply to please her mother.

Not that he disliked his future son-in-law. Evan Van Zandt was a good guy and came from a very respectable family. Delaney could do far worse. It was just that, because of Honey's overprotectiveness, Delaney had never really experienced life. Evan was the only man she'd ever dated. She'd never lived on her own, nor was she well traveled. She hadn't even worked at anything other than this little business venture she'd started, except teaching undergrads when she was working on her master's degree.

If it weren't for Honey pressuring her friends into using All the World's a Stage when they sold their houses, he doubted Delaney could keep the business afloat without tapping into the trust fund his mother had set up for her. Jim Bob couldn't help feeling that his daughter deserved so much more out of life.

But how could he advise Delaney on marriage when his own was in such rocky shape?

Where had things gotten so messed up?

He looked at Honey. A sweep of blond hair had fallen across her cheek, and his heart wadded in his chest. The past was gone, and he felt the future ebbing away like hourglass sand. God, he'd screwed things up so badly.

"I've let you down," he said to Honey.

"Excuse me?" She looked up, assessing him with cool green eyes that revealed nothing. The same inscrutable eyes Delaney had inherited.

"Over the years, I haven't been the kind of husband you deserved."

She stared at him for a long moment then said, in the oddest tone of voice, "I got exactly what I deserved."

"You didn't deserve an alcoholic."

"James Robert, you've been sober for fifteen years. It's all in the past. Forget about it."

"I'll never be able to forget it. Or what I did to you and Delaney," he said. "I haven't really made full amends."

"Yes, you have."

"If I'd truly made amends then why haven't you forgiven me? I'm so sorry I hurt you, Honey. So very sorry."

"You're forgiven. Now can we stop talking about this, please?"

"You should have divorced me."

"I'm going to keep this veil," she said, getting up and crossing the room to put the veil in her closet. "If Delaney wants it back, she's going to have to ask me for it."

It irritated him that she pretended to forgive him when he knew she hadn't. She punished him every day. Like she was doing now. By not allowing him to say what he needed to say. By dismissing his apology as inconsequential.

"I want things to be better between us," Jim Bob said. "Like they used to be when we were first married. Remember?"

"Let's go to sleep, James Robert. It's late."

"Stop changing the subject. I don't want to talk about wedding veils. I want to talk about us. How we're going to spend the rest of our lives once Delaney is married and off on her own and she's no longer the glue holding us together."

Honey looked at him with those calm green eyes that revealed nothing about what she was really feeling. "I don't know what you intend to do, but I'm planning on living my life exactly as I have been."

"Filling it up with what? Charity events and Pilates and spa dates with your friends?"

"Why, yes."

"Where do I fit into your plans?"

"What is it that you want from me?"

I want you to love me the way you used to! He wanted to grab her by the shoulders and shake some feeling into her. But you couldn't force people to feel something for you if they didn't.

His chest constricted. "What happened, Honey? What happened to the girl I married? The one who had big dreams and an even bigger heart? The one who used to laugh at my jokes and let her hair down once in a while? The one who told me we were a team and as long as we were together, nothing could break us?"

She reached across the bed and stroked his cheek with her index finger, the unexpected tenderness in her eyes cutting straight to his heart. "Delaney's grown now. We're in our mid-fifties. What's past is past. I can't be something I no longer am, and I can't bring Skylar back. Now please, can we just go to bed?"

He wanted to shout. He wanted to throw something against the wall. Anything to get her attention.

But he did not.

Jim Bob put the crossword puzzle aside, turned out the light, and slid down in bed. He reached for Honey and pulled her into his embrace. She did not resist, but she held her body so stiffly against him, he could take no comfort in her arms.

She was an ice queen. Beautiful, but untouchable. Impossible to know even after thirty-four years of marriage.

There was no getting through to her. He'd been trying

for years. She had her idea of the way things were supposed to be, and Honey refused to budge. The terrible
thing was, much as he still loved her, Jim Bob didn't
know if he could live with that anymore.

Divorce was an ugly word, but he was almost ready to
say it.

When Honey had finally fallen asleep, Jim Bob got
up, went to the closet, took out the wedding veil, and put
it back underneath his daughter's bed.

Someone in this family damn well deserved to hold
on to their dreams.

On Monday, after seeing Evan off at the airport, Delaney guided her silver Acura south toward Galveston Island to meet Lucia Vinetti. Her mind wandered during
the fifty-minute drive and for some inexplicable reason,
she found herself thinking about the man she'd thrown
the tarp over outside Evan's office. The man from her
mysterious vision.

Why did she keep thinking about him?

She liked well-groomed, well-bred men. Not scruffy,
tough guys who stared at her as if they could see every
thought that passed through her head.

Even now, just recalling the way his dark eyes had
stared at her caused Delaney's body to tingle.

She shivered. She didn't like feeling this way. It upset
her equilibrium. And she had spent her life putting on a
calm face. Passive nonresistance had taken her this far in
life, and she was sticking with it.

*Forget the guy. He's just an illusion. An image of mas-
culine perfection you've conjured in your own mind.
Focus on the job at hand. This is what you want. Your*

own base of clients and referrals, so you can prove to your mother that you don't need her interfering in your life.

Although it was just a small step, this new project represented the freedom she'd longed for, but had just been too afraid to reach out and grab. Winning this contract was a huge deal for her, and she wasn't going to let the memory of some studly guy she'd briefly brushed up against distract her from her goal.

She longed to make her business something special. Something that was hers alone, but until now she'd been floating along, just letting her mother make things happen for her. Taking the path of least resistance. It was her pattern.

Delaney crossed the bridge onto Galveston Island and traveled the main thoroughfare. At the next red light, she consulted her notes for the correct address. Lucia's place was several blocks north of the beach.

When she turned onto Seawall Boulevard, the sight of the Gulf of Mexico made her smile. Her mother hated Galveston, with its scandalous island history and touristy atmosphere, precisely the two things Delaney loved most about the town.

She found the adorable old Victorian residence without any problem. The lawn, while trimmed short, was not landscaped with any particular design in mind. A hedge here, a flower bed there, a clump of coconut-bearing palm trees thrown in.

The house was painted an outdated color of canary yellow and trimmed in powder blue. Wind chimes dangled from the porch and pink flamingos decorated the yard. Whimsical, kitschy, and cute, but definitely not for the more upscale clientele willing to pay top dollar for an island retreat. Delaney took out her notebook and jotted: *work on curb appeal.*

She parked in the driveway beside a white ten-year-old American-made sedan and hurried up the sidewalk. Before she even had a chance to knock, the door was thrown open, revealing Trudie Klausman dressed in a pink Bermuda shorts set and a bright red fedora and beside her stood a kind-faced woman in her early seventies. She wore a floral-print housedress covered with a well-worn, faded blue gingham apron.

The sight of the woman conjured images in Delaney's mind of chocolate chip cookies and pastries made from scratch with loving hands. Lucia looked like the grandmother Delaney had always longed for, but never had. Her mother's mother had died before Honey had even married her father. And her father's mother had been infirm with a debilitating illness, living the remainder of her years in a private care facility. Delaney had never known her grandmother when she'd been spry and healthy.

"It's so good to see you," Trudie said. "This is my friend Lucia. Lucia, meet Delaney Cartwright."

She held out her hand to Lucia, but the elderly woman ignored her outstretched palm and instead enveloped her in an embrace that smelled like vanilla extract and lavender soap. "Welcome to my home, Delaney. It's so nice to meet you. Trudie's told me so many wonderful things about you."

A glow of warmth at the woman's friendliness stole through her. After meeting Lucia, she wanted the job more than ever. "Thank you, Mrs. Vinetti. I'm honored that you're considering hiring All the World's a Stage."

"Please, call me Lucia."

"Lucia it is." Delaney smiled.

"Come inside," Lucia invited. "I can't wait to see what you think of the house."

In true Victorian fashion the rooms were small, but plentiful. While the house was exceptionally clean, and the woodwork phenomenal, it was a little worse for the wear. Fifty-two years of family living jam-packed the house with knickknacks and photographs and keepsakes.

It looked as if Lucia never threw anything away, and apparently a lot of people had given her many things over the years she felt obligated to display. Her homey style, while wonderful for living in, was too jumbled for enticing buyers. Nothing was cohesive. Not design or color schemes. Not furniture style or window treatments. If Lucia were to show the house in its present state, potential buyers would see it as overcrowded, old-fashioned, and out of step.

Delaney, however, loved it.

Lucia's house presented her first real decorating challenge. Her mother's friends and acquaintances were the kind of women who redecorated every few years. They were well aware of trends and fashions. Staging their homes for sale had usually consisted of little more than rearranging furniture for the best layout or bringing bits of nature indoors to create a breezy feel or simply giving the place a good cleaning.

"Trudie tells me you're engaged to be married," Lucia said.

"Yes, August fourth."

"That's wonderful." Lucia beamed. "How did you and your fiancé meet?"

"We've known each other since we were small children. Before that really. Our mothers met in Lamaze class."

"So you don't really have a story about how you two first laid eyes on each other?" Trudie asked.

"No," Delaney admitted. As far back as she could remember, Evan had been there. Like a security blanket.

"It's almost as if you're marrying your brother, huh?" Trudie asked.

"No, no." Delaney forced a laugh. Trudie's statement disturbed her because her relationship with Evan *was* more like brother and sister than passionate lovers. "It's nice. Marrying someone you know so well."

"I guess I could see it. Built-in trust and all that," Trudie said. "But I'd be afraid I'd miss the sparks of really falling madly in love."

"This window seat is adorable, Lucia," Delaney said, purposefully directing the conversation off herself as they entered one of the bedrooms on the first floor that had been converted into a library.

Bookcases lined the walls. Delaney took a peek at the titles. Georgette Heyer, Jane Austen, Mary Stewart, Daphne du Maurier. Many of the same books that lined her own shelves at home.

"My Leo made it for me," Lucia said with a sigh in her voice. "So I could curl up and read and still look outside to keep an eye on the children chasing butterflies in the backyard flower garden."

"The window seat is definitely the highlight of this

room," Delaney said, relieved that she'd seemed to have sidetracked Trudie from talk of romance.

Lucia ushered her down the hallway, Trudie bringing up the rear. "And here's the kitchen. I raised six children of my own here and then my four grandchildren, after my daughter-in-law died and my son, Vincent, needed help with the little ones. They're all big ones now, but they come back to visit me often."

Delaney surveyed the room.

The wallpaper was faded. It would have to be replaced. The appliances were all circa the mid-eighties. The dining table was even older than the appliances and bore the scars of too many children banging on it with silverware and toys. The linoleum was peeling in the corner by the refrigerator, and there was a burn mark the size of a saucepan bottom on the Formica countertop.

"This is the heart of the house," Delaney breathed, surprised at the nostalgia welling up inside her. But that was silly. How could she be nostalgic for something she'd never had? She wished with all her might she could have grown up in such a home where kids were allowed to spill and sprawl and their growth spurts were marked in colored pencil on the wall beside the back door.

She immediately felt disloyal to her own family at such a thought. She'd had all the privileges the Cartwright money could buy. But that had included hired cooks and maids. She missed the boisterous camaraderie of cousins and siblings, of the numerous aunts and uncles and grandparents that this house clearly boasted. The Vinettis had what Delaney had always longed for. A close-knit, extended family.

"For sure," Trudie said. "This is where the family congregates when they visit. And it can get pretty rowdy in here, with all the laughing and teasing and eating. Lucia's an excellent cook, and she makes the best Stromboli you'll ever put in your mouth."

"So what do you think?" Lucia asked. "What needs to be done? Can you give me an estimate for what this might cost?"

"Just let me jot down a few notes."

"Sit," Lucia invited. "I'll make coffee and we'll have some tiramisu I baked this morning."

Delaney sat, took her calculator and her notepad from her purse, and crunched numbers while Lucia served up espresso and the ladyfinger cake.

Lucia settled in across from Delaney, anxiously pleating her apron with her fingers.

"I have some good news and some bad news." Delaney took a sip of her coffee. "Which would you like to hear first?"

"Oh, definitely I want the good news first," Lucia said.

"You have a beautiful home. I can feel the love in every room. Once we get it in shape, it's going to sell very easily."

"And the bad news?" Lucia gnawed her bottom lip.

Delaney longed to tell her that there was no bad news. That this warm, welcoming home was absolutely perfect as it was. But unfortunately, in a competitive real estate market, that simply wasn't the truth. "Trudie tells me you're on a limited budget."

Lucia nodded.

"In order to get the top asking price, I'm afraid you're going to have to invest about twenty-five thousand dollars in getting the house fixed up before we're ready to start staging it."

Delaney saw the hope fracture out of Lucia's face. "I don't have that kind of money."

"Could you borrow it until the house sells?"

"I was going to borrow the down payment for the Orchid Villa condo so I didn't lose my chance at getting the unit across the courtyard from Trudie. I don't have enough collateral for both loans," she said.

"Don't give up yet. Where there's a will, there's a way." Delaney reached across the table to touch the woman's hand. And then she had a brilliant idea that would give both of them what they wanted.

One of the programs on a cable home improvement channel, *American Home Design*, was running a contest to find the best home makeovers. The rules were simple. Send in "before" and "after" videos of your home improvement project. The winning entry would be selected for the most improved space. She had seen the advertisements on television, but she had never entered because she'd never made over a place with as much potential as Lucia's.

Now, with Lucia's home as her ace in the hole, even if she just made the finals, it would take her fledgling business to a whole new level and launch her career. Thinking about the potential got Delaney excited.

"Do you think your children and grandchildren and nieces and nephews would be able to pitch in to help you get the place ready?" she asked.

"Oh, yes, yes. Especially my grandson Nick. He's an undercover cop for the Houston Police Department, but he injured his leg on the job and he's been off work."

"But can Nick do the work with an injured leg?"

"What he can't do, his brothers can."

"Good, good. Here's my plan." Quickly, Delaney told them about her idea for entering Lucia's house in the *American Home Design* contest. "If your family can provide the labor in place of my usual crew, I'll be willing to waive my fee until after the house sells. All you would have to pay for are the supplies."

"Yes!" Lucia clapped her hands. "I love it. It's the perfect solution."

"Are you sure your family will be on board? Especially the grandson you mentioned? It sounds like most of the burden will rest on his shoulders."

"Why don't you ask him yourself?" Trudie interjected. "His truck just pulled up in the driveway."

"Come meet him," Lucia said.

Her mind lighting up with ideas, Delaney followed Lucia back into the living room. She couldn't wait to get started.

Footsteps sounded on the front porch. A man's voice rang out, "Nana, I'm here. Who does the swanky car in the driveway belong to?"

Delaney was standing with her hands clutched behind her back when she realized Lucia and Trudie had slipped out of the room and left her standing there all alone.

Where had they gone?

She turned her head to look, but before she had much time to ponder this question, the door opened and Lucia's grandson walked over the threshold.

He drew up short the second he spied her.

Their eyes met.

Delaney's heart stilled, and she felt a crazy, out-of-control sense of utter serenity.

Together, they gasped in one simultaneous breath.

"Oh, it's you."

Chapter 5

"What'd I tell you?" Trudie whispered to Lucia. "I knew it. They're smitten."

"It seems like they already know each other," Lucia said. "Imagine that."

They were secreted in the small closet underneath the staircase. Lucia looked at the shelves around her, crowded with memories. It hit her. This was going to be a huge undertaking, clearing out a lifetime of living. The closet door was open, giving then a great and completely undetected view of Nick and Delaney.

Lucia had to agree, her friend was right. There was no denying the combination of surprise, delight, confusion, and distress on the young people's faces as they stared at each other.

"It's the whammy," Lucia whispered. "The way they are looking at each other is exactly the way I felt when I first saw Leo."

"Toldja." Trudie giggled gleefully.

"Delaney is so beautiful," Lucia breathed.

"And your Nicky is quite handsome in that rough, tough way of his. They're going to give you the most gorgeous great-grandchildren."

"Let's not put the cart before the horse," Lucia said. "Remember, Delaney's engaged to someone else, and Nick's ego is still smarting over what Amber did to him."

"Yeah." Trudie sighed. "There is that. But what's a good romance without a little conflict?"

As Lucia and Trudie spied on the couple, Delaney glanced from Nick to her wristwatch. She tapped the face of it, shook her wrist, and then looked again before holding it up to her ear.

"Funny, my watch must have stopped," they heard Delaney say. "Which is a bit strange because I had the battery replaced just last week. Could you tell me what time you have?"

"Three thirty-five," Nick replied.

Lucia and Trudie stared at each other.

"You hear that?" Trudie nudged Lucia in the ribs with her elbow. "Her watch stopped! Just like the clock with you and Leo. It's a sign. There's no doubt about it. Those two are fated."

Hope rose in Lucia's heart. Could it be true? Was Trudie right?

But Trudie must have spoken too loudly because Nick raised his head and glared in their direction. "Nana? Are you and Trudie hiding under the staircase?"

"Uh-oh," Lucia whispered. "Busted."

Seeing the pink-raincoat woman standing in his grandmother's living room totally blew Nick away. He stared at her and she stared at him and he had no idea what to say or do next.

And then he heard whispering and giggling from behind the staircase and realized his grandmother and her best friend must be up to something. They'd tried to play matchmaker for him before, but it was beyond his comprehension how they'd found out about Raincoat Woman and lured her here.

One thing was for sure, she seemed as surprised to see him as he was to see her.

Nick strode past her, heading for the small storage closet underneath the staircase where he used to hide as a kid to spy on the grown-ups when they entertained guests in the living room.

"Okay, you two, what's going on here?" Nick asked. His head was still reeling, but he was trying hard not to show it.

"Um, nothing." His grandmother had a guilty look about her.

"Who is that woman?" he whispered urgently, jerking a thumb over his shoulder.

"That's Delaney Cartwright," Nana said. "I just hired her to stage the house. Isn't she beautiful? Such a face."

"Do what?" Nick couldn't believe the strangeness of the coincidence. His grandmother hiring the woman he'd been fantasizing about for the last three days and trying his damnedest to forget.

Maybe it's not coincidence, a disturbing voice in the back of his head whispered. *Maybe it's kismet. Maybe it's the whammy.*

Except Nick no longer believed in all that true love, soul mate, Italian-strength romantic whammy stuff his grandmother had spoon-fed her grandchildren along with her macaroni, pizza, and tiramisu. Amber had knocked the faith right out of him.

"I've talked to a real estate agent, and she said if I wanted the house to sell quickly then I should hire someone to stage it. So I interviewed Delaney. I like her and I hired her." Nana crossed her arms over her chest and gave him a look that just dared him to argue.

What? His grandmother had already talked to a real estate agent? Without waiting to discuss it with the family? This impulse of hers to sell the house was more serious than he'd guessed. "I don't get it. What's a house stager?"

"A house stager is a person who comes in and fixes up your place so that it will appeal to a wider range of buyers."

"Remember when Artie died and I couldn't sell my house?" Trudie added. "It sat on the market for over two years until I hired Delaney. She staged my house, and it sold three days later for three thousand dollars more than the original asking price."

That sounded impressive, but Nick didn't want Nana to sell the house. Everywhere he looked, the past beckoned. Whenever he glanced around the living room, he saw the windowpane that he, his brothers, and his cousins had once busted out playing baseball with a pair of rolled-up socks and a red plastic bat on a rainy day when they'd been cooped up indoors. Who knew that socks—properly whacked—could rocket through glass like that?

In his mind's eye, he could see the Christmas tree, drowning in presents for the huge Vinetti clan. Or the fireplace where they'd hung their stockings. He pictured the archway leading into the kitchen where Grampa Leo always strung mistletoe so he could catch Nana around the waist and kiss her in front of everyone.

Nick smiled, recalling the time his baby sister, Gina, had sneaked a kiss from her boyfriend when she'd thought no one was watching and their braces had gotten locked together. He had teased her unmercifully for weeks afterward.

He saw the kitchen, full of life and laughter, as his family gathered around, cooking and eating and swapping stories. The scents were in his nose—onion and garlic, oregano and basil. The tastes filled his mouth— marinara sauce, pesto, mozzarella.

The memories hung in his mind like a drop of rich honey, thick and sweet, caught in the cleft of time and held preserved in this house. He'd always imagined bringing his own children here someday—at holidays, during the summer, to visit their great-grandmother and give them a glimpse into his history.

Tight-lipped, Nick battled to keep his emotions in check. His chest tightened.

Delaney Cartwright stood with her arms crossed over her chest. Her clothes were a far cry from what she'd been wearing the first time he'd seen her. Her pale green suit was simple and tailored, but obviously expensive. She wore sensible one-inch heels. Tall, willowy, long straight hair that was either light brown or dark blond depending upon your definition. Her cheekbones were high and her eyes were green as the Gulf. Eyes a guy could dive into without a look back.

Charlize Theron had nothing on this woman.

Although sans the raincoat and risqué lingerie he'd seen her in before, she possessed the same regal aura as the actress. She had delicate bone structure and a way of holding herself that suggested blue-blood breeding.

What had happened to the hotsie-totsie who'd ambushed him outside of Doc Van Zandt's place? That was who had fired his engines. This sophisticated-looking woman flat unnerved him with her old money aura rising up from her like the scent of freshly minted hundred-dollar bills. Her serenity and his unwanted attraction to her set his teeth on edge.

He searched for a reason to dislike her.

She looked like the kind of woman who had been floating through life on her gorgeous looks and her stacks of money, never having to take a stand or fight for something she believed in. He knew the Cartwright name. It was familiar to everyone in Texas. No doubt about it. This one had been handed the world on a silver platter.

He inflated his resentment, hunting for anything that would let the air out of this powerful attraction. She was too polished. Too perfect. With a woman like her, a guy would always be on the hot seat, never able to live up to the expectations of Daddy's little princess.

"I don't understand why you have to sell the house," he said, turning back to his grandmother.

"Without your grandfather, the magic is gone. It's just a house now, no longer a home. It should be a home again, filled with laughter and love and lots of children," she said.

"You shouldn't be making such a major decision

when you're still grieving, Nana. It's only been a little over two months."

"It's time to move on, Nicky. Wallowing in grief isn't going to bring your grandfather back. I'm lonely here on the island, and there's finally an opening at Orchid Villa in a condo right near Trudie's."

"Why didn't you tell me you were lonely? I can get the family together. Make sure someone comes over to spend time with you every day."

"All you kids have your own lives to lead and besides, someone comes to visit almost every weekend. But I need to socialize with people my own age. I need to start a new life."

"At seventy-three?"

"What would you have me do? Curl up in bed and wait to die? Leo would be pretty mad if I did that."

Nick knotted his hands into fists. He felt so damn helpless. Over the course of the last thirteen months so many bad things had happened, and he desperately needed for something to stay the same.

"I just hate to see you make a mistake."

"Nicky." She took his hand in hers and patted it. "It's okay to let go. Clinging serves no one."

"I'm trying."

"There's something else I have to tell you that you're probably not going to like."

He arched an eyebrow. "Oh?"

"I can't afford to hire Delaney's crew, so I promised you'd help her do the renovations that need to be done before the house can be put on the market."

"You did what?"

"Don't look at me that way. You told me yourself

you're bored out of your skull. Well, now you have something to do."

Nick couldn't stop the disappointment, hurt, resentment, and regret from building up inside him.

Don't be a selfish jerk. Think about what Nana needs. Back her up. But did his grandmother actually know what was best for her? Or was she simply making decisions based on blind grief and loneliness? He might not be able to stop her from putting the house on the market, but maybe he could find a way to slow down the whole process. Keep it from selling too quickly and buy some time until he could talk sense into Nana.

Turning back around, Nick saw Delaney waiting patiently for him to break up the huddle under the staircase. She looked as if nothing could ruffle her steadfast aplomb.

It set his teeth on edge and stirred in him a mighty urge to do whatever it took to sabotage the project and chase this house stager far away from his grandmother's home.

He sauntered back toward her, eyes narrowed, lips cocked sardonically, arms crossed over his chest in an I'm-gonna-throw-you-out-of-here-on-your-ear stance. Delaney had overheard enough of his conversation with his grandmother to glean the gist of it. He was not happy about Lucia's decision to sell her house.

He trod closer.

Too close.

Crowding her space, making it hard for her to think straight. His shoulders were wider than she remembered, but her memory more than adequately recalled his muscular athletic body. How could she forget when he'd had it pressed against the length of her?

Delaney realized convincing Lucia to hire her was not the test she had to pass. Here was the challenge. Here was the threshold guardian. If she wanted this job, Nick was the one she was going to have to convince.

She thought of the opportunity she'd be missing out on. A shot at publicizing All the World's a Stage on television and making it a rousing success. A prospect to spread her wings and fly. A chance to prove that she wasn't just a spoiled Cartwright princess.

Years of kowtowing to her mother, of repressing her opinions, of being the good girl and doing the right thing boiled up inside her.

This time she refused to keep quiet, refused to back down. This time, she was going to get what she wanted.

Clearing her throat, Delaney gave him her most professional smile. "I didn't mean to eavesdrop, Mr. Vinetti, but when you were speaking to your grandmother I got the distinct impression you're not in favor of investing money to have the house staged."

"Your assumption is correct, Ms. Cartwright."

"If you give me the chance, I can prove to you the value of my services."

"Oh, you can?"

"Yes."

"How's that? By showing up on my doorstep in a pink raincoat?" His gaze took a deliberate road trip down her body.

He was bringing that up? She couldn't believe his audacity. She was mentally halfway to the door when she realized that was exactly his intention. To chase her off.

She ignored his comment, opened up her briefcase, and pulled out the glossy, tri-fold brochure for All the World's a Stage.

He looked it over, quickly flipping to the back page to find her fee structure. "Kinda pricey. I think maybe you're peddling your wares in the wrong neighborhood. Try The Woodlands. They can afford to be gullible up there."

"As I told your grandmother, I'm willing to defer the payment of my services until the house sells, and if it does not sell in a specified period of time, I don't get paid at all." She raised her chin.

A suspicious glint shaded his eyes. "Now why would you do that?"

"Your grandmother's house presents an exciting opportunity to expand my business." She told him about the *American Home Design* contest.

"Yes, I see what's in it for you, but what's in it for my grandmother?"

"Quick sell of her house for an asking price that will more than offset what I charge."

"Maybe we don't want a quick sell. Maybe we'd rather have the right buyer, one who could love this house as much as we do over someone with deep pockets."

"Your grandmother needs a quick sell in order to purchase the condo she's interested in."

He glared at her suspiciously.

"There's just one catch to my proposition."

"Of course there's a catch." He was looking at her mouth and it unnerved her. "There's always a catch. What is it?"

She regretted having to say this. Dragging the words from her mouth was almost painful. "In order to save your grandmother money, you're going to have to stand in for my crew."

Just what in God's name had she gotten herself into? She couldn't believe she'd be working so closely with the one man in the world she had hoped never to see again.

Delaney lay in bed, staring up at the ceiling. One pillow under her head, the other clutched to her chest. She must be out of her mind.

"I did it to stretch my wings. To prove I can take on new challenges. Who knows? This might lead to a whole new angle to my business, especially if I can win the *American Home Design* contest."

"That's not the reason."

The voice startled Delaney. She looked over and saw Skylar perched on her vanity and realized she must have fallen asleep.

"What do you want?" She sighed.

"Dropped by to get the goods on the hottie you spent the afternoon with, and here I find you talking to yourself." Skylar tsk-tsked. "Keep that up, and people are going to start thinking you're crazy."

"I am crazy. I see dead people in my dreams."

"You don't see dead people. You only see me."

"You're dead."

"Yeah, but I'm not people. I'm a person. Singular. You see a dead person in your dreams."

"So that means I'm not crazy?"

"Please, you were raised by Honey Montgomery Cartwright. Of course you're crazy on some level."

"Touché."

"Wanna know why I think you took the Vinetti job?" Skylar grinned. "Hey, I like the sound of that. Vinetti job. Like you're in with the mob."

Delaney sighed again and pulled the covers to her chin. "I'd say no, but you'd just tell me anyway, so go ahead."

"You're hot for her hard-bodied grandson."

"That's not it. You are so far off base." Delaney laughed but it sounded hollow, forced.

"You want to prove yourself to him. He thinks you're a spoiled rich Cartwright, and you want to show him he's wrong."

Now that was probably the real truth. Delaney didn't have a comeback.

"Personally, I think taking the job was a great move. I mean, did you check out his butt? Makes a girl feel faint just looking at it." Skylar fanned herself.

"You're a ghost; haven't you gotten past physical lust?"

"Hey, indulge me. I never got to have sex when I was alive."

"Really? That's sad."

"Don't feel sorry for me, just let me live vicariously through you a little." Today Skylar was wearing a tie-dyed T-shirt and a blue-jean miniskirt and fisherman's wading boots.

"What's with the boots?"

"Borrowed 'em from Granddad. He said to say 'hi,' by the way."

"Tell him 'hi' back."

"Will do."

"What do you need wading boots for in whatever place it is where ghosts hang out?" she asked.

"You keep getting this all wrong, Laney. I'm not really a ghost. You're dreaming me up. Whatever I wear, you're the one who dressed me in it. For whatever weird reasons are churning around in that disturbed brain of yours."

"So I can change you out of wading boots?"

"Sure. Give it a try."

Delaney imagined Skylar in glass slippers, and darned if the wading boots didn't fade away and glass slippers take their place.

"Cinderella, cool." Skylar stuck her legs out in front of her to admire the shoes. "Now all I need is a Prince Charming."

"Okay, this is officially freaky."

"No, it's not. There's nothing more natural than dreaming. So anyway, back to the hottie. He's so much cuter than Evan."

"Evan's cute," Delaney said defensively.

"Please, Evan looks like he's been popped from a cookie-cutter mold. Handsome rich doctor from central casting, anyone? Come on, wouldn't you rather have a real man like that delicious Nick Vinetti?" Skylar licked her lips.

"You're not being fair to Evan."

"Yes, okay, he is a nice guy. But I remember the time when he was twelve and dropped a pocketful of change on the ground so he could get a good look up my skirt."

"Evan's not like that."

"Maybe not now, but he was back then. Believe me, I was there."

"How can I trust that tidbit of information if, as you claim, everything you say is something I'm making up in my head?"

"Good question." Skylar propped her chin in her palm. "Keep it in mind whenever you're talking to me."

"You're messing with my head."

"No, you're messing with your own head."

"Maybe you should just go away."

"Maybe you should just wake up."

"Maybe I will."

"Fine with me."

Delaney flopped over onto her side, refusing to look at Skylar anymore.

"You're not waking up."

"You don't know Evan the way I do. You don't know how he was there for me after you died. He comforted me. Helped me through it. He was my only real friend until I met Tish. He liked me when I was ugly, Sky. Before the surgery and the weight loss and the braces."

Skylar lay down on the bed next to her, stacked her hands under her cheek, and gazed into Delaney's eyes. "He's a compulsive helper, Delaney. He'll always be where someone needs help, and as soon as they're emotionally strong enough not to need him anymore, he'll find someone who does need him."

"Evan would never cheat on me."

"I'm not saying he would. I'm just predicting he'll always be standing you up in favor of his work. Unless you're in a crisis. Then he'll be there."

"He's a doctor, for Pete's sake. Surely you get that his patients must come first."

"My point exactly. You'll always play second fiddle."

"It would be pretty petty of me to be jealous of sick people," she said.

"You say that now, but what about when you have children? He can't ever make the Little League games or the dance recitals. Your Thanksgiving dinners and Christmas Eves are interrupted by hospital emergencies."

Delaney had never thought about the long-term repercussions of Evan's career. Honestly, she'd never even imagined what it would be like to have children with him. That was strange, wasn't it? She was marrying him, and she'd never pictured having his babies.

"Very strange indeed," Skylar whispered, reading her mind.

"I'm doing the right thing by marrying Evan," she said defensively.

"Even though you have zero sexual chemistry together?" Skylar asked.

"Sex is overrated."

"You only think that because you've never had great sex. Or great love."

"You never had sex at all, so buzz off with that advice." Delaney glowered.

"Don't you want to know what great sex is like? Why Tish and Jillian and Rachael talk about it with such passionate enthusiasm?"

"No. I like things just the way they are with Evan. Calm, sweet, tender."

"And orgasmless."

"I have orgasms." Delaney furrowed her brow. "At least I think I do."

"If you're not sure, then you probably don't."

"Once again, you would know this how?"

"It's going to be tough, working on Lucia's house with her gorgeous grandson Nick hanging around, keeping his suspicious eyes on you. And all the while Evan is far away in Guatemala."

Concern winnowed through her. This was what she'd been worrying about ever since taking the job. Knowing that she'd be around Nick Vinetti every day for the next several weeks.

"I have to back out of the job."

"No, you don't. I say explore it to the hilt. Find out if the chemistry you feel with this guy is real or just a passing fancy."

"What about Evan?"

"What about him? He's the one who took off for Guatemala just weeks before your wedding."

"That's lovely. My fiancé is away helping poor children to have a better life, and you want me to screw around on him with some cocky cop."

"I didn't say screw around on him."

"It's what you meant." Delaney glared at her.

"I'm going to go now. You're upset and need time to think. Besides, your alarm clock is about to go off." Skylar started fading away, getting smaller and smaller, dimmer and dimmer.

She lay there, watching Skylar go until her glass slippers were all that remained.

Her sister was right. She couldn't back out of the job. Lucia was counting on her. She was such a sweet woman, and she'd just lost her husband. It would be wrong to go back on her word now.

Delaney blew out a breath. One way or the other, she would just have to suck it up and learn to suppress her lusty feelings for the sexy Mr. Nick Vinetti.

Chapter 6

Honey Montgomery Cartwright ran a lint roller over her peach-colored Italian silk suit even though she'd just taken it from the dry cleaner's bag. She checked the sticky roller paper and spied a hint of fuzz. Hmm. She made a mental note to change dry cleaners. Clearly, they were not doing the job she'd paid them to do.

Squaring her shoulders, she double-checked her teeth in the bathroom mirror. She'd already flossed and brushed twice this morning, but she wanted to make sure she hadn't missed anything. She was having lunch with Delaney's future mother-in-law, Lenore Van Zandt, to discuss preparations for the wedding rehearsal dinner. Lenore, a noisy chatterbox, made Honey nervous, but she'd be damned if she would show it.

She scrutinized her reflection. Fifty-three, but none of her friends would ever guess it. Honey considered herself both smart and lucky. She religiously avoided the sun, worked out two hours a day, six days a week, spent a small annual fortune on antiaging potions and creams, and she had her dermatologist programmed on speed-dial.

When they were dating, James Robert had said that with Honey's platinum blond hair, high cheekbones, flawless complexion, well-toned body, and rigorous self-discipline, she was like Princess Grace in boot camp. These days, he no longer commented on her looks, just grunted and asked her how much her spa treatments had set him back. As if he didn't clear twenty million a year. What was it about the ultrarich that made them such tightwads?

Resolutely pushing thoughts of her husband aside, Honey snugged the clasp of a three-carat diamond and emerald necklace around her neck, added matching ear-rings, and then bestowed her mirror image with her most brilliant, practiced smile.

There. Everything was perfect.

No one, especially not her husband of thirty-four years, would ever guess the real truth.

With a regal toss of her head, she walked like a run-way model down the stairs of the sweeping Colonial-style mansion that had been in James Robert's family for three generations. Her four-inch heels clicked smartly against the granite tile. She might be over fifty, but she wasn't over the hill. Honey refused to trade in her Manolo Blahniks for Birkenstocks. She would rather break a hip first.

She grabbed a bottle of Evian on her way out the door. Honey carried bottled water wherever she went. She was convinced that was one of the reasons she had such a youthful complexion. Sauntering out to the garage, she paused a moment to smooth down her skirt before sliding across the Cadillac's plush leather seats. Once outside the security gate, she stopped to pick up the mail. Leaving the engine running with the air-conditioning blasting, she minced to the mailbox, collected the day's correspondence, and got back inside.

Quickly she leafed through the pile. Bills, a sales circular, a party invitation, a couple of catalogs, a fitness magazine.

And then she found it.

A plain white envelope with no return address or postmark. Her name was printed in block letters with a primitive hand.

It hadn't been mailed. Someone had placed it in their mailbox.

Honey sucked in her breath, flipped the letter over, and tentatively slipped a fingernail underneath the envelope flap. She opened it up and pulled out the sheet of notepaper.

I KNOW YOUR SECRET. IF YOU DON'T WANT YOUR HUS-BAND TO FIND OUT THE TRUTH, COME TO THE ENTRANCE TO THE GALVESTON ISLAND AMUSEMENT PARK ON SEAWALL BOULEVARD. NOON TOMORROW. BRING TWENTY THOUSAND DOLLARS IN CASH.

That was it. No signature. Nothing else.

Feeling fragile as a dried-up autumn leaf, Honey stared at the note, not wanting to understand what she was reading. Someone had learned her terrible truth.

The past had caught up with her at last.

Air left her lungs. She gasped, felt the color drain from her face.

The deception had started out as nothing more than a

little white lie, but it had become Honey's entire life. Day by day, for thirty-four years, she'd steeped in her secret until it eventually permeated every corner of her soul.

Hand over her mouth, Honey flung open the car door and, contrary to the ladylike delicacy she'd perfected over the years, vomited in the gravel.

When she was finished, she rinsed her mouth with the Evian and in a great inhalation of breath calmly drove to her luncheon date with Lenore. The blackmail note she crumpled and stuffed in the glove compartment.

She didn't want to go, but if she didn't show up, Lenore would wonder why. And Honey had spent a lifetime doing her best to keep people from wondering about her. As she searched for a parking place, dark questions plagued.

Who had sent the letter? Why had this person only asked for twenty thousand? And after all these years, how had he or she managed to track her down?

She could guess the answer to the last question. The blackmailer must have seen her picture with Delaney in the recent *Society Bride* article on society weddings. Why, oh, why had she allowed herself to be photographed for a national magazine?

Her stomach roiled again and she closed her eyes, fighting back the nausea. So much time had passed, she'd foolishly thought she was safe.

Idiot. You can never, ever let down your guard. There's no room for mistakes. Not now, not ever.

Not with the secret she harbored.

But here was this letter, threatening to ruin the life she'd built. Threatening to destroy not only her marriage, but her daughter's chance at happiness. Honey simply could not allow that to happen.

She would meet with the blackmailer and she would pay.

What other choice did she have?

The following day, Delaney took Tish with her to video Lucia's house.

Luckily, Tish had been able to rearrange her schedule so she could film the "before" video of the house so Delaney and Lucia's family could get started on the renovations as quickly as possible. Time was of the essence, both for Lucia's financial situation and for entry in the *American Home Design* contest. They had four weeks to get the house renovated and decorated before the July 9 deadline.

When they arrived at Lucia's house, Delaney was surprised to find so many cars in the driveway. She parked along the curb behind Nick's red pickup truck, and her stomach did a loopy little swoon.

She spun her engagement ring on her finger. *Remember what you swore to yourself last night? Get over your attraction to the guy. You're taken.*

"This house totally rocks," Tish exclaimed. "I can see why you're so excited. It's got such great potential."

"I know," Delaney breathed.

Tish collected her equipment while Delaney gathered up the briefcase chock-full of plans, computer printouts, and sketches she'd prepared after she'd returned home the night before. Tish filmed everything as they went up the walkway. The tiled roof, the palm trees, the pink flamingos on the lawn.

Delaney rang the doorbell and a gorgeous black-haired woman in her late twenties, with coltishly long legs, answered the door. She looked a lot like Nick, possessing the same intelligent brown eyes and long, thick, dark lashes.

"Hi," she said, greeting them. "You must be Delaney. I'm Gina, Nick's baby sister; come on in. Most everyone is in the kitchen waiting for you to film the house before we start packing up Nana's things."

"Packing?" Delaney asked.

"Nana's moving over to Trudie's while the renovations are going on. She put a retainer down on the condo this morning, and Nick's taking her to apply for a bank loan tomorrow afternoon. With any luck, you guys will be finished renovating this house before she has to close on the condo."

Feeling concerned that Gina had unrealistic expectations about what she could achieve, Delaney touched the other woman's arm. "You do understand that the house might not sell immediately."

"Don't be modest. Nana and Trudie swear you're a miracle worker. Our family has complete faith in you."

Did that include Nick? she wondered. Yesterday, he hadn't struck her as being very trusting.

"That's more than you can say about your own mother," Tish whispered to Delaney as they followed Gina into the kitchen.

They found the place pleasantly chaotic with a dozen people all talking, teasing, and laughing at once.

"This is Delaney, everyone," Gina introduced her.

They all applauded.

Delaney blushed.

Gina introduced her to everyone. Cousins and siblings, aunts and uncles, plus Gina's own identical twin seven-year-old boys, Zack and Jack.

There were too many Vinettis for Delaney to keep straight. But she was happy to meet Nick's dad. Vincent Vinetti was a big bear of a man who owned his own shrimp boat and was still handsome in middle age. He clapped her on the shoulder. "We appreciate so much what you're doing for my mother."

Some of the relatives hugged her. Some shook her hand. They all told her how much they valued her help. Oddly, she felt more welcome in this roomful of strangers than she did in her own home.

That wasn't fair. By nature her family just weren't huggers and touchers. They didn't get together in big groups, although her father's brothers and their children lived in the Houston area. She should not compare the phlegmatic Cartwrights to the lively Vinettis. It was apples and persimmons.

Delaney introduced Tish, and she also received a rousing welcome.

"Jeez." Tish pulled Delaney aside. "You didn't tell me you'd formed your own fan club."

"What can I say? They're an affectionate group."

"Apparently. Can you keep the fan club entertained while I start filming the house unencumbered by onlookers?" Tish asked.

"I'll handle it."

With her camera rolling, Tish disappeared back the way they'd come in.

"Where's Nick?" Delaney found herself asking Gina, then cringed inwardly. Why had she asked about him?

"He went with my husband, Chuck, to rent a moving van."

Well, that was a relief. She had a little extra time to compose herself before she saw Nick again.

Delaney's eyes found Lucia's in the crowded room and she held up her briefcase. "I've got the renovation plans with me to show everyone."

"Tony, get up, please," Lucia instructed the lanky young man in his late teens sitting to her right. "Let Delaney sit here."

Tony popped up and Lucia patted the chair beside her. "Sit, sit."

"Would you like something to drink?" Gina asked Delaney as she settled in next to Lucia.

"A cannoli?" someone else offered.

Delaney smiled and nodded. Who wouldn't be happy around this bunch?

"Coffee, tea, soda, water?" Gina offered.

"Whatever you've got on hand will be fine."

"We've got it all on hand."

"Coffee would be nice, and one of those cannoli does sound delicious."

"They're to die for," Gina said. "Nana baked them fresh this morning."

Delaney tried to remember the last time her mother had baked anything from scratch and came up with that disloyal feeling again. To distract herself, she took the plans from her briefcase and spread them on the table.

Everyone crowded around for a look. It was a bit disconcerting to have a dozen pairs of eyes peering over her shoulder. But as she explained what needed to be done to the property in order to achieve top dollar, everyone seemed to approve of her plans. Consensus by committee, just the way she liked doing things. Heartened by the unanimous acceptance, she looked up to see tears shining in Lucia's eyes.

Anxiety had her fingering the papers. "Oh, my goodness, there's something you don't like. Please, if you don't agree with my proposal, tell me and I'll change it."

Lucia shook her head, pulled a handkerchief from her pocket, and dabbed at her eyes. "Your proposal is wonderful. That's not why I'm crying."

"The reality of leaving your home is finally hitting you."

"Yes." Lucia pressed her lips together in an attempt to stay the tears from spilling down her cheeks. "Leo and I had such wonderful memories here. I can't believe it's over."

"Are you sure selling the house is really what you want to do?" Delaney had to ask.

Lucia nodded. "I have to let go in order to move on. It's the right thing to do."

Delaney looked into the older woman's eyes and knew Lucia needed to talk about Leo. Her family surrounded her, yes, and she could talk to them, but they knew all her stories. Lucia needed a fresh audience.

"Tell me about your husband." Delaney placed her hand on top of the older woman's.

Soon Lucia was regaling her with stories of her life in this house with her husband, Leo. The children they'd raised, the hard times they'd endured, the fun they'd had, the love that had grown deeper and richer with each passing year.

"How did Leo propose to you?" Delaney asked.

A smile flitted across her face. "He didn't."

"You proposed to him?"

Lucia looked scandalized. "No, no. I was a demure girl. I would never have done something so bold."

"So how did you two ever get together?"

There was that knowing smile again. "He kidnapped me from the chapel on my wedding day."

"What?!" Now it was Delaney's turn to look scandalized. "You married your kidnapper?"

Lucia giggled. "It was very romantic. I was engaged to marry the man of my parents' choosing. They were very old-fashioned. Frank's family had money, and my father had a struggling business."

"Your parents were basically selling you to Frank?"

"It sounds so bad when you put it like that," Lucia said, "and I'm certain that's not the way they intended it. They just wanted to make sure I would be taken care of."

"Did you love Frank?"

"I tried," Lucia said. "And then, a week before the wedding I met Leo at a party, and I just knew he was the one for me. But he was a penniless student who came from a poor family, and my parents would not hear of me marrying him. Leo knew what my papa was like. That he would never give him my hand in marriage. I felt so much family pressure to marry Frank. I'd known him since I was a child. We'd grown up in the same small village together, and I was not a young woman who voiced her own opinions. I'd been taught to be a dutiful daughter."

Dutiful.

That was exactly how she felt. Dutiful and damned. Delaney fingered her engagement ring and thought of

Evan. He was off in Guatemala helping people, and she was here having serious doubts about their relationship.

"Leo knew there was only one way he could have me. So he kidnapped me from the chapel on my wedding day. We took jobs on a cruise ship to get to America, and the captain married us at sea."

One of Lucia's daughters started singing "That's Amore," and soon everyone joined in. Singing and crying and laughing.

Including Lucia.

"Come on, Delaney," Lucia invited. "Sing with us."

To her knowledge, no one in her family had ever broken into impromptu song, much less the whole bunch of them singing in unison. She liked it, even though it felt like she had a walk-on part in *Moonstruck*. She half expected Nicolas Cage to saunter through the doorway at any minute.

Instead, it was Nick Vinetti who came traipsing through the back door.

"People, people," he said. " 'That's Amore'? You must be talking about the time Grampa kidnapped Nana. Knock it off. Eighty percent of you are off key. Face facts, you guys ain't the Von Trapps."

And then he spied Delaney. He stopped talking and stabbed her with his gaze.

Wham!

She felt it deep inside her. The forbidden pull. The taboo attraction. It made him all the more desirable.

"That certainly is a beautiful engagement ring that you're wearing," Gina said. "So tell us, Delaney, about the man you're going to marry."

"Yeah," Nick said, still holding her gaze. "Tell us.

Everyone likes the story of a good romance." His tone was sardonic. The look in his eyes inscrutable.

"I . . . I . . . think we should go over the renovation plans. Map out the tasks in phases. The sooner we get to work, the sooner we sell the house and the sooner Lucia gets the money for her condo," Delaney said.

Lucia got up from her chair. "Here, Nick, take my seat. You're going to be the one doing most of the work. See what Delaney has come up with."

Before she could protest—and how could she?—Nick plunked down beside her.

She reached for the papers, eager to have something to occupy her hands and purposefully ignored the nutmegy scent of his cologne. Clearing her throat, she launched into a thorough explanation of what she felt needed to be done to achieve the highest selling price for the house and the estimated cost of materials if the Vinettis provided all the manpower.

Nick took the papers from her and studied the list for a long time. It wasn't going to be as easy to persuade him as the rest of the family. "Why should we strip off the wallpaper and paint all the walls white?"

"Wallpaper dates a place. It's a fact of the real estate business, plain white walls sell better."

"But plain white walls have no zip. Nothing to make it special," he said. "No magic."

"That's precisely the point. The more people who can imagine themselves living here, the quicker the house will sell. We could do an off-white if you prefer. Ecru. French Vanilla. Eggshell."

He leaned forward. "Let me guess. The walls in your house are all stark white."

She took offense at the way he said it. Like he was criticizing her for having no personality. She raised her head to scowl at him, but got distracted by his face. His hair was wind-tossed, his jaw strong and stubborn, his eyes dark and challenging. "As a matter of fact they are. Do you have a problem with that?"

"Noncommittal."

"Excuse me?"

"White is a color chosen by someone who is afraid to commit," he said.

"And you obtained this information from what psychology textbook?" What was it about this guy? She was never confrontational. In fact, she avoided confrontation like the flu. But around Nick the contrary side of herself popped out. He was an instigator.

"No textbook. Eight years as a cop."

"So what color are your walls?"

He shrugged. "Varies from room to room."

She found herself wondering what color his bedroom was painted, but didn't dare ask. "Look, whoever buys the house can paint it any color they want."

"If they're going to paint it after they buy it, why are we wasting time and money painting it?"

"You really don't get the concept of presentation, do you?"

"If you mean that I can look through a fancy exterior to the truth beyond, then no, I don't get the concept of presentation. It's all bullshit."

"Nick," Lucia chided. "No cursing in mixed company. I know you're a cop, but save that kind of language for the streets."

"Sorry, Nana." He looked chagrined. "By the way," he

said to Delaney, "I accept your compliment. I take pride in my ability to ferret out bull . . ." He slid a sidelong glance at his grandmother. "You know what."

"I didn't mean it as a compliment."

"I'm aware of that."

Acutely cognizant that they were being scrutinized by a bevy of Vinettis, Delaney forced a smile. Presentation is everything. Or that was her mother's mantra. Nick had a whole different mantra that apparently involved an excess of cattle manure.

"Well, then," she said and looked at the people standing around them. "Shall we get started? Who's got a pickup truck? We need to make a run to Lowe's for the initial supplies while Tish finishes videoing the house."

"I'll take you," Nick drawled.

Dammit. Why him? Delaney slapped a hand across her mouth, worried that she might have spoken her thoughts aloud.

Nick was staring at her pointedly. As if he knew what she looked like naked.

He practically does.

Her cheeks heated.

Don't blush, don't blush.

He pulled his keys from his pocket. "Ready for a ride, Rosy?"

Rosy?

She put a hand to her cheek. Dear God, her face must be flaming red. She didn't want to go with him, but she didn't want to stay here and keep blushing in front of his family either.

Delaney stuffed the papers back in her briefcase. Stay cool. Presentation is everything. "Let's go."

"You'll need a check," Lucia said.

"I've got this one, Nana," Nick said and hustled Delaney toward the back door.

"Dominic, you come back here and get a check. I'm not going to let you pay for the renovations on my house."

"I grew up here. I'm responsible for some of the nicks and bruises this old house has suffered."

"You didn't take me to raise," Lucia argued.

"No, you took me to raise. Let me pay my due," he called to his grandmother over his shoulder as the screen door slammed behind them.

When they reached his red pickup truck, Nick opened the passenger-side door. "Climb in."

Feeling as if she'd just made a pact with the devil, Delaney got inside.

Chapter 7

"Where should we start?" Delaney asked Nick when they walked through the door at Lowe's. "I always lose my sense of direction in these warehouse stores."

Commandingly, Nick snatched the piece of notepaper from her hand and ran his gaze down the list. "Paint department. We can shop for the rest of the items while they mix our paint."

His proprietary manner agitated her, even though she knew it was her own fault. She'd acted helpless and asked his opinion; he was just taking over as bossy men had a tendency to do. Well, to heck with that. Surprising herself, Delaney snatched the notepaper right back. "White comes already made up."

Amusement played across his full lips. "We should at least get beige. I'll go nuts painting all those walls stark white."

"The condition of your nuts is not my problem," she said tartly, shocking herself. Dear God, why had she said that? What was the matter with her? What were these absurd impulses he stirred inside her?

"Why, Rosy, are you flirting with me?" His eyes twinkled mischievously.

"No, and stop calling me Rosy. We're painting the rooms white because they're small. Traditional wisdom dictates pure white walls will make the space appear larger."

"Are you shutting off my opinion?"

She didn't answer, just gave him a look that said "I'm the professional here."

Nick didn't quite know what to make of her. She had this sweet, go-with-the-flow way about her, but if you pushed her in the wrong direction, she dug her heels in with surprising stubbornness.

Delaney breezed past him, heading toward the big overhead sign pointing out the paint department, and in the process her shoulder lightly brushed against his.

His head reeled from the unexpected contact. His body stiffened and his gut clenched in a thoroughly enjoyable way.

Damn, he thought. *Damn. She smells like morning glories, fresh and pink and perfect.*

He tried to keep up with her, but his bum leg slowed him down. God, he hated feeling weak.

She glanced back over her shoulder, saw he was limping, and slowed her pace to match his.

Nick hated even more that she had to slow down for him. "Go on," he said. "I'll get there."

But she didn't. She waited. Patiently, politely. And it pissed him off.

"I'm sorry," Delaney apologized when he caught up with her. "I forgot about your injured knee."

"Were you stalking transvestites in dark alleys behind seedy strip bars?"

"What?" Startled, her eyes widened and she stared at him as if he were ordering takeout in Japanese.

"Were you knifing he/shes in parking lots?"

"No . . . no . . . ," she stammered.

He knew he'd confused her. That had been his intention. His defense mechanism. Keep your enemy off guard. "Then what do you have to be sorry for?"

"I'm sorry I wasn't more considerate of your . . ." She glanced at his leg. "Disability."

"My disability, as you put it, is not your problem. So don't apologize."

"I was just trying to express my concern. Go ahead, be a cold loner with a huge chip on your shoulder. See if I care." She turned away, but not before he saw the hurt expression on her face. "Obviously you don't want or need my concern, and that's fine with me."

"Obviously," he mumbled.

What the hell is wrong with you? She is just trying to be nice and you've hurt her feelings. Feel better now, asshole?

The truth of it was she knocked him off kilter. Nick found himself wanting her sympathy, and that was a dangerous thing to court. Better to deflect her than allow her to slip under his skin. He was already hellaciously attracted to her. He didn't have to like her as well.

They picked up ten gallons of pure white satin paint. They lined the cans up in the bottom of the shopping cart, along with drop cloths and paintbrushes and rollers and trays.

Delaney consulted her list. "What's the tool situation?"

Nick reacted without thinking, glancing down at his zipper to see if she'd noticed the state of semi-arousal he'd been in from the moment he climbed into the pickup truck beside her.

She followed his gaze, and that adorable pink glow rose swiftly to her cheeks. She flustered so easily. Her embarrassment tempered his own and restored his self-confidence.

Nick cocked a grin, ramping up the sexual tension, trying his best to embarrass her. Maybe if he made her uncomfortable enough, she'd quit the job. "Healthy."

"Mr. Vinetti," she said, clearly shocked by his retort. "I was speaking about the tools we'll need to repair your grandmother's house. Since you apparently pride yourself on being a Neanderthal, I'm assuming that you have the requisite hardware."

Nick arched an eyebrow and started to make a joke about requisite hardware, but she rushed to finish her thought before he got a chance to gig her.

"Like hammers and screwdrivers and wrenches and such," she said.

"I can assure you, Rosy, I'm a card-carrying caveman. It's not an idle boast. I own a fully equipped tool chest, and I know how to use it."

"I'm so happy for you. Now shall we continue with our shopping?"

"We shall."

She scowled. "You're making fun of me."

He measured off an inch with his thumb and forefinger. "Just a little bit."

"Are you going to keep giving me a hard time during the entire course of this project?" She primly squared her shoulders.

"Depends on what you mean by a hard time." He lowered his eyelids and sent her his most charming smile. He was bad. He shouldn't be toying with her like this, but he just couldn't seem to help himself. He got a kick out of shaking her cool.

"Will you please stop with the sexual innuendos?"

Nick held up his palms. "Hey, I can't help it if you're reading things into what I say."

She narrowed her eyes. "Be honest. Do most women really find this troglodyte stuff charming?"

"You'd be surprised."

Delaney tossed her head and skirted around him, wheeling the shopping cart toward the plumbing department.

Didn't she realize how easy she was making it for him to tease her unmercifully? Clearly, she had not grown up with brothers. She had no clue how to defend herself against verbal sparring.

"Hey, Rosy, wait up."

"Feel free to gimp along at your own pace," she called out over her shoulder.

Nick burst out laughing. Feistiness. All right. He knew she had it in her, and he loved provoking it. Chasing her off was going to be a lot more challenging than he'd first thought, but also a lot more fun.

When her left hand shot up over her head with the

middle finger extended, he laughed so hard he almost choked. Now that was a sight worth seeing.

Miss-Butter-Wouldn't-Melt-Between-Her-Thighs-High-Society flipping him the bird.

Delaney Lynn Cartwright, the daughter of a Montgomery blue blood, does not stoop to common vulgarity.

She heard her mother's chiding voice in her right ear, and the small sense of satisfaction she'd just derived from flipping off the arrogant Mr. Vinetti evaporated instantly.

Don't feel guilty. It's about time you showed some spunk, Skylar's voice countered in her left ear.

Terrific. Her highly developed superego, represented by her mother's voice, was pulling her in one direction. While her much-ignored id, in the form of Skylar-speak, was yanking her in the opposite.

Apologize to Mr. Vinetti for your rudeness, Honey's voice demanded. Delaney stopped, turned, and faced Nick.

He was standing at the end of the aisle, eyebrows cocked slyly, and a knowing smile playing across his lips.

To hell with that. Look at him. He's so damn sure of himself. He deserved the bird, Skylar's voice argued.

Delaney whirled back around and marched in the direction she'd been heading.

Just like when her sister had been alive, Delaney felt caught in the middle between two warring personalities much larger than her own. As a child, whenever Honey and Skylar went at it, Delaney hid in the closet or under the bed to avoid the fray. Her mother the perfectionist, and her sister the free spirit.

What am I? she wondered.

You're the people-pleaser, the Skylar voice and the mother voice echoed in stereo.

Feeling overwhelmed, Delaney clamped her hands over her ears to drown out the conflict.

When did she get to please herself? She was twenty-five years old, pampered and protected. How was she ever supposed to know what she really wanted if she kept letting other people tell her what to do?

Plumbing. Concentrate on plumping supplies and the repairs to Lucia's house.

She stared at the shelf in front of her, not seeing anything because her mind was in turmoil.

"Are you okay?" a deep voice curled through both her ears as a masculine hand touched her shoulder.

Startled from her reverie, Delaney leaped, hand splayed across her heart. "Eek."

"Sorry, I didn't mean to frighten you." Nick dropped his hand, but very slowly, and in the process grazed the length of her arm with his fingertips.

"No, no, I'm sorry." She wasn't prepared for the full consequence of being touched by him again. Her breath simply flew from her lungs, and she was left with her mouth hanging open at the razor-sharp jolt of awareness blasting through her body. Quickly she stepped closer to the shelf and farther away from him.

He was staring at her intently. As if he could make her disappear merely by focusing his mind on the task. He left her feeling tongue-tied, weak-kneed, and totally inadequate. "Don't apologize. You didn't do anything."

Her eyes met his. Prickles of primal excitement skidded up her spine. "I flipped you off."

"Yeah." He grinned. "You did."

"That was rude of me."

"Sometimes rude is justified."

Not according to my mother.

Their gazes were fused to each other, her pulse firing like a piston.

"Which size pipe do you think we'll need to replace the leaky one in your grandmother's upstairs bathroom?" Delaney pulled her gaze from his and ran her hand along the smooth hard length of metal plumbing pipe on the shelf in front of her.

"One and three quarters," he said.

"That doesn't seem thick enough."

"I measured it."

"Are you sure?"

"I know if I measured something or not."

"No, I mean are you sure you measured correctly."

"Go with this one, Rosy." Nick leaned around her to reach for the pipe and his chest brushed against her shoulder. The sleeve of his T-shirt rode up, revealing a wicked scar high up on his bicep.

Delaney felt something inside her start to unravel. She gasped. "What happened?"

"Huh?" He turned his head and saw her staring at his bicep. He was so close she could smell the clean linen scent of his soap. "Oh, that. Got shot."

Her whole body went cold. "You got shot?"

"Long time ago. Rookie mistake."

She swayed, imagining him hurting and in pain. She

couldn't stand the thought of it and bit down hard on her bottom lip.

"You're looking pale, Rosy. You gonna faint on me?"

"Your job is very dangerous."

"Most of the time, no."

"But you got shot on the job, and your grandmother told me you hurt your knee on the job as well. That seems pretty perilous to me."

He laughed and gave her a droll stare. Apparently her distress over his risky employment amused him. "Don't worry. Two injuries in eight years is not that bad. It's not like I'm an Alaskan king crab fisherman or anything."

His eyes hooked hers. He was so alive, so raw, so electric. So the opposite of Evan.

If she were a braver woman, she would have met the challenge in his eyes. But she wasn't brave. His overt masculinity scared the heck out of her.

"Go with this piece of pipe," he repeated, straightening and placing the pipe in her hand.

She dropped it into the shopping cart. "This is enough for now," she said, anxious to get outside where she could draw in a breath of fresh ocean air and clear her head. "We've got enough to get started. We can always come back for more supplies later."

Nick paid for the purchases and they left the store.

On the drive back to Lucia's place, tension permeated the cab of the pickup. Sexual tension. Taut and hot. Delaney stared out the window, focusing on the scenery. Condos and beach cottages and seagulls and tourists in brightly colored clothes.

But no matter how hard she tried to direct her attention outside, every cell in her was attuned to what was happening inside. Both inside the cab and inside her.

Her hands lay fisted against the tops of her thighs. Her throat felt tight, the set of her shoulders even tighter. Restlessly, she wriggled her toes inside her sandals. Even way across the seat, Delaney could feel the heat emanating off Nick's body. The truck smelled of him— musky, manly, magnificent.

The plastic hula girl, mounted on his dashboard, swayed her hips with the vehicle's movements. The faster he drove, the faster she danced the hula. Hula, hula, hula.

Her mother would have labeled the hula girl tacky and lowbrow. She supposed it did seem a bit chauvinistic, sort of like the silhouette of naked women on eighteen-wheeler mud flaps. But she liked the whimsy of it. Watching the plastic doll's undulating hips had a mesmerizing effect.

She reached out to touch it.

"No, no," Nick growled. "No touching Lalule."

She drew back her hand quickly as if he'd smacked her.

"Sorry," he apologized. "Didn't mean to snap. Reflex. The nieces and nephews are always trying to monkey around with her, and I'm so used to warning them off, I forgot it was you. Lalule means a lot to me."

"Why is that?"

"My mother gave her to me," he said gruffly. "Not long before she died."

"Oh."

He didn't say anything else.

Delaney didn't mean to be nosy, but she wanted so

badly to understand him. Because she thought that if she could understand him, maybe she could figure out why she was so attracted to this man. And then she could sublimate that attraction in a healthier way. "What was your mother's name?"

"Dominique. I'm named after her."

"How did she die?"

"Brain tumor. When I was seven." He stared out over the hood of the truck, and Delaney knew his mind was rummaging around in the past.

"That must have been so difficult for you," she soothed.

"Yeah."

"You must have felt abandoned."

He drummed his fingers against the steering wheel, and she thought that was all she was going to get out of him. She didn't press. If he didn't want to talk about it, he didn't want to talk about it.

But then a few minutes later, he surprised her. "Mom's dying wish was to go to Hawaii. Dad maxed out the credit card and took us to Maui for three weeks on one last family vacation."

He paused again and glanced over at her. The raw pain on his face was almost unbearable. Nick was far more complicated than she'd guessed.

In that moment, she saw past his looks, beyond the dark eyes that were often hooded to hide his thoughts. Beyond the high, masculine cheekbones, the thick black eyelashes, the nose that looked as if it had been broken a time or two. She peered beyond the promise of his beautiful mouth, which wasn't too full or too thin, but very well shaped with a distinctive cut to the borders and a curious firmness in the way he held it. As if if he were to relax his hold, it might give away too many secrets.

Delaney thought that was all he was going to say on the subject of his mother, but then he said, "I was a cowardly kid. I wanted so badly to learn to surf, but I was afraid of the water. I didn't even know how to swim."

It touched her that he would confess this vulnerability, that he trusted her not to judge him for his childhood fears. Most macho guys refused to admit any kind of weakness. But in Delaney's point of view, Nick's willingness to acknowledge his foibles only made him stronger.

"You?" she said, treading lightly in this swamp of emotion. "Detective Bullet-Riddled a 'fraidy cat? I don't believe it."

"Yep. I was. My little brothers could swim, but I was afraid of sharks, of drowning, of getting taken away from my mother."

"Do you think she knew that?"

"I know she did. She bought Lalule and told me she was my guardian angel. Whenever I got scared, Mom told me to just give Lalule a shake, and she would remind me to shake things up," he explained.

"Shake things up?"

"Mom said I could sit on the beach, play it safe, and feel sorry for myself, or I could be brave, learn how to shake things up, and make my life happen. With Lalule's help, in three weeks I'd learned not only how to swim, but also how to surf."

"Your mother knew she wouldn't be around to inspire you herself, and she gave you the doll as a reminder of her indomitable spirit," Delaney said softly.

"Yeah. I suppose she did. My mother was sweet on the outside, but tough on the inside. Sort of like you."

That sounded dangerously close to a compliment. Except Nick was dead wrong. Delaney wasn't tough inside at all. She was a total marshmallow through and through.

He took a deep breath. "Mom died just four days after we got back home."

Delaney's throat clotted with emotion. "Nick—I—"

"So you see why I don't like anyone messing with Lalule," he rushed in to say. She could tell he was struggling to sound casual.

She wanted to touch him, to comfort him for that long-ago pain, but she had no business, no right. Still, she couldn't just leave him with his shoulders tensed, his jaw clenched, his mind hung up in the past. She skimmed his forearm with her fingertips—briefly, lightly, just enough to let him know she cared.

"I understand the hurt. The confusion a young child goes through when they lose someone close to them. You blame yourself. You think that if you'd been a better kid, the person you loved wouldn't have died. That if you had done just one thing differently, you could have saved them."

He looked startled. "You too?"

"My older sister," she said. "When I was eight."

Nick made a noise, half empathy, half sorrow. His eyes glistened. "Life's a bitch sometimes," he said to be macho, but he reached across the seat and tenderly took her hand.

Every muscle cell in her heart ached. She looked over at him. This shared intimacy forced a deeper understanding, a bonding between them.

"Losing Skylar changed me forever, you know." She swallowed. "While losing your mother made you braver, losing my sister made me more afraid."

"You seem brave to me."

"I'm not." She ducked her head. "Not at all. You have no idea how scared I am ninety percent of the time."

"What are you so scared of?"

"Of everything, but mostly of being scared." She laughed at herself. "Of not really living."

"If that's true, where did you find the courage to dress up in that bustier and raincoat and attempt to kidnap your fiancé?"

"I needed to feel something. Needed some magic in my life, I guess. But you saw how well that turned out."

"I thought it turned out very well. It made me damn jealous of your fiancé."

Delaney couldn't handle the swell of emotions flooding through her. She couldn't keep looking at him. Instead, she directed her attention out the window and told herself to breathe.

They were traveling down Seawall Boulevard. Sunlight streamed through a break in the soft covering of clouds, sparkling off the blue waters of the Gulf of Mexico. The water shimmered, rolling in toward the seawall.

For a split second, Delaney felt the way she'd felt the night she found the wedding veil. Caught up in a special sort of magic that could change everything. And then the feeling vanished, disappearing as quickly as it surfaced.

She saw a carnival-style amusement park situated at the end of the beach. The rides looked old and shaky, the garishly painted skins peeling and rusting in the salt air.

Delaney was at once both charmed and repelled by the rinky-dink amusement park.

When she was a kid, she'd always wanted to go to a carnival or an amusement park. Ride those scary rides. Eat sticky candy apples and funnel cakes dusted with powdered sugar. Breathe in the air rich with the smell of frying grease. Get taken in by the sideshow barkers. Play games of chance and win a giant teddy bear.

Her mother had hated carnivals and amusement parks with a passion verging on phobia. "Carnies are common street thugs," she'd tell Delaney. "You'll get germs from the rides. They'll cheat you and steal your money. Stay away from carnivals and fairs and small-time amusement parks."

So she had.

But her mother had made carnivals such a taboo, that whenever Delaney saw one, she experienced the lure of the forbidden deep in the center of her stomach. Calling to her. Urging her to defy her mother. To sin by climbing on the Ferris wheel and floating high above the crowd and then slowly coming down to earth. She had imagined it a thousand times.

She latched on to the amusement park with her gaze, using it to pry her awareness off Nick. Realizing that in spite of having grown up a very rich girl, she had missed out on a lot of the simple things. What she would have given for a Lalule of her own.

Then Delaney saw something totally unbelievable.

Her smartly dressed, perfectly coiffed mother.

No way.

But she could have sworn it was Honey Montgomery Cartwright standing on the seawall beside the entrance to the amusement park, talking to an elderly woman in a babushka and wading boots, wearing a black eye patch over her left eye.

The pickup truck sailed by.

Delaney blinked. No, it couldn't be. She must have imagined it. She couldn't conceive of a single reason that would compel her mother to visit a run-down amusement park on Galveston Island.

"Wait, wait," she exclaimed.

"What is it?"

"Back up, back up," she yelled at Nick, frantically making counterclockwise motions with her hand.

"Huh?"

"Put it in reverse, go back, go back."

"I can't back up in traffic."

"Make a U-ey. Hurry, hurry."

"Okay, okay, keep your shirt on." His grin turned wicked. "Unless, of course, you want to take it off."

Any other time she would never have said what she said next, but she was so stunned at seeing her snooty mother slumming at an amusement park that she was not her normal self.

"Shut up and drive, Vinetti," she snarled.

"Yes, ma'am." He obeyed and made a U-turn at the next traffic light.

She was amazed at his acquiescence. Hmm, maybe that was the way you handled a guy like Vinetti. If she'd growled "shut up" at Evan, it would have hurt his feelings so badly he would have pouted for an hour. Nick, on the other hand, seemed to respect her for it. Then again, Evan had never given her any reason to snarl "shut up" at him.

"Drive slower."

"Cars are on my ass, Rosy."

"Tough."

"When'd you get so bossy?"

When indeed? She wasn't acting like herself, but right now that felt like a good thing. Delaney undid her seat belt and scooted over to Nick's side of the truck and craned her neck to peer out his window. She was sitting so close she could hear him breathing.

They crept along Seawall Boulevard, cars piling up behind them, drivers honking their horns in irritation.

"What are we looking for?" he asked.

"I thought I saw someone I know."

"And that's worth snarling traffic over?"

"In this case, yes."

"What? Do you think that you saw your fiancé with another woman?"

"No."

"Then what on earth could you have seen that would make you holler like a banshee with her hair caught in a chamois wringer?" Nick asked.

"That's none of your business."

"I hate to disagree with you on that, but your sighting is the reason these cars are kissing my bumper. You owe me an explanation."

"I saw my mother, okay? Happy now?"

"With a man other than your father?"

"What's with you and the cheating-loved-ones scenarios? Oh, oh." She tapped his shoulder. "Slow down even more, we're almost there."

They inched past the amusement park entrance.

Teeth clenched, Delaney scanned the area. She looked

first left toward the Gulf, then right toward the collection of ragtag carnival rides.

Nothing.

No one.

Her mother had vanished.

Chapter 8

Shaking with fear and revulsion, Honey climbed into her sleek white Cadillac and sped out of Galveston as fast as she dared, desperate to reach home and take a long, hot, cleansing shower to wash away her sins. Her heart was in her throat, her stomach was a tight knot, and her hands smelled of the twenty thousand dollars she'd just counted out. She felt very dirty.

Blackmail was an ugly business.

Then again, so was the thing she had done.

All these years, she thought she'd gotten away with it. Thought she had fooled everyone. Thought no one would ever discover her terrible secret.

In retrospect, she'd been both foolish and arrogant.

Now she was trapped. Forced to pay to keep her shame quiet and never knowing how long the blackmailing would continue.

And she had to keep it quiet. For her daughter's sake. No one must ever discover the truth.

At least until after the wedding. When Delaney was married to Evan and safely out of harm's way.

Nick didn't know why he'd told Delaney about his mother. He rarely talked about Dominique anymore. He wasn't the kind of guy who liked stirring up the past, and he certainly didn't like examining his feelings and talking about them.

Unfortunately, once the memories of those old feelings had been aroused—feelings of loss and anger and sadness—he could not easily stuff them back down into his subconscious. Even after he'd gone home for the day, he kept replaying his afternoon with Delaney over and over in his head. To relieve the pressure, Nick was back at the gym, pushing himself, exercising his body in an attempt to free his mind.

It wasn't working.

Almost always, when things got too emotionally tough, exercise provided him with the release he needed. During the whole Amber/Gary Feldstein fiasco, he shed nine pounds, ended up running a five-minute mile, and bench-pressed two-sixty. Thanks to Gold's Gym, he'd been able to put the scandal out of his mind and get through the humiliation.

But this was the second time exercise had failed him where Delaney Cartwright was concerned.

He lost count during bicep curls because he kept thinking about Delaney's soft voice and the way her deeply green, intelligent, expressive eyes encouraged him to spill his secrets. He forgot how many laps he'd done in the pool and had to go around again to make sure he wasn't shortchanging his routine because he'd vividly imagined kissing that slightly crooked little mouth of hers. He forgot to put the timer on the treadmill and ended up staying on fifteen minutes longer than he intended because he kept wondering how her silky hair would feel slipping through his fingers.

What was it about Delaney that loosened his lips? Why did he feel this need to explain himself to her?

He didn't like it. He didn't like it at all. She seemed to hold some kind of magic key to the trunk where he kept his vulnerabilities locked up tight. She knew just how and when to slip that key into the lock and turn it. Nick barely knew the woman, and he had already told her things he'd never told Amber. Not even after being engaged for eighteen months.

He'd never even told his ex-wife the story behind Lalule.

When she'd run off with Feldstein, Amber had cited Nick's inability to communicate as the reason she'd left. Ha! If she could see him now. With Delaney, he was communicating like Geraldo Rivera in the Middle East, spilling everything he knew. How laughably ironic.

Then it suddenly occurred to him why he would share his deeper feelings with Delaney and not with Amber. For one, Delaney was an empathetic listener, but he suspected that was secondary. He could talk to her because with Delaney, he had nothing to lose. She was engaged to someone else. He didn't see her as a threat to his self-image. With her, he wouldn't forfeit any macho points for revealing his tender side.

Once he realized that, he felt better.

Okay, he didn't have anything to worry about. If tears

had misted his eyes a little when he'd talked about his mother, no harm, no foul.

Except whenever he thought about Delaney, something tightened in the dead center of his chest, and that disturbed him. A helluva lot. The woman was engaged to another man. He couldn't, *wouldn't*, have these feelings for her.

Clearly, he had to find a way to chase her off. Not only because he didn't want her succeeding at selling Nana's house, but for his own mental health as well. He had to be subtle about it. Nana loved her. Hell, the whole family was smitten with her. If he didn't handle this right, he'd come off looking like the bad guy.

Quitting the job had to be Delaney's idea. But how to accomplish that goal? What he needed was an underhanded plan.

A smile broke across his lips as the perfect plot popped into his head. He'd turn on the charm and pretend he was trying to win her away from her fiancé. That ought to do the trick. Pleased with his solution, Nick breezed through the rest of his workout.

Yep, Delaney Cartwright's days as his Nana's house stager were numbered.

"You've got to be mistaken. Our mom? At an amusement park? Talking to a one-eyed carny woman?" Skylar scoffed when Delaney dreamed of her again.

"Yes."

Tonight, Skylar was dressed in scarlet cowgirl boots and a fawn-colored suede jacket with fringe on the sleeves. "I can't imagine in what universe that scenario is even remotely possible."

"I'm telling you, it was her."

"Did you ask her about it?"

Delaney blew out a breath. "Yes . . . no."

"Did you or not?"

"I tried to, but I couldn't get the words out. I did mention that I had a job on Galveston Island."

"Well, that was straightforward and to the point." Skylar picked up a tube of lipstick off Delaney's vanity, plunked down in front of the mirror, and rolled some on. "Ick! Too pale. Ditch the pink and get some red."

"If you don't like my lipstick then don't use it."

"I don't have a choice. You're the only one who dreams about me."

"Mother and Daddy don't dream about you?"

"Not much. Not anymore." Skylar uncapped Delaney's mascara and leaned forward to brush it across her eyelashes.

"Then why do I keep dreaming of you?"

"Who do I look like, Sigmund Freud? How would I know? Anyway, back to Mother."

"I don't know why she was there, but I'm telling you it was our mother."

"If you're so certain, then you should have confronted her, not wishy-washed around. If it had been me, I would have just come right out and said, 'Hey, Mom, spied you on Galveston Island chatting up a one-eyed carny chick; what gives?'"

"Yeah, well, that's you."

Skylar propped her cowgirl-booted feet up on the vanity and cocked back in the chair until only the two back legs were left on the floor. "Remember how Mom used to carry on about the evils of carnivals and street fairs and amusement parks? What was her deal? If it wasn't for Uncle Lance and Aunt Maxie taking me with their kids, I would never have even gone to Sea World."

"I never did get to go to Sea World," Delaney said. "By the time I was old enough, you were dead and Mom wouldn't let me out of her sight."

"Wonder what her deal is with carnivals? A rock concert phobia I get, but carnivals? Come on. Everyone loves carnivals."

"Not our mother."

"So what are you going to do about it?"

"About what?"

"Finding out what Mom was doing there."

"I'm not going to do anything about it."

"Why not? Scared of the one-eyed woman?"

Truthfully, yes. "What would be the point?"

"So you'd have something over on Mother. We spent our lives totally under her control, and now you have the opportunity to prove she was not only hanging out at an amusement park, but that she lied to you about it. And besides, aren't you just a wee bit curious as to why?"

"Why *would* she be there?"

"Maybe she was buying drugs. Mother always told us that behind the scenes, carnivals were a hotbed for drugs."

"Mother? Doing drugs? Please."

"Yeah, you're right. If she was doing drugs, she wouldn't be so uptight."

"I've been thinking about it all day," Delaney said. "It makes no sense."

"Maybe she went there to meet a lover."

"Hello, I saw her with a woman."

"Eeps! Mother's a lesbian? That's her big secret."

Skylar leaned back too far and the chair hit the ground. She rolled on the floor, laughing hysterically. "Good thing I'm not real. Otherwise, that might have hurt."

"Until now, I never realized how silly you were."

"I'm forever trapped in your imagination the way I was when I died. Of course I'm silly. I'm sixteen."

"When I was a kid I thought you were so mature and sophisticated."

"We all have our shattered illusions. Like Mother at an amusement park. Life will never be the same."

"You're making fun of me."

Skylar shrugged. "Have you told Mother about the wedding veil yet?"

"No."

"Wanna get to wear it with impunity?"

Delaney eyed her sister. "What do you have in mind?"

"Go talk to the one-eyed woman. Get proof it was our mother you saw at the amusement park. Then tell her you want to wear the veil. If she refuses, you whip out your trump card and inform her that you'll tell Dad about her clandestine trip to Galveston if she doesn't put her stamp of approval on the veil."

"But that's blackmail."

"Uh-huh."

"I can't blackmail my own mother."

"No? Why not? She's been doing it to you for years."

"What are you talking about?"

"Using my death to keep you in line. Be perfect, live up to her expectations, or you'll end up dead. That's emotional blackmail. She's kept you from being the person you were truly meant to be. This, my sis, is the ideal time to declare your independence and break free. All it requires is a little daring on your part. You up for it?"

"I don't know."

"Yes, you do." Skylar winked, and then Delaney woke up.

Honey couldn't sleep.

She'd spent the night tossing and turning beside a snoring James Robert, thinking of what she'd been forced to do the previous day and fretting over something Delaney had said at dinner the night before, about having a house to stage out on Galveston Island. She'd announced it quite out of the blue and then stared at Honey as if she knew something.

Could Delaney have seen her at the amusement park?

She had to find out.

Just after dawn, she got up, dressed, and went to Delaney's room.

She knocked on the door, and before her daughter could tell her to come in, Honey was already pushing her way over the threshold. She found Delaney sitting at the vanity in her bathrobe, flatironing her hair. Delaney's hair, without the proper products and styling techniques, looked shockingly unruly.

"You're up early," Delaney said mildly.

"I thought maybe we could have a heart-to-heart." Honey made Delaney's bed and stiffly sat down on it.

"Is this about the wedding preparations?" Delaney eyed her from the mirror.

"No. Not really. We just haven't had much of a chance to talk lately, and I was feeling we were a bit disconnected. You've been busy with this new project, and I've been busy too." Honey came over to pat her shoulder. "Here. Let me have the flatiron. You missed a spot along your nape."

Dutifully, Delaney handed her the ceramic styling iron and Honey breathed a sigh of relief. The insurrection had been a small one.

"Sit up straight; you're slouching."

Delaney sat up, but kept her eyes lowered so Honey couldn't peer into the mirror and read her thoughts. But she could feel tension tightening the muscles along the back of her daughter's neck.

"Busy doing what?" Delaney asked.

Alarm spread through Honey. Was her daughter being cagey? "Why, planning your wedding of course."

"Right," Delaney said in that calm, unemotional tone of hers that at times Honey found slightly demeaning.

You're the one who stressed the importance of learning to manage her emotions. She's just doing what you taught her.

Ah, but she'd learned too well. Honey feared she never really knew what her daughter was thinking or feeling behind those enigmatic green eyes so much like her own.

The price of controlling her youngest daughter had been high, but it was a cost Honey had no choice but to pay. She refused to let Delaney end up like Skylar. Even after seventeen years, the memory of her oldest child painfully wrenched Honey's heart. Haunting guilt sent her gaze flicking over Delaney, looking for any problems to nip in the bud. She took in the serene sophistication of her daughter's large bedroom with its cool sage green walls, cherrywood sleigh bed, and haute couture–inspired accessories.

"Did you have a wedding-based errand at the amusement park on Galveston Island yesterday afternoon?"

Honey froze. *Don't reveal a thing. Keep your face emotionless.* "I don't know what you mean."

"Come on, Mother, I saw you."

The words, once spoken, were as powerful as a slap. Honey's cheeks stung. She gulped. How was she going to handle this?

Lie through your teeth. It's the only way to survive.

Grappling to control the terror mushrooming inside her, Honey laughed, trying to sound carefree, but she only ended up sounding nervous. "Don't be absurd. You know how much I hate Galveston and amusement parks."

"Yes, I do, which is exactly why it struck me as so odd to see you there."

"I wasn't there," Honey denied. "It wasn't me."

The flatiron hissed in the silence between them, steam rising up from Delaney's hair. The silence lay heavy. An accusation.

"Are you having an affair?" Delaney asked.

This time her laugh was honest. "Don't be silly, darling. I would never jeopardize my marriage for a fling. I love your father with all my heart. I've never loved anyone the way I love him."

"You couldn't prove it by me." Delaney's voice was flint.

"Excuse me?" This change in her daughter bothered Honey immensely. Skylar had bucked her, spectacularly and often, but Delaney? Never.

"You nag Daddy constantly. He can't ever seem to do anything to please you."

Honey was taken aback. "I do not."

But it was true. She did nitpick James Robert. It was for his own good. Without her he would just drift along, never taking a stand, never feeling strongly about anything.

"I know things between the two of you fell apart after Skylar died, but Mother, it's been seventeen years. Hasn't Daddy been punished enough?"

"I'm not punishing him."

Delaney's accusation was ludicrous. Wasn't it?

"No?"

"I'm helping him to improve."

"What if he doesn't want to improve? What if he likes being the way he is? You married him that way. How come he isn't good enough for you anymore? You criticize me all the time too. How come I'm not good enough either? What's this impossibly high standard you're trying to reach? Face it, Mother, we're never going to be good enough for you."

Shocked to her very core, Honey sucked in her breath. "Darling," she whispered, "I had no idea you felt this way. I only correct you because I love you so much. I want to see you excel. To have a rewarding life."

"Have you ever considered your definition of excellence might differ greatly from Daddy's and mine?"

"Please don't get me wrong. I'm not putting you down. You're a wonderful daughter, and you've accomplished so much. You've started your own business and it's thriving. You're about to marry one of the most eligible bachelors in Texas, who just happens to be a really nice person as well. People are going to be talking about this wedding for years to come."

Using the curling iron, Honey pointed to Delaney's framed "ugly duckling" picture she encouraged her to keep on her dresser as a reminder not to slip up and go off her diet. "See how far you've come. You were a size eighteen in that picture, and now look at you, a perfect size four. I'm so proud."

"Uh-huh," Delaney muttered. "That's what I thought. As long as I stay thin I have your approval, but let me dare to gain weight, and I risk losing your love. Gotta tell you, Mother, conditional love doesn't feel so swell."

Honey had to bite down on her tongue to keep from lecturing her about mumbling and saying "uh-huh" and "gotta." Truth be told, her feelings were hurt. How could her own daughter misunderstand her intentions so completely?

"There." She forced a smile. "All done."

"Thank you." Delaney unplugged the flatiron and headed into the adjoining bathroom.

Suddenly feeling exhausted, Honey sank down on the bed. She thought once she'd raised Delaney to adulthood, everything would be so much easier.

But it was not.

She had imagined they would be fast friends, going shopping, calling each other several times a day, sharing fashion tips and diet recipes, and laughing together.

But they did not.

Honey thought that preparing for this wedding would be the glue that would finally bond them, that once Delaney was engaged and on the road to becoming a married woman, she would finally understand the sacrifices Honey had made. That she wanted only the very best for her.

But it had not.

If anything, the impending wedding seemed to be pushing them farther and farther apart, with Delaney growing more apathetic with each decision made. She didn't seem to have any sort of opinion on the cake or the reception menu or the invitations. Her reaction to everything was a bland, "Whatever you like."

What was wrong with her daughter?

The staunch reserve she'd perfected over the years slipped, and tears she hadn't cried since losing Skylar sprang from her eyes and slid down her cheeks. In spite of trying her very best, she was a terrible mother who couldn't love her own daughter unconditionally. God was punishing her for her lies and deceptions.

What would happen if Delaney found out about the blackmailer? What if she learned the truth?

Fear thrashed inside her. She struggled not to give in to it. She kept her hands knotted tightly in her lap, her shoulders set straight, and with catlike concentration willed the tears to stop. She was not a weak person. She was strong, she was a survivor. She and Delaney would weather this storm and come out stronger at the other end.

The tears dried on her cheeks. Yes, yes. Everything would be okay. This was fixable.

She had to believe it. Had to believe she would not lose Delaney.

Otherwise, if she dared let herself think that her surviving daughter had withdrawn from her completely, Honey would totally fall apart.

Her mother was lying, but Delaney had no idea why. She sat parked in her Acura beside the Galveston seawall, her father's black Bushnell binoculars resting in her lap. She stared at the amusement park sprawling out across the beach below. She couldn't believe she was doing this—checking up on her mother.

Curiosity nibbled at her.

At ten A.M. on a Thursday, only a few tourists haunted the rides and concession stands. Lucia wasn't expecting her until noon, when they were meeting with Lucia's real estate agent, Margaret Krist, to discuss Delaney's plans for the house.

She had two hours to locate the patch-eyed woman and quiz her about Honey. She'd brought cash in case the woman expected to be paid for the information. Delaney might be sheltered, but she wasn't dumb. She watched television. She was aware of how these things worked.

The main thing keeping her butt welded to the car seat was this inbred fear of carnivals and amusement parks that her mother had instilled in her.

Stay away from carnies. Those people are scoundrels and crooks and pickpockets and thieves. They will rob you blind, and that's if you're lucky.

Delaney scooted over to the passenger seat, rolled down the window, propped her elbows on the sill, and raised the binoculars to her eyes. She surveyed the area for the one-eyed woman, but saw no sign of her.

This wasn't getting her anywhere. She was going to have to face her fear, walk into that amusement park, and ask someone about the woman. Too bad confrontation made her nervous. She took a deep breath.

If you can flip off Nick Vinetti, you can do this.

Smiling, her courage bolstered by the memory, she got out of the car, tucked her purse under her arm, and strolled down the seawall toward the cement staircase leading down to the beach. Almost immediately, she realized how inappropriately she was dressed for a stroll along the shore. White silk slacks, a silk navy-blue V-necked blouse, and high-heeled sandals. What had she been thinking?

Well, when she'd dressed that morning she'd been thinking about her meeting with Lucia's real estate agent, not a powwow with the carnival woman. It was only after talking to her mother and Honey acting so suspiciously that she had made up her mind to do this.

Carefully, Delaney picked her way down the staircase, holding tight to the railing. The minute she veered onto the walkway leading to the amusement park entrance, the wind blew sand into her open-toed shoes.

She ambled along through the grounds, trying to look casual as she studied the faces of the amusement park workers. Surprisingly, a pleasant feeling stole over her. The sound of the ocean was so peaceful, she almost forgot why she'd come.

After trailing up and down the walkway and not seeing the one-eyed woman, she realized she was going to have to ask someone if they knew her. Taking a deep breath to bolster her courage, she sidled up to the bored-looking guy manning the Whack-a-Mole. No one else was around. He leaned across the counter and leered at her as she approached.

She forced a smile. "Hello, I was hoping you could tell me where I might find someone who works here. She's an older woman and wears an eye patch."

"What's it worth to you?" His look was lascivious and his gaze fixated on her mouth.

She pressed her lips together in a firm line. "I'll give you ten dollars."

He held out a palm.

Delaney dropped a ten-dollar bill into it.

"You're talking about Paulette Doggett." The man spat a stream of tobacco into the sand not far from her foot. "It's her day off."

"Do you have any idea where I might find Ms. Doggett?"

The leering man shrugged. "I 'magine she's out chasing the hounds."

"Excuse me?"

"Paulette came into a wad of cash yesterdee, and she likes betting on the greyhounds."

"Thank you." Grateful to be out of the man's company, Delaney hurried away. She had two choices, go to the greyhound track and try to find Paulette in the crowd, or return to the amusement park another day. Since she had a meeting planned for noon, she chose the later option.

"Well, well, well, will surprises never cease," said a familiar voice from behind her that made the hairs on her arms stand up. "If it isn't Miss Rosy."

Chapter 9

Delaney turned to find Nick Vinetti standing behind her, his grin wide and wicked. She felt a little woozy, like all the air had been leaked from her lungs.

"Hi," she said breathlessly.

"Hi."

"What are you doing here?"

"I asked first."

And that's when she noticed the boys standing on either side of him. "Gina's kids, right? Jack and Zack."

"We're twins," one of the boys said.

"I can see that." Delaney smiled at them.

"Identical," the other added.

"I can see that too."

"We're seven," they chimed in unison, charming Delaney with their gap-toothed grins, crew cuts, and skinned elbows. She could easily imagine Nick at their age, dark-eyed and full of mischief. Although she had no idea why that image would make her chest feel all tight and knotty.

"I'm keeping them occupied while Gina and Nana are packing up Grampa Leo's personal effects," Nick explained. His voice sounded as tight as her chest.

Her eyes met his. "That's got to be difficult for your grandmother."

Nick shrugged. "Yeah, that's why they didn't need these little sea monkeys around. With school out for the summer, Gina didn't have anyone to babysit, so I volunteered."

Delaney's heart twisted. Nick acted all macho and nonchalant, but one look at his face told her it was hard on him too, and he was happier watching the kids than being the one sorting out his grandfather's belongings. "That was nice of you."

"I don't mind. Sea monkeys can be a lot of fun."

"Hey," Zack, or maybe it was Jack, protested. It was really tough to tell them apart. "We're not sea monkeys."

"You sure squirm around like sea monkeys."

The twins made faces and jumped around, letting their arms flop loosely as if they had no bones in them. Delaney smiled. They were so cute, and Nick was adorable with them.

"How about you?" Nick asked her. "Why are you here, looking decidedly out of your element?"

She didn't miss the gaze that he slid down her body in a disconcertingly intimate fashion, and then his eyes lingered on her inappropriate footwear. The intensity of his stare should have made her uncomfortable. Instead it ignited the sparks that had been simmering between them from the day he'd flipped her onto her back in the grass outside Evan's building.

Delaney didn't want to tell him the truth, so she skipped over his question. "Did your grandmother tell you that she and I are having lunch with her real estate agent to discuss the renovations and a time schedule for listing the house on the market?"

"Yeah, she told me, but that still doesn't explain why you're at the amusement park looking like you stepped from the pages of some fashion magazine."

"We wanna go on the Ferris wheel." Jack tugged on his uncle's hand. "You promised."

"Would you like to come with us?" Nick inclined his head toward the biggest ride in the carnival that jutted high into the cloudless blue summer sky. "Plenty of time before your lunch date. Unless you have something else going on."

She hesitated.

He'd leaned in close, his face just to the side of hers. "Come on," he coaxed. "Have a little fun."

Was it her imagination, or was he standing just a bit too close and pushing just a bit too hard?

"I . . . I . . ."

"I gotcha. You're too fancy for Ferris wheels."

"I'm not," she denied indignantly. He had a way of pushing her buttons.

A half smile hovered at the edges of his lips. His warm breath fell against her neck, heating her all the way through. Was he doing it on purpose? Was he *trying* to make her uncomfortable?

"Come on. What do you say? Please, don't leave me alone with the sea monkeys."

Delaney was about to refuse his invitation and then she thought, *Why not?* She was twenty-five years old, and she'd never been on a Ferris wheel because her mother had made her afraid of them. It was pathetic really.

He gave her such a winning smile she decided she must be reading more into his body language than he actually intended. He was a cop; crowding people was probably just second nature. Nothing personal. Right?

"Pretty please." His grin widened.

"Well, when you put it like that, sure," she said. "I would love to."

The sun shone brightly on her face, and rather than worry that she hadn't put on sunblock and was exposing herself to the risk of premature wrinkles, she simply threw back her head and laughed. Then, she stumbled over a thick extension cord running across the midway and fell against Nick's side.

"Whoa there, Rosy," he said and put a hand on her shoulder to steady her. "You okay?"

"Fine," she chirped, feeling finer than she'd felt in a very long time. She couldn't explain where this sudden exuberance was coming from, but it sure felt good.

Nick said nothing. He angled an odd look her way just before he bought their tickets. The twins climbed into one of the cars of the Ferris wheel ahead of them, leaving her alone in the second car with Nick. They were the only customers on the ride.

The operator lowered the restraining bar, locking them in together. He stepped over to the controls and started the ride.

The cars jerked forward.

Delaney squealed and grabbed on to Nick's elbow.

He chuckled and slid his arm around her shoulder. "Scared of Ferris wheels?"

"Never been on one."

"You're kidding me."

"My mother was a bit overprotective."

"I'll say. It's not like it's a roller coaster."

"I've never been on one of those either."

For the first time, she realized how high up they were and that they were just dangling in the air. She eyed the ground, feeling decidedly nervous. Were they supposed to be this high up? It didn't seem right.

"Have no fear, Nick is here," he teased. "I'll protect you."

Sitting so close to Nick with his arm draped around her shoulder, she felt too giddy and way too free.

"Do you have any idea how tempting you are?" he murmured and touched the simple gold hoop earring at her earlobe.

"Um." She raised her left hand between them, flashed him her engagement right. "Just a reminder, I'm engaged."

"So I see." He said it with such regret in his voice. She searched his face for the emotion behind his words. His smile turned tender, wistful.

What was with him? He was acting as if he wanted to date her.

Delaney huddled into herself. His arm felt too good resting over her shoulders. She felt safe and protected. But she shouldn't be feeling this way. It was wrong. In just over six weeks she was marrying Evan.

Around and around and around the Ferris wheel churned.

Her head spun dizzily. Her stomach clenched. She thought of all the horror stories her mother had told her over the years about carnivals and amusement parks. About people getting hurt or killed on the rides. About safety violations and bribed inspectors and drunken ride operators.

Around and around and around.

The ride seemed to be lasting forever. It wasn't supposed to be this long, was it?

Colors were more vivid. Sounds intensified. Time stretched. What should have been only seconds felt like an hour as the rusted old bucket of bolts creaked and groaned.

She heard the twins laughing in the car ahead of them. They were having fun. This was supposed to be fun. How come she wasn't having fun anymore?

They circled around to the bottom. This was it. The ride operator had to let them out now. She shifted, getting ready to stand up.

Get out of here and far away from Nick Vinetti.

But the ride did not stop; it whizzed on by the operator and swiftly climbed back into the sky.

Delaney's mouth went dry. Her muscles contracted. She wrapped her fingers around Nick's forearm.

"Stop," she squeaked and laid a hand against his upper thigh.

"Stop?"

"You're a cop. Do something. Stop the ride."

"I can't. We're in midair."

She peeked over at him. He was trying hard not to laugh at her. She dug her fingers deeper into his flesh. Her breathing was fast and raspy. "Get me off this thing."

"You're serious," he said, his body tensing beside her. "You're really scared?"

She nodded.

Nick leaned over the edge of the ride just as they were cresting the top. "Hey," he shouted down at the operator. "We want off."

"Thank you," she whimpered. "Thank you very much."

His pulled her close against him. "It's okay. I'm here. I'm sorry for laughing at you. I didn't realize you were really scared."

Delaney went stock-still as his chest made contact with her breasts and a surge of unwelcome desire ripped through her. His body heat warmed her and the connection of his raw, masculine power overwhelmed her. Even more unsettling, his comforting scent of nutmeg and leather invaded her brain.

She wanted him.

Desperately.

Oh, this was a terrible state of affairs.

Nick tilted her chin up, forced her to look him in the eyes. "Are you okay?"

Emotions she couldn't deny, but had held in rigid check ever since she'd met him, surged inside her. Stunned, she could barely nod.

"You're safe," he murmured. "I promise."

The thing of it was, she did feel safe. He made her feel safe. Safer than she'd ever felt with anyone. And that was far scarier than the Ferris wheel ride. She was loopy and frightened and she wanted him to kiss her even more than she wanted off this contraption.

He dipped his head toward her and she was already opening her lips. Already eager and ready for him.

He's going to kiss me, yes, yes, yes.

But he didn't kiss her.

Just as his lips were about to softly brush against hers, the ride stopped.

And so did Nick.

Leaving her hanging, quite literally, her mouth open and wet and wanting him.

He pulled back, raised his head, removed his arm from her shoulders, and did not look at her.

Her mind spun with sensory overload. What was happening to her? The taste of frustrated anticipation lay bittersweet in her mouth. The lonely sound of the metal bar clanking echoed in her ears. The feel of the empty space between them as he got out of the car stretched long and lonely. The smell of ocean breeze and cotton candy came rushing in to fill the void left by his leaving.

But Nick did not stray far. He turned and reached back for her. Offering his hand to help her step out. His touch was a furnace, his body heat seeping into her skin.

She took his hand and he pulled her gently across the seat toward him.

Delaney felt the material of her pants tug tightly across her bottom. She heard a soft ripping sound, like the tearing of silk. She jerked her head around and saw that the seat of her pants had snagged on a small jagged hole in the aging metal. When she stood up, she felt the air against her bare skin and put a hand behind her to examine the damage.

The tear was much bigger than she'd feared. She gasped at the six-by-six-inch square of nearly severed material that had once been covering her left butt cheek, but was now flapping in the Gulf breeze. Unfortunately, she also happened to be wearing thong underwear.

"Hey, Uncle Nick, that was fun." Nick's twin nephews came walking toward them.

"Please, you've got to help me out here," Delaney whispered urgently to Nick. "Before the boys see me."

"What is it?" He ducked his head.

"Put your hand on my backside and you'll find out."

"An unorthodox request," he said, "but okay." He pressed his large palm flush against her bare flesh. "Uh-oh."

"Uh-oh is an understatement."

"Here, boys." Nick reached into his pocket with his free hand and pulled out several one-dollar bills. "Go get yourselves some cotton candy."

"Mom said we can't have any junk," Jack said. "She says it'll spoil our lunch."

The boys were peering at her curiously. Delaney gave them a shaky smile. "What kind of kids is your sister raising?" she whispered out of the corner of her mouth. "They can't be bribed with cotton candy?"

"Kids that will have all their teeth?"

"Look at them, they've already lost teeth."

"Baby teeth."

"This isn't funny," she said.

"Yes, it is." He grinned.

Her initial impulse was to get upset. Torn pants that had cost her a fortune. A blow to her dignity. Then she realized it *was* funny, and to get huffy was exactly like something her mother would do. It was just a pair of pants. No major catastrophe. As for her dignity, big deal. She was loopy from a cheap amusement park ride. Dignity didn't figure into it.

Delaney giggled. "Any suggestions, Detective? On

how to make an exit without everyone"—she waved her hands at the twins—"seeing my . . . er . . . exit?"

"I've got you covered. I'll send the boys on ahead of us and I'll walk with my arm around you, holding up the flap of the loose material with my hand."

"I'm going to need a new pair of pants. I can't meet with the real estate agent and your grandmother looking like this."

"You and Gina are about the same size. I'm sure she's got something at Nana's that you can wear. Maybe not as snazzy as your outfit, but at least you won't be naked."

"Stop teasing," she pleaded. "I can't hold still while I'm laughing."

"Where's your car parked?"

"Along the seawall about a block up."

"Come on, boys, we're walking Delaney to her car. You guys lead the way to the seawall." Nick's arm circled snuggly around her waist and his big palm rested hot and heavy on her butt.

Animal instinct tussled with her sophisticated demeanor. Her pulse pumped. Her skin tingled. Self-control had been drummed into her from birth, but nature was nature. Polished manners and civilized etiquette didn't stand a chance against pure animal magnetism.

Delaney wanted to scurry back to her car as fast as her legs would carry her, but with Nick's leg in the knee brace, he couldn't move fast, and she was left plodding along at his pace.

"Ask him," Jack whispered to Zack.

"No, you ask him."

"You."

"No, you." The boys pushed each other.

"Ask me what?" Nick said.

Jack and Zack cast looks over their shoulders at Delaney and Nick. "Is she your new girlfriend? We hope she's your new girlfriend 'cause we heard Mama telling Nana that if you didn't get a new girlfriend soon, you were going to turn into a grumpy old man and she'd have to go find Amber and kick her skinny butt for breaking your heart."

"My heart's not broken," Nick growled.

"But you are grumpy," Zack pointed out.

"Who's Amber?" Delaney felt Nick's arm tighten around her waist.

"Nobody important."

"Amber was his old wife," Zack said.

"Mama says she ran away on their honeymoon," Jack added.

"With a famous guy from TV," Zack supplied.

Delaney looked at Nick. "What's this?"

Nick rolled his eyes. "I'll never live this down."

"What?"

"Gary Feldstein. My wife left me on our honeymoon for Gary Feldstein. Can we drop it?"

"I'm sorry."

"Hey," he said. "Don't apologize. You weren't the one doing the horizontal tango in our stateroom with Feldstein. You have nothing to be sorry about."

She could tell he was embarrassed. She remembered hearing something on one of the tabloid television shows about the fact that comedian Gary Feldstein's new bride-to-be had met him during her honeymoon with another man. To think that Nick was that man made her heart ache.

"Your sister sounds really protective of you," she said softly.

"So is she your new girlfriend?" Jack asked. "Or not?"

"Delaney's just a friend."

Just a friend.

Why those words would make her feel sad, Delaney had no idea. She couldn't be anything more to Nick than just a friend. She didn't want to be anything more than just a friend because she was engaged to another man. A sweet, kind, generous man who would be tremendously hurt if he could see her now, strolling down the seawall with Nick's arm around her waist, his hand splayed across her bottom.

She didn't know how to deal with this conflict of emotions. Wanting Nick to like her as more than a friend, but very glad that he did not. Guilt over the fact she was here with Nick, instead of with Evan, and not feeling very badly about it.

Honestly, she was a little miffed. Evan had gone off and left her for six weeks just before their wedding. But being miffed made her feel guilty again because Evan was doing such great work in Guatemala. What kind of person was she to be jealous of that?

A small, petty person, that's what she was.

She started to draw away from Nick, eager to remove herself from his proximity, but then she remembered he was the only thing standing between her and revealing her bare butt cheek to the tourists strolling the seawall.

Her stomach was in turmoil, her mind a mess. She wanted to sprint to her car and sit down ASAP, but of course she could not. She had to smile and walk slowly and pretend that she wasn't turned on by the feel of

Nick's calloused hand. Meryl Streep couldn't have done an acting job this good. Luckily, years of trying to please her perfectionist mother came in pretty handy at times like these.

After what seemed an eternity, they finally reached her car.

"This you?" Nick stopped beside her silver Acura.

"Yes, yes."

"Boys," he said, "stay here on the seawall while I walk Delaney around to the driver's side." Thankfully, the twins were arguing about Hank Blalock's batting record and not paying them any attention.

"You asked me why I was here," she said. "Do you still want to know?"

"Sure, if you want to tell me."

"Remember when we were driving past and I told you I thought I saw my mother here?"

"Yes."

"She was talking to a patch-eyed woman and I came here to find her to ask her why my mother was talking to her. I found out her name was Paulette Doggett."

"Why don't you just ask your mother?"

"I did. She lied."

"Did you talk to Paulette Doggett?"

"No. It's her day off. But I was wondering, since you're a cop, if you could do a little investigating for me and find out exactly who this woman is before I approach her."

"I could do that," Nick said.

"Thank you. Thank you so much."

"Don't mention it. Apparently this is my day to be chivalrous."

Delaney unlocked her car door while Nick's hand

stayed firmly in place. Heart thumping crazily, she turned her head to look at him. "I'm going to sit down now, you can let go."

"Ah," he said. "All good things must come to an end."

Blushing, she sank down into the seat.

"See you later, Rosy." Nick shut the car door and walked back to the boys, who were now seeing who could spit the farthest over the side of the seawall.

She sat there with the engine running, watching Nick corral the kids and feeling an emotion she couldn't describe. She hadn't found the one-eyed woman or her mother's secret reason for visiting the amusement park, but what she had found was a part of herself she never knew existed.

What she didn't know was if she liked what she had discovered about herself.

Or hated it.

Nick brooded through Happy Meals at McDonald's with his nephews. His maneuverings at the amusement park had backfired spectacularly.

When he'd seen Delaney standing in the midway, looking out of place and a little forlorn, he'd made up his mind to put his plan into action. He'd flirted with her and crowded her personal space. He'd coaxed her onto the Ferris wheel ride. The torn pants had been an added bonus. He'd felt her tension, knew he'd unsettled her.

But she'd unsettled him just as much.

Using sex appeal to chase her off definitely had its drawbacks. If this was going to work, he would have to keep his mind on his objective—talking Nana out of selling the family home, while at the same time keeping his mind off this powerful attraction to Delaney.

Nick plowed a hand through his hair. How had he gotten himself into this ugly kettle of sharks? He wanted a woman he could not have.

His sister, Gina, would call it fate.

Nana would call it the whammy.

But Nick didn't believe in all that bologna. Not anymore.

And yet, in a matter of days, Delaney Cartwright had burrowed deep under his skin and he couldn't figure out why. Why her? Why now? Why did he think she was so special? Once upon a time, he'd thought Amber was special too.

Maybe it's you. Maybe subconsciously you're looking to turn the tables and get even with fate by falling for someone who's already spoken for.

Nick grimaced. He hated to think that.

And yet, here he was, pining for a woman with a huge engagement ring on her finger.

Aw, crap. The truth of it was, he was too screwed up for this. Even if Delaney wasn't engaged—which she was—he had a lot of baggage he needed to unload before jumping into another relationship.

The knee, for one thing.

His grandfather's death, for another.

Delaney's watch did stop the minute that you met her. Just like the clock on the wall at the party stopped when Nana and Grampa Leo met.

Yes, but that wasn't the first time he'd ever met her. If it really was the whammy, wouldn't her watch have stopped when she threw the tarp over his head?

He didn't have the patience for this whammy nonsense.

"Uncle Nick, the Ching Bada in my Happy Meal broke," Zack said, handing him the pieces of a cheap plastic toy.

Nick didn't even know what the hell a Ching Bada was, but from the looks of it, the thing was some kind of weird cartoon character on wheels.

Nick examined the shattered pieces. "Sorry, buddy, but I don't think I can fix this."

Zack's lip pouched out sorrowfully. "But I want it."

"I know, but sometimes we can't always have what we want."

Strange thing, the forlorn expression on his nephew's face was exactly how he was feeling about Delaney. He wanted her, but he couldn't have her. The situation was broken beyond his ability to fix it.

One thing was for certain. Time wasn't on his side. He had to get rid of Delaney and get rid of her fast, before he did something totally stupid. Like fall in love with her.

In order to chase her away, he was going to have to turn up the heat and make sure he checked his heart at the door. He knew of only one way to accomplish his goal. Tackle getting rid of Delaney like she was an assignment. Use the three-pronged approach he'd developed. It had never failed to keep his professionalism in place undercover and his emotions tucked deeply away.

Chapter 10

For the rest of the week, Nick and his family worked to move Nana in with Trudie. They put the bulk of her things in storage, leaving only a bare minimum of furniture—at Delaney's advice—in the house for the staging. Once they had her possessions relocated, they spent the weekend cleaning the place from top to bottom.

By Monday morning, everyone else had gone home. Nana was ensconced at Trudie's, and Nick was alone at the house. He would be living there during the renovations. It felt hollow and sad with everything gone and the sound of his footsteps bouncing off the vacant walls.

Nana kept insisting this was a new chapter in her life, but to Nick, it felt like an epilogue. As he stared around the bare rooms, a moody thrust of emotions pushed against his throat. The book of his grandmother's life was coming to a close, and he couldn't do anything about it. He hated feeling powerless.

This house—and his grandparents' love—had been

the sanctuary that had saved him after his mother died. For the house to go out of the family made him feel as if he were losing both his mom and his grandfather all over again.

Being here alone strengthened his determination to undermine the house renovation process, no matter what it took. With the family dispersed and Delaney on her way over for their first real day of tackling the repairs, Nick paced the kitchen, rehearsing what he'd planned. The initial phase of "Operation: House Stager Ouster, Tactic #1—Know Thy Enemy" was now in play.

Delaney appeared on the doorstep at eight A.M. dressed in a sleeveless floral V-neck tee, flip-flops, and clam-digger-style blue jeans. Her hair was pulled back in a carefree ponytail that swished about her shoulders whenever she moved. She had a sack of bagels and two cups of Starbucks coffee in her hands. The smile on her face wrapped him like an unexpected hug.

"Good morning." She beamed. "I brought breakfast. We need fuel to start the day."

Ah, clearly she was a morning person. Nick made a mental note. You never could tell what information would prove useful. "Come on in."

He held the screen door open and let her in through the mudroom, then led the way into the kitchen. He'd raised all the windows to let in the Gulf breeze—the house had never been equipped with air-conditioning—and while it was cool now, by noon the temperature promised to be in the high eighties.

"It's just me and you today?"

"Yep." *And you have no clue what you're in for.* "No one else can afford any more time off from their jobs.

We're flying solo until the weekend." He held out his arms and said mischievously, "I'm your crew. Do with me what you will."

She set the bagels on the kitchen counter. "It looks so empty," she said. The word "empty" echoed in the room, underscoring her point. "It makes me feel a little sad."

Nick nodded. *Yeah, try having it be your grand-mother's house and see how that feels.*

"I figured you for straight black." She held out a grande cup of coffee to him. "No fancy blend."

"You pegged me." He eyed her. "Let me guess. You're a low-fat hazelnut latte with artificial sweetener."

She canted her head. "I guess stereotypes are stereo-types for a reason."

Reaching out to take the coffee from her, their fingers touched briefly against the cup and he almost fumbled it. Nick was very aware of how close they were standing, but he wanted to move even closer. *Careful. Not too soon. That's Tactic #2. We're not there yet.*

"Bagel?"

"What kind?"

"Plain, cinnamon-raisin, and poppy seed. Not know-ing what you like, I got all three."

"Plain."

She took a bagel from the sack. "Cream cheese?"

"Why not?"

She slathered the bagel with cream cheese and then held it out to him. Rather than taking it, Nick boldly leaned over and took a bite of it right out of her hand.

Okay, so he was blurring the edges between Tactic #1 and Tactic #2. It was an intimate gesture calculated to throw her off balance, but as his head went down and Nick got a whiff of her sweet, gentle-smelling cologne, he was the one thrown off.

"You've got cream cheese on your chin," she said as calmly as if men ate from her hand every day of the week.

Nick gulped. Where had his blushing Rosy gone?

She reached over with her thumb, then dabbed his chin with a Starbucks napkin. "There."

Then Delaney raised the bagel to her mouth and nibbled off a chunk right where he'd bitten into it.

She did it with such finesse he had to wonder if she possessed a few undercover tactics of her own. Blood pooled low in his abdomen. He stood there feeling awkward and unsure of himself, when just seconds before he'd been the one trying to unsettle her. How had she managed to turn the tables on him so swiftly? It was almost as if she knew what he was up to and was secretly paying him back.

She glanced down and he followed her gaze to see her staring at his knee. "Exactly how did you injure it?"

He shrugged. He didn't like talking about it. "I'd rather not say. It's sort of embarrassing."

"Hmm, sounds intriguing."

"Why, Rose, what in the hell are you thinking? Are you imagining me in a compromising position?" he teased. "Say, busting my knee falling from a chandelier during adventuresome sex?"

"No, I wasn't."

Ah, ah, she couldn't hide it. He saw a pink tinge creeping over her cheeks. He knew it. She wasn't as bold as she was pretending.

"Sorry, sweetheart. You can't lie. Your rosy red cheeks give you away."

"How did you hurt your knee?" she badgered, and he could tell she was determined not to let him get the best of her. He admired that. He made her nervous, but she wasn't going to let him steamroll her.

"A few months ago someone was assaulting transvestites in south Houston."

"Don't tell me you were having kinky sexcapades with a transvestite?" she teased.

He lifted his eyebrows and cocked his most seductive grin her way. "Now, Rosy, that's just wrong."

She acted immune—setting down the unfinished bagel, folding her arms over her chest, assessing him mildly. But she didn't fool him one bit. Nick saw the way her breath quickened, how the pulse at the hollow of her throat jumped.

"I've got it." She snapped her fingers. "You were assigned to dress as a woman, weren't you?"

"How did you know?"

"What else could make a tough guy like you blush?"

"I'm not blushing," he denied.

"Yes, you are."

"My face is turning red because whenever I think about what happened, I get pissed off all over again."

"Have a temper, do you?"

He snorted. "My captain gave me the assignment as punishment for not following orders on another case. He hates it when I don't follow orders and still end up making a good clean collar."

"Oh, you're one of those kinds of cops." She picked up her coffee and peered at him over the rim of the cup.

"What kind of cop?"

"The maverick-loose-canyon-Mel-Gibson-*Lethal-Weapon* kind of cop."

"More like Mel in *Lethal Weapon 3* and *4*. I'm not suicidal. I just don't like following orders when they're ill-conceived and could get me or my partner or an innocent bystander killed. And the dress the captain picked out for me to wear, good God, it looked like something from *Boogie Nights*. Cheap, polyester, and sequinned."

"So what happened?" She leaned in, obviously intrigued. Nick had to admit her interest flattered his ego.

"It's midnight. In a seedy part of Houston. Dive bars and strip joints and crack houses." He stopped and looked at her. "You have no idea what that part of town looks like, do you?"

"No," she confessed. "I'm from River Oaks."

"Somehow I'd guessed. You're one of *those* Cartwrights. Richer than God."

"Yes," Delaney admitted. "But let's not get sidetracked by the fact that I'm an oil heiress. About your story. You're in an unsavory section of the city late at night. Now what?" She took another sip of coffee.

"Don't you dare laugh."

She held up two fingers. "Scout's honor."

"You were a Girl Scout?"

"No."

"So your vow not to laugh has no oath to back it up."

The corners of her lips twitched and her eyes twinkled. "Nope. You're just going to have to trust me."

"Okay, here goes. I'm wearing gold lamé spandex, four-inch stilettos, and panty hose. By the way, how in the hell do you women walk around in those damn things? Panty hose are the most god-awful torture device ever invented. The Geneva Convention should have weighed in on those puppies."

"Next time try a bronzer on your legs instead."

"Trust me, there ain't gonna be a next time."

She laughed.

"It wasn't funny. And remember, you promised not to laugh."

"Sorry." She tried to school her features, but couldn't completely dampen her smile. "But I would have given anything to see you in that outfit."

"Trust me, it was ugly. My partner and I are strolling down the street looking like Jack Lemmon and Tony Curtis from *Some Like It Hot* and this guy jumps out of the alley, grabs my partner, puts a knife to his throat, and starts dragging him back down the alley."

Delaney sucked in her breath, splayed hand across her heart, and looked sincerely concerned. "Oh, my goodness."

"It was a little hairier than oh-my-goodness," he said. "I went after the guy, but he threatened to stab my partner in the throat if I didn't step off."

"What did you do?"

"I threw my purse at the guy's head. My partner took that opportunity to bite the guy's wrist. The perp lost his grip on my partner, realized he was in trouble, dropped the knife, and took off down the alley. Stupid me, I just had to go after him. Word to the wise, don't sprint down a dark alley, in a seedy part of town, wearing four-inch stilettos."

Delaney hissed in her breath through clenched teeth. "Ouch. I can see where this is headed."

"Believe me, ouch doesn't begin to describe the words that came out of my mouth. The guy tried to scale a fence. I jumped to grab for him and came down hard on my right leg. My heel caught on some garbage and slipped out from under me. I had my hands locked around the perp's ankle when my knee gave way. I heard this horrible crackling sound like an elephant stomping on a big bag of pork rinds. To make matters worse, I pulled the punk down on top of me. What damage the fall hadn't done, the weight of a two-hundred-pound meth-head finished off. I tore all the ligaments and fractured my kneecap."

Delaney's face paled and she made a low noise of sympathy.

"So here I am in the emergency room, gold lamé skirt hiked up to my waist, panty hose twisted around my privates, howling like a werewolf at the moon."

She reached out a hand and touched his arm. "I'm sorry that happened to you."

"Hey, don't be sorry. It wasn't your fault." He didn't want to admit it, but he liked the way her hand felt against his skin. "Your turn."

"My turn for what?"

"Confession time. I tell you my most embarrassing moment, and you have to tell me yours." He'd been blabbing away, trying to gain her confidence so she'd confide in him, but so far he hadn't learned anything personal about her. If Operation: House Stage Ouster was going to work, he had to get her to talk about herself so he could figure out her Achilles' heel.

"You were present for my most embarrassing moment."

"Ah, yes, the tarp incident. That's the most humiliating thing that's ever happened to you?"

"I don't usually put myself in embarrassing situations."

"Tell me, what inspired you to dress in a raincoat and bustier to bag your fiancé and drag him off for an afternoon of hot sex?"

"Truthfully, I didn't really want to do it."

"No? Then why did you?"

"It was my friends' idea."

"I'm going to need a little more to go on. Fair's fair. I told you about the panty hose."

"It's embarrassing."

"More embarrassing than my story?"

"You're going to make me go through with this, aren't you?"

"Absolutely. We can't have the ledger go unbalanced."

"Okay, here goes." She inhaled. "I was telling my friends that my fiancé and I had entered a celibacy pack before our wedding. We haven't had sex in six months and I was feeling—"

"Horny."

She blushed. "Well, yes."

"What kind of red-blooded American male agrees to a celibacy pact?" Nick raked his eyes over Delaney. "Especially with a woman like you?"

"It was my fiancé's idea. Anyway, my friends came up with the scenario to kidnap him from his job for an afternoon of hot sex. To prove to myself I wasn't a stick in the mud, I decided to go through with it."

"Are you sure your fiancé isn't gay?" Nick cocked an eyebrow.

"He's not gay."

"Asexual then?"

"Maybe," she admitted. She wouldn't look at him.

"Do you love the guy?" Nick had to ask.

"I've known him since I was a child."

"That's not what I asked."

"I love him," she whispered. "But I'm afraid the love I feel for him is not the right kind of love. That's what I was trying to find out with the whole raincoat and bustier thing."

"If you don't love him that way, then for God's sake, do the poor schlub a favor and don't marry him," Nick said sharply.

"You don't understand. It's very complicated. My mother, she's a stickler for all that social registry stuff. Wants to make sure I marry the right kind of man."

"Meaning rich and well bred."

"Yes."

"What century are you living in?"

"You don't know what it's like. Coming from high society."

"Sounds like a pain in the ass to me."

She laughed. "It is."

"So you thought you were bagging your boyfriend and instead you bagged me. You must have felt like you were angling for whitefish and came up with a carp instead."

"I was so nervous about the whole thing that I threw

the tarp over the first guy who came out the door. It never even entered my head that you weren't Evan."

He felt as if he'd been kicked squarely in the bread basket. His breath left his body in one long whoosh. "Evan? Your fiancé is Dr. Evan Van Zandt?"

Her eyes widened in surprise. "How did you know?"

Nick groaned. Of all the freakin' luck. His gut fisted and his pulse knocked for no good reason.

"What is it? What's wrong?"

"Trust me to get myself in this kind of situation," he muttered under his breath.

"What are you talking about?"

He tapped his knee. "Evan? Your fiancé. He's my doctor."

Nick's revelation rattled Delaney to her core. Evan was his surgeon?

"We better get to work," she said, ignoring the feelings churning inside her. She couldn't meet his eyes. She was still trying to deal with the implications of what he'd told her. Nick knew Evan. Evan had treated Nick. "Did you get to the plumbing repairs yet? Are we ready to move on to putting down the kitchen tile?"

"I finished the plumbing," he said. "Just waiting for you to help me pull up the old linoleum; the new tile is stacked up on the porch, ready to go."

Delaney worried her bottom lip with her teeth. Being so close to him was unsettling. "Maybe we could skip to the painting today instead. You can do one room, I can do another."

"Wouldn't it be more effective if we worked together?" he asked, sizing her up with one long, cool stare. "And I thought you wanted the kitchen finished first, since it requires the most work."

She cleared her throat. "Um, I'm thinking it's better if we're not in the same room."

"What's the matter, Rosy? Scared you can't keep your hands off me?" he taunted her. "Scared Evan will find out we were in a room alone together? Shh, I won't tell if you won't tell."

"There's nothing to tell," she denied stridently.

"No?" He stepped closer, crowding her space, chasing all the air from her lungs.

"Absolutely not," she bristled.

"You're going to deny there's chemistry going on here." His gaze nailed her to the spot.

"I will not jeopardize my relationship with a man I've known for twenty-five years over a lusty affair."

"Whoa." He held up both palms. "You're moving a little fast for me. Who said anything about an affair? What makes you think I'm the kind of guy who would have an affair with an engaged woman? I'm outraged."

"You're teasing me?" She eyed him.

"I'm testing you."

She didn't know what to make of that. "I don't trust you."

He shrugged. "So quit."

"What?" Her eyes narrowed. "You want me to quit, don't you? That's what this is all about. That's why you've been coming on so strong."

He didn't say anything, his silence confirming her suspicions. He didn't want Lucia to sell the house so he was coming on to her, hoping to make her leave.

"I'm not quitting." She hardened her jaw.

"Fine by me."

"I've got work to do." Drawing herself up to her full height, she went over to the corner, picked up a putty knife, and started tackling the aged linoleum.

Nick came up behind her. "Why did you offer to wait to get paid until after the house sells? That doesn't sound like good business to me."

She didn't answer him for the longest moment. She was trying to decide if he even deserved an answer. "Because I needed this job as much as your grandmother needed it done."

"You?" He made a dismissive noise. "You're an oil heiress. You're engaged to a prominent doctor. You're stunningly beautiful. Why would you need a job?"

"It's complicated." Her face was burning red again as she felt the telltale flush creep up her neck. No matter how hard she tried to suppress it, he seemed to have a magical ability to make her blush.

"I've got two good ears."

She ignored him. She'd already talked too much, gave him too much ammunition to use against her. Darn her need to be liked. She wished she didn't care what he thought about her, but she did. Disgruntled with herself, she grabbed a chunk of linoleum and yanked it up from the subflooring.

"You blush every time I give you a compliment. Why is that?" He came over to lean one shoulder against the wall in front of her.

"You're in my way."

"I know that."

She raised her head and glared at him point-blank. "I realize you're a cop and interrogating people just comes naturally to you, but I'd appreciate it if you dropped this whole line of questioning and helped me get this old flooring up."

He grabbed a piece of linoleum from the opposite end of the kitchen and pulled up a long hunk of it. He opened the back door, chucked the brittle strip out onto the back lawn, and then started again. In half an hour, they met in the middle of the room, the floor sticky and raw from the glue of the old linoleum.

They looked at each other, but neither of them spoke. Two people standing in the middle of a vacant room, uncertain what to make of each other.

"I was unattractive as a child," she said, not knowing why she was telling him this. "The proverbial ugly duckling."

Nick tilted his head and studied her. "Well, I'd say you've blossomed into a hellaciously beautiful swan."

"No, I haven't."

"You want me to haul you over in front of a mirror and prove to you otherwise?"

"What you're seeing isn't real, Nick. It's all packaging."

"What are you talking about? Don't you notice the heads swiveling and the tongues drooling when you walk down the street?"

"Nose job." She touched her nose with fingertips. "Until I was fourteen I resembled the Wicked Witch from *The Wizard of Oz*."

"No way."

She put a hand to her waist. "Or you could say I looked like the Pillsbury Doughboy's blind date. And then there were the teeth." She raised her upper lip, revealing her teeth that she knew were perfectly straight and dazzlingly white. Five grand worth of veneers could do that for you. "I could have given Bugs Bunny a run for his money, except I stuttered like Porky Pig. Oh"—she snapped her fingers—"I almost forgot the Coke-bottle glasses."

"I'm sure you're exaggerating. Women have a tendency to denigrate their looks."

"It's true. Just ask my mother. She'll be the first to tell you I was a total train wreck." Under her breath she mumbled, "Lord knows she's told me often enough."

"I think I get it," he said.

"Get what?"

"Why you lowballed your bid on my grandmother's house."

"Really?"

"Lack of self-confidence," he said.

"Partially," Delaney conceded.

"And you lack self-confidence because your mother never believed in you until you had your nose done, lost weight, underwent LASIK surgery, got braces, and stopped stuttering."

Her eyes widened. "How did you know?"

"Why else would you be so hard on yourself?" His voice was kind, his eyes kinder still. "Come on, Delaney, it's way past time to stop beating yourself up for your sister's death. You didn't kill her. You weren't responsible. Let go of the blame."

Dammit, just when he was making it easy for her to resist him, he turned sweet. She couldn't bear the understanding expression on his face. It was too much. She could handle feelings of lust for him. Lust was just lust, but this feeling—this was dangerous stuff.

"I've just remembered something," she said, feeling bad about lying but knowing she had to get out of here before something really dangerous happened.

"Yeah?"

"I've got an appointment to give a bid on a house in west Houston at ten. With the traffic, I'll be lucky to make it. Sorry to bail on you like this, but we made a good start."

"You've been here less than an hour," he said.

"I know, I'm sorry." The way he was looking at her was making things worse. "I gotta go."

"See you tomorrow?"

"Uh-huh." She forced a smile, grabbed her purse, and ran from the house while she still had the strength of will to tear herself away.

Chapter 11

Okay, phase one of Operation: House Stage Ouster had been a rousing success. Nick had gotten Delaney to reveal her doubts and fears and insecurities. He knew where her vulnerabilities lay, knew just how to wound her. Problem was, he didn't want to wound her. In fact, he felt an overwhelming urge to protect her. From her mother, from her fiancé, from the entire world.

Shit. Shit, shit, shit.

Tender feelings were not part of the plan.

Last night, unable to sleep, he'd tiled the entire kitchen by himself in spite of the pain in his knee. This morning, he was tired and achy and ready to abandon his plans to chase her off. Face facts, he wanted her around. And that thought was scary as hell.

"Come on," he muttered. "You can't let your feelings for her derail your own needs. She's marrying someone else. It's not like you have a chance with her. Hell, you don't want a chance with her. You're through with all that romantic mumbo jumbo."

Oh, yeah?

"Yeah."

Then prove it, Vinetti. Tactic #2—Undermine Your Enemy. Start it today.

Right. He could do this.

To rev himself up, he thought of his toughest undercover assignments. If he could maneuver criminals and thugs and the underworld, he could certainly handle one high-bred young house stager.

What to do? How best to undermine her without really hurting her feelings?

He plotted. He schemed. He connived and came up with a kind yet devious plan. He would goad her into causing her own demise.

Nick took a trip to the souvenir shops on Seawall Boulevard and after striking out in several stores, finally found what he was looking for. Satisfied with his purchase, he had it gift wrapped. Then he hurried back to Nana's and found Delaney standing on the back porch, looking sumptuous in a red tank top and a blue-jean skirt, and all the underhanded subterfuge just flew right out of his head.

Delaney had given herself a good talking to after what had happened the previous day, and convinced herself she could indeed work around Nick Vinetti without succumbing to this charms. Donning her mental armor, she arrived at Lucia's house with a professional smile plastered on her face.

She was pleasantly surprised to find that Nick had

tiled the kitchen and done a superb job at it too. The man was skilled with his hands, she'd give him that. She bragged on him, but not too enthusiastically. She didn't want to give him any ideas. Didn't want any repeat of yesterday's familiarity. Happy to have another thing ticked off her to-do list and encouraged by the progress they were making, Delaney decided to accelerate her plans. Painting was next on the agenda, and she ambitiously aimed to get two bedrooms done that day.

An hour and a half later, they were deeply into painting the bedroom Lucia had used as a library. They'd already completed the first coat on three walls and were working on the final one.

She and Nick stood next to each other, not speaking, just painting. Surprisingly, in their work, the silence felt uncomplicated and easy.

Then Delaney went and spoiled the peace by noticing they were painting in tandem—starting high and then pulling downward in slow, easy strokes. Her stomach dipped at the realization they were operating in total sync.

The rhythm was hypnotic. Sexual. Almost like foreplay.

Dip, brush, sweep, dip, brush, sweep.

Disconcerted, Delaney broke the pattern. She stopped painting and lifted the tip of her brush from the wall. She waited—for what she could not say—hand hovering, paint dripping. Splat. Splat. Splat. Onto the plastic drop cloth.

Nick stopped painting too and looked over at her, his bold stare caressing her intimately.

The sharp crackling of erotic current running between

them raised the hairs on Delaney's arms. She shifted her gaze to the wall, pretending to assess the paint job.

"It looks good," he murmured, but he was not studying the wall. She could feel the heat of his gaze on her face. He was looking at her. "Real good."

His words echoed in the empty room.

Real good.

Closing her eyes, she willed herself not to shiver, then quickly opened them again. "Uh-huh."

He reached out and took the paintbrush from her, his fingertips barely grazing her skin, and then balanced her brush, along with his, over the top of the paint can.

"You thirsty?" he asked.

She nodded and noticed perspiration had plastered his cotton muscle shirt against his toned chest. She was sweating too, but it wasn't from the summer heat. She could smell the salt air blowing in on the cool breeze. Hear the sounds of seagulls in the distance, calling to one another above the neighborhood noises. A car chugging up the street, children playing tag in the alley, a dog barking in the yard next door.

He disappeared for a minute and then came back with two ice-cold beers. He twisted off the tops, tossed them onto the drop cloth, and walked back across the room. His limp was barely noticeable. He handed her one of the longneck bottles.

It was cold and damp in her hand, and Delaney realized she'd never drunk beer directly from the bottle, only in an iced mug, and even then, only twice. Beer, Honey was fond of saying, was a middle-class beverage and best left for the middle class.

Without ever taking his eyes off her, Nick tilted his head and took a long swallow from his bottle.

Her gaze tracked from his lips to his throat. She watched his Adam's apple work and this time she did shiver.

Anxiously, she shifted her attention away from him, looking for something else to focus on. She surveyed the paint job.

It looked fresh and white and . . .

Bland.

All the personality of Lucia's house was being white-washed.

"What's the matter?" Nick asked, coming up behind her. He was standing so close she could feel his body heat.

"You were right." She crossed her arms over her chest.

"In what way?"

"The room looks so generic. Like it could be in any house in America."

"I thought that was the point. It's what you said would help the house sell better."

"It is."

"But you want more."

"I want the house to sell for Lucia."

"Is that the real reason?" he asked. "Or are you just more comfortable playing it safe?"

She looked at him. There was challenge in his eyes.

"We could take the paint back," he continued. "Get another color. You could give your creativity full rein and not worry about what some upscale yuppie buyer wants in a vacation home. You could really do this house justice if you just allowed yourself to shake things up."

He was tempting her, egging her on, but the truth was she wanted to do it. Wanted to use Lucia's house as a canvas to create a bit of magic.

"We could do a Tuscan theme," Nick suggested. "Reflect Nana's heritage."

"But the research I've done tells me . . ."

"Screw research." He took her by the shoulders and turned her around to face him. He placed his hand over her heart. It thumped erratically. He was the devil, pure and simple.

"What does your heart tell you?" he whispered.

"I can't be selfish about this."

"The right person will find the house charming."

"But your grandmother needs to sell the house as soon as possible."

"Wouldn't it be better if the house went to someone who could love it the way my grandparents did? Someone who could appreciate all the love that went into it?"

It sounded so good. She wanted to believe it was possible. She wanted to let go. To take a chance. But she was also afraid.

"Hang on," he said. "I've got something I want to give you. I was going to give it to you later, after you finished the house, but I think it might be better for you to have it now."

"You bought me a gift?"

He pointed a finger at her. "I'll be right back."

Puzzled, Delaney watched him leave the room. She heard the back door creak open and then slam closed again a few minutes later.

Nick was back. Holding a pretty pink box wrapped with red ribbon.

He'd bought her a present. She was touched.

"Here. Maybe this will help you decide."

She untied the ribbon, lifted the lid. There, nestled in tissue paper, she saw his hula doll. Stunned, she raised her head and met his gaze. "Oh, Nick, I can't accept this. Your mother gave you Lalule to help you deal with your grief."

"It's not Lalule," he said. "I bought you your own hula doll. She's to remind you that when life gets too bland and predictable, you need to shake things up."

Delaney took the hula doll out of the box and gently thumbed her hips. The doll shook and shimmied.

Shake it up.

She looked at the white walls.

Shake it up.

She thought about what she wanted, but it was hard trying to figure out exactly what she did want. She'd spent so many years pleasing everyone else. Delaney had forgotten how to express her own desires.

Shake it up.

She looked at Nick and put the doll back in the box. She wasn't convinced shaking things up was the smart way to go. "Thank you. I'll treasure this."

"So what's your decision?" he asked. "Do we keep on painting white? Or do we make another trip to Lowe's and exchange the paint for something exciting?"

"I want to help your grandmother sell her house."

"Forget about that for a moment. If you could do anything with this house, what would you do?"

"I'd go for it. I'd make this place special. I'd make magic."

"Look out, Lowe's, here we come." He laughed and

the sound warmed her from the inside out. Nick reached over, took the box from her hand, and then walked over to set it on the windowsill along with his beer.

He turned back to her, grinning his cocky grin, eyes glistening with the same out-of-control impulses that were simmering through her blood. He took a step closer. She did not move away.

Nick took another step and then another.

Her heart pounded.

He reached out a hand.

She stopped breathing.

His thumb came down to rub the tip of her nose. "Smudge of paint," he explained.

She exhaled heavily.

"If we were in a romantic movie," Nick said, "this would be the point where I'd kiss you."

"But this isn't a movie."

Their gazes fused.

"No."

"And you're not going to kiss me."

He leaned forward until his lips were almost touching hers. "No."

"That's very good," she said, "because I'm engaged to be married."

"I know. I've seen the rock. It's big enough to choke a two-headed Clydesdale."

She smiled. "It is rather ostentatious, isn't it?"

"From a cop's point of view, it's dangerous. You might as well wear a neon sign that says, 'Rob me.' You're just asking to have your finger cut off for that thing." He reached over and picked up her left hand. "And I'd sure as hell hate to see any harm come to that hand. Whenever you're in an unsafe area you should turn your ring around to the palm side and close your fingers around it."

He turned the ring to demonstrate. Closed his hand over hers. Over her engagement ring. His touch shook her. Fully. Completely. Upside down and inside out.

"Chopped-off fingers are not romantic," she said. "It isn't even remotely like something Tom Hanks would say to Meg Ryan. You are not making my knees weak."

"Good," he murmured and looked her straight in the eyes. "Because mine are weak enough for the both of us."

Now *that* was romantic.

"You *do* want to kiss me," she said. "Admit it."

"Woman," he answered softly, "you have absolutely no idea how much."

A thrill blitzed down her spine. His warm breath tickled her skin. He smelled so good Delaney could scarcely remember her own name, much less Evan's.

You can't let Nick kiss you. You mustn't let him kiss you. This cannot happen.

She raised her hands and clutched them together in front of her chest, building a barrier between them. It was weak, but it was all she could come up with.

"Please . . . ," she whispered, meaning to add "don't," but her throat was so tight and his eyes were so dark and she was caught up in the strange magic surging between them.

He reached for her hand again and he turned the ring back where it belonged. Back where they could both see that she was spoken for and could not forget it.

"If you didn't have the ring on your finger . . ." His

eyes flashed a promise of the wonderful things that could happen if she were unattached.

"But I do."

He nodded, took a deep breath. "Yeah."

"It's an engagement ring," she said, not really knowing why she said it. "Not a wedding ring. Not yet."

"Marriage is supposed to be for a lifetime," Nick said. "Like with Grampa and Nana. The vows don't read, 'Until some guy you like better comes along.'"

Sympathy tugged her heart. He was thinking about his ex-wife. What was her name? Oh, yes. Amber. She could tell by the way he screwed his mouth up tightly, absent-mindedly rubbed his injured knee, and stared off into the distance. Delaney wanted to make things better for him. She wanted to take away his pain.

It was the only excuse she could come up with for what happened next.

She was acutely aware of a very important line being crossed, but she couldn't seem to stop herself from crossing it. The question was, how far across that taboo line was she willing to go?

Delaney touched Nick's shoulder.

He looked at her and their eyes wed.

She felt everything all at once.

It was like an earthquake rocking her chest. Lust and chemistry. Longing and yearning. Guilt and loneliness. Hunger and sadness and hope. It fell in on her, heavy and warm and too much, too soon.

What had she gotten herself into?

His gaze was hot. Lightning that lingered.

The look made her lips tingle.

Neither of them moved.

He cupped his palm under her chin and tilted his head, his eyes never leaving hers.

She stiffened. Wanting him to kiss her, but scared, scared, scared of where it might lead.

He dropped his hand, backed up.

No, something inside her whimpered.

Compelled by a force she couldn't understand or explain, Delaney stepped forward. She just knew that she had to kiss him or die, but it wasn't in her nature to act so boldly. She was accustomed to finding roundabout ways to meet her needs. She couldn't bring herself to initiate the kiss, but she could make him kiss her.

Wantonly, Delaney slipped her fingers through the belt loops of his blue jeans and held on tight.

He arched his eyebrows, making sure he understood what she wanted.

She swallowed, moistened her lips. Nodded.

His eyes lit up and a smile tipped his mouth. It was like watching a drawbridge drop. And behind the door of the fortress, hidden beneath the tough-guy image, Delaney spied a center of tenderness she'd never imagined.

"Aw, Rosy," he murmured and lowered his head.

Her pulse danced, light as the sunshine dappling the freshly painted walls.

The kiss was quieter than she thought it would be, languid and deep, a slow opportunity to taste and smell and feel. A chance to settle, by layers, into a dreamy ease. The teasing of his tongue against hers brought a helpless response so acute, she felt faint, like she was falling.

Delaney locked her fingers in his hair and made him kiss her harder, deeper and harder still.

The taste of him!

Like returning home from a long, arduous journey. Recognizing every part of him with her lips and hands and body and yet at the same time he felt fabulously foreign—and strangely familiar.

While the world shrank down into the minute width of mouths, she opened herself up to possibilities as yet undreamed. She was completely disarmed. With any other man the quick intimacy and astonishing sensuality would have appalled her, but with Nick everything was different.

Her lips shuddered against his mouth and her body molded to his. His hands roved over her back and she strained into him, her breasts crushed against his chest. Instantly, she experienced a sense of peace and safety. In Nick's arms, she felt special.

And that very sensation scared her.

In her need to put some magic in her life, was she grasping at straws? Was she mistakenly reading something into this kiss that wasn't really there? Was she confusing passion for something substantial? How could she begin to compare the history, companionship, and compatibility she shared with Evan to this explosive, red-hot rocket of sensation with a man she'd only known for a little over a week?

Delaney dithered, caught between doubt and desire. She did not like this push-pull of emotions. For years, she'd been living life on autopilot, melding with her mother's wishes, putting on a pleasant face, getting through life by putting things in soft focus. She did what felt safe.

But the power of Nick's kiss drove home the fact that she'd done so at the price of her vitality and aliveness. That's what scared her most. This arousal of aspects of herself she'd always chosen to ignore.

"I'm sorry, I can't do it. I wanted you so badly I thought I could ignore my conscience, but I can't." She splayed a hand against his chest and pushed him away.

"Because of your fiancé," he said, fingering her engagement ring again. "That you love. But not in the right way."

She nodded.

"Leave him."

"You're talking crazy. We don't even know each other."

"Forget about me. Leave him for your sake. For his sake. You can't marry this guy if you want me that badly."

Panicked, Delaney pressed a hand to her forehead, still tingly from where his lips had branded her. It was true, but it was not that simple. "I've been dating Evan since I was sixteen. We were high school sweethearts. I've never been with anyone else but him. You're just . . ."

"Just what?" Nick pulled back, his eyes glinting darkly in the light. "Exactly what am I to you, Delaney?"

"Just something to get out of my system."

There was no mistaking the hurt on Nick's face. Without another word, he turned and walked away.

*   *   *

"I've done a terrible, terrible thing," Delaney told Tish and Jillian and Rachael early the next morning as they struck the warrior pose on side-by-side yoga mats at a chic, women-only gym in downtown Houston.

"You?" Tish, who was positioned on Delaney's left, tipped her body into perfect alignment. "What did you do? Eat dessert with your salad fork at your mother's latest dinner party?"

"I'm serious, Tish."

The teasing expression on her friend's face changed. "What's wrong?"

"There's a guy."

"A guy?" Jillian said from Delaney's right.

"What did she say?" asked Rachael, who was on the other side of Jillian. She was having trouble hearing over the Eastern-flavored music.

"She met a guy," Jillian relayed.

"But she already has a guy. She's engaged." Rachael broke her form to lean around Jillian and glare at Delaney. "What are you thinking?"

"I know." Delaney's legs wobbled as she struggled to hold her pose. Trust Rachael to be the voice of her conscience. "I'm a horrible, horrible person."

"You're not horrible," Tish said. "You're human."

"Trust me. I'm horrible. You haven't heard the worst of it," Delaney said.

"What's the worst of it?" Jillian dared.

"It gets worse?" Rachael groaned.

"I kissed him. No, he kissed me. No, we kissed each other. Oh, I don't know what happened. I'm so confused." Delaney pushed away a stray strand of hair that had fallen out of her ponytail and into her face.

All three of her friends lost their poses as they turned to stare at her. Delaney looked straight ahead, keeping up the pose, keeping up appearances.

"What?" Rachael gasped.

"Naughty girl," Tish said.

"I didn't believe you had it in you." Jillian shook her head. "Way to go."

"Don't encourage her," Rachael snapped. "This is serious. Delaney has broken her vow to Evan."

"Lighten up, Rach. They're not married yet," Jillian said. "She just had to get it out of her system."

"That's exactly right. That's what I told Nick." Delaney nodded.

"Evan's the only guy she's ever been with," Jillian said. "Cut her a break. It was just a little kiss, right, Del?"

Just a little kiss? That was like calling the Grand Canyon a little crack in the ground.

"I feel terrible about it," Delaney said. But not so terrible that she could wish it never happened.

"Up dog," the yoga instructor called out as the music changed tempo, becoming more languid. They all made an attempt to follow her command.

"Okay, so you kissed him. It's not the end of the world." Tish stretched her spine upward.

"It wasn't just a kiss," Delaney confessed.

"You slept with him too?" Jillian, who never sounded scandalized, sounded scandalized.

"No, no. It was just the best damn kiss of my life."

"She's cussing," Rachael said. "Delaney hardly ever cusses. He's got her cussing now." She frowned deeply. "Who is this guy?"

"Up dog," the instructor said again.

Everyone dipped their heads down and stuck their butts in the air, stretching their hamstring muscles.

"Breathe deep, class."

Delaney drew in a deep, upside-down breath. "That's the problem. He's the grandson of the woman I'm doing the renovations for, and I can't avoid him because he's the one who's filling in for my crew since Lucia can't afford them."

"Oh, my God," Tish said. "It's that gorgeous undercover cop, isn't it? When I was at Lucia's house filming I thought I detected a vibe between you two." To Rachael and Jillian, she said, "He really is hot. You should see him. He's got the tightest butt that's just begging to be pinched."

"Tish!"

"I'm just saying." Tish shrugged and tilted her head toward the ceiling.

"There's vibes now?" Rachael exclaimed, clearly upset. "You're all vibey with the guy, Delaney?"

"And muscles out to here," Tish waxed rhapsodically and measured off a thick chunk of space behind her own bicep.

"Shh." Delaney frowned at her.

"Evan's got muscles," Rachael said.

"Not like these." Tish's eyes rounded in appreciation. "Evan has run-of-the-mill, work-out-on-the-weekend muscles. Nick's got oh-my-god-he-could-have-been-a-cover-model muscles. I bet anything his abs are equally amazing. What are his abs like, Del? Can you bounce a condom off them?"

"I don't know what his abs are like," Delaney cried,

embarrassed by the attention they were drawing. Most everyone in the class had stopped striking poses and was staring at them. "I haven't seen him naked."

The music picked that moment to shift into another song, and for one brief second the only sound in the room was Delaney yelling, "Naked."

"Ladies," the instructor said sternly, "if you're not going to concentrate on yoga, could you please leave the room so that the rest of us who want to relax and enjoy our exercise can do so?"

"Let's get out of here," Jillian said, yanking up her yoga mat. "Who's for coffee?"

"Delaney is wrecking her life and you're thinking about coffee." Rachael shook her head.

"Maybe she's claiming her life, not wrecking it," Tish said.

"Oh, yeah, like what you did with Shane?" Rachael asked. "Maybe you're not the most qualified person to be giving Delaney relationship advice."

Delaney saw Tish freeze at the mention of her ex's name. Although Tish denied it, they all suspected she was still in love with her ex-husband. "That was really cold, Rachael."

"Ladies," the instructor said sharply and pointed at the door.

Chastised, they gathered up their yoga mats and trooped out into the hallway.

Eyes flaring, Rachael faced off with Delaney. "I can't believe you're doing this to Evan. He's such a nice, caring man. Why would you do this to him?"

Rachael was asking her the same thing that Delaney had been asking herself ever since Nick kissed her. It was wrong. So very wrong. She knew it. Regretted it and yet she still wanted to kiss him again.

"Hey," Jillian said, hopping to Delaney's defense. "Evan took off for Guatemala just before their wedding, and he was the one who came up with that celibacy thing. What did he expect her to do?"

"Unlike some people," Rachael said pointedly and glared at Jillian, "I thought Delaney could control her hormonal impulses."

"You calling me a slut?" Jillian challenged. "Is that where this is going?"

"If the stiletto fits . . ."

Delaney's pulse leaped as she realized the consequences of her actions on her friends. It distressed her that they were fighting over her. This wasn't just about her. She'd involved them and upset them, and now she had to step in and make things right before either Rachael or Jillian said something they couldn't take back.

She stepped between them. "Please, you guys are my best friends in the world. Don't do this to each other. Rachael is right, Jillian. I shouldn't have kissed Nick."

"You shouldn't be marrying Evan is what you shouldn't be doing," Jillian said. "No matter how nice and caring he is, he's wrong for you, and your heart knows it even if your head doesn't."

Delaney thought of Nick, whom she had known for only a very short time. There was chemistry there, yes. Lots of it. But what did they have in common beyond the attraction? Absolutely nothing. She tried to imagine him fitting in with her high-society world and failed miserably.

Then she thought of Evan, whom she had known her entire life. He was the man who'd been there for her during the bad times. He'd held her in his arms when her sister died. And when a bully at school made fun of the way she looked, Evan had punched him out, defending her honor. She and Evan were so much alike. They came from the same world. Knew the same people. Liked the same things.

She twisted her engagement ring on her finger. How could she throw away the history they had, the security Evan offered, for physical lust and sexual attraction with Nick?

And there was the issue of her mother.

At the mere thought of having to tell Honey she'd decided not to go through with the wedding, Delaney felt physically sick.

She couldn't. She wouldn't. Jillian was right. Nick was just something to get out of her system. This need for magic, for something special, was a childish impulse. Her experimentation had already caused discord between her friends. She had to stop this daydreaming and wishing for something more before it ruined her life and hurt those she loved.

Tish touched her arm. "You okay, Del?"

Delaney forced a smile. "I'm all right, or I would be if you guys would stop sniping at each other. I never meant to cause trouble in our little group. I just value your support so much, I had to tell you. Please, forgive me for dumping my problems on you."

"There's nothing to forgive," Tish said.

"I'm sorry too," Jillian apologized. "I'm far too reactionary at times."

"Group hug!" Rachael held out her arms.

Grinning, they all came together for a hug.

"Now," Jillian said, "let's go for coffee. I'm buying."

They walked over to the nearby Starbucks and Tish fell into step beside Delaney. "So, what *are* you going to do about Mr. Hard-Body Cop?"

Delaney sighed. "There's only one thing I can do."

"You're going to break it off with Evan?"

"No!" She stared at her friend, and then lowered her voice. "Of course not. I'm going to have to tell Lucia I can't stage her house."

"But what about the *American Home Design* contest and your own dream of taking your business out of the realm of your mother's friends and controlling destiny?"

"For now," Delaney said, "I've got to let that dream go. For the good of everyone involved, I simply can't trust myself around Nick."

Chapter 12

"What are we going to do?" Lucia asked Trudie as they pushed their shopping cart through the handy little community grocery store located two blocks from Trudie's doorstep. Just before they'd walked out the door, Delaney had called with the bad news she was resigning as Lucia's house stager.

"I'm telling you, Luce, you're worrying for nothing. Delaney is a Pisces. Nick is Scorpio. They're one of the most compatible matches in the Zodiac. Trust me on this."

"Not to offend you, Trudie, but I don't have much faith in astrology."

"That's fine, but what about your faith in the whammy? You do believe in that, don't you?"

"I don't know what the problem is," Lucia fretted. "Delaney said she didn't have enough time to do the house justice with her impending wedding plans. She never said a word about Nick. But I know that's the real issue. But what if she's telling the truth and she's simply overwhelmed?"

"She's only overwhelmed because the whammy has her rattled and she doesn't want to tell you she has the hots for your grandson, especially since she's engaged to someone else. She doesn't want you to think badly of her."

"But how are she and Nicky ever going to get together if she's not going to help me sell my house? And besides that, now who's going to help me sell my house?" Lucia turned their cart down the cereal aisle. "I knew we should never have meddled."

Trudie took a box of Lucky Charms off the shelf and tossed it in the cart. "It's not meddling when it's kismet."

Lucia fished the box of sugary cereal out of the cart and handed it back to Trudie. "You're as bad as Leo with the sweet tooth. Get the All-Bran."

Grumbling under her breath, Trudie put the Lucky Charms back and replaced it with bran flakes. "Happy now?"

"No, not at all. I'm worried about Delaney and Nick. I'm worried about selling my house."

Trudie waved a hand. "You worry too much."

"You don't worry at all."

"And that's what makes us such good friends. We balance each other out. Can I get some fruit roll-ups?"

Lucia sighed. "Go ahead."

Trudie scampered to the fruit roll-ups and brought a box to the cart. "You want Delaney back as your house stager?"

"Of course I do. Didn't I just say that? But how can we get her to come back?"

"We're going to have to meddle. Oh, and you might have to tell a little white fib or two."

Lucia desperately wanted to see her grandson happy. He deserved the same kind of happiness she'd known with Leo. She wasn't so sure of Trudie's interfering, but she didn't know what else to do. If Delaney married the man she was engaged to, Lucia knew the young woman would live to regret it.

She'd been there herself. She understood the pressure to comply with her family's wishes, especially if you were the kind of girl who took great care not to hurt people. If it hadn't been for Leo boldly taking matters into his own hands, she would probably be living in a hovel in Tuscany, waiting for Frank Tigerelli to get out of prison.

Lucia couldn't stand by and watch Delaney make a terrible mistake. Her gaze locked with Trudie's. "So what do you have in mind?"

Nick was caulking the front windows of Nana's house when he looked up to see Trudie's corvette pull into the driveway with his grandmother riding shotgun. Nana climbed gingerly from the low-slung sports car and then marched toward him, looking like she used to look just before she stuck his nose in the corner for bad behavior.

Uh-oh. Something was up.

He laid the caulking gun down on the window ledge and cocked a disarming smile. "Hey, Nana."

"Don't you 'Hey, Nana' me, young man." She glowered darkly and shook an index finger under his nose. "What did you do to that girl?"

"What girl?"

"Don't play dumb," Nana snapped.

Surprise widened Nick's eyes. His grandmother rarely lost her temper, but when she did, she got really steamed.

"I know what you're up to, young man."

His shoulder muscles bunched defensive protest. "I'm not up to anything."

"Flirting with Delaney to chase her off so I can't sell the house. She called me up and quit today."

He felt a mix of relief and regret. The regret startled him. He had nothing to feel sorry about. "Is that what she said? That I was flirting with her?"

"Delaney has too much class and respect for other people's feelings to say that. She laid all the blame on herself. But I know the real truth, mister. Don't forget who raised you."

"I didn't chase her off," Nick mumbled and ducked his head. Nana had a way of making him feel seven years old all over again.

"You can't fool me, Dominic Vincent Vinetti. You've done it before."

"Done what before?"

"Ran off a perfectly nice young woman because you were getting too close, feeling too much, and couldn't deal with it." Her eyes sparked angrily and she reached over to snap the head off a dead bloom on the rosebush beside him.

Nick gulped.

"Yes," she said. "I know about your tactics. Probably more than you know yourself. For instance, I know you're at least fifty percent responsible for what happened between you and Amber. Maybe even more than fifty percent."

Now that was a low blow. Nick narrowed his eyes.

"Amber left me. On our honeymoon. To run off with another man."

Nana sank her hands on her hips. "And why was that?"

Fear slid down his spine. Nick clenched his jaw, dropped his gaze, and picked up the caulking gun. "I've got to get this caulking done before it rains."

"That," Nana crowed. "Right there. That's why Amber left you."

"What? Amber left me because I like to caulk?" Was his grandmother losing it?

"Don't play dumb."

"Maybe I am dumb."

"Humph. You run away from your feelings, that's what you do."

"I married Amber, didn't I? How could I run away from my feelings if I married her?" he growled. "And look what happened."

"You married a woman you *knew* would break your heart. You damn well did it on purpose. Subconsciously, of course, but still purposefully."

His mouth dropped open and he stared at his grandmother, bewildered by her accusations. She *was* losing it. "Think whatever you want to think," he said, not knowing how else to respond. He'd never seen his grandmother like this and didn't know what to make of it.

"You're terrified," she accused. "Scared to death that if you really let yourself love a woman who truly deserves your love, she'll end up dying on you the way Dominique died on your father."

Nick studied the window casing, trying to ignore his grandmother, who was now systemically snapping the heads off all the dead rose stems and slinging them viciously to the ground. Hmm. Looked like he'd missed a spot with the caulk.

"Stubborn," Nana muttered, and he heard the crisp snap of another dried bloom being broken off.

Nick dabbed a white bead of caulk into the spot he'd overlooked, cocked his head, studied his handiwork. Nice.

"Arrogant." Snap, snap.

Let's see. There were three more windows in the front. Would he have enough caulk? Or would he need to make another run to Lowe's?

"I swear you're just like your grandfather. He would rather putter around in the garage than express what he was feeling."

"What are you taking about? He kidnapped you from your wedding. That sounds like he was expressing his feelings to me."

Nana waved a hand. "Grand gestures came easily to him, it was the quiet moments—the moments that count to a woman—where he froze up. I loved your grandfather with every beat of my heart, Nick, but he was so stubborn. He never told me about his heart condition. Arrogantly, he wanted to shoulder the burden alone, spare me the worry." She snorted and then tears sprang to her eyes. "I never knew he was dying. He robbed me of the special conversations we could have had. The extra moments we could have savored. The ones your father and mother got to share."

Awkwardly, Nick wrapped his arms around his grandmother and she sank her head against his chest. He didn't know how to deal with Nana's tears. He patted her shoulder, his own emotions a tight clot in his throat.

Nana pulled back, dabbing at her eyes. "I'm sorry. I shouldn't have broken down on you like that."

Rattled, Nick ran a hand through his hair. "Um . . . it's okay."

"I shouldn't have gone off on you either. It's just that I want you to understand how you're sabotaging your chance for happiness."

"Yeah?" The question came to his lips even though he hated to ask it. "How's that?"

"All you've got to do is stop denying how you really feel."

Nick sucked in a deep breath. The heat of her gaze warmed his cheek. "You wanna know how I really feel?"

"Yes."

He opened his mouth, but he couldn't say the words. Couldn't tell her how betrayed he felt because she was selling the house out from under him. Couldn't tell her why he'd felt so compelled to chase Delaney Cartwright away.

"Well?"

Anger sent his pulse throbbing through his veins. Fear tightened his lungs. Denial squeezed his stomach. "Never mind," Nick mumbled, turned on his heels, and walked away.

Before he reached the corner of the house, he heard his grandmother muttering, "Men. Hardheaded as cement. Every last one of them."

Lucia and Trudie caught Delaney as she was leaving the office that afternoon. The minute she saw the two elderly ladies, her heart sank. Via the telephone it had been difficult enough to quit the job, but to reject Lucia to her face would be next to impossible.

"Lucia, Trudie, it's so good to see you," Delaney greeted them in the parking lot of her office. The silver Acura sat three spots away from the front door, taunting her. If she'd just parked a few feet closer, she would have already been driving away when they pulled up. "Were you in the area and decided to drop by?"

"No, no." Lucia beamed. "We made a special trip just to see you."

"It's over fifty miles," Trudie said. "And my driving's not what it used to be."

"You can say that again," Lucia chimed in. "We were lucky to make it here alive. She almost hit a seagull. Twice."

"Pesky creatures," Trudie muttered.

"I was just leaving for the day," Delaney said, hoping that might deter them.

"We brought cannoli," Lucia said and held up a paper bag smelling deliciously of baked goods. "I made them myself."

"They're an especially tasty batch," Trudie said. "I had two on the drive over."

"That's why you almost hit the seagulls. Eating and driving don't mix."

"It's your fault. You're too good of a cook."

Delaney bit back a sigh. "Would you ladies like to come into my office?"

"We would love that." Lucia smiled. "Thank you."

Delaney took out her keys, opened the office back up, and ushered the women inside. "Have a seat," she said, inviting them to sit down on the love seat while she took the plush-cushioned chair positioned beside it.

"Nice office," Trudie said. "Informal, cozy. I like it."

"Thank you." Delaney smiled and braced herself for what she knew was coming next. "How can I help you, Lucia?"

Lucia reached across to take Delaney's hand in hers. She looked her in the eyes. "Come back, stage my house. I don't know what I'll do without you."

Delaney took a deep breath to bolster her courage. "Like I said when we spoke over the phone, Lucia, I should never have agreed to take on your project in the first place. Not with my wedding so close. I just have too much to do. I apologize for any inconvenience I might have caused you. I have the name of another house stager I can recommend."

"This is about Nicky, isn't it?" Lucia wasn't pulling any punches. "You can tell me the truth. He likes you. I can tell, but I promise he won't get out of line with you again. It hurt him so badly last year when Amber cheated on him on their honeymoon. He would never do anything to cause your fiancé to suffer like that."

"Lucia . . ."

"If being alone with Nicky is the only thing that's worrying you, we can take care of that."

Delaney paused. She still wanted to renovate that house. Still hoped to get on *American Home Design*. But she couldn't do that if she had to work alone in the house with Nick. She simply couldn't trust herself to keep her hands off him.

"This is very important to me," Lucia said lowering

her voice. "Because you see . . ." She let go of Delaney's hand and splayed her palm across her heart.

"What she's trying to say," Trudie interjected, "is that her ticker isn't in the best of shape. She wants to get the house sold and settled before . . . well, you know, she kicks the bucket."

Delaney scooted to the edge of her chair. "You're sick? Lucia, why didn't you tell me?"

"She's proud," Trudie said.

"Please, Delaney," Lucia whispered. "Finish the house. Trudie and I will be there every day to act as chaperones. We promise you that."

"But is that good for your heart? Shouldn't you rest?"

"Doc says it's good for her to get out. Stay busy. She just needs to avoid any emotional distress. Right, Luce?"

Lucia nodded. "Please?"

When she presented it like that, how could Delaney say no? "Under the circumstances, of course I'll finish the job for you, Lucia."

"Oh," Trudie said. "One other thing. You can't tell Nick about her heart condition. He doesn't know."

Delaney captured Lucia's gaze. "Doesn't he deserve to know?"

Lucia looked uncomfortable. "It's just that he's had so much to deal with over the past year. I thought it best to keep it from him for now."

Delaney didn't agree, but she had to respect Lucia's wishes. "I won't say a word to him about it," she promised.

"That," Lucia said to Trudie as they left Delaney's office, "was completely underhanded. I feel like such a liar. I just had a physical two weeks ago, and the doctor told me I had the heart of a thirty-year-old."

"It worked though, didn't it? Pretend heart problems get 'em every time. How do you think I con my kids into coming home for the holidays?" Trudie winked. "Now it's all up to the whammy."

Nick sat at the Sandpiper, an outdoor seaside bar near the entrance to the amusement park, his injured leg propped on an adjacent stool, nursing a longneck bottle of beer and idly watching a game of beach volleyball featuring bikini-clad coeds. He wished he could stop thinking about Delaney and what Nana had said to him.

He had chased Delaney off—fully, intentionally. Not because she was staging his grandmother's house, like he told himself, but because he was terrified of his growing feelings for her.

And he had done the same thing with Amber, albeit subconsciously. Nana had him pegged.

It was a painful thing to face. His denial. The way he'd been sabotaging himself. He was still doing it. Allowing himself to be attracted to a woman who was engaged to marry another man, knowing he stood no chance with her.

"You're one sick puppy, Vinetti."

"Excuse me?" the bartender said. "Need another beer?"

Nick waved him away. He didn't want the one he was drinking; he'd just needed to get out of the house and away from the renovations and Nana's on-target assessment to clear his head. "I'm good."

The guy nodded, swiped the bar with a towel, and

slipped a bowl of cocktail peanuts in front of him. Nick reached for a handful, then stopped with the peanuts halfway to his mouth with he spied an elderly woman with a patch over one eye amble up to the bar.

He sat up straight.

Was this the woman he'd promised Delaney he would investigate and had completely forgotten about? Just his luck, the one-eyed carny woman drew herself up on the bar stool beside him, slanted her head Nick's way, winked, and said, "Buy an old gal a drink, handsome?"

Nick was painting the shutters on Lucia's house the next morning when Delaney drove up. She didn't see any signs of Lucia's car, and for one breathless moment when she looked across the lawn at him, she almost panicked and drove away.

He must have sensed her hesitation, because he looked up from his work and gestured her over.

Lucia had promised Delaney she would be here and she trusted her to keep her word. She could handle being alone with Nick until Lucia arrived. It wasn't like she was going to rip his clothes off his body and have her way with him on the front porch. But even as she thought it, she pictured it. What in the heck was wrong with her?

Putting the smile she'd perfected in charm school on her face, she strode up the sidewalk.

"Delaney," he said when she reached the porch.

"Nick."

"I've got some news for you."

Worry gripped her. What kind of news? Had he found out about Lucia's heart condition? Had something bad happened to Lucia? "Yes?" she asked and laced her fingers together.

"You remember that matter you asked me to check out for you?"

"What matter?" She was so busy worrying, his words didn't fully register.

"The patch-eyed woman from the amusement park."

"Huh?"

"You asked me to find out who she was."

"Oh, right, yes, yes."

"I should have followed up sooner, but we were so busy with the house that it slipped my mind."

"That's okay." Truthfully, it had slipped Delaney's mind too. "What did you find out?"

"All I learned is that she hasn't been working at the amusement park long, and in fact, she's leaving town soon."

"Where's she going?"

"Pensacola."

"Is that all?" Delaney curled her fingers into her palms.

"I asked a PI friend of mine to do a little more digging. See if he could find out where she came from. I'll let you know if he finds a connection to your mother."

"Any clues as to why my mother would be meeting her?"

"No idea."

"I'm sure it's nothing. Now that I think back on it, I was probably mistaken. I don't see how my mother could have a secret life where she slipped off to islands to visit carnivals." She laughed.

"I'm sure you're right about that."

"It's preposterous, really. Maybe we should tell your friend not to bother." Delaney tried not to notice how delicious Nick looked with the morning sun glinting off his muscles. She swallowed. "Thank you anyway. I appreciate it. I'll give you a check so you can pay your friend for the trouble he's already gone through."

"Don't worry about it. He owes me a favor. I'll just give him a call and tell him you decided not to persue the matter."

"Thanks," she said again.

They looked at each other.

"We should talk about what happened the other day," he said. "I'm sorry about my behavior. I was out of line."

"So was I."

"I can promise nothing like that will happen again."

"It's okay. I talked to your grandmother. She and Trudie are going to come over every day and act as our chaperones."

"That's pretty pathetic. We're adults, and we can't be trusted in the same room alone together."

"Things just got out of hand."

"I apologize for kissing you," he said. "But I don't regret it. It was bound to happen."

"I'm sorry if I hurt you. I'm sorry I said you were just something to get out of my system. The way I said it made it sound like you didn't matter, but you do matter and that's precisely the problem. You're a good person, Nick, and you deserve a woman who's free to love you, wholly, completely. In another time, another place . . ." She let her words trail off.

"Yeah." He nodded, but did not look at her. Restlessly,

he ran his hands down the sides of his jeans. "It would be a lot easier if this was just an itch that needed scratching."

That was the hell of it. Underneath the guilt, her heart was breaking from the desolation of knowing she would never again feel the pressure of his lips against hers. If he had just been something to flush from her system, she wouldn't have felt such shame. But the kiss they'd shared held too much meaning to dismiss as a simple hormone rush.

"So we understand each other?" She looked deeply into his eyes. "Nothing more can ever come of this."

"Never," he croaked.

Chapter 13

Since she couldn't shake things up with Nick, Delaney shook things up by decorating Lucia's house in a Tuscan style. Lucia heartily approved and her input was invaluable. She told Delaney stories, reminiscing about her childhood in Tuscany, describing the countryside, the food, the people. Through her narrative, Delaney fell in love with a country she'd never seen, but soon felt as if she knew by heart. It sounded like a magical place, and she hoped someday to visit.

Her creativity took on a whole new facet as she explored aspects of color and lighting, texture and dimension, that she'd never before explored.

Most of the walls they painted using Venetian plaster technique. It was time-consuming, but the results were well worth it. In the kitchen, they installed new appliances, replaced the Formica countertops with Italian tile, and refurbished the cabinets. Delaney selected Roman shades as window treatments for the rooms. They added crown molding for visual flair, installed scroll casing around the doors, and exchanged the small baseboards for wider ones. They put in rounded archways and atmospheric lighting.

Lucia and Trudie helped out in what ways they could—refilling paint trays when they ran low, handing Nick tools as he worked to repair leaky pipes, making lunch, tending the flower garden.

Other members of the family put in appearances when possible, mainly on weekends, pitching in wherever they were needed. Delaney loved being around when the whole group got together. Even when they were arguing, the Vinettis had fun together. Teasing and disagreeing, laughing and squabbling and loving one another in ways Delaney envied.

Throughout the whole restoration project, Nick and Delaney kept a respectful distance from each other. Making sure they never accidentally touched or brushed up against each other, which was sometimes difficult in the confines of the small rooms. But even though it was possible to maintain their physical distance, it was almost impossible to keep from bonding emotionally.

Nick was a passionate man, yes, but he managed to retain his cool when things went wrong. Delaney admired that about him. He had a tolerance for the tedious and a willingness to start over from scratch if a project wasn't working out. His patience surprised her. She hadn't expected it.

Besides tales of Tuscany, Lucia told Delaney stories of Nick and his siblings when they were growing up in this house. How Nick had gone through an *Untouchables* phase when he was six—dressing up like Eliot Ness complete with suit, tie, hat, and plastic tommy gun. Even then, he was a cop in the making. She told of how he climbed up the chimney one Christmas to see if he could find Santa. And how he slid down the banister, crashed into his sister, and knocked out her front baby tooth.

On the long Fourth of July weekend, the Vinetti clan returned for one final big push on the project. It would be the family's last holiday in the house on Galveston Island, and no one wanted to miss it.

For four days they worked and joked and ate and drank. Teased and cried and laughed and sighed. At times it was something of a madhouse with all the activity. But miraculously, on the final day almost all of the renovations had been completed. Delaney and Nick would be left with only touch-ups and strategic decorating before the house was ready to display. Delaney's job was almost done, and oddly enough, she found herself feeling as nostalgic for the house as the rest of the family.

"I'll see you after the Fourth," Delaney told Lucia as she got ready to leave for the day. The family was standing in the kitchen, admiring how well it had all turned out. All except for Nick. He'd disappeared somewhere, and Delaney had to force herself not to look around for him.

"You're not coming to our barbecue tomorrow?" Lucia asked, disappointment in her voice.

"My mother . . ." Delaney waved a hand. "She has this event she sponsors for the Houston Symphony every year. I'm expected to attend."

"Can you get out of it?" Gina asked. "The party won't be the same without you."

Delaney's heart squeezed, and for some weird reason she felt like crying. "I always go."

Trudie clicked her tongue. "Tsk. Such a shame. You haven't lived until you've had Fourth of July with the Vinettis."

"We have fireworks," Zack said.

"And homemade ice cream," Jack added.

"And watermelon," lanky, teenage Tony threw in. "It's a blast."

She wanted so badly to say yes, but from the time she was little more than a toddler, Delaney had been attending the annual Fourth of July Symphony Under the Stars bash her father funded and her mother orchestrated. And all that time, she'd wished for the simple pleasure of backyard barbecues and fireworks.

There's no law compelling you to go to that symphony event. Tell Lucia you'll come and deal with Mom later. It was Skylar's voice whispering in the back of her head, urging her to misbehave.

"We'll miss you," Gina said.

Delaney smiled gently. "There's over two dozen people spending the night in this house; I seriously doubt I'll be missed."

"You underestimate yourself," said a deep voice from the doorway. "The party won't be the same without you."

Her pulse spiked. She looked over to see Nick standing there with an enigmatic look in his eyes.

"You want me to come?" Delaney murmured, unable to take her gaze off him.

"I'm just saying you'll be missed." His tone was grave, and he broke their eye contact.

Delaney's breath hitched in her lungs.

"Don't pressure her," Lucia scolded. "If she's got a previous engagement, she's got a previous engagement."

"I'd love to come to your barbecue, Lucia," Delaney surprised herself by saying. "I've been attending that boring symphony thing for as long as I can remember. I can skip one year."

"Really?" Lucia's face brightened so significantly, Delaney knew she'd made the right choice. If Honey got upset with her for skipping the event, she could just lump it.

"Really."

Her announcement to Honey that she wasn't going to the symphony turned out to be amazingly anticlimactic. Her mother seemed very distracted about something, and while she expressed displeasure over Delaney's absence from the program, she didn't badger her the way she'd expected. So it was with a light heart Delaney arrived at the Galveston Island house at midmorning on the Fourth. But when she got out of the car and headed up the sidewalk, arms laden with grocery sacks filled with offerings for the barbecue, her legs started to quiver.

She spied Gina and her husband, Chuck—partially hidden by an overgrowth of bougainvillea along the fence—kissing like teenagers. Chuck's hand tenderly cupped Gina's bottom, and her arms were entwined around his neck.

The sense of jealousy-tinged sadness that swept over Delaney was so intense it almost brought her to her knees. Would Evan be pulling her in the bushes for a passionate kiss after they'd been married for ten years?

He doesn't do that now, why would he do it in a decade? muttered Skylar's annoying voice again.

Mentally, Delaney shook herself and tore her gaze from the amorous couple. What was the matter with her?

"Need a hand with that?"

And then there he was, coming up the sidewalk behind her, the source of all her internal distress.

Nick Vinetti.

Looking as if he was the answer to all her most subversive fantasies, in his tight white T-shirt and black shorts.

He'd replaced his knee brace with an Ace wrap and his limp was barely discernible. He looked very strong and incredibly handsome, and Delaney was feeling as if she possessed the moral resolve of a jellyfish.

Suddenly she wished like hell she hadn't come.

"Here." Nick reached out and plucked the two heaviest plastic bags from her hands. His fingertips brushed against her skin and heat rushed her cheeks.

She was achingly aware of every nuance between them. His manly nutmegy scent collided with the delicate lavender of her own perfume, producing an intoxicating clash of woodsy and floral. The sharp differences in their bodies—his sinewy muscles versus her supple softness. The emotional vastness of the very short distance between them—the tips of her sandals almost touching the toes of his sneakers.

"Where's your brace?" Delaney asked, fixing her gaze on his knee so she wouldn't have to meet his eyes and find out if he shared the same awareness of her that she did of him. She didn't know which thought scared her more. That he felt it too, or the possibility that he didn't.

"I don't need it any longer."

Helplessly, her gaze was drawn up past his hard-muscled thigh, to his narrow hips, to the flat of his belly barely hidden by his thin cotton T-shirt.

She raised her lashes and slanted a coy glance at his face and was caught in the trance of his bemused smile.

He lowered his head.

He's going to kiss me!

The thought set off a fire alarm in her head. *No!*

Please let him kiss me.

She lifted her chin, held her breath, eyes locked with Nick's, and waited. "Don't you dare kiss me, you scoundrel," she said, sounding exactly like a woman who desperately needed to be kissed.

From behind her, she heard Gina and Chuck giggle, and thankfully that broke the spell.

Delaney sucked in air and held up the remaining sack in her hand. "Meat. For the barbecue. Needs refrigerating."

Oh, gosh, how pathetic. He'd so rattled her that she couldn't even speak in complete sentences.

With that, she hurried past him, grateful that she was almost finished with the house and would soon be far away from the temptation of Lucia's maddeningly mesmerizing grandson.

Nick would have kissed Delaney and broken all the promises he'd made to her, if Gina and Chuck hadn't come strolling from the bougainvillea bushes with self-satisfied smirks on their faces.

It was a good thing they were there, he told himself as he frowned at his sister and her husband lounging against the fence, arm in arm. Otherwise, there was no telling what he might have done.

Then, unable to keep himself from watching her, Nick turned his head and enjoyed the view of Delaney's hips swaying as she hurried toward the house.

He thought about how her cheeks had turned red when he'd touched her while reaching for the grocery sacks. He grinned. Aw, Rosy. She disappeared around the side of the house, headed for the back door that the family used, and his grin widened.

Delaney was astute. He was a scoundrel. And he wasn't proud of it. But he wasn't ashamed of it either. Okay, he was a little ashamed, but only because she was engaged to his doctor.

But what if she wasn't engaged to Evan Van Zandt?

She is, so stop thinking about it, he rebuked himself.

It was easy to say, but not so damn easy to do. Because ever since he'd kissed her, Nick hadn't been able to think of anything else.

By midafternoon the food was ready and everyone had assembled. The backyard picnic table was laden with food. Barbecued chicken, grilled Italian sausages, and hamburger patties. There was potato salad, cole slaw, corn on the cob, and baked beans, along with cold macaroni salad, an assortment of cheeses, antipasto, and tomato bruschetta. Dessert was a bountiful selection of fresh fruits, homemade brownies, and tiramisu. Two ice-cream freezers churned batches of homemade peach ice cream. There was lemonade for the children and iced tea or cold beer or chilled white wine for the adults.

Nick, Delaney noticed, was in rare form. Playing with the kids, charming his sisters-in-law, guy-talking with his brothers, his cousins, his father, and Chuck. He sur-

prised her. She thought he'd be gloomy today, on this last
Vinetti family holiday in Lucia's house where they'd all
shared so many memories.

The food was delicious, the company even more so.
They lingered long over the meal, until the kids started
begging to go swimming. Everyone pitched in to get
ready—the women putting away leftovers and cleaning
the kitchen while the men packed up the cars with cool-
ers and blankets, fireworks, lawn chairs, beach towels,
and a boom box. Even Trudie and Lucia went along for
the trek to the secluded beach outside the Galveston city
limits that only the locals knew about.

Delaney soon found herself—toes dug into the sand—
sitting under a big beach umbrella. She watched the kids
shriek gleefully as they ran through the surf, chased by
Nick, Chuck, and Nick's brothers Richie and Johnny.
Vincent was manning the boom box. Causing the
teenagers, who were too cool to play in the ocean with
the younger kids, to roll their eyes and groan when he
put in a CD of the Beach Boys.

Then, for absolutely no reason at all, a lump rose to
Delaney's throat, forcing her to swallow back the salty
taste. She was happy. Why the sudden urge to cry?

From childhood, she'd been trained to control her
emotions, to repress her feelings, deny her impulses.
She'd been taught that appearances were paramount, and
she should conduct herself based on what others thought
of her.

Growing up rich and privileged, Delaney realized,
was like living on an island with other people who were
exactly like you. The lifestyle imposed upon children of
the wealthy and powerful entailed certain duties and

conditions unknown to the rest of the population. In high society there was no blending into an anonymous background—which was one of the reasons Honey had been so strict with her. Delaney had been required to watch every step. No one trod easily on the emotions of others where money and manners mingled. This need for caution, this intricate caretaking, resulted in an inbreeding of the spirit. Too much held in. Too much regret. Too much silent brooding.

And she wanted out.

But she wasn't going to get out if she married Evan. He was too much like her.

The thought twisted her stomach.

Is this really about Evan? she had to ask herself. *Or your attraction to Nick?*

Her gaze tracked back to the man frolicking in the surf with his nieces and nephews, and it was her heart's turn to twist. His shirt was off and he was silhouetted against the backdrop of ocean and sunset, aglow in the ending day. Orange rays of light licked his body. Every muscle was ripped, rock hard, and clearly defined.

One look at him and she could feel the simmering chemistry. In her lungs. In her throat. Tight around her wrists like shackles. Light as a breath. Thick as blood.

He must have felt the heat of her gaze, because he turned his head and like a proud, regal wolf stared at her.

Delaney squeezed her eyes shut, and in that pop of difference between the setting sun on the horizon and the darkness behind her lids, she experienced the strangest sensation of falling down a long, black, empty tunnel. Her eyes flew open and she curled her fingers around the arms of the lawn chair to ground herself. Blinking, she glanced around. Vincent was lighting tiki torches, and his brother, Phil, was starting a campfire. Somebody's mom was dishing out mosquito repellent. But no matter how hard she tried to find something else to look at, time and again she found her eyes drawn back to Nick.

Honestly, even if she weren't engaged to Evan, she and Nick didn't stand a chance as a couple. They were simply too different. He was rugged and streetwise; she was pampered and polished. He valued directness and honesty, and she'd spent her life putting a perfect spin on reality. Gingerly, she reached up to finger the bridge of her nose—living a lie, pretending to be a beauty when she was not. Face it, she was insecure and he was self-confident. He was bold and she was timid. She could not view Nick as a way out of her circumstances. He couldn't rescue her. He was just a guy with problems of his own. Like it or not, she was engaged to another man.

Don't fill your head with dreams of him, she warned herself.

Nick's brother Johnny's wife pulled up a lawn chair beside Delaney. Her name was Brittany, Delaney remembered, and she was holding her new baby daughter in her arms. She was a slender woman about Delaney's age, with an elfin face and long dark hair she kept pinned back with a thick barrette. "Mind the company?"

"Not at all." Delaney shook her head.

Brittany tossed a receiving blanket over her shoulder and modestly began nursing her daughter. Delaney's attention drifted back to the shoreline, her eyes hooked on Nick.

"Gorgeous, huh?" Brittany said.

"What?"

"The Vinetti men."

She couldn't deny that. "Yes."

For a minute the only sounds were the rush of the surf, the Beach Boys singing about their little Deuce coupe, and the baby suckling.

"You're engaged to be married, right?" Brittany said after a long moment.

"Uh-huh." Delaney glanced over to find Brittany studying her speculatively.

"So how come you're not with your fiancé today? Wait, that was rude; you don't have to answer that."

Delaney smiled. "It's okay. Evan is in Guatemala." She told Brittany about Evan's medical mission to Central America.

"He sounds like a great guy."

"He is."

"Nick knows you're engaged, right?"

"Yes. Why do you ask?"

"We're all crazy about him, you know. He's a great uncle and a terrific cop and an all-around good guy. After what Amber did to him . . ." Brittany paused a moment to reposition her baby. "Well, we're pretty protective. The last thing we want is for Nick to get hurt again. He's been through a lot, what with his knee and being forced off the job and everything else that's happened."

"I understand."

"Do you? Do you really?"

Delaney met Brittany's gaze. "What are you trying to say?"

"The way Nick looks at you when you're not looking at him . . ." She trailed off again.

"What way is that?" Delaney felt her body tense, and she curled her fingernails into her palms.

She shrugged. "I dunno, sort of wistful and sad. It worries me and Johnny."

"I can assure you, Brittany, I have no designs on Nick."

"And Nick knows that?"

"Yes, he does."

Brittany blew out a breath. "Okay. Just wanted to make sure. Because we all really like you, but Nick, you know, he's family. Nothing is more important than family loyalty. Right?"

"Right," Delaney echoed, suddenly feeling incredibly out of place. It was time she said good-bye and left the Vinettis to their celebration. She looked around and realized she was going to have to ask someone to drive her back to her car. Why hadn't she driven herself?

At that moment, Brittany's five-year-old son, Logan, came running up, soaking wet and grinning. "Mama, can we shoot off some Black Cats now?"

"Only if your daddy or Uncle Nick or Uncle Richie or Uncle Chuck helps you with them."

Logan zoomed over to Vincent, who was sitting on the tailgate of Nick's pickup truck with Lucia and Trudie, changing the Beach Boys to Ira Gershwin.

Nick came trotting up after Logan. Droplets of water caught in his dark, curling chest hairs glistened in the waning sunlight. Delaney looked up at him and he looked down at her, and immediately she understood why Brittany had come over to warn her off. The look in Nick's eyes was undeniably hungry.

He flopped down on the ground dangerously close to Delaney's sand-dusted toes.

Up the beach some other picnickers had already brought out their fireworks. Kids twirled sparklers spewing yellow, red, and green heat into the gathering twilight. Fireflies had gotten into the act, blinking on and off among the dunes, Mother Nature competing with man-made pyrotechnics.

"That looks like such fun," Delaney said, drawing up her knees to her chest and resting her chin on them as she watched the sparklers dance and sizzle.

Nick lay propped up on his elbows. "You've never played with sparklers?"

"Always spent my Fourth at the symphony. They have a magnificent fireworks display after the concert."

"You never, ever shot off any firecrackers of your own?"

She shook her head.

"Now, that's just shocking." Nick grinned. "You've been so deprived."

"Tell me about it." Delaney grinned back.

"Would you like to correct that oversight?" He arched one eyebrow speculatively.

"What? Shoot off fireworks?"

He got to his feet, held out his palm. "Come with me."

She looked up at him.

He nodded encouragingly. "Yes?"

Swallowing hard, she committed herself by taking his hand.

He closed his fingers around hers and hauled her from the lawn chair. Brittany watched them with narrowed

eyes and a disapproving expression on her lips that made
Delaney quickly glance away.

Nick's hand was firm but gentle. A warm sensation of
sweet security washed over her. *You are important to me,*
his grip seemed to say. *I will take care of you.*

But she didn't need to be taken care of. She'd been
taken care of all her life. Everyone telling her what to do,
how to think, what to believe, and she'd complied with
their wishes. What she really needed was someone who
would challenge her, urge her to grow. A tender tether,
not a ball and chain. Bonded but not bound. Could Nick
be all that?

*You're reading too much into this. He's just leading
you to the fireworks. Stop overthinking things and enjoy
the moment.*

Sensible. Now, if only she could heed her own advice.

With his fingers loosely laced through hers, Nick
guided her to the back of the pickup where Vincent was
doling out small doses of fireworks from a large card-
board box to the excited children.

"We'll start with sparklers," Nick told Delaney.
"They're the least intimidating."

Just as he said that, Zack lit off a Black Cat a few feet
away, and the loud bang caused Delaney to jump and
Brittany's baby to start crying.

"Go on down closer to the water with your dad," Vincent instructed his grandson. "And be careful not to burn
yourself with that punk."

Nick retrieved a box of sparklers and a couple of
punks from his father, took Delaney's hand again, and
walked her down to the edge of the Gulf.

He handed her a sparkler. Then he lit the punk with a

match and once it was going, touched the punk to her sparkler.

There was a quick hiss, and then a magical sizzle of light as the sparkler sprang to life in her hands.

"Oh, oh!" Delaney gasped. "It's going, it's going. What do I do? What do I do?"

"Circle your wrist," he said.

"What?" She was so disconcerted by the fact she was holding a sparking, spitting fire stick, she couldn't get what he was trying to tell her.

"Like this."

Nick reached around her, his bare chest grazing her back, his damp swimming trunks pressed against her hip as he slid one hand down her arm to her wrist and encircled it with his big, masculine fingers. He moved her hand in a circle. The sparks showered into a sweeping arc, decorating the night air.

This was fun!

She giggled as Nick changed the circles into zigzags, and then into figure eights, blurring the sparks into one smooth, rapid ride of light until it sputtered and died.

That's when she realized she was holding a spent but red-hot metal stick, and Nick was still pressed up close against her. She could feel the heat of his breath fanning the hairs on the nape of her neck. Delaney turned her head and peeked at him from behind lowered lashes.

A full moon had risen, bathing the shore in a soft white radiance. Nick's eyes were alight with a rarefied glow, the smile at his lips beatific. He had a passion about him. A sense of adventure. A childlike wonder when it came to play. He had what she longed for. The ability to let go and enjoy life.

Idly, she wondered if this was what his face looked like when he was having sex. Totally absorbed, blissfully engaged. That irreverent thought caused her whole body to tingle.

This was serious trouble.

Nick's lips brushed softly against her temple. She felt the erratic rise and fall of his chest, knew his breathing was as labored as her own.

Then the sky lit up with fireworks.

She and Nick turned in unison to see the Vinetti family gathered around as Vincent set off rockets. They were laughing and joking and hugging and talking.

Nick's arm went around her waist and Delaney's heart was pounding so hard she could barely hear the Roman candles screaming toward the stars in an explosion of color.

And in that moment, she knew she was going to miss the entire Vinetti clan in general—and one special Vinetti in particular—something awful.

Chapter 14

Once the renovations had been completed, Tish came back to tape the "after" video for the *American Home Design* contest, and they mailed it off just in time for the deadline.

But now Lucia's house had been on the market for a week, and no one had shown the slightest interest in it.

"No problem," the real estate agent Margaret Krist insisted. "It's only been seven days."

But Delaney couldn't stop worrying. The potential buyers that Margaret ushered through complained the house was too brightly colored, or too provincial, or not elegant enough, or too themed.

Delaney feared she should have listened to conventional wisdom and painted the walls white, with chic but generic decor. She shouldn't have listened to Nick. She shouldn't have tried to shake things up. Her experiment had failed.

Lucia told her not to worry, that they just hadn't found the right buyer who could really fall in love with the place.

Unfortunately time was running out for Lucia, and Delaney felt responsible.

The impulse to buy Nana Vinetti's house herself was strong, but how could she? She was marrying Evan, and he would never go for it. Not even for investment property. A house this old would require a lot of TLC. Something he had neither the time nor the inclination to pursue.

The third week the house was on the market, Delaney started to sweat. Another week and Lucia would be closing on the condo. But she couldn't close on it until her home had sold. Determined that her friend would not be left high and dry, Delaney took matters into her own hands and began contacting her mother's friends, telling them about the fabulous island home for sale. But the women in her mother's circle weren't impressed with Galveston. They had second homes in Florida and California and Hawaii and beyond.

She'd run out of options.

Glumly, she sat in her office, trying to figure out what more she could do, when the telephone rang.

"Ms. Delaney Cartwright?"

"This is she."

"This is Winn Griffin from *American Home Design*."

"Yes?" Her voice went up an octave as her grip tightened around the receiver.

"I'm pleased to inform you that your entry of Mrs. Lucia Vinetti's Galveston Island home has won second place in our contest."

Excitement shot Delaney to her feet. "Really?"

"You and Mrs. Vinetti will share the twenty-five-thousand-dollar second prize, and the video you submitted will be featured on the next installment of *American Home Design*."

"That's amazing. Thank you, thank you."

"The renovations you did on the home were charming. Your entry really captured our judges' imaginations. Tuscany meets Queen Victoria. Brilliant work."

She wasn't the one with the brilliant idea. It had been all Nick's doing. Shake it up, he'd told her, and he'd been so right.

"You're a truly talented designer, Ms. Cartwright, and I'm sure this exposure will skyrocket your house-staging business."

"How soon will we get the money?" she asked, thinking that the money would be enough for the down payment on Lucia's condo.

"It takes six to eight weeks to process payment through our accounting firm."

That was too bad. The money wouldn't arrive before Lucia was due to close on the condo.

Maybe this time Lucia would accept a loan from her. She'd tried to get her to borrow the down payment from her before, but Lucia's fierce pride would not let her take Delaney's money. Perhaps knowing that the money was coming to her eventually would sway Lucia's thinking. Especially since she had that heart condition.

She'd told herself she would worry about that later. Right now, she had good news to share. Lucia's house was going to be featured on *American Home Design*.

*   *   *

The Vinetti clan along with Delaney and Tish gathered at Lucia's house for an *American Home Design* watching party.

Nick hadn't seen Delaney since they'd finished the house, just a few days after the Fourth of July party.

The minute she walked through the door, everyone was on their feet to greet her, welcoming her like part of the family.

She looked elegant as always—expensive and classy in a beige skirt cut from some kind of soft flowing material that made it look like water parting when she moved. Her top was simple, black and sleeveless, showing off her well-toned arms and smooth, creamy skin. The minute she saw him, her soft green eyes crinkled along with her perfectly straight nose and she smiled slightly, shyly.

And Nick couldn't take his eyes off her.

That smile was a missile launched straight into his heart.

It was over, he realized. After tonight he would probably never see her again.

Nick was going to miss her more than he'd ever thought possible. She'd brought lightness into his life at a time when everything looked dark and dismal. She'd made him believe in possibilities again, even though she was way beyond what he had any right to fantasize about.

He fought the feeling. Fought it hard. He didn't want to fall in love again. Couldn't fall in love again. Not with a woman who was marrying another man.

*   *   *

It was easy enough to avoid Nick in a room crowded with people, but Delaney couldn't seem to stop her gaze from straying over to him throughout the broadcast of *American Home Design*. He caught her studying him a couple of times. She would duck her head and will the heat not to rise to her cheeks. She didn't want anyone else noticing what he could do to her with just one meaningful glance.

When the first-, second-, and third-place winners of the contest were announced, the room broke into applause. The program ran the video of the third-place winner first. It was a house built among the trees near the Oregon coastline, and then they went on to Delaney's entry.

"Great video footage," Gina told Tish.

"Great house decorating," Nick's brother Richie said.

"It was a great idea to go with the Tuscan style, Nick," Delaney said, her eyes on him. "I'm glad you nixed the stark white."

He met her gaze with his intense stare, and she couldn't stop herself. This time she did blush.

The television show went to commercial before the final winner was announced, but the Vinettis had already seen the winning home. Everyone was talking at once. Someone broke open a bottle of champagne. Someone else muted the television and turned on a recording of Italian love songs. Lucia brought a tray of antipasto into the room. Zack and Jack trailed behind her with another tray of mini-pizzas and finger sandwiches made from prosciutto and provolone.

It was officially a party.

Delaney avoided Nick and Nick avoided Delaney.

They stayed at opposite sides of the room, both pretending not to notice that they were noticing each other. Restlessly, he prowled his corner, shooting quick, searing glances at her from time to time.

His leg was almost healed. She hadn't seen him limp in a long time. She was glad for Nick. He'd be returning to work soon, and that should make him happy. He deserved to be happy.

Except that he did not look very happy.

He looked tormented, and she had the most awful realization that she was the cause.

Unnerved by the black look in his eyes, Delaney escaped into the kitchen to see if Lucia needed any help. The older woman was standing at the stove stirring a simmering pot of marinara sauce that smelled like Tuscan heaven.

Lucia turned to smile at her and slipped an arm around her waist. "Delaney, I can't thank you enough for what you've done for me and my family."

A warm glow of affection for Lucia filled her up. "You don't have to thank me. It's my job."

"It's more than a job and you know it. The amount of love you poured into this house is exceptional. You've taken the heart of this place and made it bigger than anyone thought it could be. You're an artist, and I'm so pleased you chose my house as your canvas."

"I only hope that by expressing my creativity I didn't ruin your chances of selling the house. It got us on *American Home Design*, yes, but it doesn't achieve your ultimate goal."

In the distance, below the noisy hubbub of the Vinettis' celebration, the phone rang. A few seconds later

Gina came into the kitchen wagging the cordless in her hand. "Delaney, it's for you."

She took the phone. "Hello?"

"Delaney, I've got fabulous news," Margaret Krist, the real estate agent, exclaimed.

"What's up?"

"We've had a bid on Lucia's house. The potential buyer saw the *American Home Design* and they just have to have it so they called me on my cell phone. Get this, they offered fifty thousand dollars over the price we were asking before the program aired."

Emotion overcame her—relief, happiness tinged with a dose of sadness that it was over. "That's wonderful news."

"Oh, that's not all."

Delaney could feel the excitement in Margaret's voice. "How much better can it get?"

"My phone has been ringing off the wall with clients wanting you to stage their houses. Check your messages. I'm sure you've received a lot of phone calls as well. This is it, Delaney. Your career has just been made. All your dreams are coming true."

Delaney looked through the archway from the kitchen into the living room, saw Nick playing with Zack and Jack, and her heart just sank. Margaret was wrong. There was one dream she knew would never come true.

"Thank you, Margaret," she said. "I'll let the Vinettis know." She hung up the phone and broke the joyous news to the family. The crowd let out a shout of happiness.

She found herself deposited breathless and laughing

in the kitchen right next to Nick, who looked moody and disgruntled. She reached out to touch his arm.

"We did it," she said. "We restored your grandmother's house and got an offer just in time for her to close on the condo."

Nick hardened his jaw. She saw the emotion play across his face. Sadness, regret, anger.

Was he mad at her? She didn't understand. "You're not pleased?"

He didn't say anything. He just removed her hand from his arm, got up, and walked out the back door.

Now this was ridiculous. She was tired of his moodiness. She knew he'd been through a lot. But enough was enough. He needed a good, swift kick in the seat of his pants. He'd lost a lot, yes, but the man seemed to have no idea what he had. And she was going to give him a piece of her mind.

Delaney went after him.

He was already climbing into his pickup truck.

What was his problem? Her hurt and rejection turned to fury. How dare he spoil his grandmother's party? Determinedly, she followed, yanking open the passenger door and hopping inside as he started the engine.

"Where do you think you're going?" he snarled.

"With you."

"You're not invited."

"Too bad." She thrust out her chin and folded her arms over her chest. "I'm going anyway, I . . ."

"Get a clue; I don't want you here," his deep, belligerent voice cut her off, his face looking like a volcano about to erupt. She half expected to see plumes of smoke

THERE GOES THE BRIDE

rising out of his ears. He was steamed, and as far as she could see he had no excuse for his behavior.

"I'm not leaving until you talk to me."

"If you don't get out of here, be forewarned, woman, I can't be held accountable for my actions."

"What's the matter with you?" she scolded. "You're acting like a butthead."

Some of the family had come out on the back porch and were staring at them as they sat in his truck.

Nick swore loudly, put the pickup truck in reverse, and blasted out of the drive.

"What's your deal?"

He shot Delaney a visual bullet with enough power to arm a dictator-toppling death squad. Nick gripped the steering wheel so tightly she feared it would snap off in his hands. Grinding his teeth, Nick was headed for Seawall Boulevard, his brow furrowed. He did not speak a word.

Delaney shrank back against the seat, uncertain what to do next.

They drove in silence, past the main drag, away from the cluster of lights toward the secluded beach where the family had picnicked on the Fourth of July. He took the sandy road too fast and the truck bottomed out.

Delaney clutched the seat belt with both hands, hanging on for dear life. They bumped out onto the beach. There was no one else in sight. Nick pulled up on the hard-packed sand just short of the water, shut off the engine, and got out.

He went around to the passenger side and flung open the door. "Out," he commanded.

Her eyes widened. What was going on here? He was so forceful, so masculine. It both scared and thrilled her.

"You're going to leave me here?"

"You wanted to come, you wanted to hear this, well get out of the truck and listen."

"Why couldn't we have had this discussion while we were driving?" She glanced nervously around the dark, empty beach. "Or back at your grandmother's house?"

"Because I needed to move." He fisted his hands and paced the sand. "Because I'm so filled up with . . . with . . ."

"Rage?"

"Jealousy."

"Jealousy?" she squeaked. It was not what she expected him to say.

"Jealousy," he confirmed. "We're sitting in my grandmother's living room, watching your ideas on television, and then the phone rings and we find out you've sold her house."

"I thought that's what you wanted. What we all wanted."

"No," Nick shouted. "I wanted to be the one who took care of her. But you . . . you . . . come into her house, into our lives, and you changed everything."

"It was your idea to decorate the house in a Tuscan theme. I wanted to do it in something simple and chic. I wanted to make it look like some house from a glossy magazine. You're the reason her house sold, not me. You have no reason to be jealous."

He jammed his fingers through his hair in frustration. "You don't get it, do you?"

"No, I don't." She sank her hands on her hips and

watched him stride back and forth, back and forth, a caged animal desperate to break free.

He stopped pacing and came over to glare at her. "I'm jealous of that ring you have on your finger and of the man who put it there. I had to sit across the room from you tonight, watching you, wanting you, being so proud of you, and knowing I can't have you. You fit in so well with my family. It's like you belong there more than I do. And every time you looked over at me, smiled in my direction, it was ripping my guts out."

His words were ripping her apart too.

"I tried the very best I could to control myself," he said. "And whether you realize or not, you've been toying with me. Flirting and confiding in me, but then using that damn diamond ring as a shield from getting close." He ground out the words.

Was it true? Had she been leading him on? It wasn't a pretty thought. She reached out her hand to touch him. "Nick, I'm so sorry, it was never my intention to lead you on."

"Don't touch me," he threatened. "If you touch me, I'm going to lose it. I've been hanging on by a thread ever since we kissed, and I can barely keep my hands off you."

Silence strummed the heavy salt air, stretching between them vast as the ocean.

She felt sorry for him. And for herself. They had met at exactly the wrong time in their lives. She was spoken for and he, on the rebound, hurting from his knee injury and his grandfather's death, couldn't really trust what he was feeling for her.

Nick was an intensely physical guy cursed with a

strong moral compass. He wouldn't let himself act on his desires. No matter how difficult it was for him to keep them in check. She understood then why he'd gone into law enforcement. The attraction such a dangerous job held for a man like him. To Nick, the combination of a job that let him move and breathe and the justice it meted out would be the best possible career.

It would be wrong to touch him now. So very, very wrong. Compounding the problem. Making things worse.

Helpless, unable to hold herself back, she reached up and ran her fingertips along his jaw.

"You're playing with fire, Delaney." His eyes were dark and deadly. "I'll burn you up."

A hot rush of overwhelming desire surged through her. Her knees trembled. "Burn me," she cried.

He cupped her chin in his palm. "Be very careful what you ask for, Rosy."

"Nick." His name slipped past her lips on a sigh.

He captured her mouth without a moment's hesitation, fast and deep and hot.

Her lips parted for his. Eager and excited.

He splayed one hand against the back of her head, stabbing his fingers through her hair and hauling her closer.

They were chest to chest and she could feel his heart leaping against hers, quick and thrilling.

The reckless wildness startled Delaney. The stunning intensity of her feral need. Raw nature. Their passion was a brewing hurricane, threatening to roll ashore and decimate everything in its path.

How she wanted to ride out the storm! To let it over-take her, bring her down. Ruin her.

She wanted him here and now. Nothing else mattered. All she knew was that nothing in her life had ever felt so right.

Sighing, Delaney sank against him, swept up in the feel of his calloused palms against her bare arms, the force of their tangling tongues and raspy breaths. Who would have guessed they'd be so hot together? The cool heiress and the fiery cop.

His lips trailed from her lips to her cheeks, to her fore-head, to her temple where his mouth rested quietly against her throbbing pulse. The sweetness of the gesture in the wake of that fever-pitched kiss left her breathless and trembling.

She couldn't think, could barely remember her own name. The civilized part of her brain was numbed with lusty hormones. The animal part took over. Claimed her. Each and every sensation in her body dominated by the rough, decadent touch of him.

"Take me," she whispered.

Nick needed no more invitation than that.

He pushed her into the sand, not caring that it was damp. He was as hard as a man could get and growing harder by the second. His heartbeat spiked. It was a sud-den kick in his chest, a vigorous thudding in his groin.

Any doubts he might have had about what he was doing vanished in the hazy heat of the moment. He for-got that she was engaged. Forgot that they were on a public beach where anyone could come upon them at any moment. He was consumed by a hunger so elemental it transcended everything else. He felt it to his soul, this wanting. He'd never felt anything quite this intensely.

She made him feel so real. So alive. He hadn't realized how shut off he'd become.

And when she slipped her arms around his neck and drew him closer still, the pupils of her eyes widening darkly, he surmised she was just as startled as he was by the power of this thing between them.

He'd grown so cynical over the years and he thought he was immune to these kinds of feelings, especially after Amber. But here he was aching with the need to explore her fully, to burrow his way deep underneath her perfect facade.

Blindly, without purposeful thought, Nick trailed his fingertips over the nape of her neck and leaned his head down to kiss the throbbing pulse at the hollow of her throat. Her silky skin softened beneath his mouth and a tight little moan escaped her lips.

His hand crept from her neck and down the hollow of her throat to her breast heaving with each inhalation of air. A simple but lingering touch that escalated the intimacy between them and felt extremely erotic.

The air smelled of electricity. The ocean crashed loudly with the darkness of his deed. Stealing another man's woman. Time hung, suspended as they looked into each other's eyes.

Nick could not fully comprehend the hold Delaney had over him. She made him want to chuck all his values and morals and just do what felt good. He was a lost soul, vanquished by her kiss. Nick could think of nothing else but being melded with her in any way that he could.

She rocked her pelvis against him, lithe and graceful.

Blood dove through his body, pouring out from his heart and pooling into his crotch, setting his erection in stone. He closed his eyes, grappling for some semblance of control, but it was nowhere to be found.

He kissed her again, his clashing tongue hot against hers, enjoying the glorious taste of her.

She shivered in response, a tremor quaking through her slender body. He pulled his lips from hers and ran his tongue over the outside of her ear and she shuddered even harder.

Her quick intake of breath, low and excited, in the vast openness of sea and sky, ignited his own need, sending it shooting to flaming heights.

She lightly bit his chin.

The feel of her teeth against his skin rocketed a searing heat to all of his erogenous zones and he groaned. God, she was one helluva woman, willing to walk out on this limb with him.

Nick's lips found hers again and as they kissed, he raised a hand to touch her breast.

Her nipple poked through the material of both her silky lace bra and her silk top.

His thumb brushed against her hard little button and she responded by wrapping her legs around his and sliding her bottom against his upper thigh. The feel of her panties against the leg of his jeans was highly sensuous.

When he bent his head to gently suck at her nipple through her shirt, she gasped and clutched his head to her.

This wasn't good enough. He had to touch her bare skin or go insane.

Sliding his hand up underneath her shirt, he unhooked her bra from behind and set her breasts free. She moved against him, mewling softly. Her usual reticence was gone, replaced by a stark hunger that shoved his libido into overdrive.

No way could he resist the mounting pleasure, nor the sweet little sound slipping past her lips.

And yet, even as he succumbed, he couldn't help thinking that he was pushing her into this, no matter how eagerly she responded. He wanted her. But not like this. He wanted her to come to him once she had faced the problems in her life and untangled herself from Van Zandt. He didn't want their joining to spring from his anger or jealousy. Or from her desire to please him. He wanted her to want him unequivocally, with all her heart and soul. He would play second fiddle to no other motive.

"We've got to stop," he gasped, wrenching his mouth from hers. "I can't do this. I won't do this. You belong to someone else, and I won't violate your commitment. It's wrong and we both know it."

She drew in a shuddering breath. "Nick, no . . . please . . . don't stop. It feels too good."

"I made a promise to you. We can't do this." He shook his head. "Not as long as another man's ring is on your finger."

Delaney got home around midnight, her clothes damp and filled with sand. Her mind in turmoil, her soul filled with a dark roaring, like a house in a hurricane. Buffeted by a destructive force she could not control.

Thankfully, her parents were in bed. No Honey to deal

with. No need to explain the wild, desperate look she knew was etched into her face.

Delaney undressed in her bathroom and stared at her reflection in the mirror, felt the cool tile beneath her feet. Who in the world was this woman? She was morphing into someone she no longer recognized.

Tonight, she'd almost been unfaithful to Evan. Delaney would never have believed herself capable of such a thing. Of violating her most basic principles. She shuddered to think what would have happened if Nick hadn't had the moral courage to put on the brakes.

Searchingly, she raised her fingertips and traced the outline of her lips, raw and aching from the imprint of his mouth. Trying desperately to make sense of the emotions commanding her.

The map is not the territory, she thought. It was a piece of paper marked with symbols and lines, a representation of a place. *You are here.* But when you were actually there, the space around you did not look like the map drawings. There was undocumented terrain and surfaces not captured. There were scents and sounds and tastes and textures no map could denote. There were secret alcoves and gradient shadows and varying shades of light and hue.

On the outside, Delaney's external map was a glossy image—perfected by scalpel and etiquette, but her internal map of reality was distorted by her changing values and beliefs. By the filters life as a Cartwright had placed on her sense of self.

What did she want?

Where did she fit?

Who was she really?

Unable to answer these disturbing questions, she blocked them out and hopped into the shower, eager to wash away her sins.

She turned the water as hot as she could stand it and let it roll over her in heated waves, but no amount of steaming water could drown her guilt. When the water finally ran cold, she got out of the shower, dressed in silk pajamas, and climbed into bed.

Her mind kept going back to Nick and what had occurred on the beach. She tried to barricade her heart against him. To tell herself these feelings weren't important. That hormones couldn't be trusted, but she knew it was all a lie to salve her aching soul.

The phone, which was a private line into her bedroom, rang. She checked the caller ID. Out of area. Who was calling so late? She picked up the receiver.

"Hello?"

"Delaney, it's Evan."

Guilt rushed her. Guilt, guilt, and more guilt, combined with a strange sense of relief and gratitude. Thank heavens he had called. She needed so badly to hear his voice. So desperately needed for him to bring her back to the values she had almost thrown away in the heat of passion.

"Evan, it's so good to hear your voice. I'm so happy that you called." She crossed her legs into a semi-lotus position.

"It's not too late to be calling? Did I wake you?"

"No, no."

"I've missed you so much, Delaney," his voice cracked with emotion.

"I've missed you too." And she had missed him, in her

way, missed that he hadn't been here to stop her from making a huge mistake.

"I was thinking about you tonight," he said. "I think about you every night and all through the day."

"I think about you too."

"I can't wait to see you. We've got so much to discuss."

"When will you be home?"

"A week from Sunday."

"I can't wait."

"Neither can I." She heard the smile in his voice. "Remember when we were kids, when we were each other's best friend?"

She swallowed hard. "I remember."

"I wish we were still friends in that same way."

"But we are still best friends," she protested.

"No, we're not. You have Tish, and I . . . I have my work," he said.

Delaney's heart pounded with hope. "Is there something bothering you, Evan? You sound different somehow."

"No, no, not at all," he denied. "Just thinking about how long we've known each other and how very much I love you. I do love you deeply, Delaney. You do know that."

Oh, dear God, the guilt was ripping her apart. "I know."

"You're a very special person."

"Not so special," she said, fresh pins of guilt pricking her.

"Very special," he disagreed. "You believed in me when no one else did. My parents didn't want me to be a doctor, remember? They wanted me to follow Dad into the oil business. You alone encouraged me to follow my dreams. You were the one who told me I'd make the best doctor in the world. You remember that?"

"I remember."

"I owe my success to you."

"You don't. You did all the hard work. I was just your cheering section."

"And I love you for it. You matter to me. You matter in my life. Being with you makes me happy."

"Oh, Evan." She sighed.

They were the magic words. He couldn't have said anything that would have convinced her more that she was doing the right thing by marrying him.

"I better go," he said. "Surgery around here starts at five A.M. I just needed to hear your voice, touch base with you. Everything okay there?"

"Fine, just fine."

"And the wedding plans?"

"Perfect."

"With your mother handling the arrangements, of course they are. I love you."

"I love you too," Delaney whispered. *Even if it's not in the way you deserve.*

But it was going to be okay, she convinced herself. He needed her. She mattered to him. Ultimately, that's what she needed most. No chemistry, no sparks, not that certain magical something.

Because it was easier for her to pretend that what they had was enough rather than risk her security on the outside chance that she could have it all.

Chapter 15

Nick tried not to think about Delaney while he sat in Evan Van Zandt's waiting room, but it was like a drowning man trying not to think about oxygen. She was in his brain, in his blood—like a virus he couldn't shake.

To distract himself he picked up a copy of *Texas Monthly* and leafed through it, only to find an article about high-society summer weddings and there, smiling back at him from her engagement photograph, was Delaney. Evan had his arm around her waist, and they both looked so happy it was all Nick could do to keep from ripping the page out of the magazine and shredding it into a hundred little pieces.

Instead, he tossed the magazine aside, got to his feet, and began to pace. Hell, even if she wasn't already engaged to his doctor, there was no way he and Delaney could have a future together. She got her picture in *Texas Monthly*, for crying out loud. She was cool, she was rich, and she was beautiful. He was hotheaded, middle class, and scarred in more ways than one.

"Mr. Vinetti," the nurse called from the doorway. "Dr. Van Zandt will see you now."

Nick clenched his jaw. He couldn't do this. Couldn't walk in there, look at Van Zandt's smiling mug, and not ache to coldcock him for running off to Guatemala and causing this whole mess in the first place.

It's not his fault, it's yours. You kissed Delaney when you knew she belonged to someone else. If you get your heart broken, you're responsible. No one else.

"Mr. Vinetti?" the nurse called again, and he followed her into the back offices.

Five minutes later, Nick was on the examination table, stuck in that damn yellow paper gown again, when Evan Van Zandt strode through the door. He looked tanned and lean and happy. Apparently, Guatemala agreed with him.

Van Zandt plopped down on the rolling stool and scooted over to the exam table. "How's the leg?"

"Improved."

"That's good to hear. Let's have a look." Van Zandt flipped up the corner of the paper gown and prodded Nick's knee. "How's that feel?"

"Doesn't hurt," he said. "A little sensitive to pressure, but no real pain."

"Excellent, excellent, and the swelling is gone. You really took my advice to heart. Nice progress." Van Zandt nodded, then rolled back over to the counter where he made some notations in Nick's chart.

Don't ask him about his trip. Don't ask about his up-

coming wedding. Don't ask about Delaney. Get your release form and get the hell out of here.

"How was Guatemala?" Nick asked.

"Oh, terrific, wonderful." Van Zandt put down his pen and an expression came over his face that could only be described as transformational. "I've never felt so alive. We were in the wilds of the jungle, doing primitive surgery on children, most of whom had never even seen Americans. We were changing lives. These kids had horrible deformities, and when we were finished with them they looked normal. Their families were so grateful. I've never experienced anything like it."

The way Van Zandt was looking now was the way Nick felt whenever he thought about Delaney. If Van Zandt preferred getting off on his God complex to being with Delaney, in Nick's opinion, he was seriously delusional.

"There was this one little fella . . ." And Van Zandt was off, regaling him with the specifics of his trip.

Nick shifted uncomfortably on the table and indulged Van Zandt's riff for several minutes. Finally, he couldn't take it any longer. "What does your fiancée think about all this?"

"Oh, well, you know, I just got in late last night and I was so exhausted, to tell you the truth, I haven't had a chance to see Delaney."

"You haven't seen her since you got back?" Nick couldn't believe it. If he'd been gone from Delaney for six weeks, he'd immediately run to her house, sweep her into his arms, and make love to her all night long.

"I know, it sounds odd, but she's busy preparing for the wedding, and I'm busy catching up with my patients, and we've known each other since we were little kids. It's not like the crazy, can't-get-enough-of-you breathless kind of love that you see in the movies. Ours is a quieter, more mature relationship."

"Don't you think you deserve the breathless kind of love?" Nick surprised himself by asking. It was all he could do to keep from smashing his fist into Van Zandt's clueless face.

Van Zandt looked startled. "But that's not love. That's just a romanticized version of lust."

"Have you ever felt it? That breathless variety."

Van Zandt moistened his lips. "Well, no."

"That's what I thought."

Their gazes met and Nick saw a flick of doubt in Van Zandt's eyes and it made him feel stronger. "Can I go back to work?"

"What?" Van Zandt blinked.

"You'll sign my release form? Let me get back to work?"

"Yes, sure." Van Zandt shook his head. "I've got the form right here. A man does need his work."

A few minutes later, after getting dressed and settling up his bill, Nick found himself on the sidewalk outside the building. The same place where Delaney had first thrown the tarp over him—the release form clutched in his hands.

Scrawled in Van Zandt's strangely legible hand were the words, *Mr. Vinetti may return to full active duty.*

He looked at the form and an arrow of sadness pierced straight into his heart. He'd gotten what he'd come here for. How come he didn't feel the least bit happy about it?

*　　*　　*

The packages arrived like swarms of locust. Everyone in Houston, it seemed, was eager to curry favor with the Cartwrights by sending Delaney and Evan wedding gifts.

Now that she no longer had Lucia's house to worry about and had closed her office until after the honeymoon, Delaney was stuck opening wedding presents and writing thank-you notes. Honey oversaw the operation like General Patton reviewing his troops. Delaney sat at the kitchen table, glumly wielding a calligraphy pen while her mother opened the day's arrivals.

"That's the sixth food processor you've gotten," she sniped. "Doesn't anyone follow the wedding registry? How difficult is it to go to Neiman's online and type in your name?"

"It's okay, Mother," Delaney said. "I don't mind exchanging them."

"I think it's just inconsiderate."

"You have to realize not everyone stresses over proper etiquette the way you do."

"Etiquette? I'm talking common courtesy."

Delaney sighed. "Just let it go."

"Excuse me?"

"Let it go, Mother. Stop trying to control everything."

"I'm not. I just think it's—"

"You are."

Honey drew herself up. "Well, what's wrong with trying to control things in order to have the best outcome?"

"It's my wedding. I should have some say in it."

Honey sat down beside her and reached out and took her hand. "I just want this to be the most perfect wedding ever. You deserve it. I can't tell you how much it means to me and your father. We love Evan so much. And you know how I've dreamed of this day. Especially since I never got to do this for Skylar."

Her mother's eyes misted with tears, and she fumbled in the pocket of her linen suit for a crisply starched and pressed monogrammed handkerchief. She dabbed carefully at the corners of her eyes, taking care not to smear her makeup. "How I wish your sister could be here for this celebration."

Seeing her normally composed mother tear up wrenched Delaney's stomach. In a flash, she was thrown back seventeen years to the day when they first heard the news that Skylar had been killed. It was the first time she'd ever seen her mother fracture, cracking like an egg, collapsing sobbing onto the floor.

Delaney had vowed then and there to do everything in her power to make everything all right. To do what it took to be the perfect child, to make her mother smile again. She packed down her anger, packed down her own desires, and devoted her life to being good. Her mother had taught her it was not okay to assert herself, and she'd lifted the lesson to virtuoso status.

The defense mechanism had served her well.

Following her mother's advice had transformed her from a chubby, unattractive, socially awkward child into a thin, pretty woman with lots of friends. But now, as she stood on the verge of marrying Evan and entering a life not of her own making, Delaney couldn't help feeling it had crippled her too.

All these years, what she longed to hear was that her presence mattered. That she was as important to her mother as Skylar had been.

But she'd never heard it.

Instead all she'd heard was that it was not okay to be who she really was, to assert herself.

Her mother put the handkerchief away and forced a bright smile. "Enough regrets. Since the other bakery we were using inconveniently went out of business on us, Sunshine Bakery graciously agreed to stand in at the last minute. They just e-mailed a picture of the cake they've specially designed for you based on the qualifications I sent them. I think you're going to love it." Honey reached inside the portfolio she carried stuffed with wedding details and passed her the computer printout. "The other bakery's going out of business turned out to be a blessing in disguise."

Disappointment stole over her as she studied it. Delaney had wanted a traditional wedding cake with lots of tiers and roses and beading made of frosting.

This three-tiered cake was simple, sleek, and smooth. While it was stylish, it had no personality, no heart.

"Isn't it perfect?" Honey looked at her expectantly. Delaney knew what she was supposed to say; she was supposed to echo "Perfect."

But her success with Lucia's house gave her courage. She moistened her lips and met Honey's eyes. "Mother, I'm not sure this is the right one for me."

"Of course it's the right one. I know you think the wedding cake is a bit plain, but darling, it's simple and elegant. All those colored flowers and excess layers and cream frosting you wanted looked so trailer park."

"I'm not speaking of the cake."

"No?" Honey tilted her head. "Is there something else you wanted to weigh in on?"

For years her mother had been able to quell her with

a single look that said, *I'm disappointed in you.* Delaney saw the awakening of that look now. One wrong word, and Honey's face would shift into full-blown disapproval.

"The wedding . . ." Delaney swallowed. *Come on. You can do this. Tell her the truth. Tell her you're not sure you're really ready to get married.*

"Yes?" Honey crossed her arms over her chest, warning her with her change in body language.

The childhood fear that her mother would no longer love her if she expressed an opinion dogged her.

Don't let her run over you. Say it.

"I'm not sure . . . August is so hot, and . . . while I love Evan to death, I'm not sure he's the right one for me."

"Young lady," Honey said and sternly pointed a finger at her. "Enough with the cold feet. It's time to grow up. You are *not* postponing this wedding again. The last two postponements have already cost your father in the neighborhood of twenty thousand dollars. He doesn't complain because he loves you, but I will not tolerate another postponement. You are marrying Evan Van Zandt on August fourth at three P.M., and I will not hear another word about it."

"It's time," Skylar told her that night, "to play your trump card. Mother might have issued an edict about your marriage to Evan, but you can still rattle her cage enough so she'll have to let you wear the veil."

Delaney, who had been growing more and more upset as the wedding plans progressed, was susceptible to Skylar's words. She climbed out of bed and as she made her way to the closet, she bumped against the dresser where she'd installed the hula doll Nick had given her.

The hula girl wildly shook her hips, and darn if she didn't appear to be winking.

Shake it up.

She flung open the closet door, took out both the consignment shop veil and the one her mother had bought for her at Bergdorf's. Using great care, she sat down at her vanity table, snapped the label from the Bergdorf's veil, and painstakingly stitched it into the hem of the veil Morag had tatted three hundred years ago.

As she worked, Delaney felt the power of the veil suffuse her. On this one thing, she would have her way. She might not get the chapel she'd hoped for or the wedding cake or the invitations or the dress or the groom of her choice, but by God she would wear Morag's veil. One way or the other she would have some small bit of magic in her life.

After she finished sewing the label in the veil, she crept downstairs to the closet where Honey kept the wrapping paper. She put the veil in a Bergdorf's box and then went back to her room to print off a note from her computer. Delaney racked her memory for the name of one of Honey's Philadelphia relatives and could only recall one. A great-aunt Maxie whom she'd never heard from nor met. Delaney had no idea if the woman was even still alive or not, but at this point she did not care. The note she typed read:

> To Delaney—so sorry I cannot attend the wedding. Please accept this veil in lieu of my presence. Wear it in good health—Your Great-Aunt Maxie.

Pleased with her handiwork, she wrapped the veil in elegant gift-wrapping paper, adorned it with a lavish bow, and sneaked back downstairs to put it with the stack of presents yet to be gone through sitting on the dining room table. She couldn't wait to see the look on her mother's face when Delaney opened that veil in the morning.

Honey could not believe Delaney was trying to back out of the wedding a third time. Children could be so ungrateful. No matter how much you did for them, it never seemed to be enough. They criticized and complained and generally behaved in a disagreeable manner.

She was going to take the high moral ground and forgive her daughter. Cold feet was an unpleasant affliction. Not that she could empathize. Marrying James Robert had been the best thing that had ever happened to her. She'd never had second thoughts. Even years later, when he'd developed a drinking problem. She knew you had to take the good with the bad.

Delaney was just nervous. That was all. Everything would be fine as long as Honey did not allow her to consider postponing as an option. This wedding was happening. Honey would not be embarrassed again.

"Mother," Delaney told her at breakfast, "I want to apologize for my behavior yesterday. You were right and I was wrong."

Honey smiled. There now. That was the daughter she knew and loved. "It's all right, darling. I really do understand that this is a stressful time for you."

"Will you help me go through the gifts that arrived

since yesterday? I want to keep abreast of the thank-you notes."

"Absolutely." Honey beamed. Yes, this was what she'd been wanting from Delaney. Full participation in the process. Honey retrieved the embossed stationery she'd had printed up just for the wedding and her Mont Blanc pen and joined her daughter in the dining room.

The packages that had arrived in the previous day's afternoon deliveries were stacked beside the boxes they'd already opened and gone through. Honey pulled out her list and settled at the table to write down who had given what while Delaney unwrapped the packages. She brought her orange juice with her from the breakfast table. It rested on a coaster to her left.

"Oh," Delaney said after she'd pulled the wrapping paper off the first gift. "It's in a Bergdorf's box."

"Who's it from?" Honey asked, picking up her glass of orange juice for a sip.

"I don't know. Let me see if there's a card in the box." Delaney lifted the lid and took out a wedding veil.

No, not just a wedding veil, but that hideous consignment shop wedding veil Honey had found under Delaney's bed. The one she'd hidden in her own closet.

She felt the blood drain from her face. What was going on here?

"Isn't it beautiful? And it has a designer label," Delaney said, shooting Honey a cool, calculated gaze.

"Who . . . sent it?"

"There's a note right here. 'To Delaney—so sorry I cannot attend the wedding. Please accept this veil in lieu of my presence. Wear it in good health—Your Great-Aunt Maxie.'"

Maxie. The name she'd never expected to hear again.

All the air left Honey's lungs. The glass of orange juice slipped from her hand and crashed to the tile, splattering her white slacks like a Jackson Pollock painting.

"Goodness, Mother, are you okay?"

Honey met her daughter's gaze, and she couldn't believe the cunning expression she saw there. It was as if Delaney was channeling Skylar.

"Fine," she managed to whisper. What was going on?

"Wasn't that sweet of Great-aunt Maxie?" Delaney clutched the veil to her chest. "I simply have to wear this veil at the wedding. I'm sure you won't mind if we return the veil you bought me. Right, Mother?"

"Right," Honey croaked.

And that's when she realized it was the beginning of the end of her life as she knew it.

On Thursday evening, at the Orchid Villa retirement community, Trudie and Lucia threw Delaney a bachelorette party.

Still flying high on her victory with the wedding veil, Delaney brought it with her to the party.

Everyone oohed and aahed over it as they passed it around. Then Tish told them about how wishing on the veil was supposed to make the deepest desires of your heart come true. Then, of course, everyone wanted to try it on and make a wish. As if it were a birthday cake or a falling star or a wishing well.

Delaney cringed as it was passed from head to head. "Please, you guys, I promised the lady I bought it from that I wouldn't wish on the veil."

"You promised you wouldn't wish on the veil," Jillian

pointed out, just after she wished to win an important court case she was in serious danger of losing. "We didn't."

Delaney wrung her hands. "It still feels wrong."

"You don't seriously believe in it?" Tish said and then wished to get out of debt, before passing the veil to Rachael.

"The issue isn't whether I believe in it or not, but the fact that I promised Claire Kelley."

"But like Jillian said, that was your promise, not ours." Rachael settled the veil on her head.

"*Et tu*, Rachael?"

Rachael shrugged. "I wish for a grand romance."

"It's not Aladdin's lamp, you guys."

"We know. We're just having fun." Trudie accepted the veil from Rachael. "I wish to find a red-hot stud in my bed," she said, then passed it to Gina, who wished to get pregnant.

That brought an "aah" from everyone assembled.

Everyone except Lucia.

Lucia met Delaney's eyes. She was the only one who appreciated the power of the veil. When Gina passed the veil to her, Lucia said, "I wish you would all respect Delaney's wishes."

She got up and said to Delaney, "I'm just going to put this in Trudie's bedroom so no one else is tempted to monkey with fate. Don't forget it when you leave."

Delaney smiled gratefully at Lucia.

"Okay," Trudie said, rubbing her palms briskly together. "Who's up for Jell-O shooters?"

"I'm in," Tish said.

"Me too," Jillian chimed in.

"None for me." Gina patted her flat belly. "Chuck and I are working on giving the twins a little sister."

"I'm the designated driver," Rachael explained. "I'll have to pass as well."

"Delaney?" Trudie coaxed. "It's your next to last night as a free woman. Gotta shake things up and cut loose."

"No Jell-O shooters," Lucia said, coming back from the bedroom. "Until everyone has some food in their stomachs. There's Stromboli in the kitchen."

They all crammed into the kitchen, and soon they were laughing and talking and eating and drinking and doing Jell-O shooters and telling worst-date horror stories.

"I went out with a guy who, instead of going in for a good-night kiss, licked my face." Jillian shuddered.

"Ugh!" everyone shouted in unison.

"A guy took me to the movies, and when I came back from getting popcorn, he was necking with the woman sitting across the aisle from us," Gina said.

"What a pig." Rachael shook her head.

"Sex addict," Jillian diagnosed.

"Anyone wanna talk brushes with celebrities?" Trudie asked.

Lucia sighed. "Trudie had sex with Frank Sinatra when she was eighteen, and she's just dying to tell the story to a fresh audience."

"No kidding?" the younger women exclaimed. "Tell us, tell us. What was old Blue Eyes like in bed?"

"First let's set the stage. Anyone for poker?"

Five minutes later they had Sinatra on the stereo. Trudie was dealing Texas Hold 'Em, and Tish was passing around a bottle of peppermint schnapps because they'd run out of Jell-O shooters. Everyone seemed to be having a great time.

In Delaney's estimation, it was a pretty cool bache- lorette party and she was glad no one had hired a male stripper. That would have been so embarrassing.

But then halfway through the game, there was a knock at the door. "Get that for me, will you, Jillian?" Trudie asked.

Jillian pushed back from the kitchen table just as an- other knock sounded.

"Houston PD," came a rough, masculine voice. "Open up in the name of the law."

Delaney's heart leaped.

And when Jillian opened the door to reveal a very buff masked man in a police uniform, for one crazy second Delaney thought it might be Nick.

The minute he walked over the threshold, her hopes were shattered. "We've had reports of disturbing the peace."

"Please, Officer Goodbody," Trudie said. "Don't ar- rest us. We're having a bachelorette party."

"Well, why didn't you say so?"

In an instant someone killed Sinatra and put on strip- per music and Officer Goodbody whipped off his Velcro pants. "Who's the bride-to-be?"

Delaney good-naturedly endured the striptease and to please her friends pretended to like it. But the thing was, the fake cop made her think about the real cop in her life.

Nick's not in your life.

Her heart hit the floor. Sadness filled her, and she had to force herself to keep smiling as Officer Goodbody waggled his groove thing. She missed Nick so much.

What would it be like? she wondered. If it was Nick she was going to meet at River Oaks Methodist Church on Saturday afternoon instead of Evan?

Inside her head, wistful longing warred with loyal duty. Sexual chemistry duked it out with steadfast stability. Desire versus dignity.

She couldn't take it anymore. "Excuse me," Delaney said, got up from the table, and left the room, leaving Officer Goodbody looking surprised.

"Hey, what gives with her?" he asked. "Don't she wanna see the finale?"

"You can show us," Delaney heard Jillian say as she hurried into Trudie's bedroom, looking for solitude so she could collect her thoughts.

The minute she walked into the room, she saw the veil stretched out on Trudie's bed, looking more magical than ever.

Wish on me, it whispered to her. *Make the deepest wish of your soul come true.*

Delaney paced Trudie's small bedroom, casting frequent glances at the veil.

You can't wish on the veil. You promised Claire Kelley.

But it was a promise Delaney couldn't keep. The veil was her only way out. The single salvation left to her. She knew no other way to get out of the marriage that should have been so perfect and yet loomed like a total disaster. She had to rely on the magic of the veil. She had to believe.

With trembling hands, Delaney put the veil on her head.

"I wish . . . ," she whispered, drawing in a deep breath, inhaling courage. "I wish to get out of this marriage."

Immediately a strange tingling spread over her scalp and her entire body grew hot.

She felt it once more, that wavery suspension of time that she'd experienced the first time she'd touched the veil and she'd had the vision.

The one where she was marrying Nick.

She saw it again. In minute detail.

Dizziness spun her head. She had to sit down hard on the edge of Trudie's bed to keep from falling.

"I wish to get out of this marriage," she said again, stronger, more certain this time.

"Do you really want to get out of it?" a voice asked.

Delaney's eyes flew open and she saw Trudie standing with her back pressed against the closed door.

"Yes."

"So why don't you just call it off?"

"I can't. Evan is so good. I've known him since we were kids, and I don't want to lose his friendship. Plus there's my mother. She'll be crushed. And the money my father has spent." Delaney shook her head.

"It's better than spending a lifetime married to a man you don't love."

"I don't know how to tell them so they'll hear me. No one really listens to me." *Except for Nick,* she thought. "I've spent most of my life letting people push me around, bending to their will, going with the flow to avoid confrontation. I can't stand the thought of hurting someone's feelings to their face."

"Too bad you don't have a Leo to come rescue you from the altar the way Lucia did."

"Yeah," Delaney echoed. She could wish all she wanted, but she knew Nick wouldn't come save her. He had too much integrity to steal another man's wife. "Too bad."

"You could hire someone to kidnap you."

Delaney looked up. Possibilities raced through her. If she hired someone to kidnap her from the wedding, then her family would have to listen to her. It was dramatic. It was bold. And Delaney saw it as her only way out.

"Remember my nephew Louie?" Trudie said. "You met him when you staged my house."

Louie had been a little rough-looking, with lots of piercings and tattoos, but he'd seemed like a nice enough guy. "Yes."

"For the right price, he'll kidnap you."

Chapter 16

Someone was beating on his front door.

Nick pulled himself from slumber, squinted at the clock on his bedside table, and groaned. Who in the hell had the audacity to show up on his doorstep at three o'clock in the morning? One of his brothers? A cousin?

Growling his displeasure, Nick threw off the covers.

"Coming, coming," he called out, searching in his closet for the bathrobe he hardly ever had the need to wear. Even though his knee was almost completely healed now, he didn't want to push it and move too quickly too soon. "Hold your horses."

He ambled to the living room, turned on the front porch light, and looked through the peephole to find Trudie Klausman, dressed like a twenty-year-old party girl in a belly-baring tank top and a short skirt that showed off her wrinkled knees and with sparkle glitter on her face, swaying in the night air. At first, he thought something must have happened to his nana.

Terrified, Nick yanked open the door. He stared Trudie in the eyes and realized she'd been drinking.

Horror squeezed his heart as another thought occurred to him. Holy shit, what if Trudie was here for some kind of perverted, middle-of-the-night, Mrs. Robinson booty call?

Nick gulped. "Um, hello, Mrs. Klausman."

"Nicky, we've got an emergency situation on our hands." She rushed into his apartment.

Dear God in heaven, she *was* here for a booty call.

"Emergency?" The word came out high and squeaky, the way it did when he was thirteen and his voice was changing.

She wrapped her hand around his wrist and Nick stopped breathing. "I've got a very dire problem, and you're the only one who can solve it for me."

Nick had had a few booty calls in his life, but none he'd ever had to turn down before. He didn't know how to go about deflecting his grandmother's best friend without hurting her feelings.

"Mrs. Klausman . . . I . . . ," he stuttered. "I'm very flattered, but . . but . . ."

Trudie gave him an odd look and quickly let go of his hand. "Oh, my God, you thought I came here for a booty call."

"No, no."

"Don't lie." She shook her finger under his nose. "And just because you are one handsome devil doesn't give you the right to assume that just because I'm an ex–Vegas showgirl and that I had a little too much to drink and I'm wearing something sexy, that I would want to have sex with you. You're far too young for me, and besides, your grandmother is my best friend. What do you take me for? A complete hussy?"

Mortified, he ducked his head. "Trudie, I'm truly sorry."

"If Delaney didn't need your help, I'd turn around and walk right out of here."

Nick's head shot up. "Delaney needs help?"

"I've done something kinda illegal and I'm having second thoughts, but Delaney was so desperate to get out of this wedding tomorrow, she asked me to hire my nephew, Louie, to kidnap her from the chapel."

Delaney wanted out of her marriage to Evan Van Zandt? Hope was like a gift, sprung in his chest, resurrecting the feelings he'd tried so hard to bury. "You're kidding."

"Do I look like I'm kidding?" Trudie glared and sank her hands on her hips.

No, she did not.

"Delaney's planning on standing Evan up at the altar?"

"In the most dramatic way possible. Poor girl, she's such a people-pleaser. Can't bear to hurt her fiancé's feelings, can't sum up the courage to face her overbearing mother. She feels backed into a corner with no way out. That's why I offered to contact Louie for her. She's such a good-hearted person, but she's never learned to stand up for herself."

"She's stood up to me a few times," Nick said, recalling the arguments they'd had. The time she flipped him the bird.

"Which is why you're so good for her. You inspire her to be more. You let her speak her mind and don't squelch her. You don't put her in a box or up on a pedestal. You actually like it when she's not perfect. You give her the freedom to be herself. You're exactly what she needs."

"Did you contact Louie already?"

"Yes."

"Has money exchanged hands?" Had a crime already occurred?

"I don't know. Delaney was on her way to meet him when I left her."

Nick blew out a breath and shoved a hand through his hair.

If what Trudie said was true and Delaney wanted out of the marriage so badly that she'd hired Trudie's nephew to kidnap her from the wedding, it meant she didn't have the courage to tell Evan the truth.

It must also mean she finally recognized platonic love was not enough to sustain a marriage.

While he admired Delaney for not going through with the wedding when she knew it was wrong, he was disappointed that she was taking the easy way out. And he wasn't going to let her get away with it. He was going to make her face up to her feelings.

"Call up your nephew," Nick told Trudie. "Tell him his services are no longer required."

"But if Louie doesn't kidnap Delaney from the chapel, she'll end up married to Evan. And you of all people should know how miserable it is to be married to the wrong one."

"I'll handle it. Just call off the kidnapping."

"Oh," Trudie exclaimed, her eyes flashing with excitement. "Are you going to do for Delaney what your grampa Leo did for Lucia? Are you going to whisk her away and save her from marrying the wrong man?"

"No," Nick growled. "She's spent most of her life looking for a magical solution to her problems. Rescuing is not what she needs. What I'm going to do is be there to make sure that Delaney saves herself."

The members of the wedding party and their families gathered outside the River Oaks Methodist Church for the wedding rehearsal. Delaney had driven over with her parents, and she regretted the decision. Her mother's constant nit-picking of every little detail had given her a headache.

"Don't worry, it'll be over soon." Evan smiled and squeezed her hand. "Your mother means well."

"I've got to get something for this headache," she said. "I think there's some ibuprofen in the glove compartment of the Caddy. Go on in, I'll be right behind you."

Head throbbing, Delaney headed back out to the parking lot, angling for her mother's Cadillac. It wasn't just her mother's nit-picking that had given her the headache, and she knew it. Guilt was the thing pounding through her veins. She didn't want to go through with this wedding, but she didn't have the courage to tell Evan to his face. She had written him a long note, explaining how she felt and begging his forgiveness. She still hadn't figured out how to handle her mother.

Delaney thought about all the people she was going to hurt and felt physically ill.

She plunked down in the front passenger seat of the Caddy. The humidity plastered her panty hose to her legs. She wouldn't have worn them, but her mother in-

sisted. Apparently in Honey's book it was gauche to go
bare-legged to a wedding rehearsal.

After resting a moment to let the nausea subside, she
popped open the glove compartment and rummaged
around until she found the ibuprofen. She pulled the bottle out, and a crumpled-up note fell out with it.

What was this?

Delaney unfolded the note, read what was written
there in stark black block letters.

She let out a gasp and plastered her hand over her
mouth. Her mother had been lying. At last, she knew
the reason her mother had gone to meet the patch-eyed
woman at the amusement park on Galveston Island.

Honey Montgomery Cartwright was being blackmailed.

What she didn't know was why.

"Invitation, sir." The security guard posted outside the
River Oaks Methodist Church held out his palm and
waited expectantly for Nick to paper it with a wedding
invitation.

But he didn't have one.

"No invite?" The guard arched an eyebrow.

"No."

"Sorry." The guard moved to block the door. "Without
an invitation you don't get in."

A few people were still trickling in from the parking
lot, but they were rushing as if late, flashing their invitations to the security guard, then slipping inside through
the heavy wooden door. The sun beat down hot, pooling
sweat under the collar of the only suit Nick owned. The
suit he'd bought for his grandfather's funeral.

"You don't understand," Nick said. "It's imperative I get in. The bride is about to make a huge mistake."

"If you ask me, anyone who gets married is making a huge mistake." The guard shook his head. "Can't go in."

The sounds of the wedding march began. He had to get in there before it was too late. Louie wouldn't be showing up to kidnap Delaney as she expected, and if Nick wasn't there to intervene, he feared she'd just go ahead with the ceremony.

"I have to get in there."

"You want me to call the cops?"

"I am the cops."

"Prove it."

Grinding his teeth in frustration, Nick fumbled in his pocket for his badge and shoved it in the guy's face. "Now get the hell out of my way."

"Jeez, fella, why didn't you just say you were a cop in the first place?" the guard grumbled and stepped aside.

Nick tore into the building.

The contrast from the bright sunlight to the darkened interior of the church had him blinking. Disoriented, he stood in the entryway while his eyes adjusted.

Flowers invaded the foyer, filling his nose with their fresh summer scent. He heard the rustling of clothes, the muted coughs of the spectators, and the wedding march. The song was already half over.

The doors leading into the chapel were thrown wide. He hurried toward them and saw Delaney on the arm of a man he presumed was her father, moving toward the altar.

Instinct had him wanting to shout her name, but he

would wait for the right moment. When the minister asked if there were any objections, that's when he would say his peace.

He looked around for a place to sit, but he was out of luck. The chapel was crammed to the rafters. This shindig was costing her father a boatload of money. Boy, was he going to be upset when everything blew up in his face.

But probably not as upset as Evan Van Zandt was going to be. Nick actually felt sorry for him. He knew what it was like, getting dumped by the woman you loved.

Heart clogging his throat, Nick went to stand against the back wall, watching the proceedings with a surreal feeling of detached anxiety. It was as if he were in a dream, knowing he was dreaming but unable to wake up. What if, when the time came, he shouted out his objection but no one heard him?

Goose bumps broke out on his arms. He was too far away. He needed to move closer. Nick started creeping around the back of the church, picking his way past the other attendees who'd been too late to find a seat, all the while craning his neck to follow what was going on up at the altar.

Delaney looked absolutely, totally stunning in that white dress and wedding veil.

Nick stared at the veil. When she walked, it looked as if a hundred white butterflies were fluttering up around her. She looked like magic, pure and perfect. And he wanted her with the same seven-year-old fervency he had wanted his mother not to die. If he didn't stop her from marrying Van Zandt, he feared his heart would never, ever recover.

Delaney's father put her hand in Van Zandt's and stepped back to take a seat in the front row.

Nick stopped making his way around the side of the packed pews, every muscle in his body tensed as he heard the portly minister say, "Dearly beloved . . ."

But that was as far as the man got.

A loud noise, like someone tripping over tin cans stacked high behind the exit door to the left of the altar, drew everyone's attention in that direction.

The minister paused.

The exit door flew open and a man dressed in black jeans, a long-sleeved black button-down shirt, black boots, and a black ski mask came tumbling out. He looked as out of place as a chunk of charcoal in a basket of marshmallows.

The guests heaved a collective gasp.

Anger shook him. Dammit. Trudie must have forgotten to cancel her nephew, Louie. Either that or she hadn't trusted Nick to get Delaney out of this mess of her own making. That was a fine state of affairs. Now what was he going to do?

Before Nick had time to formulate a plan, Louie was at the altar waving a gun around. He hoped like hell it was a prop gun, because if it wasn't, whenever he got his hands on Louie he was going to make him sorry he ever agreed to this fake kidnapping.

Poor Van Zandt looked scared out of his wits. He was trembling and blinking and just standing there impotently letting it all play out. If Nick had been up there, he would have charged the guy.

So charge him anyway. Put a stop to this nonsense.

Nick ran.

But some woman had her purse in the aisle and he tripped over it. His knee crumbled. He cursed but immediately got back up.

Louie was already dragging Delaney out the exit. The crowd was on their feet, everyone following after them.

The mob bottlenecked at the exit door, and Nick knew it was time for another plan. Ignoring the pain shooting through his knee, he did an about-face and headed back in the direction he'd come, dodging the guests surging forward.

Somehow, he made it out to his pickup just in time to spy a white delivery van careening out of the parking lot with Louie at the wheel.

Nick started his engine, popped the clutch into gear, and sped off after them.

The nondescript white delivery van roared from the church parking lot. Jim Bob Cartwright stared after it, his mind numb. "Someone call 911. My daughter's been kidnapped!" he intended to shout to the clump of tuxedoed crowd gawking at him, but his throat squeezed so tight he could not speak.

Honey wrapped her hand around his wrist. "We've got to get out of here, James Robert. Right now."

"No, no," he gasped and clung to her arm. "Must call police. FBI. Delaney's been kidnapped."

Honey lowered her voice. "Listen to me. We can't call in the authorities."

Jim Bob stared at her, uncomprehending. "What?"

"We can't call the police."

Was his wife afraid of public embarrassment? The vein at his forehead throbbed suddenly, violently. He let go of her, stepped back, and fisted his hands. Was Honey actually worried about how this was going to reflect on her? Was she more concerned about appearances than her daughter's safety?

Disgust sickened his stomach. "Why in the hell not?"

"Please, James Robert." Her eyes beseeched him. It had been a very long time since he'd seen her this vulnerable, and it scared him. "Just take me home."

"No, no. We have to call the authorities. Someone just kidnapped our daughter."

"We *can't*." Fear drew her mouth tight, creased the fine wrinkles around her eyes. She looked haunted, hunted.

"What is it, Honey? What's wrong?"

"I know who took Delaney."

He watched her—confused, nervous, heart pounding. Beneath his tuxedo, sweat plastered his shirt to his back.

Honey hitched in a fragile breath that sounded strangely like the frantic beat of hummingbird wings. "And I know why she took her. She took her because of me."

"She? It was a man who kidnapped Delaney."

"Hired thug."

"What?"

Honey swayed and Jim Bob was afraid she would collapse. Instinctively, he circled his arm around her waist. "Are you all right?"

"This heat. Get me out of here."

"We have to call the cops," he said. "I'm going to call the cops."

"No." Her voice was soft, yet shrill.

He ignored her protest, turned to the crowd around them. The longer they waited, the farther Delaney got from them. "Does anyone have a cell phone I can use?"

A half dozen people thrust cell phones at him, but before Jim Bob could grab one, Honey tugged him in the direction of their car, her fingernails digging into his skin.

He balked, digging his heels into the pavement.

"James Robert," she said through gritted teeth, "don't buck me on this."

He studied her face, regal, proud, well preserved yet suddenly looking every bit of her fifty-three years. This was the first time in years he'd seen her looking so unguarded, so full of pain and hunger and desperation. She was a mystery to him. Always had been and he feared she always would be.

"I'm tired of tiptoeing around you, Honey," he growled. "Tired of pretending we don't have a big problem with our marriage. Tired of kowtowing and trying to please you. It's impossible. Nothing pleases you."

"Stop," she hissed, shifting her gaze to the gawking crowd gathered behind them.

"Why? Afraid of a little public embarrassment? Is that it? You'd rather save face than save your daughter?"

Honey's cheeks blanched so pale Jim Bob thought she might faint. He felt like an utter shit and rushed to slide his arm around her once more.

His wife rested her head against his shoulder, pressed

her lips against his ear, and whispered hoarsely, "We can't call the cops because I'm being blackmailed."

"You're not Trudie's nephew," Delaney exclaimed to the man who'd snatched her from the chapel.

"Surprise, surprise."

"Where's Louie?"

"I dunno. Who's Louie?"

"You're not working for Trudie?"

"No."

"I think you've abducted the wrong bride."

"No, I haven't." He pulled a piece of paper from his front pocket. "Delaney Lynn Cartwright. That's you, right?"

"Pull this van over right now and let me out of here," she commanded in her best imitation of her mother.

"Sorry." He shook his head, thick with dark, shaggy hair. "No can do."

"You're kidnapping me for real? This isn't some prank?"

He eyed her in the rearview mirror. "What do you think?"

How had this happened? What was going on? "Who in the hell are you?"

"There's no need for you to know my name."

"So what am I supposed to call you? Here, kidnapper, kidnapper, kidnapper?"

He laughed. "Cute, but it's not going to work. You ain't getting my name."

"Maybe I'll just call you Little Dick," she said, feeling a million miles away from her old self. In spite of being kidnapped, she was feeling spunky and relieved.

This guy didn't know her. She could say anything. Be anyone. It was a surprisingly freeing thought.

"Hey!" he snapped. "Five and a half inches is average-sized!"

"Little Dick."

"Stop saying that."

"Why? What are you going to do? Kill me?"

"Not if you don't give me a good reason. Word to the wise, calling me Little Dick is bordering on a good reason."

"You're right," she said. "Excuse me. My bad manners."

How ridiculous! Here she was, apologizing to a kidnapper. It took a lot to totally shake off a lifetime of indoctrination in proper etiquette. Although, she doubted Emily Post had penned anything on kidnapping protocol.

"Where are you taking me?"

"It's a surprise."

"I don't like surprises."

"Too bad."

"Remove these handcuffs," she demanded and then added, "Please."

"Nope."

"They're hurting my wrists."

"You'll live, princess."

"Let me go. I'll pay you."

He didn't answer.

"I have money."

"It's not just about that."

"No? What else is it about then?"

"Not my place to tell you."

"Are you an enemy of my father? Is this some business deal gone awry?"

"Nope." He sounded too damn casual. "Now be a good girl and just sit back and relax."

Oh, God, this guy really was kidnapping her for real. What were the odds of someone plotting to kidnap her on her wedding day? The exact same day she'd already hired someone to kidnap her? Impossibly high and suspiciously coincidental.

Suddenly the kidnapper sped up and Delaney was thrown backward onto the floorboards again. Real terror struck her then. Hard and coppery-tasting.

"What is it? What's going on?"

"Some asshole is chasing us."

"Where?" Delaney twisted around and tried to peer out the back of the van, but a dirty window and the lace veil blocked her view. She'd wished on it for a way out of her impending marriage and she'd gotten her wish, but certainly not in the way she had expected.

What was it Claire Kelley had said? You get your most heartfelt wish, not necessarily the thing you wished for most. Maybe this was cosmic punishment for wishing on the veil when she'd promised Claire she wouldn't.

She crawled to the back of the van with an unformed plan for escape, her handcuffed wrists held out in front to brace herself in case she fell over again. The progress was slow because the train of her dress kept wadding up underneath her. She would shuffle forward a bit, stop, pull the nest of collected material out from under her knees, and shuffle forward again. Just as she reached the back window, the nut job behind the wheel swerved crazily and she went down, weeble-wobbling into the side of the van.

"Drive like a human being," she hollered. "My parents won't pay you a single dime if I'm dead."

The word "dead" echoed in the empty confines of the van, and for the first time the true reality of the situation struck Delaney.

"He's trying to cut me off," the kidnapper whined.

Hope vaulted into her chest. Was it someone from the wedding party out to save her? Could it be her daddy? Was it Evan? Oh, dear, how could she ever look her fiancé in the eyes again once he learned she'd hired someone to kidnap her? "Who's trying to cut you off?"

"Some son of a bitch in a red Ford pickup truck. Friend of yours?"

That tenuous hope blossomed into full-blown optimistic joy. Her heart sang.

Nick!

But how could it be Nick? He hadn't been invited to the wedding. He didn't even know where it was being held.

He's a cop, he could figure it out.

But why would Nick be after her?

Her mind spun a crazy fantasy worthy of *The Graduate*. Nick had come to rescue her from an ill-conceived wedding in the tradition of Leo and Lucia. Only to discover she'd already hired Louie to take her hostage. Except that had gone haywire, and now she was being spirited away by some unknown kidnapper. What the hell kind of wish-fulfilling magic threads was the veil made out of?

She had to get a look out that window and see if it was

indeed Nick. Delaney finally made it over to the back window for a peek outside just as the red pickup truck pulled into the left lane beside the delivery van. All she could see was the bumper.

Bummer.

"The red truck," she called to the driver, "can you see the dashboard?"

"Lady, it's taking all my concentration to keep us from getting run off the road."

"Look in your side-view mirror. Can you tell if there's a hula girl shimmying away on his dashboard?"

"I can't tell. Hold on. I see something. Yep, there's a hula girl shaking it up on his dashboard. Mean something to you?"

Hello, it was her Nick! Shaking things up.

Her insides knotted with emotion. She felt giddy and scared and happy and surprised and so many other things she couldn't even name them all.

The right front and back tires of the van veered off the road and rattled along the shoulder. Delaney ended up toppling over again. At this rate, she might as well stay on the floor until Nick got her out of this mess.

The van was making ominous noises, tires thrumming against the uneven asphalt. The smell of tar melting hotly in the August sun burned her nose. Delaney's mouth tasted of dry anxiety. Her knees and elbows stung from carpet burn. The driver was twisting the van to and fro, trying to outrun Nick.

Fear spun her head. Her heart slammed her blood through her veins as rapidly as a six-piston pump.

"This bastard's crazy!" The driver accelerated. "Hang

on, I'm gonna cut across the freeway, and it ain't gonna be pretty."

The van swerved dramatically. Car horns blared. Tires squealed. Delaney shrieked before the van ever slammed the concrete median separating the southbound lane from the northbound lane.

The impact jarred her teeth as they bumped over the barrier. Her heart stilled suddenly and her chest felt tense and cold. She was going to die like this. Handcuffed. Wearing an outrageously overpriced wedding dress that she'd chosen for her wedding to a man she didn't love in the right way, while she secretly longed for another man. A different man.

Her heart stirred restlessly. The very man who was risking his life to come after her. Closing her eyes, she prayed Nick would have sense enough not to follow them over the median.

"He's still coming after us."

No, Nick, no, she thought, but could not contain her elation. He was coming after her. No concrete median or big-city traffic was going to stop her brave, daring cop.

"Holy shit!"

"What, what?" Delaney's eyes flew open. She struggled toward the back window again, desperate to see what was happening. An eighteen-wheeler's horn blared. Brakes screamed.

"Your boyfriend in the red pickup . . . holy shit . . ."

"What is it, what is it?" she cried.

But the loud noise of metal smacking metal said it all.

"He just wiped out."

Chapter 17

After an SUV sideswiped his bumper, Nick battled physics to keep the pickup truck on the road. He squeezed the steering wheel in a death grip and his right leg quivered from the adrenaline rush and quick tromping from the brake to the gas pedal.

Cars swerved, drivers flipped him off. He spied a couple of people with shocked expressions on their faces, grabbing their cell phones, no doubt phoning 911.

Good. He could use all the help he could get.

In the meantime, he was hell-bent on catching up with the bastard in the white van who'd taken off with Delaney before the vehicle disappeared from Nick's sight. His heart was willing; his pickup truck, however, was made of weaker stuff. The tires shimmied as he turned on his blinker and guided the clattering vehicle into the middle lane. His muffler had been knocked loose in the impact, but he had no time to worry about it.

Delaney needed him.

His pulse pumped hard and fast. Who had taken her hostage and why?

Why? Well, her father was one of the richest men in Houston. That was motive enough.

Nick's cop mind wasn't buying it. The kidnapping was too much of a coincidence, what with Delaney already hiring her own abductor. There had to be another connection, something important that he was missing.

But he couldn't think. His emotions were strangling him, pushing him forward, stamping out caution and common sense. He was ready to fight. To battle anyone who got in his way. He was getting Delaney back.

He tromped on the accelerator, anxious to close the widening gap between him and the white van. In the distance, he heard the sound of sirens. He didn't slow down. Nothing was going to keep him from his woman.

His woman?

What the hell was that?

Nick's chest tightened. Okay, he was ready to admit it. He felt possessive of Delaney.

Up ahead, the van took the exit ramp. Nick tried to coax more power from the pickup, pushing the gas pedal to the floor, but nothing doing. The engine rumbled ominously. Nick swore.

He changed lanes, swerving around a slow-moving Caddy, and followed the van off the freeway.

There was a traffic signal up ahead turning from yellow to red. The van never slowed, just sailed right through the intersection, accompanied by a cacophony of honking horns.

"Dammit, Delaney," he muttered, cursing because he

knew no other way to deal with the intensity of his feelings. "Hang in there, babe, I'm coming, I'm coming."

But just as he declared it, the pickup sputtered and died right in the middle of the crossroads.

Honey made James Robert take her home before she would tell him the truth. But even once they were there, she realized it was the hardest thing she would ever have to admit. She had no idea how to explain to her husband that the woman he'd been sleeping beside for thirty-four years had never really existed. That she'd been living a lie, that their marriage was a sham.

They'd sent the maid home and turned off the ringer on the phone. The neon numbers on the answering machine blinked wildly. Twenty-seven messages. Everyone wanting to know what had happened to Delaney. Honey wondered if any of the calls were from Evan, but she didn't have the energy to think about him. She had enough problems on her hands. Evan and the Van Zandts would just have to wait.

James Robert sat on the leather sofa in the living room while Honey paced in front of him, still wearing her stiff, uncomfortable mother-of-the-bride dress and high heels. *Tap, tap, tap,* went her shoes as she moved back and forth, top teeth sunk into her bottom lip as she tried to decide how to begin.

"Just tell me," James Robert said. "Why are you being blackmailed?"

Honey cleared her throat and glanced over at him. He looked at her with haunted eyes, pleading for her to deny everything. But her past had finally caught up with her. It was time for the truth. He deserved the truth. Even if

afterward he told her he wanted a divorce. That he never
wanted to see her again.

Her heart cleaved. This was a mess of her own making and she knew it. The rubber had smacked up against
the road. Time for the truth.

"I'm not who you think I am," she said at last.

James Robert blinked. "I don't get it."

"I'm not Honey Montgomery."

"What are you talking about?"

Fear of losing everything in the world she loved ce-
mented her throat. She shook her head. "I . . . I . . ."

"If you're not Honey Montgomery, who are you?"

She took a deep breath and spoke the name she hadn't
said aloud in over thirty years. "My real name is Fayrene
Doggett."

"I don't understand. How? Why?"

Honey sat down across from him, hands clasped in
her lap, shoulders razor-straight the way she'd taught
herself to sit. She wanted to duck her head to look away,
but that wasn't her style. She might be a liar and a fraud,
but she wasn't a coward.

James Robert's eyes searched hers. He looked bewildered, confused, but not judgmental or angry. That
would change. When he learned how she had deceived
him, discovered who she really was deep inside.

"Let me get this straight. You're not in the social registry? You're not a Philadelphia blue blood?"

"No."

He didn't say a word—just studied her intently, as if
she were some alien pod person who'd kidnapped his
wife. In a way, she was. Honey wished he'd yell at her or

curse or slam his fist into the expensive coffee table imported from Germany. But he did not.

The lie, her admission, his shock, her betrayal, cohered into a thick, dark wall of emotion and tension, vibrated the bleak air between them.

Honey spied the slightest quiver in his hands and her own body quaked in response.

The long moment of silence stretched between them. Sweat beaded on Honey's upper lip in spite of the air-conditioning cooling their vast home to a balmy seventy-five degrees. She noticed how the lines around her husband's eyes had deepened with the years. How the loss of their daughter had etched pain into his face. She wanted to reach out to stroke his cheek, but she didn't dare. She didn't deserve to touch him. Not after what she'd done.

"Well?" James Robert prompted. "Just who the fuck are you, Fayrene Doggett?"

His rough language made her cringe, but she reveled in it. Ah, there it was. The anger. The emotion that meant he still cared, that he hadn't given up on her completely. "I was born the daughter of carnival workers," she began, and it hurt so much to say those words she thought her lips must have cracked.

"Carnies?"

"Yes," she whispered.

James Robert snorted and dragged a palm down his face. "That explains your violent hatred of carnivals. I always wondered about it."

His response seemed so incongruous to Honey that she almost laughed. Except nothing was funny.

"So how did you get from there to here?" he asked,

anger growing in his eyes. A chill chased over her, raised goose bumps on her arms.

"We moved in caravans from town to town. It was a rough life. My parents were essentially grifters, con artists. I was forced to pickpocket and beg for money. From the time I was very small, I dreamed of a better world. I would cut pictures from magazines and paste them in a scrapbook. I promised myself one day I would escape. I would become a great lady. I would live in a beautiful house and have a loving family and lots and lots of money. Everything would be perfect and then I could finally be happy," she said.

Tears pressed at the back of her eyelids, but she blinked them back. After so many years of disciplined self-control, she had no idea how to just let them fall. How to show her vulnerability to the man she loved more than life, but had never been able to share her true self with.

Her mind scalded with the thought of all she'd hidden from him. She felt strangled, weighted down, burdened by her lies. A great hopelessness washed over her. How could she ever expect him to forgive her? How could she ever forgive herself for cheating them of the closeness they could have had?

But if he'd known you were from carny stock, you'd never have had a chance with him at all.

Her husband stared at her, unmoving, hands clenched atop his thighs. She could see him processing what she had told him, trying to understand. But he could never really understand. His life had been blessed from the beginning. Charmed. James Robert had no idea what it took to crawl up from the gutter.

Nervously, she cleared her throat. This was a good sign, right? That he was even hearing her out. That he hadn't already thrown her from the house?

"I never even finished high school," Honey admitted. "My parents never stayed in one place long enough. But wherever we went, I found the local library and I read and read and read. Reading was my escape from reality. The safe haven I ran to when things got ugly. I took the GED when I turned seventeen and scored one hundred percent on the test."

Her hands trembled. She was afraid to look him in the eyes, but she couldn't stand not knowing what was in his eyes. The look on James Robert's face was empty, unmoving. Honey's soul ached. He hadn't thrown her out yet, but the potential was there.

"My father had a heart attack that same year." She smoothed her fingers over the skirt of her dress, ironing out wrinkles that weren't there. "We were in Philadelphia then and my mother couldn't handle it. Her drinking spiraled, she started dating a really rough character and dabbled with drugs. They fought all the time." Honey swallowed. She had blocked the details from her mind so long ago. It was difficult to call them up again. "It was ugly. I tried to get my mother to leave him, but she was too deep into alcoholism to drag herself out, and I was terrified her boyfriend was going to turn his violent temper on me if I stayed. So I ran away."

Guilt and shame suffused her as the truth spilled out of her. She told him all the things she should have told him years and years ago. She talked and talked and talked and when she was done, she sank back against her expensive leather couch, drained and exhausted.

She peeked over at James Robert, who hadn't moved a muscle during her recitation. She wanted him to take her in his arms, kiss her gently, and tell her it was all right. The past was over, and he loved her no matter who she was. But she couldn't hope for that. She didn't deserve his forgiveness.

"I'm sorry you suffered," James Robert said, but his tone was devoid of emotion. He sounded flat, dead inside.

Honey lifted her chin. Always the fighter, always the survivor. Never give up, never surrender. He didn't ask her what happened next, but she told him anyway. "I survived. I went to a homeless shelter and they got me a job as a live-in companion taking care of a wealthy elderly woman with Alzheimer's, who'd been a recluse for years."

"Abigail Montgomery," James Robert said.

"Yes. She had no immediate family left. Her only child, a daughter named Honey, had died years before in a skiing accident in the Alps."

"So when did you decide to assume the daughter's identity?" He spit out the words. His jaw muscles clenched tight.

"It was never a conscious decision. She'd call me by her daughter's name and when I tried to correct her, she'd get upset. It was easier to humor her and let her call me Honey. In the beginning Abigail had her lucid days where she was more lucid than others, and even when she wasn't lucid about the present, she still remembered her debutante days. She taught me the ways of high society. How to speak. How to act. Proper etiquette.

The right way to do things. She was lonely and enjoyed my company."

Honey stared off into the distance, remembering who she used to be and the path she'd taken to become who she was now. "As Abigail's condition worsened, she started calling me Honey all the time. She'd kept her daughter's clothes and gave them to me to wear. It was easy to pretend I was her daughter, who'd been living abroad for some years and had returned home to care for my ailing mother. It took little effort to fool the boy who delivered the groceries or the mailman or the local pharmacist. Remember, by this time, I was walking the walk and talking the talk of a woman raised in the lap of luxury."

"And Abigail," James Robert said, "because of her condition and her lack of immediate family, was no longer active in her social circle. I'm guessing her friends had long ago abandoned her, so it made it easier for you to pretend. There was no one to ferret you out as a fraud."

"That's right."

His gaze hardened. "So you formed a plan to become Honey Montgomery, and you started trolling the University of Pennsylvania campus, looking for a rich husband. You knew Abigail's gravy train wouldn't last forever."

"No, no," Honey denied. "It wasn't like that. On the one day I had off from caring for Abigail, I took a class at the university. I was interested in an education, not getting married. Marriage was the last thing on my mind."

"I find that hard to believe." His eyes were cold, unfeeling. "Coming from a liar like you."

Real fear pushed bile into her throat. She curled her fingernails into her palms. She was losing him. He wasn't going to forgive her. But she couldn't fault him. She'd done an unforgivable thing.

"And the day I met you?"

She sat up straighter. "That was the day I killed Fayrene Doggett, and Honey Montgomery was resurrected from the grave. I knew that a man like you, from a rich, successful family, could never love a common carny pickpocket like me. I became what you needed me to be, James Robert."

"I guess you're pretty lucky Abigail Montgomery died when she did, or you wouldn't have been able to fool me for long. If we'd stayed in Philadelphia, I would have eventually found out the truth. Unless, that is, you killed her."

Honey gasped as if he'd slapped her. "Do you actually believe that of me?"

"How would I know? I have no idea who you really are."

"I'm not capable of murder." Her voice quivered, half with anger, half with fear.

"I didn't think you were capable of lying and cheating your way into marriage, either, but apparently I was wrong. I always knew you were one determined woman. That you never let anything stand in your way. It was one of the things I admired most about you." He gave a rough, humorless laugh.

"I'm not denying that Abigail's death, two weeks after we met, made my deception much easier. And the fact she left me a small inheritance gave credence to my story that medical bills and bad investments had wiped out the family fortune."

Honey felt the familiar ache of loss and loneliness deep within her heart, a void that plunged straight through to her soul. A single tear slid down her cheek. Wet and hot. She didn't swipe it away, just allowed it to roll until it dried at her chin.

"You tricked me into marriage. You were the one who insisted on a quick elopement." Resentment was etched into every corner of her husband's face, and she couldn't think badly of him for it. He had every right to his resentment, his anger, his hatred for her and what she had done.

"I did it only because I loved you so much," she murmured.

He made a harsh, unforgiving noise. "You irrevocably altered the course of my life, without my knowledge, without my permission. You cheated me."

"Please," she begged for his understanding, even though Honey Montgomery Cartwright never begged. "I couldn't bear the thought of living without you, and I knew if you found out who I really was, your family would pressure you to dump me."

"You're probably right about that." His eyes were cold as flint, the look in them striking her through the heart. The gulf between them loomed impossibly wide. And she realized there was no bridging this canyon. There was no going back.

"And you would have done it because you had a hard time standing up to your family, James Robert."

"Just like Delaney does," he said.

The mention of their daughter's name brought them

out of their muddled past and back into the room, back to the reality that their daughter had been kidnapped from the chapel on her wedding day. Honey wanted to reach over and touch her husband's hand, but she was so terrified he'd shake off her comfort. She couldn't bear that.

"You've lived in fear all these years. That the world was going to discover your dark secret. That's why you were so insistent on things being perfect. That's why you pushed the girls the way you did. Everyone was watching. You couldn't risk a misstep, nor could your children."

"Yes," Honey admitted.

"Lying turned you into something you're not, into someone you're not. I've watched you change over the years, and I never understood why you did the things you did. At times I felt like you were doing your best to push me away."

Her husband was right. She had pushed him away with her demands of perfection. She'd known she was pushing him away, forsaking intimacy for secrecy. Honey thought of all the love she'd missed, all the joy she'd negated. In her desperate need to forsake her past, she'd hopelessly maimed her future.

Despair seized her. Turned her inside out as the world as she knew it flipped upside down. And nothing would ever be the same again.

"And now," she whispered, "I'm being blackmailed by my own mother. She saw my picture with Delaney in *Society Bride* and demanded twenty thousand dollars or she was going to the police. I paid her off."

James Robert got up from the couch.

"Where are you going?" Honey asked, nervously lacing her fingers together.

"To phone the police."

Terror gripped her. "You can't. If you call the police everyone will find out about me."

He stared at her. "Keeping your secret is more important than our daughter's life?"

"No, no, of course not. It's just that I'm sure my mother is behind this kidnapping. She won't hurt Delaney. We can pay her off and still keep things quiet."

Hatred flared in his eyes. "Good God, woman, you can't keep living this lie. It's over. Everything is over."

Honey closed her eyes. He was right. She'd been hiding and lying for so long, her values had gotten completely screwed up. Her eyes flew open. Mentally, she braced herself. "Call them."

James Robert reached for the phone at exactly the same moment it rang. He picked it up. "Hello."

Honey sank her teeth into her bottom lip.

"Evan," James Robert said on a sharp intake of breath.

Hand splayed over her chest, she got to her feet and went to stand beside her husband. He had a short, one-sided conversation with Evan that she couldn't decipher, then he hung up and turned to look at her.

"Delaney left Evan a note."

Honey blinked. "A note."

James Robert pursed his lips and glared at her. Honey felt his rage all the way to her bone marrow. "I guess it was a good thing you didn't let me call the cops."

She frowned. "I don't understand."

"Seems our daughter was desperate to get out of the marriage, but because of you and your inflexible demand for perfection, she had no idea how to tell us she didn't want to marry Evan. Congratulations, you officially pushed her over the edge."

Misery lay like granite in Honey's stomach. "What are you saying?"

"Delaney hired someone to take her hostage."

Nick had been in a car accident racing to rescue her. He could be hurt. He could have been killed.

Delaney felt a shock of fear and dread unlike anything she'd ever experienced before. The white-hot pain of sorrow rocketed into her heart, so intense she thought she was going to be sick.

She had to get out of this van. Had to get to Nick. She had to make sure he was unharmed. Had to let him know how much she loved him.

Because she did love him. Loved him so much she could scarcely breathe.

She had loved him from the moment she'd seen him in her vision that evening in Claire Kelley's consignment shop. She just hadn't known it then. But there was no denying it. They were fated. He simply could not die.

Please, God, she prayed. *Please, let my Nicky be okay.*

How to get out of here? How to get away from this kidnapping creep? What she needed was a plan.

But she had nothing.

Do what you do best, Skylar's voice whispered in the back of her head.

What was that? She wasn't brave or bold or intrepid. She wasn't particularly smart or cunning. Most of her life she'd been motivated by the need to live in harmony with those around her. She'd preferred blending in to rocking the boat, to accommodate others and put her own needs on hold.

She had nothing that could help her out of this fix.

You've got empathy. It was Skylar's voice again. *And you're patient and nonjudgmental.*

Okay, she could do that. Pretend to be on the side of her kidnapper.

Delaney heard sirens wail from somewhere in the distance behind them. Her heart jumped into her throat. Nick!

Do something! Now!

"Whew," Delaney said as calmly as she could and tentatively raised her gaze to meet the eyes of her kidnapper in the rearview mirror. "Thank heavens we shook him."

The man behind the wheel narrowed his eyes suspiciously. "Whaddya mean?"

"The guy in the red pickup was my bodyguard. I'm so glad he's out of the picture. You have no idea what a pain in the neck it is having your every move monitored."

"You kiddin' me? I've been in the pen, girlie. You're the one with no idea what it's like to have your every move monitored for real."

"I'm sorry. I had no idea. You're right. It's completely inappropriate for me to compare my pampered life to prison."

"Damn straight."

"It'd be really awful if you had to go back there."

"I'm never going back."

"Well, you might. Kidnapping is a felony."

"I ain't getting caught."

"You might."

"I'm not going back to jail," he said stubbornly.

"I bet it's hard," she mused. All the while she was talking to him, Delaney was edging up the floor of the van toward the seat that separated her from the driver. Getting him to talk was one thing, but she needed a better plan. Needed to shake things up, but at the right moment, when it would do her the most good. "Starting all over again after prison. Is that why you turned to kidnapping?"

"Pays better than working at Wal-Mart."

"What did you do for a living?" she asked. "Besides kidnapping, I mean. Before you went to jail."

"I'm a barker at the Whack-a-Mole on Galveston Island," he said proudly.

Ah, now she knew why he looked familiar. Was that how the kidnapping had come about? He'd seen her at the amusement park and recognized her as a Cartwright?

"You like that work?"

"Outside, near the ocean, no boss. What's not to like?"

Closer, closer. She was just a few inches from the back of his seat, although she wasn't quite sure what she was going to do once she got there. Her hands were cuffed. It wasn't like she had a whole lot of options.

She scooted forward. Her veil fell across her face, blurring her vision with a curtain of lace.

And then she knew what to do.

In a soothing voice, she coaxed the driver to talk, while the seconds ticked away and they drove farther and farther from where Nick had crashed his pickup. It took everything she possessed to keep herself from acting immediately. If she was going to be successful in her escape attempt, she had to time things right.

He turned on his blinker and changed lanes. Up ahead lay a freeway ramp. She couldn't let him get back on the freeway. Her plan would be far too dangerous to execute on the expressway.

The time was now.

She was positioned directly behind the driver. With her cuffed hands she reached over her head, while simultaneously rising up on her knees. Briefly, her eyes met those of her kidnapper in the rearview mirror at the very same moment she flipped the long veil up over his head.

The guy swore, swerved violently. The van shot back across the lane they'd just left.

He batted at her veil.

The van rocked.

Delaney fell back on her butt.

The van bounced hard up onto the curb.

He cut the wheel tight, brought the van down on the road with a solid smack. The jarring impact caused the back door to swing open. Hot air rushed in.

A horn sounded and Delaney looked up in time to see a delivery truck headed straight for them.

She screamed. The kidnapper twisted the steering wheel, sending them careening around a corner and up over a second curb.

Delaney somersaulted across the floor of the van, and the next thing she knew she was free-falling out the door.

Chapter 18

While Delaney was tussling with the kidnapping Whack-a-Mole barker, Nick pumped the foot feed and twisted the key in the ignition. He grunted with relief when the engine fired up again.

He took off after her, not knowing for sure where the van had gone. It might be back up on the freeway by now, completely out of reach. That thought fisted his gut. No, no, he wasn't that far behind them. He'd only lost a few seconds, maybe a minute, but no longer. He had to believe they were still on this access road.

Resolutely, Nick goosed the ailing pickup and ignored the rattling and groaning noises coming from the rear end. Lalule shook on the dashboard, urging him onward.

He sped over the rise in the road, eyes desperately scanning the area in search of the white van.

Then he saw something that stopped his heart. The van, maybe eight blocks ahead of him, spinning around a corner with the back door flapping open.

In horror, Nick watched as the woman he loved fell out onto the pavement.

Ouch. That was going to leave a bruise. Delaney lay on the ground, breathing hard as she watched the van disappear in a blinding blur around the corner.

She heard the squeal of brakes and the sound of tires sliding in gravel. She felt pebbles pelt her skin. Delaney pushed herself up, winced against abrasions on her palms.

A car door slammed.

She shook her head and the veil fell to one side. She saw someone running toward her.

Nick! He was all right!

Delaney had never seen a more welcome sight. She grinned in spite of cuts and scrapes.

He was at her side, picking her up, dusting her off, his face knitted with concern. "Are you all right? Are you okay?" He sounded breathless and scared.

"Fine, fine. How about you?"

"I'm okay."

"You sure?" She touched his face, needing proof.

"Are you sure?" His brow furrowed with concern.

"What in the hell is going on with Trudie's nephew? Why did he run from me? When I get my hands on that punk . . ."

"That wasn't Louie," she said.

"Then who the hell was it?"

Delaney shrugged. "Your guess is as good as mine."

Nick stared her in the eyes and felt such a surge of gratitude, he couldn't even speak. Ignoring his weak knee, he scooped her into his arms and carried her to the pickup, even though she protested the entire way.

She looked okay, kept demanding he put her down so she could walk, but he wasn't taking any chances. He held her tightly against his chest and maneuvered toward the passenger side of his truck. Her hair was pressed against his nose. She smelled like sunflowers, and she was trembling like a fawn abandoned by its mother.

His heart jerked hard. If that kidnapper had hurt her in any way, shape, or form, he would strangle him with his bare hands in a crime of passion. He put her in the truck, snapped the seat belt around her, and realized he was trembling too. She could have been killed. He could have lost her.

Taking a deep breath, Nick walked around to the driver's side and got in beside Delaney. He sat there a moment staring out across the hood of the pickup. He couldn't look at her. If he looked at her and thought about what could have happened, he would lose it completely.

Nick Vinetti didn't cry. Not when his wife left him. Not when he hurt his knee. Not when his grandfather died. The events of the past fifteen months were all knotted up inside him. One little chink in his armor and the dam would burst and he would bawl like an infant.

And that little chink was sitting next to him, looking as vulnerable as Bambi and twice as cute.

They were both breathing raggedly, sliding down off the adrenaline high. She was staring straight ahead too, as if trying to reconcile her own emotions. Cars were chugging slowly past, curious rubberneckers staring through their tinted windows at them, trying to guess at their story. They must have made a sight. A handcuffed bride and a limping man in a black suit more fit for funerals than weddings.

No one could guess this.

Once he'd collected himself, he got on his cell phone, called the Houston PD, alerted them to the kidnapping, and had them put out an all-points bulletin on the white delivery van.

"Where to?" he asked and started the engine.

"Away from here."

"Back to the chapel?"

"No!"

"To your parents' home."

"Definitely not."

"To your fiancé?" He said this last part with difficulty and dread.

"Evan is no longer my fiancé."

"No?"

Instead of answering his question, she held up her cuffed wrists. "Can you help me out of these?"

"I believe I can help you with that." Nick leaned over her lap to dig in the glove compartment for the spare handcuff key he kept stowed there. He was acutely aware of her, and from the way her body tensed, he knew she was just as aware of him. He unlocked the cuffs and straightened in the seat as she rubbed her wrists.

Delaney dumped the handcuffs on the dashboard beside Lalule and slipped off her veil. She carefully folded it up and settled in on the seat. Amazingly, the veil appeared no worse for the wear, although her dress was stained with dirt, tar, and grass.

"Does Evan know he's no longer your fiancé?" he asked, determined to know the answer.

Delaney nodded. "I left him a note where he would find it after the ceremony. I explained why I took the easy way out and had Louie kidnap me. Except, of course, it wasn't Louie."

"That's because I told Trudie to cancel Louie."

She jerked her head around sharply to pin him with those sea green eyes. "Why did you do that?"

"For one thing, you were involving Trudie's nephew in a crime."

"What's the crime? I was having myself kidnapped."

"Filing a false police report. Wasting government agency funds to search for you. Remember the brouhaha over Jennifer Wilbanks, the runaway bride?"

It fully hit her then, what she'd done. How she'd been unable to deal with her problems head-on. She'd cheated, taken the easy way out. Delaney uttered a bleak laugh, but nothing was funny. "I'm just like her, aren't I?"

Nick reached across the table to touch her hand. "Don't feel ashamed. Your family sort of cornered you into it."

"That's no excuse. I was a coward."

"Don't be so hard on yourself. You're not a coward so much as someone who hates to hurt other people's feelings. You let their needs come before your own, and then you feel trapped by their expectations and don't know how to get out of it."

He knew her so well. Better even than Evan, who'd known her all her life. It was as if he could see past the glossy surface her mother had polished and honed to the real Delaney beneath.

"Still, it was such a dumb thing to do." She dropped her face into her palms. "What must you think of me?"

"Everyone makes mistakes, and I'm sure from the time you realized your kidnapper wasn't Louie that you were feeling pretty punished by yours."

This didn't sound like a cop talking. He was making excuses for her, acting like someone who cared. Delaney held her breath. She didn't dare hope he cared as much for her as she did for him. A pall of tension hung in the air as they gazed at each other.

"But if you canceled Louie, then who kidnapped me?" Delaney asked. "Maybe more important, why?"

"That's the big question."

Puzzled, they looked at each other.

"It could have been a real kidnapping," Nick said. "You are an oil heiress."

"But that's awfully coincidental," she said. "Unless . . ."

"Unless what?"

"Unless the kidnapper is involved with the same person who's been blackmailing my mother. He did work as a barker at the Whack-a-Mole booth at the Galveston amusement park."

"You figured out that she's being blackmailed?" Nick didn't look surprised.

Delaney stared at him. "You knew?"

"I didn't know for sure, but I can guess why."

All the blood seemed to drain from her body. Her skin felt at once icy cold and blistering hot. "Why's that?"

"Because your mother isn't Honey Montgomery Cartwright."

* * *

Jim Bob Cartwright sat on a stool in a dark, dank-smelling bar not far from the oil refinery his family had owned and operated for three generations until economics had forced them to join forces with corporate America. He was a figurehead these days. No real power. His seat on the board of directors was little more than a commitment to the contract he and his brothers had signed. Jim Bob still made lots of money, but he had no real duties, no real influence in the company his grandfather had built. Without the Cartwright name, he was nothing.

Not even a good husband.

The place was almost empty. A couple of barflies hung off the other end of the bar, engrossed in a golf tournament on television. The jukebox was playing a Dwight Yoakam song.

Jim Bob stared at the double shot of Crown Royal he'd ordered. Stared and licked his lips and thought of Honey.

Correction. *Fayrene.*

He gritted his teeth as fresh rage swept over him. He closed his fist around the shot glass. How could she have deceived him so thoroughly? Everything they'd built together had been based on a lie.

His stomach roiled.

He loved her so damn much, but how could he love her? He didn't even know who in the hell she was. Fuck, but he felt like crying. His wife was a stranger, and his daughter had arranged her own kidnapping simply because she hadn't been able to tell him she didn't want to go through with her wedding.

Both his wife and his daughter had hidden their secrets from him. He'd failed them both. Failed them spectacularly. Jim Bob hadn't felt so alone since he'd given up drinking.

He eyed the beautiful amber liquid, and then lifted the whiskey to his lips. The smell of it was like an old, familiar friend. How easy it would be to swallow it back, allow it to take him under.

It's not the answer. Remember your vow of sobriety. Remember the night you swore it?

Until he took his dying breath, Jim Bob would remember the day he'd hit rock bottom.

It was the first anniversary of Skylar's death, and the Dallas Cowboys had been scrimmaging the Buffalo Bills in the Super Bowl. Honey had planned a memorial service for eight P.M., and the Wildcatters bar was hosting a Super Bowl party with two-for-one whiskey shots.

He hadn't purposely chosen the Super Bowl over his daughter's memorial service, but the thought of putting himself through more emotional pain had overwhelmed him. He'd stopped by Wildcatters after leaving the office, intent on one shot of liquid courage before heading home to change into the black suit and tie Honey had laid out for him that morning.

A handful of his drinking buddies had been at the bar, rowdy and well on their way to getting drunk. He'd been jealous of how happy and pain-free they looked, and he wanted to join them in that blessed state of oblivion.

One shot of Wild Turkey had turned into two and two into three.

The next thing he knew it was almost eight o'clock, and the Super Bowl was starting and he was too drunk to drive. Guilt and grief had burned inside him. To kill the feelings he'd had another shot and then another.

But it couldn't drown out the image of Honey standing at the front of River Oaks Methodist Church waiting and waiting and waiting for him to appear. In a whiskey-soaked stupor, he'd called a taxi.

He arrived at the memorial service ten minutes before nine and stumbled into the church in his khaki Dockers, plaid western shirt, and scuffed cowboy boots.

The altar was still set up with candles burning, pristine white lilies, and a big color poster from Kinkos with Skylar's picture on it. But the pews were empty. He dropped to his knees at the altar. The smell of the cloying lilies, reminding him too much of the day he'd buried his precious baby, turned Jim Bob's stomach.

Where was everyone?

You're too late; they've already gone home.

But he knew Honey wouldn't leave Skylar's portrait behind. She had to still be here.

Then he heard the sound of muted voices somewhere in the distance, and he remembered about the reception Honey had put together.

Staggering to his feet, he swayed a moment, fighting off the nausea, and then lumbered to the rectory.

He pushed open the door and stepped inside.

Everyone was dressed in black. They stopped talking the minute they spied him, his family and friends sizing him up with barely disguised disdain.

"Jim Bob." His brother Lance had come toward him, but Jim Bob shoved him aside and barreled straight for his wife.

He would never forget the look of horror that crossed Honey's face. It was as if someone had doused everything she owned in gasoline and set a blowtorch to it.

Grief and disgust and embarrassment and fury flashed across the face she normally kept pleasant and controlled.

"My precious baby's dead," he wailed and fell against her, hoping she'd gather him up in her arms and hold him close. But she had not. "I'll never love anyone the way I loved her."

He sank to his knees, clutching the hem of her skirt in his hands. He'd cried, pathetic and maudlin, clinging to Honey as she tried her best to retain her dignity. She was the most stoic woman he'd ever known, and he was jealous of her ability to detach herself from her pain.

Jim Bob had looked up to see chubby little Delaney standing in the corner staring at him, her thumb in her mouth at age eight, her eyes wide as quarters. Shame engulfed him.

And then he'd thrown up all over Honey's shoes.

The next morning he'd joined AA and hadn't had a drink since. Hadn't even come close.

Until now.

Temptation coaxed. *Drink it. Everything's changed. Honey's not who you thought she was. Your marriage is a sham. Your daughter doesn't trust you to keep her confidences. You've no real purpose. Come on. Slide back inside the bottle.*

Hand trembling, he touched the rim of the shot glass to his lips. The smell of the whiskey was nauseating now.

He gulped, opened his mouth.

And set down the shot glass. He couldn't do it. He couldn't cross that line, couldn't throw away his hard-won recovery.

Just then, his cell phone rang. He pulled it from his pocket, flipped it open, saw it was Honey calling.

He didn't want to talk to her. Not when he was sitting so close to temptation.

But she wouldn't stop ringing him. Not even when it forwarded to voice mail. She just hung up and called again. Four times, five, six.

What if it's about Delaney?

He knew he had to answer. He pushed the TALK button. "Yeah?" he said gruffly.

"Jim Bob," Honey said, startling him by calling him by his nickname. In the whole thirty-four years of their marriage he couldn't recall a time when she'd called him Jim Bob. The sound of her voice, desperate and scared, wrinkled his heart. "Please, you've got to come home right away. I just received the ransom note. My mother's threatening to kill our daughter if we don't pay her ten million dollars."

Chapter 19

"What do you mean my mother isn't Honey Montgomery Cartwright?" Delaney blinked at Nick.

"We need to go someplace more private for this conversation," he said. "It's not the kind of thing you discuss sitting on the side of the road."

She met his gaze. The serious look in his eyes scared her. "That bad, huh?"

"It's probably going to rock your world."

She considered the implications of that. "Let's go to Galveston. Get away from the city. Sit on the beach and get rip-roaring drunk on umbrella drinks."

They didn't talk on the drive to the island. But Nick stretched his right arm out across the seat palm up, and Delaney rested her hand in his. He squeezed her fingers lightly, comfortingly. They held hands and watched Lalule dance and by the time they reached Galveston, Delaney was feeling somewhat better, even if anxiety over her mother's identity was sitting squarely in the middle of her chest.

"Where to from here?" Nick asked. They couldn't go to Lucia's. The house was in escrow.

"I need someplace quiet where I can think."

"I know just the place."

He took her to a quaint little bed-and-breakfast close to the beach but a little out of the way of the usual tourist crowd. "I'll get you a room for the night," he said. "Until you can make up your mind what you want to do."

"Thank you." She smiled at him.

The proprietor of the B&B, June Harmony, was a plump middle-aged lady with a mischievous smile and an unexpected mane of glorious auburn hair that curled halfway down her back. She immediately assumed they were married from the way they were dressed and showed them to the honeymoon suite. After the woman gave them the usual welcoming spiel and details about the B&B, she turned to Nick and asked, "Where's your luggage? I'll send my husband, Henry, to bring it up to you."

"Luggage got lost," Nick explained.

"Well then." June winked. "I'll just leave you two alone to settle in."

"Why don't you take a shower," Nick said. "And try to relax while I head over to one of those souvenir shops on the seawall and pick us up shorts and T-shirts."

It was as if he'd read her mind. "Thank you."

He leaned over to kiss her lightly on the cheek. It was the sweetest kiss she'd ever gotten, but it upped her anxiety. If he was being so sweet, what he had to tell her must be bad indeed. "Be right back."

Nick left and Delaney shed her bedraggled wedding dress. Just looking at it lying in a heap on the floor made her feel wistful in a way she'd never quite felt before. It was a sadness tinged with relief and regret, concern and longing. Part of her wanted to pick up the phone right now, call her mother, and tell her everything. But another part of her, the rebellious part she'd hidden for years, needed to hear what Nick had to say before making any phone calls or drawing any conclusions.

She got out of the shower and wrapped herself in one of the thick terry-cloth robes provided by the B&B. BRIDE was embroidered across the pocket in maroon stitching. The matching robe said GROOM.

Pulling a comb through her wet hair, Delaney walked to the French doors leading to the balcony. She opened them up and a draft of sultry Gulf breeze blew back the thin white sheers. The sound of the water lured her out onto the little terrace barely large enough for two chairs and a bistro table.

On the bistro table sat two champagne flutes, a metal bucket filled with ice and a bottle of champagne. A note card propped against the bucket said: "To the Happy Couple, complimentary champagne to start your new life in style. Best wishes, June and Henry Harmony."

For no good reason Delaney's eyes misted and that sad, wistful feeling blocked up her chest again. She might not be part of a happy couple, but she was ready to start her new life in style. She pocketed the comb, picked up the bottle.

She'd just poured herself a glass of champagne when Nick returned, carrying a paper bag and wearing rubber flip-flops. She looked at his bare toes sticking out from under the cuff of his suit pants and smiled.

"Those dress shoes were killing my feet."

"Still," she said. "I'm betting they're not as bad as stilettos."

"You got me there." He grinned. "Hey, champagne."

"Compliments of June and Henry. I thought a drink was in order, considering the serious discussion we're about to have. Pour yourself a glass while I change."

She took the sack he passed to her and went into the bathroom to change out of the robe. He'd bought her a form-fitting, spaghetti-strap pink T-shirt, white denim shorts, and a pair of pink-and-white flip-flops. When she sauntered back to the balcony, she felt her cheeks warm as his eyes raked boldly over her body.

He too had changed into a T-shirt and shorts. His knee wasn't wrapped, and for the first time she saw the network of purple-red scars. She sucked in her breath, startled by the extent of his injury.

His eyes tracked the direction of her gaze. "Ugly, huh."

"No." She shook her head. "Not ugly. Vulnerable."

"Great. Just what every guy wants to hear." He plunked down onto one of the chairs and self-consciously pointed his knee away from her. She found his embarrassment touching.

"You don't have to hide from me."

"Better sit down." He waved at the chair beside him and ignored her last comment. "We've got a lot to discuss."

She drained her champagne, poured herself another glass, and slid into the chair next to him. They watched the tourists walk along the seawall for a few minutes, then Delaney took a deep breath and plunged in. "Okay," she said. "What's this about my mother not being my mother?"

"She's your mother. She's just not Honey Montgomery."

"I don't understand how that can be." From the moment he'd first told her that, she'd been trying not to think about it. The idea was so ludicrous she couldn't really wrap her head around it.

"Her real name is Fayrene Doggett. She's been pretending to be Honey Montgomery."

"I find that hard to believe. How can she possibly be someone else?"

"Identity theft is not indigenous to the computer age."

"There's got to be some kind of mistake."

"I'm afraid not. I have proof. Birth records. Fingerprints. The real Honey Montgomery's death certificate."

"May I see it?"

"It's back at my apartment. I know you told me to stop investigating, but my PI friend had already collected the information and I knew I couldn't leave it alone."

Delaney pushed her hand through her hair. How could her mother not be who she thought she was? What about all that high-society, blue-blood stuff Honey had drilled into her head? How could it all be a charade? "But that means she's been living a lie for thirty-four years."

"That's right."

She glanced at Nick. His eyes were full of understanding and compassion. That look, along with the second glass of champagne, caused her to feel a little dizzy. "Do you think my father knows?"

"I'm guessing he doesn't."

She could barely comprehend that her mother had been living a lie. All her mother's rules, her proper code of conduct, had been based on big fat lies. For years she'd been toeing a false line. Trying to live up to an image that was exactly that and nothing more. An image. An illusion. She felt totally betrayed. Her mind spun in turmoil.

Pushed by anxiety, fear, and confusion, she reached to pour another glass of champagne. Nick closed his hand over hers. "You don't need any more of that. It's not going to change things."

His fingers rested across the knuckles of her left hand, and they both ended up staring down at Evan's engagement ring on her finger. Delaney took it off and slipped it into her pocket, and then she raised her head and met Nick's eyes. "There's no other man's ring on my finger now."

Desire glazed his eyes. He reached up to cup her chin in his palm. "You need time," he said. "To sort out your feelings. I won't take advantage of you when you're so susceptible."

His thumb brushed her bottom lip and she shivered. "Nick," she whispered softly. "Nick."

He leaned in close. "Yes."

They hung there, leaning over the table, staring into each other's eyes, his thumb on her lip, his hand on hers, Delaney's heart beating crazily in her chest.

If he didn't kiss her she would come unraveled. He had to kiss her. He was the only solid thing she could trust, the only sure thing in her life right now. Everything else was quicksand under her feet.

"Nick."

"Delaney."

He took both his hands and interlaced them with hers on the table, his body heat radiating through her. The act of joining hands was highly underrated, she decided, as the current of possibility flowed between them, electrified.

His gaze searched her face and she searched his. Her heart just bloomed big as roses in springtime. Looking into his eyes she forgot about her parents, about her mother's true identity, about Evan, about the wedding, about everything.

Nick had so many layers she had yet to peel back, so many things about him she did not know. The edges of his mouth were angular and unyielding, but she knew his lips were soft. The contradictions in him were exciting. She felt as if she was teetering on some great chasm and he was her only ally.

She was caught up in the moment and the sweet vortex of Nick's dark eyes. With a groan, he pulled her to her feet, took her from the table to the balcony railing, and then his mouth was on hers, tasting of champagne and raw vulnerability.

Who was he trying to kid? Nick was as susceptible as she. Maybe even more so. He was the one who'd been hurt in so many ways. She was merely confused about her place in the world. He had a lot more at stake than she did.

His kiss was tender, almost reverential. Delaney wanted wild and impudent, but she would take whatever he was willing to give. For almost two months she'd been fighting the attraction, and now she was finally free to give in, let passion sweep her away.

Ah, yes, this was what she craved. Sexual oblivion.

His hands were at her back, smoothly sliding down her spine. She arched into him. He didn't close his eyes and neither did Delaney. They stared into each other, searching deeply and both finding what they were looking for.

Acceptance.

Delaney couldn't stop looking at him. She felt like the bride off a cake topper, but instead of going home with the perfect plastic groom, she'd tumbled off the cake and fallen into the arms of a very sexy bad boy. She told Nick this and he laughed.

She liked making him laugh.

"There goes the bride," he said ruefully. "But this time it's into my arms instead of away from them."

He undressed them both, slowly, seductively. First came her top. Then his T-shirt. Followed by her shorts and his. Her bra was a showstopper. He groaned softly at the sight of her breasts and had to dip his head to kiss first one and then the other before he could continue with the undressing. Delaney felt a hot flush rise to her cheeks at his careful attention.

"Ah," he said and traced a finger over her blushing cheek. "There's my Rosy."

Nick kicked off his flip-flops and then knelt before her in his underwear. He kissed her navel and sent a jolt of awareness angling straight for her crotch. She fisted her fingers in his hair and gasped when he took her white lace panties between his teeth and pulled them down the length of her body.

She shuddered against him and he buried his face in the triangle of her hair.

"Get out of your underwear," she commanded.

He obeyed, whipping off his briefs. Delaney stood before him totally naked.

"I know you have trouble believing this, but Delaney, you are so beautiful." He breathed in a reverential sigh.

When he said it, she did feel beautiful. He made her feel beautiful with the way he looked deeply into her eyes. Without taking his gaze from her face, he held out his hand and led her to the bed.

The sweet magic of the moment of their first time together made her heart ache. In her head, she heard music. Soft and low. Irish music. The music of the veil. Morag's song. It was low and lyrical and haunting.

He looked at her so long and deep she thought he must have heard it too—the sound of Celtic harps and flutes binding them together.

It occurred to Delaney her wish had come true. She'd wished on the veil, wished to get out of marrying Evan and she had.

Nick lay down on the bed and pulled her gently on top of him, holding her close, smiling into her face. She curled into him. He made her feel cherished, treasured. He made her feel like she mattered.

He touched his lips to hers. Time spun away from them, ceased to exist. Such exquisite tenderness.

Delaney had thought she wanted raw sex but this was so much better. Ten times better, this leisurely journey of discovery. Touching each other softly, lingeringly, finding the spots that made each other wriggle and wiggle.

He held up his palm. "Press your palm against mine."

She did as he asked, and she could feel the powerful strum of energy flowing between them. Their hands were fused, and it was as if there had been no other before them, nor would there be any others after.

Magic. There was no other word for the sensation she was feeling. Unbelievable magic.

Except she was a believer—fully, completely, unequivocally. In the veil, in Nick, in magic.

He kissed her and then his lips slid down her throat to her breast. He kissed each nipple, then after a time began to suckle them with his mouth as his hand crept to the apex between her legs. Gently he pushed her legs apart and began to do amazing things with his fingers, finding tantalizing spots she never knew existed.

He kept touching her there and tenderly nibbling her nipples, and the next thing she knew she was moaning softly and slipping toward oblivion. Lost in the wonderful moment of discovery.

Slowly, he drew his fingers up the sensitive underside of her arm and took her hand in his. She watched transfixed as he brought her knuckles to his mouth, kissed each one separately, then opened her hand and moved his tongue in small circles around her palm.

"You taste so good," he murmured.

Delaney shivered.

Nick propped himself on his elbow and looked down at her, eyes shining with emotions she couldn't name.

Heat filled her cheeks and then abruptly embarrassed, she felt her old self again, nervous, aiming to please, but terrified of falling short of his expectations. She reached for a pillow and pulled it over her face.

Nick grabbed one corner of the pillow and tugged at it. "What are you doing?"

Delaney clung to the fluffy rectangle of goose down. Wrapped both arms around it. Buried her face in it.

"Stop hiding behind the damn pillow," he growled. "I want to see your face when you come."

"I can't . . . I don't want you to see me like this."

"Like what?"

"You know, with my mouth all twisted up and my eyes rolling back in my head. I don't want you to look down and think, 'Good God, I never noticed before, but when she's in the throes of an orgasm she's got the tackiest double chin.'"

"Come on, I'm a guy."

"Meaning what?"

"I would never think that."

"You wouldn't?" She uncovered one eye to peek at him.

"No, I'd be thinking, 'God, I love the way her tits jiggle when she wriggles.'"

"Really?" She lowered the pillow and peered up from behind a thick strand of hair that had fallen across her face. "Should I put my bra back on while we have sex? You know, so I don't jiggle so much?"

"Good grief, woman," he exploded. "I love your jiggling breasts and orgasm chin. I want to see your face while we're making love. I want to see what I'm doing to you and I want you to see what you're doing to me. That's what intimacy is all about. Sharing what's going on between us, whether we look good doing it or not. Stop being so self-conscious. You'll never fully enjoy sex until you do."

She relinquished her grip on the pillow. Nick sailed it across the room.

"There now," he said. "No more hiding from me."

She stilled and looked up at him and her heartbeat stalled.

His mouth came down hard on hers and she tasted the yearning on his lips, the urgency on his breath. Delaney's body responded with a craving so intense it stunned her.

Whenever she was around him her perfectly structured control just shattered. She didn't fully understand why, but around him she felt freer, more like the person she was supposed to be. But letting go of the old Delaney was pretty darn scary, no matter how much she wanted to let go.

Even though he'd chased after her, Nick hadn't promised her anything. He offered her nothing but his loyalty and his help facing her family.

Was it enough? Could she just surrender to him, make love to him, without any expectations? Without any need for everything to be perfect? She wanted to, but she didn't know if it was really possible.

Shake it up.

The phrase drifted into her head. Shaking it up meant letting go of everything. Of her fears. Of her old self. Of the way she'd always believed things were supposed to be. Her old world was gone forever, it was time to adapt to new situations and circumstances. Time to live in the present.

Her ache for him was undeniable, and she just stopped resisting.

She didn't need any promises. All she needed was Nick.

His calloused hands moved down her shoulders and

her body came alive with pleasure. She whimpered help-lessly into his mouth as he kissed her.

"That's right, Rosy, just let go," he said, giving her permission to do the one thing she'd been dying to do for years and years and years but hadn't known how until now.

Until Nick.

Surrendering to the moment, she became the Delaney that she was always supposed to be. Boldly, she pulled his bottom lip into her mouth with her teeth. The feel of their colliding mouths curled her toes.

This was the magic she'd been missing.

She'd been so placid for so long, not rocking the boat, letting herself be swept away by her mother's dominant personality, that she'd been unable to express her repressed will.

But Nick's blunt directness gave her the permission to discover what she needed.

Firmly, he tilted her chin up with his thumb and index finger, snaring her so he could thrust his tongue deeper inside her. He pressed his body closer until she could feel him everywhere. With each bold stroke of his tongue, he dared her to resist him, challenging her to deny what they both wanted so desperately. His kiss taunted, punishing her for provoking him.

Even through the haze of their mind-soaking arousal, there was no denying that she provoked him to levels to which he'd never before been provoked. Intensity rose off him like heat off the desert sand. His biceps nearly quivering beneath her fingertips. His hips pressed into her as if he would never let her up off this bed.

Desire ignited, hot as gasoline, and surged through

her veins, snatching her entire being on an upswell of yearning.

He kept kissing her, doing these absolutely amazing things with his tongue.

Her breasts ached, heavy and taut, eager to feel the caress of his fingers, to construct memories she would never forget. If this was the only night she spent with him, Delaney would remember it forever. They might be fated for only a hot, quick fling, but this joining would stand out as one of the greatest points of her life.

For better or for worse, she was going to make love with Nick Vinetti, and she knew without a doubt that it was going to be the most splendid sex of her life.

Her abdomen melted into a steamy puddle of hungry lust, and the most feminine part of her clenched in a desperate cry for release.

As if reading her mind, Nick pushed her legs apart with his knee and leaned forward until his erection branded her skin. The head of his penis thrust firmly against the throbbing head of her clitoris.

Delaney could not have prevented her hips from arching upward if a tornado had blown the roof right off the building, swept them over the rainbow and into Oz.

Nick groaned, his lips vibrating against her mouth. He broke their kiss, trailed his lips down to the underside of her jaw, and nipped her skin just hard enough to send a jolt of powerful need straight through her entire body.

While planting more erotic love bites along her throat, he ground his pelvis against hers, in long sinuous strokes that let her know she had not been mistaken about his potency.

He kept up the steady rocking, driving her deeper and

deeper into the savage wanting that was changing everything she had ever known about herself and what she was
capable of.

She reached up and pressed a palm to his chest, in-
tending on restraining him until her mind caught up with
what her body was doing. But instead of putting on the
brakes and telling him she needed more time, that this
was moving too fast, her head was reeling, she felt the
wild pounding of his restless heart.

He was as crazy for her as she was for him.

I'm responsible for this, Delaney thought in awe.
She'd never caused Evan to react in this manner, and she
felt as giddy as if she'd drunk a whole bottle of champagne by herself.

She couldn't get over how wonderful he looked—firm
biceps, taut abs, manly shoulders, tousled hair. Or how
powerful she felt. It was freedom of the most delicious
kind. With Nick, she didn't have to gauge her response
and adjust accordingly. She didn't have to pretend. She
could just be.

His eyes were open wide, and he was staring at her as
if she was the most incredible thing he had ever seen.
The look made her blush. She felt the hot flush.

"Rosy," he whispered. "Oh, Rosy, don't be embarrassed with me."

"But that's just it," she whispered. "That's the glory of
it. I'm not, I'm not."

"So why are you blushing?"

"Because," she said, "all my life, I've tried to be perfect and fell far short of my goal. But then you came and
I stopped trying to be perfect and now, when I look into

your eyes and see the way that you see me, I finally feel perfect at last."

Tears misted his eyes and he swallowed hard. "Damn, Rosy, that was some speech."

The pounding thrust of their lust had slipped a bit, but in its place came a softer, kinder desire. She still wanted him, oh, yes, with a need that would not be denied. But there was something deeper too. Something more than lust and hunger and wanting.

There was love.

Big and rich and true.

She didn't know if either of them was ready to say it, but she felt it to the depths of her soul. He didn't have to say it. She knew.

Happiness erupted from her lips in a giggle.

He kissed her again, swallowing her giddy sound. She tasted her joy on his tongue.

They danced together in a ritual as old as time, moving in perfect union, their bodies pressed close, smoothly, in tandem.

A heated calm seeped through Delaney's body as she experienced a blissful sense of homecoming. A wondrous peace unlike anything she'd ever known.

She understood the mystery of creation, recognized the cosmic connection between herself and Nick. They were one soul, one entity. His eyes latched on to hers and she could not look away. Did not want to look away.

They climaxed together like that, locked in each other's embrace.

And in that moment, two souls became one.

Chapter 20

They spent the entire weekend holed up in the room with only brief forays down to the beach. For two glorious days they made love. In the bed, on the floor, in the bathroom in front of the mirror, and even on the terrace late one night.

At times their lovemaking was sweet—a romantic seduction in the bathtub, complete with bubbles and candles and expensive champagne. At other times, it was hungry and fierce and raw—they tore at each other, animals unable to get enough. After one such session, they came up for air and Nick glanced around the room.

"We knocked two seascapes off the walls." He grinned. "I think we broke the glass in the frames."

"Oh, my." She grinned back and drew the covers to her chest. "Seven years' bad luck."

"No, no, that's mirrors."

"Better check the bathroom. The way we were going at it, we could have knocked the mirror off the wall too."

"You were amazing." Nick was lying facedown in the pillows. He reached a hand over and trailed his fingertips over her belly. His touch raised gooseflesh on her arms. She couldn't believe the way he made her feel. As if the very air they breathed was special.

She sat up, pushed back a strand of hair that flopped across her face. "Oh, dear."

"What is it?"

"There's scratches all over your back. How did they get there?"

His laugh was deep and rich. "You clawed me."

"I did?"

"You don't remember?"

"I remember feeling all shook up."

"Yep." He rolled over and grinned up at her. "You were wild, out of control."

"I'm sorry."

"Don't apologize. I loved it."

She leaned down and gently pressed her lips to the scratches she'd inflicted upon him in the throes of desire. She would never have thought herself capable of such passion. It renewed her excitement.

When she finished kissing the scratches she kept going, tracing her lips down the curve of his spine to the high, tight mound of his bottom. Once there, she bit down tenderly on a nice chunk of butt.

"Watch out, woman, you're playing with fire."

"Promises, promises," she teased. "We've already made love twice today."

"Are you questioning my stamina?"

"Stop bragging and back it up."

Quick as a cobra, he flipped her over. She giggled as

he grabbed her around the waist and tackled her to the mattress. "There's two more seascapes on the wall. Wanna go for double or nothing?"

Looking into his eyes, a thrill so rich and true she would never be able to express it filled her up. He kissed her and they were off again. Riding the crest of their passion.

They woke again at dawn on Monday morning, locked in each other's arms. He leaned in to kiss her.

"No, no, morning breath." She put a hand over her mouth.

"I don't care. I want to share everything with you, including morning breath."

"That's yucky."

"That's life, baby."

He kissed her, then pulled back laughing. "Okay, so maybe it's a little yucky."

Teasing each other, they filed into the bathroom to brush their teeth. They stood side by side, naked in front of the mirror, making silly faces at each other. Delaney felt lighter, freer, than she'd ever felt in her life.

She realized with a start that she had never been naked in the bathroom with a man before she'd been with Nick. How had she managed to get to the ripe old age of twenty-five without such intimacy?

Nick wandered back into the bedroom and flicked on the television. It was the first time they'd had the TV on all weekend. He channel surfed, looking for the morning news. And stopped cold when he saw Delaney's face flash across the screen.

Uh-oh.

He thumbed up the volume.

"Delaney Cartwright has been missing since she was

kidnapped from the chapel on her wedding day," said the News 4 anchorwoman. "Police departments all across the country have been looking for her. This morning we have stunning new revelations in the case. We go now to our correspondent, Joe Sanchez, outside the main precinct of the Houston Police Department."

Delaney came running in from the bathroom, her toothbrush still in her mouth, wearing nothing but her underwear. Since they'd been holed up together, she'd stopped flatironing her hair and it curled around her face. Nick said it made her look like an erotic sea nymph and she liked the sound of that.

"New revelations," she mouthed around the tooth-brush. "What new revelations?"

"Kelly," Joe Sanchez addressed the anchorwoman. "Here's what we've learned. James Robert Cartwright, Senior VP of Cartwright Oil and Gas, and his wife, Honey Montgomery Cartwright, received a ransom note asking for ten million dollars or their missing daughter will be executed."

Delaney pulled the toothbrush from her mouth and waved it at the TV. "They can't execute me," she shouted. "I'm not being held hostage."

"Your parents don't know that," Nick said quietly and the full extent of his words hit her like a slap.

Guilt took hold of her then, sharp and raw. What a horrible daughter she was. She hadn't thought about her parents or Evan from the moment Nick kissed her on the balcony. She imagined how frantic they must be and recalled how crushed they had been after Skylar's death. She thought the note she'd left for Evan would ease their minds, let them know she'd gone off on her own.

The taste of shame filled her mouth. She'd wanted to punish her mother for lying, for deceiving her all these years, but this was too cruel. How thoughtless she'd been. How selfish.

Nick loosely hooked his elbow around her neck and drew her against his chest and whispered, "Don't browbeat yourself."

"In a stunning revelation," the newscaster continued, "Honey Montgomery Cartwright revealed that she was being blackmailed by her biological mother and that her real name is Fayrene Doggett. Thirty-five years ago, she assumed the identity of a dead woman. For over three decades, Fayrene Doggett was posing as a Philadelphia blue blood. The scandal has rocked Houston high society, and the police have put out an APB on Paulette Doggett Wilson and her stepson Monty Wilson, who are suspected of holding Delaney Cartwright hostage. Their fingerprints were all over the ransom note."

Delaney's mouth dropped open and she sat down hard on the floor. "Mother went public? She admitted she's Fayrene Doggett? She'll be drummed out of the society that means so much to her. I can't believe she confessed."

"She did it for you," Nick said.

Her mother had come clean in order to get her back. Letting go of her too-high standards, telling the truth, risking everything for Delaney. Guilt and shame mixed with sadness and concern inside her. There'd been too much pain and misunderstanding on both sides of the fence. It was time for open and honest communication between mother and daughter.

She looked up at him, tears streaming down her face. "Take me home, Nick. Take me home."

As Nick drove Delaney up to the security gate of the mansion she called home, he felt decidedly out of place.

Delaney told him the security code and as he punched it into the keypad, he wished he could disappear. The driveway was crammed with unmarked police cars. Nick recognized the Feds when he saw them, standing guard outside the house. Before he even stopped the pickup, they were running toward him, guns drawn.

He got out with his hands up, identifying himself.

The FBI yanked open his truck door and pulled Delaney out. They ushered her inside the house, while another batch of agents surrounded him. Nick stood watching Delaney go, and he'd never felt more like an outsider in his life.

"Delaney!" Honey swallowed her daughter up in the tightest embrace she'd ever given.

The last two days had been a living hell. Right in front of the FBI, she and James Robert had fought and cried and argued and slammed doors and relived the day Skylar had been killed. But he'd stayed and they'd fought it out. Then they'd talked in a way they hadn't talked in years, if ever. Honey didn't hold back. She told him all her secrets, her fears, her terror of losing him. Letting down the guard she'd held up so high for so long wasn't easy.

When they could argue no more, James Robert took her in his arms, kissed her tenderly the way he'd kissed her in the early days, and told her he forgave her, but that for them to go forward, she was also going to have to forgive herself.

That was the hard part. Letting go of thirty-five years of self-recrimination and guilt. But she was trying her best.

Honey kissed her daughter's face over and over. They were both sobbing and apologizing profusely. Delaney for running away from her wedding, Honey for keeping a lifetime's worth of secrets and lies.

The FBI debriefed Delaney at her parents' home and then went off to find Paulette and her stepson Monty. Honey would eventually have to deal with her blackmailing mother face-to-face, but for now, her only concern was her daughter.

"I'm so sorry," she told Delaney. "The way I raised you was wrong. In trying to keep anyone from finding out that I was living a lie, I forced my fears and anxieties onto you. I emphasized perfection, because I couldn't afford to slip. I demanded too much from you and Skylar. I know that now, and I'll go to my grave regretting what I did to you."

"No, Mother," Delaney said. "I don't want you to have regrets. You were strict, yes, but you taught me a lot. And now that I understand where you came from and why you did what you did, it makes it easier to accept your flaws. I forgive you, Mother, and I only hope you can forgive me for hiding out from you for two days. I was just so angry when Nick told me your real identity. I couldn't believe you'd kept such a dark secret for so long. I mean, if you weren't who you said you were, then who was I? I needed time to sort it all out. I should have called you. It was so wrong of me to let you worry, fearing I was dead."

And then she told Honey about how Nick had rescued her from the kidnapper.

"Where is he?" Honey asked softly. "I'd like to meet the man you're in love with."

"Who says I'm in love with him?" Delaney's eyes widened.

"You can't hide it, sweetheart. It's in your face. You look the way I felt when I first met your father."

"I guess he wanted to give us our space," she said.

Honey reached over and squeezed Delaney's hand. "I'm so happy you didn't marry Evan. And I'm sorry you felt pressured into a wedding. I'm so glad that you knew better than I did and stuck to your convictions, even if your methods were a bit unorthodox."

The maid appeared in the dining room where Honey, Delaney, and James Robert had congregated. "There's a visitor at the door to see Delaney," she announced.

"Nick!" Delaney cried. She was up and out of her seat. She ran down the hall, threw open the door.

"Hello, Delaney," Evan said. "May I come in?"

Somewhere in the back of her mind, she'd known this moment would come; she'd just hoped it would be later rather than sooner. But here was Evan, and from the look on his face, he wasn't going away until he'd had his say.

"Evan," she said.

"Delaney." His eyes were tinged with sadness, and she just felt awful. "I'm glad to see you're all right."

She ushered him over the threshold. "Come on in."

He followed her inside and then they just stood awkwardly in the foyer, avoiding looking each other directly in the eyes. It hurt her to realize how she must have hurt Evan. He'd been her best friend for as long as she could remember.

"Evan," she started, "I'm so—"

"Shh." He raised an index finger. "Don't say it. You don't have to apologize to me."

"Yes, yes, I do. I'm so ashamed of the way I treated you. Arranging my own kidnapping." She shook her head. "It was cowardly."

"It's all right. I understand. In fact, I'm glad you had the courage to dump me at the altar. Granted, your methods were a bit unorthodox." His laugh was shaky.

"You were glad?"

"Yeah." He smiled ruefully. "I didn't want to marry you either."

Flabbergasted, she stared at him. "Then why didn't you just say something?"

"Why didn't you?"

Good question. "Because we were perfect for each other, everyone said so."

"Same here."

"Why did you ask me to marry you in the first place?" she asked.

"Because my family was pressuring me to get married, to give them a grandchild. It's a drawback to being an only child born late in life. Your parents fear they'll die before they'll get to see their grandchildren. I wanted to make them happy, and you're one of the finest women I've ever known. But after going to Guatemala, I realized I love that kind of primitive medicine. I want to move there, live there. I want to make a real difference in those children's lives. And I do love you, Laney—"

"But not in the way we both deserve," she finished the sentence for him.

"Yeah." He pressed his lips together tight.

Tears misted her eyes. He was a good man. Just not the man for her.

"I was looking for the magic that was missing between us," he said. "And I found it in Guatemala."

Delaney smiled. Tears were in his eyes too. "I understand completely."

They looked at each other and then burst out laughing, as tears slid down their cheeks.

"Friends?" Evan stuck out his hand.

She took it. "Friends."

He reached out and gently touched her cheek in a sweet brotherly gesture that she cherished but did not yearn for. "You're an amazing woman, Laney. I hope you know that, and I hope you find the same kind of happiness in your life that I've found in Guatemala."

"I've already found it," she said.

"Good for you." Evan kissed her on the forehead and then he was gone, leaving her feeling a little startled by his admission and a lot relieved. She was also stunned by what she suddenly realized about herself.

All this time she'd been looking outside for the answer to what was missing from her life. And here it turned out the magic had been inside her all along. Afraid of her own power, she'd hidden it, covered up beneath a fake facade, a false image. By trying so hard to please others, she'd denied her true essence.

Nick alone had seen her potential. He was the one who had shown Delaney her real self.

And she loved him for it.

Now all she had to do was tell him exactly how she felt.

It was a media circus around the house for the next few days. Delaney kept expecting Nick to call her, but he never did. She knew he'd gone back to work and she supposed he was too busy to make contact, and that he was trying to give her some privacy.

But when a week went by and he still hadn't called her, she began to worry.

She called Lucia and was distressed to learn not only had Lucia not heard from Nick, but that the buyer for her house had backed out of the deal and it was back on the market.

She called his cell phone. No answer. Same with the home phone.

She had to face facts. He was screening his calls and didn't want to talk to her. Heart breaking, she came to the awful conclusion their time together hadn't been as magical for him as it had been for her.

In the past, she might have accepted defeat, but no longer. She'd been through too much. She'd learned how to speak her mind and tell people what she wanted. Sure, she might get rejected, but wasn't it better to get rejected than to never express your opinion, never get what you really want, and always settle for second best because you were afraid to speak up?

She picked up the phone and called Lucia again. Delaney had a plan.

* * *

That night, Delaney dreamed of Skylar. She was wearing the same black baby-doll-style KISS T-shirt and faded blue jeans that she'd worn to the concert on the day she'd died. She was also wearing the wedding veil and carrying a pink suitcase.

"So what's up? You eloping with a KISS roadie or something?"

"Witty," Skylar said, "but no. I just dropped by to say so long."

Delaney sat up in bed. "So long? What do you mean?"

"I got my wish."

"What?"

"I wished on the dream version of your veil on the same night you wished on it, and well, the deepest desire of my soul came true."

"What did you wish for?"

Skylar gave her a wistful smile. "You can't guess?"

"You wished for me to find true love?"

"No, you had that covered."

She met her sister's eyes and saw tears shining there. "For Mother's secret to come out?"

"Not exactly."

"What exactly?"

"I wished for you to be able to let go of the past—to let go of me. I was happy to be here for you, in your dreams, Delaney, since I couldn't be here in the flesh, but you don't need me anymore. You've confronted your demons, faced off with Mother, and found your true self. You don't need me anymore. And that's a good thing."

Anxiety gripped her. She'd been dreaming of her sister almost weekly for the last seventeen years. What would she do without her? "But I don't want you to go!"

"It's okay. It's time to embrace the future, embrace your new life with Nick, and you can't do that with me hanging around."

"Skylar," her voice, brittle with tears, cracked open.

"Adios, little sister." Skylar leaned over and kissed her forehead. "Never forget I'll always love you."

And with that, her sister picked up her pink suitcase and was gone.

A week later, Nick was moping in his truck on the beach at Galveston Island where he and Delaney had almost made love, listening to sad country-and-western songs. Going to Delaney's home, seeing how she really lived in opulence and glamour, had brought out the fact that he was pipe dreaming if he thought he was ever going to fit in with a woman like that. No matter how down to earth she seemed.

He took a pull off his soda and tried to tell himself that everything was going to be all right. That they'd had a good time together, and it needn't be anything more than that. But deep down inside he knew it was a lie. He loved Delaney as he'd never loved another.

Finally, he understood why Amber had left him for another man. With Feldstein, she'd found the magic that was missing in their relationship. The magic he thought he'd found with Delaney.

But now he wasn't so sure. Would love and magic be enough to bridge the chasm between their upbringings? He feared it would not.

Despair consumed him.

He reached up to start the engine and accidentally hit Lalule. She hula danced.

Shake it up.

What on earth had compelled him to let down his guard and let her get so close to him? Why had he told her about his mother? Why had he given her a hula doll of her own?

From the minute Delaney had tarped him outside Evan's office, he'd known she had the potential to hurt him bad. He hated feeling like this—all soft and mushy. He wanted his hard outer shell back, wanted his cynical cop attitude back.

It was too late for regrets. He'd fallen in love with Delaney, but she was out of his league, out of his reach.

There was a knock on his window and Nick almost jumped a foot. He looked up and saw Trudie standing there, a deep frown on her face.

He rolled down the window. "Jesus, Trudie, you about scared me to death."

"What are you doing out here feeling sorry for yourself?"

"I'm thinking," he said.

"Well, your grandmother is looking for you. She just found a new buyer for the house, but she wants your approval first."

"She didn't want it before, why is she suddenly interested in my opinion now?"

"Don't be a putz," Trudie said. "Get over to the house."

Grumbling, Nick drove over to Nana's. Lalule did the hula.

Shake it up.

Damn that hula doll.

He parked in the driveway of the house he'd grown up in and his chest tightened. He hated that he was losing both Delaney and his home too.

"Nana," he called as he went up the steps, house keys in hand. He turned the key in the lock, pushed open the door. "Nana? What's up?"

The smell of lasagna was thick on the air. Damn, but he was going to miss the smell of this house.

He went to the kitchen.

And stopped dead in his tracks.

There at the stove stood Delaney. Wearing nothing but high heels and an apron.

What was this?

She turned to smile at him. "Welcome home, Nick."

"What do you mean, welcome home?"

"I'm your grandmother's new buyer."

Damn if his smile didn't spread all the way across his face. "You're kidding me."

"Nope. Unfortunately, this house is just a little bit too big for little ole me. I was hoping that maybe you could help me fill it with children."

"Why, Delaney Cartwright," he said. "Are you proposing to me?"

"Why yes, Nick Vinetti, I think I am."

And that's when Nick Vinetti knew all was right with the world.

Epilogue

The winter issue of *Society Bride* declared the double wedding ceremony of undercover cop Nick Vinetti to successful business entrepreneur Delaney Cartwright—and oil tycoon Jim Bob Cartwright to Fayrene Doggett—the "must crash" nuptials of the season.

Texas Monthly decreed that following on the heels of her daughter's faked kidnapping from her wedding to Evan Van Zandt, the outing of Philadelphia blue-blood Honey Montgomery Cartwright's true identity was nothing less than a Texas-sized scandal.

The *Houston Chronicle* dubbed it the best water-cooler gossip of the year.

Bouquet clutched in her hand, Fayrene walked down the rose-petal-strewn garden path in the backyard of her daughter's home on Galveston Island. Accompanied by the traditional Wagner's wedding march and escorted by Nick's father, Vincent, Fayrene wore a simple pale blue dress and the happiest smile on her face. When she got to the makeshift altar, she stopped and turned to wait for her husband and daughter to come down the cobblestone walkway behind her.

The backyard was packed with friends and family. Tish was recording it all on video. Jillian and Rachael were bridesmaids. Lucia and Trudie sat in the front row, beaming like the conniving matchmakers they were. Chalk up another one for the whammy.

The wedding march ended and the band struck up the Cars' tune "Shake It Up."

Jim Bob was dressed in a Texas tuxedo—tuxedo top, blue jeans on the bottom, and shiny new cowboy boots. Honey would have had a hissy fit over such lax wedding attire. Fayrene, however, thought he looked adorable.

Delaney wore an off-white gown and the wish-fulfilling consignment-store wedding veil that had foretold this very day. She looked to the altar where Nick stood to the right of her mother, patiently waiting for her. He looked stunningly handsome in his own Texas tuxedo. She'd never seen a more glorious sight.

Her father shifted his weight. "You sure you want to do this, princess?"

"Positive. How about you?"

Jim Bob looked to his wife. "I've never been more sure of anything in my life."

"Me either. Let's go then." She didn't even wait for her father to take the lead. Delaney was already hurrying down the aisle, pulling him along with her. She couldn't wait to marry Nick. Couldn't wait to start the next chapter of their lifelong romance.

When they got to the altar, her father put her hand in

Nick's, then he stepped over to his bride and looped his arm through hers. The minister stepped forward to renew the vows between her parents.

"You look so beautiful," Nick whispered. "I'll never forget this day for as long as I live."

Their eyes met and Delaney's heart soared. She didn't hear the minister's words to her parents, didn't smell the scent of the sea on the air, didn't see the crowd surrounding them. She only had ears and nose and eyes for the man standing beside her.

He was gazing at her with eyes so bright she thought she might stop breathing. This, then, was nirvana. Happiness enveloped her so completely she lost awareness of everything but him.

In that moment, true courage was born in her. She was not afraid of anything. Not with Nick.

For most of her life, she'd lived in the illusion of the perfect world, shielding herself from pain and the uncertainty of taking risks. But through knowing Nick, she'd learned to say "yes" to what she wanted and "no" to what she didn't.

She'd come full circle and now she was back where she's started, but totally changed. She was a fully realized person now. She could see clearly all the ways in which she'd held herself back, let her mother run her life. And she could see it in her friends too. Tish, who was afraid to admit she loved her ex-husband. Jillian, who was terrified to love altogether. Rachael, who fell in love too easily. She wanted desperately to help them all.

Her heart swelled with the exquisiteness of everything she'd learned, with the sweetness of her journey.

And as the minister joined her and Nick together, Delaney knew what she must do to help her friends.

The band played "Shake It Up" again as they went back up the aisle accompanied by applause. Tish had taken up a crouching position at the end of the back of the last row of folding chairs. She started to stand up as Delaney and Nick walked up, but ended up bumping her head on the corner of the gift table.

"Son of a . . ." Tish started to swear, realized she was recording, and clamped her lips closed.

"Wait." Delaney placed a restraining arm on Nick's hand. "There's something I need to do."

He stopped, waited patiently. He would always be there for her. She knew it as surely as she knew her own name. "Do what you have to do."

Delaney reached up, took the veil from her head, walked over, and handed it to Tish.

"What's this?" Tish asked.

"Be careful what you wish for," Delaney said, gazing happily at her new husband. "Because you're going to get your soul's desire."

"Huh?"

Delaney left her friend staring with puzzlement at the wedding veil and went back to Nick. He took her hands, kissed her tenderly, and then just before family and friends descended upon them, Delaney caught sight of someone standing at the far corner of the backyard.

Claire Kelley.

Her eyes met Delaney's,

Claire nodded at Tish, winked, and then she was gone.

And in that whisper of a second, Delaney realized

the truth of the universe. The magic of the wedding veil had been inside her all along. Faith—in herself, in love—was what had activated it.

With that, she took Nick's hand and walked into her brand-new life.

About the Author

Lori Wilde is the bestselling author of more than thirty books. A former RITA finalist, Lori's books have been recognized by the Romantic Times Reviewers' Choice Award, the Holt Medallion, the Booksellers Best, the National Readers' Choice, and numerous other honors. She lives in Weatherford, Texas, with her husband and a wide assortment of pets. You may write to Lori at P.O. Box 31, Weatherford, TX 76086, or e-mail her via her homepage at www.loriwilde.com.

Want more
Lori Wilde?

Please turn this page
for a preview of
the next book in her
Wedding Veil Wishes series.

Available in mass market in 2008

Affluence attracts affluence.

Tish Gallagher repeated her mother's favorite mantra to herself as she wriggled into a fifteen-hundred-dollar gray tweed Chanel suit. Her potential client was a banker and quite conservative.

After a quick peek into her closet, she added a lavender silk blouse to the ensemble. The color complimented her deep auburn hair. She removed four earrings from the multiple piercings in her ears, leaving only a single pair of simple gold studs. She clipped a strand of pearls around her neck and then donned four-inch, open-toed, lavender and gray Christian Louboutin stilettos. Because, hey, an artistic girl's just gotta wear *something* whimsical.

Although it was late September the weather in Houston was still in the low nineties and dastardly humid. But Tish knew La Maison Vert, the upscale

French restaurant where she was meeting Addison James and her daughter, Felicity, kept their dining room chilled like fine champagne. Hence the long-sleeved tweed jacket. This job was very important. She couldn't afford to shiver throughout the interview.

As she studied herself in the full-length mirror mounted on the inside door of her closet, Tish spied the price tag dangling from her sleeve. "Uh-oh, that won't do."

Since her divorce, she'd lived in a one-bedroom garage apartment behind a lavish manor house in the old money section of River Oaks. The apartment had once served as maid quarters and it's 1950's décor with black and white tiled floors and foam green appliances held a certain kind of retro charm. Not to mention the six hundred dollar a month rent was a salve to her strained budget. The elegant neighborhood was quiet. The only draw back was her bedroom had to double as her office. Consequently, everything was always in dis-array. Cameras hanging from hooks on the wall, a bank of editing monitors vying for space on the bedroom furniture, papers and files stacked on the floor.

A search for the scotch tape amidst the disorgan-ized, overflowing room finally turned up the dispenser lurking beneath a tote bag on her computer desk. After peeling off a strip, she carefully taped the price tag up inside the sleeve of her suit jacket so she could return it to Nordstrom's for a refund on her credit card once the meeting was over.

She took another spin in front of the mirror. Yes. She exuded money, polish and sophistication. Never mind that deep inside she still felt poor, tarnished and from the wrong side of town. "Please, please, let me get this job."

Her car payment was two months overdue and she'd been eating Ramen noodles every meal for the past two weeks. She was hoping to procure a down payment from Addison so she could zip it to the bank before the check she'd written for the stilettos ending up costing her thirty bucks in overdraft protection.

For five years now she'd been struggling to get her fledging business off the ground. She was a damned good videographer and she knew it, but she couldn't seem to catch a break. She wasn't one to give up on her dreams, but at some point didn't prudence step in? When did common sense shout that your dreams were going to destroy you and you better let go of them before you lost everything that was important to you?

Like Shane.

Tish winced and bit down on her bottom lip. The love of her life. The man she'd foolishly allowed to get away. But she wasn't going to think about him. Not today, dammit.

Sometimes, in spite of her best attempts to look on the bright side of life, it felt as if everything was slipping, spreading, festooning headlong into a disaster she could neither name, nor predict. Her throat tightened and she shook her head against the dark, creeping thoughts.

No, no. She wasn't the sort to dwell on unhappy things. Onward and upward. That was her motto. She was just about to shut her closet door when she caught sight of the wedding veil in her peripheral vision.

The three-hundred-year-old veil was carefully folded and draped over a wooden coat hanger. Her best friend in the whole world, Delaney Cartwright, gave Tish the veil for good luck after her wedding last December.

Tish remembered the day they'd found the veil in a tiny consignment shop. Delaney had immediately fallen under the spell of it, but Tish had been skeptical. Then the mysterious shopkeeper, Claire Kelley, had told them a fantastical tale about the veil that Tish did not believe. Still, it had been a compelling fable and she recalled it with clarity. For some reason, the story had stuck with her.

Once upon a time, according to the legend, in long ago Ireland, there lived a beautiful young witch named Morag who possessed a great talent for tatting lace. People came from far and wide to buy the lovely wedding veils she created, but there were other women in the community who were envious of Morag's beauty and talent.

These women made up a lie and told the magistrate that Morag was casting spells on the men of the village. The magistrate arrested Morag, but fell madly in love with her. Convinced that she must have cast a spell upon him as well, he moved to have her tried for practicing witchcraft.

If found guilty, she would be burned at the stake.

But in the end, the magistrate could not resist the power of true love. On the eve before Morag was to stand trial, he kidnapped her from the jail in the dead of night and spirited her away to America, giving up everything for her love.

To prove that she had not cast a spell over him, Morag promised never to use magic again. As her final act of witchcraft, she made one last wedding veil, investing it with the power to grant the deepest wish of the wearer's soul.

She wore the veil on her own wedding day, wishing for true and lasting love. Morag and the magistrate were blessed with many children and much happiness. They lived to be a ripe old age and died in each other's arms.

Claire Kelley had gone on to claim that whoever wished upon the veil would get their heart's deepest desire.

Delaney had believed. She'd wished on the veil to get out of her marriage to her childhood sweetheart Evan Van Zandt-and ended up finding her true love in Nick Vinetti.

Tish was truly happy for Delaney, but magical wedding veil or not, she wasn't sinking all her hopes into happily-ever-after. She'd thought she'd found true love with Shane and look what had happened. The old familiar misery rose up in her. The misery she'd struggled for two long years to exorcise.

She fingered the veil, wrestled with the idea of making a wish. It seemed silly. *But what would it hurt? Even if you don't believe?*

Good point. Tish slipped the veil from the hanger. The lace felt strangely warm to the touch.

Tentatively, she settled it on her head and examined herself in the mirror. The design was constructed of tiny roses grouped to form a larger pattern of butterflies. The veil was so white it was almost phosphorescent. Her scalp tingled. Her pulse quickened. There was something undeniably magnetic about the veil, even to a die-hard cynic.

"I wish," Tish said out loud. "I wish, I wish, I wish . . ."

Her voice tapered off. Oddly, the veil seemed to shimmer until it looked like butterfly wings were fluttering all around her. Eerie.

She swallowed hard. Goosebumps danced across her forearms. "I wish to get out of debt. I wish I didn't have to struggle over money. Oh hell, I'm just going to come out and say it. I wish for my career to skyrocket into the stratosphere and I'll become rich beyond my wildest dreams."

Instant heat swamped her body. The tingling at her scalp intensified. Her lungs felt at once both breathless and overly oxygenated. She almost ripped off the veil, but something held her back. She stared into the mirror. Stared and stared and stared.

The looking glass blurred.

She'd skipped breakfast this morning because she'd run out of Ramen noodles. Was that why she was feeling weak and a little dizzy? Tish blinked, shook her head. Her reflection swept in and out, her mirror image fading before her eyes as if she were in a slow, dreamy faint.

A face appeared. Indistinct at first. Fuzzy. A man's face.

Her gut pitched and her knees swayed. Not just any face. But a familiar one. A face she loved. Joy, full and unexpected, filled her heart.

"Shane," she whispered breathlessly. "Shane."

And then she could see all of him. He was dressed the way she'd seen him last, in his Secret Service black suit, white shirt and black tie. Her man in black. Even through his clothes she could see the steel of his muscles and she knew that beneath the tailored material his body was ripped, perfectly define.

"Tish." His jaw was clenched, his brow furrowed. Some who did not know him might think him angry. But she knew that look. She saw it in the edges of his mouth, the corner of his eyes. He was in pain. "I need you. I'm lost and I can't find my way back. Help me, Tish, help me."

Unable to believe-not what she was seeing in the mirror, but that the fact the her impossibly strong husband was calling out for her-she reached out a hand and her fingers touch the hard surface of the looking glass. Tish gasped as if she'd been splashed with cold water.

The vision vanished.

She stumbled backward, her temple pounding, eyes wide with awe and terror. She was back in her bedroom, back in the closet, gaping at the mirror, struggling to breathe. The cursed veil lay on the floor at her feet.

Her gut pitched. Her knees swayed. Impossible.

She reached out a hand and her fingers bumped into the hard surface of the mirror. Nothing was there except her own frightened reflection. Tish couldn't explain what had just happened, or where she had been, but her body hummed and ached with raw energy, rattling her to the very core of her soul.

"Holy shit," she exclaimed. "Shit, shit, shit. Today of all days, I certainly didn't need this."

THE DISH

Where authors give you the inside scoop!

From the desk of Annie Solomon

Dear Reader,

One of the fun things about writing my latest romantic suspense novel, DEAD SHOT (on sale now), is that it's my first Nashville-set book, and I enjoyed using real locations around town. My heroine, Gillian Gray, is an art photographer who comes from a wealthy family. Their estate is in Belle Meade, which is where old Nashville money lives. The original wealth in that part of town came from racing horses on the Belle Meade Plantation, a historic site that is popular with visitors. There really is a statue of prancing horses at the beginning of Belle Meade Boulevard.

Out on Highway 100, just past the Loveless Café (best fried chicken and biscuits in town), you can see the house where Gillian lived when she was seven and found her mother's murdered body. Or rather, the house I based my imaginary one on. The murderer was never caught, and Gillian's been obsessed with death ever since.

The Gray Visual Arts Center is similar to the art

museum in Nashville, in that it's new (the real museum is several years older) and the arts community worked a long time to fund it. The real museum has never been picketed, but I can't help wondering what would happen if it did exhibit Gillian's macabre self-portraits—the dead shots of the title—which inspire several murders in the book.

When Gillian is attacked over her controversial photographs and someone starts re-creating them for real, her family hires a bodyguard, Ray Pearce. Ray lives in Sylvan Park, another actual location. As in the book, the streets are all named after states, and Nebraska, Ray's street, actually exists. I pass by it on the way to Bobby's Dairy Dip for their signature chocolate-dipped cones. Yum.

I know most people think of country music when they think of Nashville. But in DEAD SHOT, it's murder and mayhem. So for a whole different take on my hometown—plus more real locations—check out my latest, DEAD SHOT. And next time you visit, you can check out the other side of Nashville, too.

Annie Solomon

www.anniesolomon.com

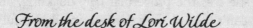

From the desk of Lori Wilde

Dear Reader,

When I first got the idea to write a series of bride-to-be stories centered on a magical, wish-granting wedding veil, I knew I had to do a little research. Google and I became fast friends as I scoured the Internet for bridal myths and legends. And then I discovered the coolest thing: There are only about eighty people left in the world who make hand-made rose point lace, and they're all in Belgium.

I unearthed so many romantic stories about lace and wedding veils, it was mind-boggling. There was even one about a mysterious woman who supposedly made veils so beautiful, they cast a spell over anyone who wore them. Those fables were the jumping-off place for my imagination as I envisioned the most exquisite wedding veil ever made that also possessed the power to grant the wearer's most heartfelt wish.

Then I thought, what if the women passed this wedding veil along from friend to friend as they each found their happily-ever-afters? What fun!

The Wedding Veil Wishes series starts with THERE GOES THE BRIDE (on sale now) and my heroine, Delaney Cartwright. Poor Delaney. As a kid she was the proverbial ugly duckling, and she still can't believe she's grown into a beautiful swan. She's got a snobby, blue-blood mama she's afraid to buck, and in her sleep she talks to the ghost of her dead sister. She's been keeping all that bottled up inside for far too long!

Until the day the veil comes into her life and changes everything. Bravely, she wishes on the wedding veil, desperate to find a way out of her impending marriage to her childhood sweetheart. That's when she meets sexy Houston PD detective Nick Vinetti, and everything starts to go completely *wrong*. . .

I hope you enjoy the book!

Lori Wilde

http://www.loriwilde.com